RELUCTA

Desire, Oklahoma 8

Leah Brooke

EVERLASTING CLASSIC

Siren Publishing, Inc.
www.SirenPublishing.com

A SIREN PUBLISHING BOOK
IMPRINT: Everlasting Classic

RELUCTANT DESIRE
Copyright © 2014 by Leah Brooke

ISBN: 978-1-62740-940-7

First Printing: March 2014

Cover design by Les Byerley
All art and logo copyright © 2014 by Siren Publishing, Inc.

Printed in the U.S.A.

PUBLISHER
Siren Publishing, Inc.
www.SirenPublishing.com

RELUCTANT DESIRE

Desire, Oklahoma 8

LEAH BROOKE

Chapter One

Charity Sanderson shivered at the feel of Beau Parrish's hands and lips moving up the backs of her legs. "Oh, that feels good."

Good didn't even begin to describe it.

Every time he touched her, she turned to putty, the decadence in the slow slide of his fingertips over the outside of her legs and to her hips created a fluttering in her stomach, while the feel of his lips and tongue working their way up her thighs sent pinpricks of pleasure racing through her.

Sprawled naked on her belly, she gripped the edge of the mattress, lifting herself into his touch, a touch that never failed to send her senses soaring. Having such a physical and playful lover was like a dream come true, a dream that she wanted to enjoy as long as possible.

Currents of sizzling delight ran up her legs as his touch moved higher, each caress, and each brush of his lips awakening every pleasure point in her body.

It had always been like this with him.

From the first touch, the first look, she knew it was something special.

Beau was every erotic fantasy she'd ever had rolled into one.

She'd lost her virginity to him, and couldn't imagine letting another man touch her.

No one could ever make her feel this way, and she wanted to savor every moment with him as long as he'd let her.

Just the brush of his fingers over her skin awakened every nerve ending, drawing her into a spell of seduction she never wanted to escape.

Every kiss inflamed her, making her dizzy.

She couldn't get enough of him, and even though she knew their loving meant nothing more than a night of pleasure to him, she couldn't stop coming back for more.

Beau nipped her bottom cheek, his hands sliding up her sides to hold her steady. "It would have felt good an hour ago if you hadn't been late."

Startled by the rush of erotic heat, Charity yelped at the sharp nip, and tried to squirm away, but Beau slid his hands to her hips and pulled her back, urging her legs wider. Gripping the rails on the headboard of his bed, she let out a moan at the feel of his warm lips moving over her back. "I had some things to do. There's a lot to be— ah—done before the club opens again. Jesus, Beau, that mouth should be illegal."

Drowning in sensation, she threw her head back and struggled for air. No matter how hard she tried to hide her response to him in an effort to appear more sophisticated, she didn't stand a chance.

He simply overwhelmed her—something she thought existed only in the erotic novels her sister devoured like candy.

Beau's teeth scraped over her bottom. "Hmm. I can tell from those moans and whimpers pouring out of you that you don't like it very much." Sliding higher up her body, he pushed her hair aside to nuzzle her neck, focusing on a particularly sensitive spot. "You're just going to have to endure it for a while longer while I reacquaint myself with this gorgeous body. I haven't seen you for two days. It seems like forever." Straddling her hips, he pressed his cock against her bottom, his fingers caressing the outer curves of her breasts.

Shivering in delight, Charity lifted her head, turning it to the side to give him better access, raising herself on her elbows, her nipples aching for attention. "Beau, oh God, how do you make me feel this way?" She tried to spread her thighs to make a place for him between them, but Beau straddled them with his, keeping them closed.

Sliding his hands under her, he cupped her breasts, running his thumbs back and forth over her nipples. "You make me just as crazy. I love playing with you. I could spend every waking moment just touching you. Everywhere. No, don't tense up. Don't I always go slow with you? I'm not in any hurry. We've got all the time in the world. I brought something from the store."

Shivering at the feel of his cock, hot and hard, pressing against her bottom, Charity moaned. "I'm scared to ask." She tried to keep her tone playful, but she knew what he wanted from her.

They'd been lovers for several months, and he wanted her ass.

Beau owned an adult toy store in Desire, Oklahoma, a town where people took sex very seriously.

Beau took playing and sex *very* seriously. He wanted to explore every aspect of it with her, which she loved, but she couldn't deny that at times, he made her nervous.

He seemed to think that it was his responsibility to test every new product that came into his store, telling her that he had to be prepared to answer questions about his products and recommend them.

She loved his toys, and loved how they played together.

He made her feel more than she'd ever thought it possible to feel—physically and emotionally.

She feared, though, that it was all physical for him, and as hard as she tried to stay away from him, she couldn't resist coming back for more.

She loved him so much, but she suspected that once he knew that, and knew that she wanted something more permanent, he would back away.

Trying to appear more sophisticated, and convincing him she wanted nothing more than these times together grew more difficult every day.

She didn't want to think about the times he'd used toys with other women, or where he'd gotten the experience that turned her into a quivering mass of need. His delightful Cajun accent made it worse, the seductive quality in his lyrical voice melting her every time.

No man should be so sexy.

No man should be so easy to love.

Beau chuckled, his hair brushing over her back as he trailed his lips to her shoulder. "You like my toys." He flipped her to her back, straddling her and leaning close. His dark brown hair, in need of a cut again, fell around his face, disheveled from her fingers. "You said you wanted to help me with my business. Toys are my business."

His smile, full of mischief, seemed to reach inside her and tug at her heart. "Don't worry, baby. No handcuffs this time. Tonight, I'm going to paint you."

Reaching across to the other side of the bed, he moved aside the pillow that he'd evidently placed there to hide his latest surprise, and pulled a tray closer. "Each color is a different flavor. The salesman assured me that the paints taste delicious, and that the brushes feel really good against the skin. Evidently, there are different textures, so we're going to have to try all of them out. The paint is supposed to wash off easily—whatever I don't lick off—and it's supposed to leave your skin soft and lightly scented."

Lifting a brush, he ran his finger experimentally over the bristles. "The salesman assured me that customers could have quite a bit of fun experimenting with the different textures for different parts of the body."

Charity shivered again, her nipples tingling with anticipation. "You're kidding, right?"

She never knew what he would do next. One time he would tie her to the bed and make her come over and over, and the next, he would torment her, not letting her come for what seemed like forever.

Grinning, he picked up a small jar of paint, and poised the brush over it. "No, Charity. I'm testing a product. Aren't you the one who's always lecturing me about not taking my business seriously?"

The hint of censure in his tone made her more nervous than she would have ever admitted to, sending a shiver of apprehension through her that excited her even more, taking her arousal to a new level.

Her opinion about things, including his business mattered to him.

Her pulse leapt at the realization that he cared what she thought, taking their relationship past merely sex.

Lowering her gaze to hide her excitement, Charity eyed his muscular chest and well-defined arms, the low light on the nightstand bathing every gorgeous inch of him in a warm glow.

She'd broached the subject about taking his business seriously several times, hoping to understand him, but every time she brought up a subject that had nothing to do with what happened in the bedroom, all playfulness fled.

Even though it was what she wanted, Beau's intensity alarmed her, and she found herself backing off, cursing herself for her cowardice.

He kept her off guard at every turn, making her feel naïve and insecure, keeping her from letting him see just how much he mattered to her.

She clenched her hands into fists, fighting the need to reach for him. She knew how warm and solid his arms would feel against her palms, and around her as he held her close. She knew the strength of them, strength he'd demonstrated numerous times as he lifted her in his arms, or adjusted her with breathtaking ease to his liking.

She let her gaze wander lower, but because the sheets had bunched around his cock, she couldn't see it.

She knew the size of it. The heat of it.

The way it filled her. Stretched her. Pleasured her.

Her pussy clenched, anticipating the first firm thrust.

Lifting her gaze to his again, she sucked in a breath, once again staggered by his striking good looks. Unable to look aware from the heat in his dark gaze, she found herself arching toward him, desperate for his touch.

He dipped the brush into the jar of paint, his mischievous smile stealing her breath. "How else am I supposed to see if these things really work the way the salesman claimed?"

Desperate for attention to her nipples, Charity arched her breasts toward him, thankful that his playfulness lightened the atmosphere she couldn't quite deal with. Watching the look of contemplation on his face as he stared down at her breasts, Charity giggled nervously, a habit she'd acquired since sleeping with Beau. "You don't care what the salesman said. You just like to play."

Beau smiled and tapped the brush against the inside rim of the jar, removing the excess. "Of course I like to play. So do you, but you don't want to admit it. Now, what should I paint first? Hmm, this looks like a good spot." His eyes danced as they met hers. "I'm probably not much of a painter, so be as still as you can."

Charity held her breath as he lowered the brush to her nipple, clenching her fists at her sides and trembling with anticipation. At the first touch of the soft brush, Charity cried out, her pussy clenching at the light friction, and the unexpected coolness of the paint on her beaded nipple.

Shaking with the effort to remain still as he continued, she looked down at her breast, watching in fascination as brushed purple paint with slow deliberation over her nipple. Unable to look away from him for long, she lifted her gaze to his again, once again struck with an overwhelming surge of love and desire.

Determined to keep the atmosphere playful, she ran her fingers through the ends of his hair and smiled. "What the hell are you doing? I thought you were just going to dab it on."

The look of concentration on Beau's face might have been one of an artist painting a masterpiece. Glancing up at her, he grinned. "Why would you think that? If I'm going to do this, I'm going to do it right. You just can't rush these things, chéri."

Closing her eyes at the erotic teasing in his tone, Charity dropped her head back to the pillow, digging her heels into the mattress as he continued to torture her with the brush. "What the hell are you painting, anyway?" Rubbing her thighs together to ease the ache at her slit, she teased herself, and hopefully him, by brushing her thigh against his cock, her stomach tightening when his hard length jumped against her thigh.

Beau lifted the brush from her nipple, dipping it into the jar again, a muscle working in his jaw. "I'm painting a heart. Now, be still, or you'll make me go out of the lines. Tell me how the brush feels." Grinning, he tapped the brush against her nipple. "Research. I need to know what to tell my customers."

Charity fisted her hands in the bedding as the brush moved over her nipple, each stroke sending ribbons of heat to her already needy slit. Quick strokes intermingled with slow ones, each enhancing her need for him and making it increasingly difficult to stay still.

She couldn't resist looking down to where his cock pushed insistently against her thigh, thrilling at the sight of it now that it was no longer covered.

Needing it inside her, she shifted restlessly and struggled to part her thighs, groaning in frustration when she couldn't. "It feels great. Okay, you tested it. Now, take me." She reached for his cock, hoping to hurry him along, but Beau knocked her hand away.

Clicking his tongue, Beau frowned. "You're always in such a hurry. You moved and made me mess up. Now, I'm gonna have to make it bigger." He dipped the brush and got more of the purple paint, his eyes dancing with mischief. "One of these days I'll get you to slow down. Now, stay still so I can do this. I still have several more colors to try."

Charity gritted her teeth, trying to remain as still as possible as he spread the cool paint over her nipple. "How many of them are there? Please don't tell me you plan to try all of them."

Beau sat back, glancing up at her before he studied her nipple. "Of course. How else am I supposed to know if they do what they're supposed to do? Be patient. There's only a few."

"Don't you think one is enough?" Charity didn't know how much more she could take. She wanted to spread her legs, but with Beau's knees on either side of them, she couldn't. Rubbing her thighs together didn't do any good. Her pussy was soaked, and she couldn't stop clenching, the need to be filled driving her insane.

Her clit felt so hot and swollen, she couldn't stand it, and the feel of his cock, only inches from her mound, made her crazy to have him.

He seduced her senses, making her want him more each passing day. He made her aware of desires she'd never known existed, somehow drawing her deeper and deeper into a decadent world of physical hungers and desires that she still didn't understand.

Beau set the paint and the brush aside, grinning down at her. "One is never enough, is it, chéri?"

Too aroused to be embarrassed by his teasing, she sank her fingertips into his muscular thighs. "I have no idea. You're the one who makes me come more than once. It's your fault."

Leaning so close that their noses almost touched, Beau gripped her chin, his eyes narrowed. "When you come, chéri, it sure as hell better be my fault."

The rare show of the domineering attitude she recognized from most of the other men in Desire sent a thrill through her, one that startled her with its intensity.

She'd always bristled at that attitude, and couldn't understand why Beau's infrequent displays of it thrilled her so much. Frowning, she met his gaze, sucking in a breath at the hint of jealousy and threat in his eyes.

Sitting back, he gave her a hard look before picking up another jar. "I play, but I don't share. I see nothing wrong with those who choose to, but I don't. Ever. I'm selfish."

He smiled, all trace of arrogance replaced by erotic playfulness. "Hmm, blue. Let's try this other brush. It's smaller and rougher than the last one. Stay still. I think I should do another heart. That way we can tell the difference in the texture." Watching her face, he dipped the brush into the paint, tapped off the excess, and touched the brush to her other nipple.

Charity jolted. "Oh, God." Kicking her legs, she dug her nails into his thighs as the rush of heat shot from her nipple to her clit.

"Tell me." Beau moved the brush over her nipple again, the rough bristles creating an intense combination of pleasure and sharp, almost painful sensation.

Sucking in a breath, she lifted a hand to cover herself, but Beau once again knocked it away. "Too much. Beau, my nipple's already too sensitive. No more."

"I have to finish. I'm only half done. Why don't you grab on to the headboard again? We need to keep your hands out of the way so I can finish testing this." He smiled, his eyes daring her to object. "You *did* promise to help me with my business, didn't you?" He dipped the brush into the paint again.

Charity couldn't hold back a moan when he stroked the brush over her nipple again. "Hurry up!" Even though he moved the brush slowly, the effect of the rougher bristles over her nipple sent her arousal soaring.

Beau shifted over her, rubbing his cock against her stomach. "Just a little more. There. Be real still. Perfect." Sitting back, he set the jar and brush aside, his smile pure sin.

"What shall we paint next?"

Looking down at herself, Charity frowned. "I look ridiculous."

"Not at all." Bending low, Beau ran his fingers through her hair, lifting her face for his kiss. Running his tongue over her bottom lip, he slid his hands beneath her shoulders, lifting her higher. Sliding his thumbs over the outer curve of her breasts, he nibbled at her lips before slipping his tongue inside, tangling it with hers.

He teased her, inviting her to play, curling his tongue around hers and leading her into the first steps of an erotic dance that made her heart leap in anticipation.

Tangling her fingers in his hair, she kissed him the way he'd taught her, earning a groan of pleasure from him.

Easing back, he brushed his lips over hers before lifting his head, his eyes dark and mysterious as he stared down at her. "You look beautiful. Sexy. Sweet." His tone, more serious than she'd become used to, cracked her composure and sent a jolt of alarm through her.

Swallowing heavily, she tightened her hold on him in an automatic and silent need for reassurance.

She loved him so much that sometimes she could hardly contain it. Scared to face the time he would decide he wanted to move on to his next playmate, Charity stiffened, earning a look of concern from him, one that eased some of her apprehension.

"What's the matter, honey?"

Shaking her head, Charity smiled as a sense of relief washed over her. "I'm aroused, and my lover wants to paint instead of taking me."

Sitting up again, he positioned himself between her thighs, spreading hers and lifting them over his. With another of those devastating smiles, he teased her curls. "I like playing with you. We still have one more color to go. Red. It's supposed to taste like cherry. It's only fitting that I use that one on your clit."

Her clit tingled in anticipation, and she tried to close her legs against the sharp awareness, but Beau kept her knees bent outward and outside of his. "Beaaaau…"

"Shh. I saved the softest brush for your clit." Holding the brush up for her to see, he grinned. "Perfect. Huh? Now, be still so we can try this out." He lifted her hips higher, using his own powerful thighs to prop her up and keep her held wide in that position.

"Beau!" Having her entire slit spread wide in front of him, and with enough light in the room to allow him to see everything, Charity thrashed, shaken by the sharp tingling in her clit.

He hadn't even touched her there, and she feared she wouldn't be able to hold back, and would come at the first touch of the brush on the swollen and already tingling bundle of nerves.

His foreplay continued the slow build to take her to new heights, something he did with alarming regularity, and shocking her with just how many ways he could arouse her.

And to what heights.

He'd never made her come before taking her, but each time he made love to her, she found herself moving closer and closer to losing complete control before he even entered her. He eyed her slit while dipping the brush into the paint, licking his lips as if he wanted a taste of her.

Feeling too exposed, she tried to close her legs, but held high and wide by Beau's muscular thighs, she couldn't, and tried to at least close her knees, but he knocked them aside without pausing in his task.

Beau shook his head, laughing softly. "There's no reason to be shy with me. I've seen it all before, chéri." He ran his fingers through her slit, brushing them lightly over her clit before sinking a finger into her pussy and startling a cry from her. "Beautiful. You're so beautiful."

Embarrassed by the amount of moisture there, Charity shifted restlessly against him, moving on the finger he held deep inside her. "Just take me, Beau. I'm ready."

Beau blinked in surprise and amusement. "Of course you're ready, chéri, but we're not done yet. It amazes me that you can be so shy with me. We've been working up to this, haven't we, cher? Little by little. One step at a time. It's all right for me to see you this way. It's all right for me to watch your face when you come. It's all right for me to see this beautiful pussy."

Charity shook her head, fisting her hands against the dizzying rush to her senses. "Turn off the light."

He'd put his mouth on her there many times before, but always in the dark. "No, baby. I want to see. Now, I know you're gonna move around a lot, so I'm gonna keep my finger inside you to hold you steady."

"Oh, God." The tingling in her clit grew, enticing her to rock her hips, which moved her on the finger Beau held inside her. She watched, holding her breath, as he dipped the brush in the paint again.

"Should I paint another heart?" Beau frowned, as though considering that. "No, you're probably gonna move and make me mess it up. I'll just paint your whole clit. It's so tiny anyway."

Charity groaned, staring at the brush. "It doesn't feel small." Her clit felt huge.

Swollen.

Throbbing.

Beau laughed at that. "I'm sure it doesn't. Needs attention, doesn't it, sweet baby? Don't you worry. As soon as I finish painting it, I'll lick all the paint off."

With the brush poised over her clit, Beau paused. "Hold on to the headboard again. I don't want you trying to cover your clit while I'm painting it. I want you to come, and I want to see your face when you do."

"Oh, God." She fisted her hands on her thighs, moaning as the tingling grew stronger. Sucking in another breath, she stared down at the brush and waited.

And waited, her thighs shaking with the effort to remain still.

Blowing out her breath in a rush, she glanced up at Beau shaking everywhere. "What are you waiting for, damn it?"

He withdrew his finger almost all the way, brushing his thumb over her clit as he slid it deep again. Smiling, but with that arrogant look in his eyes that excited her so much, he gestured to a spot over her head. "I'm waiting for you to hold on to the headboard." He met her look with a shrug, his lips twitching. "You were the one who wanted me to check the inventory, chéri. I'm just doing as you asked. I'm checking out my woman at the same time, and enjoying it immensely."

Narrowing her eyes, Charity attempted to glare at him, but the hot rush of pleasure as he moved his finger again prevented it. "You're teasing me on purpose, damn it."

Chuckling softly, he ran the blunt end of the paintbrush around her navel. "Of course I'm teasing you on purpose—another example of working and playing at the same time. You can sneak a little play into almost anything if you try."

"Stop that. It tickles." Swatting the brush away, she laughed, reaching for the headboard and holding on tight as she rocked her hips. She'd never thought that laughter and sex could coexist, but every night she spent in Beau's bed had been filled with laughter.

And pleasure beyond her wildest dreams.

Once she gripped the headboard, Beau nodded his approval. "Ready, cher?"

As always, there came a time when all laughter died.

Charity's died on a moan when Beau moved the finger inside her again and poised the brush over her slit. Stiffening, she gripped the headboard tighter, unable to tear her gaze away from Beau's face as he lowered the brush.

Jolting at the first touch of it on her clit, Charity cried out and reached to cover herself with both hands, but Beau withdrew his finger from her pussy and caught her wrists in one big hand.

"No, cher. Let me finish."

Digging her heels into the mattress, she lifted her hips. "Beau, I'm gonna come!" The sharp warning tingles she'd come to recognize burned hot, the sensation so extreme, it wiped away her inhibitions.

Beau's eyes narrowed, sharpening on hers. "So come." He touched the cold tip of the brush to her clit, his forearms pressing down on her thighs at her initial jolt.

Charity cried out at the feel of the soft bristles on her throbbing clit, and went over with a speed that stunned her. The coolness of the paint, a sharp contrast to her hot clit, made it even more arousing, the unfamiliar sensation sending Charity soaring.

"Oh! Beau!" Even though she'd expected the rush of pleasure, it always took her by surprise. Bucking against it proved futile, leaving Charity helpless to escape Beau's devious ministrations.

The slow strokes of the brush kept the sensation going on and on, the pleasure holding her in its grip for several heart-pounding moments. "Ahhh!" A cry of pleasure—of magnificent bliss—erupted from her as she dug her heels into the mattress, swell after swell washing over her.

As the pleasure began to dim, the sensation of the brush moving on her clit became too intense to endure. She fought to get her hands free to push the brush away, but Beau didn't loosen his hold on her wrists.

"Easy, chéri. Nice and slow. Yes, that's it. Nice and slow. Doesn't that feel good?"

Moaning at the feel of the brush moving with slow deliberation over her clit, Charity opened her eyes, drinking in the sight of her lover.

She loved to watch him. She loved his eyes. His smile.

Most of all, she loved the way he looked at her.

The way he looked at her now.

Lifting the brush, he stared down at her, his eyes glittering with something that never failed to take her breath away, an emotion she couldn't let herself believe.

She wished she had the courage to ask.

While the rest of his body remained stiff with sexual tension, his expression softened into one of affection and indulgence.

Setting the paint and brush aside, Beau gathered her close, brushing his lips over her chin, her cheek, and finally, her lips. "You okay, cher?"

Braced on his knees and elbows, he surrounded her, the warmth of his body and the gentleness in his touch making her feel like something precious, and easing the helpless feeling of losing part of herself she always experienced when she came.

His big body blocked out most of the light, cocooning them in a private world she'd never known with anyone else, and couldn't imagine sharing with another. "You come so beautifully."

Charity buried her face against his shoulder, needing the warm, solid feel of him. "I can't believe the things you say." It amazed her that she could be so adept and confident in every aspect of her life, but when she was with Beau, she became shy and insecure.

Lifting his head, Beau pushed her hair back from her face. "Why shouldn't I tell you how beautiful you are?" Grinning, he sat back and eyed her breasts. "Especially when you let me paint you. I have to say, though, I much prefer the natural color of your nipples. Rosy and pink."

Gripping his thighs, she wiggled against him, her nipples burning under his gaze. "Next time I get to paint you."

Beau laughed. "We're making progress. At least you admit that there *will* be a next time, and that you're planning to play with me in the future."

Bending again, he watched her face as he touch his tongue to her nipple. "For future reference, chéri, you can play with me anytime you want to."

Charity gasped at the feel of his lips closing over her nipple, arching against him as he sucked it into his mouth. "Beau, oh God!"

The pull to her clit had her writhing against him, and lifting her hips to get the friction she needed. She shouldn't have been surprised to be aroused again so soon after coming. With Beau, she'd learned that she could never get enough.

His mouth worked its magic on her nipple, creating a long, slow pull to her clit that had the swollen bundle of nerves craving his attention again, and her pussy clenching with the need to feel him inside her.

Hard and fast.

Frustrated by his teasing, Charity pulled at his shoulders, but couldn't budge him. "Beau, please!"

She tried to lift against him, wiggling her hips in an effort to get his cock inside her. The feel of it against her hip threatened to drive her mad.

Beau lifted his head, and glanced up at her, smiling as he licked his lips. "The purple tastes like grape, just as the salesman promised. Now, let's see if the blue tastes like blue raspberry."

Charity threw her head back as his lips closed over her other nipple, kicking her legs as the need sharpened. Rocking her hips, she pulled at his shoulders again, her frustration growing when she had no better luck at getting his cock inside her than she had the last time.

"Hmm." Beau sucked her nipple, taking his time as he licked the flavored paint. Scraping his teeth over the beaded tip, he slid his hands under her, lifting her against him. With a groan of pleasure, he raised his head a few inches, touching the tip of his tongue to her nipple. "Blue raspberry. Hmm, so far everything the salesman said is true. Now, for the cherry."

Charity's stomach muscles quivered under his lips as he worked his way down her body. Her clit throbbed harder, the anticipation of having his wicked mouth on her slit making it difficult for her to breathe.

Need clawed at her, the strength of it driving her wild.

She already knew how it would feel—how incredibly sharp the first touch of his tongue would be—and that after the first touch, she would be lost.

Running his tongue over her belly, he dipped it into her naval before lifting his head. "You're so soft. I'm always amazed at how soft you are. How tiny. When you're mad at me, and lose that temper of yours, I forget how delicate you really are."

Every inch he moved lower made her breathing even more ragged, her abdomen clenching as his teeth scraped over it. When his hands slid to her inner thighs, she cried out and tried to close her legs against him, and at the same time lifting into him.

Whimpering when his mouth moved lower, she clawed at the bedding, her breath catching as he slid his hands under her bottom and lifted her.

"And now for my cherry. All mine."

Jolting, she cried out at the first swipe of his tongue over her clit. The second had her kicking at him to escape the too sharp pleasure, and by the third, she was calling his name and grabbing fistfuls of his hair.

Too hot. Too intense. Too unbelievably good.

Her clit tingled and burned under his mouth, the tingling sensation growing with every brush of his tongue. Her body stiffened as the swell of pleasure hit her, and with a cry, she dug her heels into Beau's back as he tightened his hands on her bottom and pulled her against him.

"Beau!" The magic of his tongue sent sizzling heat rolling through her, the soft caress of warm velvety friction over her clit leaving her breathless.

With trembling hands, Charity grabbed clumsily for him as the swell of pleasure peaked, and slowly began to ebb, a sigh escaping when he lifted his head and moved up her body to hold her again.

"Hmm. The cherry tastes good, but not nearly as good as you. See, once is never enough, and I haven't even gotten inside you yet."

Burying her face against his shoulder, she breathed in his scent and giggled at his playful tone, still trembling with pleasure. "Bragging, Beau?"

"Just stating facts, ma'am."

Another giggle burst free, and then another when he nuzzled a ticklish spot on her neck before sitting up. Watching in fascination as he rolled on a condom, she reached out to caress his chest. "You're so conceited. I don't know why I put up with you."

She couldn't tear her gaze away from his cock, still a little amazed at the size of it, and that something that long and thick could feel so good inside her.

Beau tapped her chin, lifting her gaze to his. "Because I make you feel good." Moving over her again, he used his knees to push her legs wider, the frustration and emotion in his eyes disconcerting her. "And because you love me—even if you won't admit it."

Reeling with the knowledge that he knew, Charity gasped, and gasped again as he surged deep, her pussy clamping down on him as soon as he entered her. Digging her heels into his tight butt, she gripped his shoulders, stunned when he began to move right away, instead of pausing to let her adjust to him.

She was glad he did. She closed her eyes, unable to face him, not knowing what she could say. Unable to keep from looking at him, she opened her eyes again, struck by the gleam in his hooded gaze.

Braced on his arms, he stared down at her, his quick, shallow thrusts so unlike him, it alarmed her. "I'll. Give. You. All. The. Pleasure. You. Want."

He took her hard and fast, filling her with every thrust, the friction on her inner walls making her wild with pleasure. With one hand under her back, he arched her high, bending his head to take a nipple into his mouth. His other hand slid beneath her bottom, lifting her into his thrusts and surging even deeper. "As long as you keep coming back for more, I'll give you everything you need. Just. Keep. Coming. Back."

She couldn't seem to catch up, the pleasure so intense that she could only hang on to his shoulders and go for the ride. Her legs, too weak to hold on to him, fell to the sides, leaving her spread wide.

Thrilled and humbled at the need in his voice, Charity gripped him tighter. "Beau! Oh, God, Beau! Yes. Yes."

Their usually playful lovemaking turned primitive.

Wild.

Sweaty and hot.

Harsh groans and growls came from somewhere deep inside him, washing over her and adding to the decadent atmosphere.

Love for him made everything even more intense. Every brush of his body against hers, every breath he took, every soft murmur of approval and groan coming from him even sharper than ever.

Releasing her nipple, he lifted his head and stared down at her, slowing his thrusts, and digging at a sensitive spot inside her. With a groan, he shuddered. "Hmm, I love how your sweet little pussy grabs at me, cher. It makes me insane to know how your tight little bottom would grip me." Sliding the hand under her lower, Beau slid a finger over her puckered opening.

Stunned at his wickedness and at the animalistic surge of hunger for more decadence, Charity gasped, bucking her hips. "No, Beau. You can't!"

She could only imagine how intimate it would be to have him take her that way, and how much deeper she'd fall in love with him if she let the intimacy between them grow.

Fisting her hands in the bedding, she shook uncontrollably, holding on to the only solid thing in her world.

Beau.

Scraping his teeth over her neck, Beau growled. "One day I will. One day you're going to give me your virginity here, too."

Digging her heels into his bottom again, Charity bucked against him, crying out when her movements forced the tip of his finger inside her.

Crying out, she stiffened, arching against him, embarrassed and shocked that something so naughty could excite her so much. "No. I can't. Oh, God." She couldn't stop tightening on him, shaken by her body's demand for more.

Crying out as she came again, Charity moved on his cock and the finger he held just inside her, groaning in frustration that she moved so hard, his finger slipped free. Trembling helplessly, she wrapped herself around him, stunned by the vulnerability of being so helpless against her own body's demands.

Holding his finger against her most forbidden opening with enough pressure to keep her senses reeling, Beau buried his face against her neck and thrust faster. "Yes, cher. You can. You did, and it was beautiful." Holding her close, he thrust several more times and stiffened, groaning in her ear. "Yes. God, you feel so good. Every time I take you, it makes me hungry for more."

She couldn't hold back a moan as he circled her puckered opening with his finger, biting her lip against the urge to beg him to keep touching her there.

Bracing himself on his elbows, he stared down at her, breathing heavily and gorgeously disheveled. "Poor baby. You didn't want to like that and you did. There's nothing to be embarrassed about. It excited me as much as it excited you. You're a passionate woman, chéri. Don't be embarrassed about experimenting, or playing—with *me*."

Charity couldn't look him in the eye. With her face burning, she stared at his chest. "I don't do things like that." She couldn't believe she'd actually had an orgasm with his finger in her ass.

She couldn't believe how good it felt, or that she could be so wild.

She'd never been that sort of woman, and couldn't get over the change in herself whenever she was with him.

Chuckling, Beau nuzzled her jaw. "You didn't do a lot of things until I got you in my bed. There's a whole lot more to explore, baby."

Rolling off of her, he got to his feet and headed for the bathroom. "You worry too much about things, Charity. Just relax and have some fun." With a wink, he poked his head out. "Don't worry. I'll help you."

Smiling and shaking her head, Charity stared after him, her smile falling as soon as the door closed behind him. Sitting up, she straightened the tray of paints, putting the lids back on them and gathering the brushes to wash, doing it automatically while struggling to deal with her emotions.

He knew.

He knew she loved him.

He hadn't said he loved her, too.

Was it all just a game to him?

Why did she have to fall in love with someone who never took anything seriously except fun?

She glanced up when the bathroom door opened, inwardly wincing at the sight of the washcloth in his hand. His increasing demand for intimacy made hiding her feelings even more difficult, but she couldn't let him see her weakness for him again. "Beau, I can do that myself."

Ignoring her protest, Beau took the brushes from her hand and tossed them on to the tray. "I know you can, but this pussy is mine to care for. I like doing this." Spreading her thighs, he ran the warm cloth over her folds, his gaze holding hers. "Do you remember the night I took your virginity? I cleaned you then. The warm cloth feels good, doesn't it?"

Charity bit back a moan at the feel of the warm cloth moving over her delicate flesh. "It's embarrassing, Beau."

Shaking his head, Beau laughed. "Woman, you have the strangest way of looking at things. Despite my best efforts, you're still too uptight. Do you mean to say that it's all right if I lick your pussy, fuck your pussy, and use toys in your pussy, but I can't put a washcloth on it?"

Her face burned even hotter. "It's different."

Sitting back on his heels, he lifted a brow, a faint smile curving his sensuous lips. "How?"

Letting her gaze move over him, Charity found herself once again struck by what a beautiful man he was, and had to swallow heavily before speaking. "Because I'm not...um...aroused when you do this."

Beau tapped her chin, grinning as she met his gaze again, "So I can fuck you, stick my finger up your ass, but I can't wash you?"

Charity's bottom clenched. Mortified at the reminder of her weakness, she turned away. "Something like that."

Beau grinned, tossed the cloth on to the tray and shoved the entire thing onto the floor. Moving up to lie next to her, he traced a pattern on her belly. "You take things far too seriously."

Charity frowned, glancing up at him. "And you don't take things seriously enough. You're six years older than I am, and I happen to be the responsible one."

Beau tapped her nipple. "You can be responsible *and* have fun, cher." Rolling on top of her, he pushed her damp hair back and smiled down at her, his eyes dancing. "I like when you come out to play with me."

Sliding her hands through his silky hair, Charity crossed her wrists over each other at the back of his neck, pulling him closer. "I like playing with you." Frowning, she looked away.

She knew that Beau considered their lovemaking nothing more than play. She'd gone into this affair with her eyes wide open.

Still, she couldn't help but wish for more.

"Do you?" Leaning slightly over her with his head propped on his hand, Beau cupped her cheek, running his thumb back and forth over her chin. "We could do this all the time, you know."

Charity's heart raced even as her stomach tightened. Forcing a laugh, she lifted her gaze to his. "Then, neither one of us would get any work done."

Beau frowned. "You work too hard."

"So you keep telling me." Rolling away from him, she got to her feet. Not seeing any of her clothing, Charity cursed under her breath. Chilled now, but still weak from his lovemaking, Charity started rifling through the covers for her clothing, watching Beau out of the corner of her eye.

He rolled to his back, not bothering to cover himself, his eyes hard. "The difference between you and me is that I also play hard. Without taking some time to relax and have fun, you'll kill yourself. I'm not going to let that happen."

Distracted by the sight of him stretched out naked on the bed, she pulled the covers back on to the bed, shaking them out as she did. Finding her bra, she quickly put it on, aware of Beau's sharp gaze. "You play all the time, Beau. You're a lot like Hope. I don't know where she gets it. Our parents have always worked their fingers to the bone. That's how we were raised."

She found her pants, but not her panties. Mentally shrugging, she pulled her pants on, seeing her shirt across the room as she did. "I like playing with you, Beau, but a few hours here and there are all I can afford."

"If you marry me, cher, we can play every day."

She sucked in a breath, her heart pounding furiously. "That's not funny."

She wanted to cry. Swallowing heavily, she continued to dress.

Beau's expression hardened, and became distant. "It wasn't a joke." With a smile, he held up one of her socks, pulling it back when she lunged for it, dangling it just out of reach.

Climbing on the bed, Charity lunged again, her temper flaring. "Stop goofing off." Catching her sock, she yanked it from his grasp, her hands shaking. "Life can't be all fun and games, you know."

Beau's expression softened, the tension that had been in his eyes gone. "Of course not, beautiful, but we should all make time to play." Rolling her to her back, he held up her other sock, holding it out of reach. "I want a kiss first."

Charity's stomach knotted at the abrupt change from the man who'd asked her to marry him to the playful lover. Figuring he'd probably just been caught up in the moment, and regretted his impulsive proposal as soon as the words left his mouth, she struggled to appear unaffected. Shrugging, she lifted her face to his, swallowing a sob.

He touched his lips to hers, nibbling at her bottom lip before tracing it with his tongue. "So sweet." He deepened his kiss, sliding his tongue against hers in a warm, affectionate kiss that dispelled some of the chill, leaving her fighting to hide her response.

Lifting his head, he clicked his tongue. "Charity, you're all tense again." His eyes sharpened, and he looked as if he wanted to say something, but the tension left his body in a rush, and his expression softened again. "I've been trying to teach you how to relax and enjoy life—"

"How am I doing?" She forced a smile, not wanting to ruin the closeness she felt from their recent lovemaking, especially with him warm and solid on top of her.

As she'd hoped, Beau grinned, his eyes flashed with what she suspected to be frustration. "You're a very good student, but I think you need to stay after school." Brushing her lips with his, he kept his voice low and intimate. "Spend the night with me, cher. I can hold you all night."

Charity swallowed heavily, looking away. "You know I can't do that."

She'd already made enough of a fool of herself over him, and she didn't want anyone to find out. "You promised we could keep this private."

Wrapping his arms around her, he nuzzled her neck. "It's cold outside. Listen to that wind. Wouldn't you rather spend the night in bed here with me? I'll keep you nice and warm."

Spent and languid, she moved against him, loving the feel of his hard, warm body against hers. The temptation to stay with him got harder to resist each time he asked. "Beau, you know as well as I do that someone would see me leave in the morning and it would be all over town by noon. Mom and the dads would have a fit."

Her parents had a ménage marriage, and had always been pretty liberal, a requirement for the residents of Desire, Oklahoma, a town founded primarily for ménage relationships.

Charity and her older sister, Hope, had been born and raised in Desire, and understood how the overprotective men of Desire thought better than most people.

Beau lifted a brow. "That wouldn't be an issue if you agreed to marry me."

Charity pushed at him and scrambled from the bed. "Beau, don't."

Beau reclined against the pillows in a deceptively relaxed pose, but his eyes glittered with anger and hurt. "So I'm good to have around for the sex, but that's it?"

She didn't want to hurt his feelings, and didn't want this to end. Worn out after a long day at the club and frustrated that Beau never seemed to take anything seriously, she felt a headache starting as her temper snapped. "Stop playing. I don't want to do this right now."

Beau's hand whipped out, faster than a snake, and wrapped around her wrist. "I'm not fucking playing. You love me. Don't even try to deny it. I see it. I feel it."

Hating the hurt in his eyes, Charity blew out a breath and dropped to the bed. "Okay. I'll admit it. I love you." Glancing at him, she swallowed again at the satisfaction glittering in his eyes. "I'm scared, Beau. I don't want to rush into anything I'm going to regret."

"You think you'd regret marrying me?"

Getting to her feet, she slipped on her shoes. "Beau, please, let's not get into this tonight. I've got to get up early. I have a lot of things to do tomorrow if we're going to be ready on time. The grand reopening is two weeks away."

Her stomach knotted at his steady look, but she felt too emotionally raw to deal with the subject of marriage with him right now. She was very afraid that they'd end up fighting, and what had become so vital to her would be over. Lifting her gaze to his, she swallowed heavily. "Please." Her voice cracked, revealing her desperation.

Beau stared at her for several long seconds, his eyes narrowed, as though considering his options. Finally, his face cleared and he nodded once. "You're tired. We'll do this your way tonight, but this weekend, you and I are going to have a talk."

He slid from the bed and reached for his jeans. "Wait. I'll drive you home. You probably walked again so no one would see your car parked here."

She hated the guilt that assailed her. "What we have between us is private, Beau."

He pulled a fresh shirt over his head and sat down to pull on his socks. "It pisses me off, you know—the fact that you don't want to be seen with me."

"Damn it, Beau! It's not like that, and you know it."

"Forget it. It's late. We'll talk about it later." After pulling on his shoes, he got to his feet and gripped her upper arm. "But we *will* talk about this." With a hand at her back, he walked her down the hall and to the living room. He picked up her jacket from where he'd tossed it over the back of the sofa and held it up for her.

Wanting to lighten the mood, Charity smiled up at him over her shoulder. "You always start undressing me as soon as I walk through the door."

Instead of the teasing smile she'd expected, Beau frowned down at her. "Maybe that's part of the problem."

Charity got a funny feeling in the pit of her stomach. "Look, Beau, I'd better get out of here before one of us says something stupid. I'm tired, and I know I'm not handling this well. You stay here. I'll walk home by myself. I'll text you when I get in."

"I'll take you home."

"That's not necessary. It's not a long walk, and nothing's going to happen to me on the streets of Desire. Hell, I think Ace is on tonight. I don't want to run into him."

Beau opened the door. "I'll take you home."

"Fine. Do whatever you want to do." He'd been moody lately, and Beau was never moody. She had a feeling that something was going to come to a head soon and she wasn't looking forward to it.

She done something she'd sworn not to do.

She'd fallen in love with a man who breezed through life without a care, and couldn't be serious about anything.

She loved him, and loved their time together. Their nights together were a luxury she allowed herself, a luxury that became more of a necessity every day.

Walking down the sidewalk, they turned the corner and headed down the street she lived on, in an apartment above her parents' diner. The streets were quiet except for the music playing in the distance. "It sounds like the bar's busy."

"Sounds like."

When the wind kicked up, she dug her scarf out of her pocket, uncomfortably aware of the lengthening silence. Warmed by the hand he kept at her back, she looked up at him, her breath catching at the surge of love she felt for him.

Sometimes it threatened to choke her.

She wanted nothing more than to spend the rest of her life with him, and kept hoping he would change. "Beau, we're too different. We're total opposites. You never take anything seriously." What scared her the most was that he wouldn't take their marriage seriously.

"Of course I do, but you take things far too seriously. Life is to be enjoyed. You don't take enough time to enjoy yourself."

"We don't all have inheritances to live off of."

Beau gripped her arm, bringing her to a stop, his expression hard. "Is that what this is all about? You think that I'll blow all my money and won't be able to support you?"

Charity tried to shake off his hold, but couldn't. Looking around to make sure no one could see them, she lowered her voice to a whisper. "Don't be ridiculous. I just want a man who's steady."

The incredulous look in Beau's eyes made her feel like an idiot. "And you think I'm not?"

Charity fisted her hands in her pockets, looking straight ahead. "You like to play. You wouldn't want the responsibility of a wife."

Beau continued down the sidewalk, his arm flat against her lower back. "Don't presume to tell me what I want."

Chilled by his cold flat tone, Charity shivered. "It would never work between us."

"It has so far."

"That's because I'm always in your world. You'd never make it in mine."

"I wouldn't want to live in a world of all work and no play. Dull. And you don't know my world. You've never tried to. All you want from me is to be in my bed."

Charity shivered again, more from nerves than from the cold. "I thought that's what you wanted. You've always been anxious to get me there."

Beau's smile seemed full of self-recrimination, but it could have been the trick of the light. "Touché."

Since the subject had come up, she couldn't stop herself from asking a question that had plagued her for months. "Do you think I'm dull?"

Beau grinned, a flash of white in the near darkness, but she had a feeling he wasn't amused. "That question proves to me that you don't know me at all."

Charity shook her head, glancing around for any sign of the town sheriff, Ace, who also happened to be her overprotective brother-in-law. "See, always jokes with you. You can never be serious."

Pulling her to his side, he hugged her. "I'm *very* serious about marrying you, chéri. I want us to spend the rest of our lives together. I can take care of you, Charity. I love you."

"I love you, too, Beau. But I want more. I want children. Not yet, but one day." Terrified that the differences between them would become more apparent, and cause more tension every day, she fought to resist him.

"And you don't think I'll be a good father?"

Charity blew out a breath, frustrated and too tired and shaky to deal with this subject. "I think you'd be a *fun* father. Don't forget. Hope and I have *three* fathers and they've always worked their fingers to the bone. They've always been there for us, but it hasn't been easy. I can only imagine what it would be like for one man."

She paused as they reached the diner her parents owned, and where her mother and three fathers worked every day. The diner was closed now, but they'd be there about four thirty to get started on breakfast the next day.

She started walking again, trying not to imagine what it would be like to be married to a man like Beau. There would be lots of laughter and loving.

But she couldn't help but wonder if he would really love her once the initial excitement was gone. The honeymoon couldn't last forever, and when real life trickled in again, he'd ignore problems and she'd worry them to death. They'd fight, and he'd quickly become bored with her.

She could almost see it play out.

She started up the steps to her apartment, feeling much older than twenty-three.

Beau's voice came from directly behind her. "I understand that you were raised with three fathers, Charity, but I'm perfectly capable of taking care of you, and our children."

She unlocked the door to the apartment and opened it. As always, she'd left a low light on. Turning, she placed a hand on his chest.

"Beau—"

Shaking his head, Beau ran a hand down her arm. "Never mind. It's late, and you're exhausted."

Bending, he kissed her, brushing her hair back from her face. "I'll see you tomorrow. Sleep well."

He pushed her inside and closed the door. "Lock it, Charity."

Charity locked the door and leaned back again it, so worn out that even the thought of getting ready for bed seemed insurmountable. She *was* exhausted, but she doubted sleep would come easy tonight.

She didn't know what to do.

She was too scared to marry him—too afraid that he wouldn't be there when she needed him. Too scared that he'd quickly become bored with the idea of marriage.

But, she loved him far too much to walk away.

Fisting a hand over her stomach, she dropped her head back against the door and blinked back tears.

She needed more time to think it through. She'd never been the type to rush into things the way Beau did.

She couldn't make such an important decision about her future without knowing if they could deal with the huge differences between them.

She wanted things to stay the same until they could figure it out.

She needed time, and she had a feeling that time had run out.

What could she do?

If she walked away, she'd always wonder.

If she married him, she'd always be waiting for him to walk away.

Either way, she faced a hurt that would change her forever.

And there wasn't a damned thing she could do about it.

Chapter Two

Frustrated with himself, and with Charity, Beau emerged from the alley next to the diner, unsurprised to find Ace Tyler parked at the curb, apparently waiting for him.

Opening the door to the SUV emblazoned with the sheriff's logo, Beau got in, closing the door behind him, wincing when he realized he'd slammed it.

"Cold out tonight." Beau glanced at Ace as he put his hands in front of the vents to warm them, ignoring his friend's searching look.

After a pause long enough to indicate that he knew something was wrong, Ace put the SUV in gear. "Yep. I got a report that the blizzard's supposed to get here earlier than expected. Everybody who has a plow has already hooked it up to the front of their trucks and is on standby."

Ace grinned. "I'm glad that fundraiser we had made enough money to buy one of the big plows."

Beau chuckled. "Do you think anyone ever figured out that the money for that went into the town coffers, and you, your brothers, the Ericksons, and I bought it?"

Ace shrugged. "They can suspect all they want, but they can't prove a thing. Jesse and Hope don't even know about it." Turning his head, he lifted a brow. "You didn't tell Charity, did you?"

Beau's stomach knotted. "A series of one-night stands doesn't make us a couple."

Ace stopped at a stop sign before turning the corner. "If I thought you were having one-night stands with my sister-in-law, I would have kicked your ass by now."

Looking out the windows, Beau avoided Ace's scrutiny and scanned the deserted street, his attention sharpening when they slowed as they passed the bar. "I'm just damned glad that someone knows how to drive the damned snowplow. Boone and Chase's new partners, the Madisons, sound like they know what they're doing. They're gonna have to teach us so we can take turns."

Ace leaned forward, checking out the parking lot next to the bar. "Yep."

Beau sat back as they pulled away. "I didn't hear the weather tonight. I'll get my plow hooked up in the morning."

Ace glanced at him, and looked away, probably seeing more in one short glance than most people did by staring. "Suppose you were busy tonight."

Beau clenched his fists, frustrated at how the evening had ended. "Yeah. She was late. Stayed and worked on some stuff for the Grand Reopening." He should have been home in bed with a naked Charity in his arms. Instead, he was out on a cold night and restless. Glancing at Ace, he waved his hand. "Don't take me home. I'll ride with you a bit if you don't mind."

Ace shrugged, his expression never changing. The sheriff had always been hard to read, but Beau knew his friend well.

Ace could be like a dog with a bone while interrogating a suspect, but with friends, he waited them out.

The end result always seemed to be the same. Desire's sheriff always found out what he wanted to know.

Amused, despite his bad temper, Beau leaned back and sighed. "You're a fucking workaholic like Charity. Hope works, but makes time to play. She makes *you* play. How the hell do you work that out?"

Glancing at him, Ace shrugged again. "It's never really been an issue. Charity turn you down again?"

"Yes. Came right out and flat out asked her this time instead of working around it so I didn't scare her off." Beau blew out a breath, but the knots in his stomach didn't seem to be easing. "Says I like to play too much, and would just be bored with being a husband and father."

Ace frowned. "You still haven't told her the whole story, have you?"

Beau bristled. "She doesn't ask about things, and I sure as hell don't think I have to prove myself to her. Is it so wrong to want her to believe me? Christ, it pisses me off when she lectures me as if I was ten years old and not getting my chores done."

Ace glanced at him as they turned the corner. "Despite all the crap these women spew about taking care of themselves, a woman needs to know her man will be there for her when she needs him."

Once he turned the corner, he glanced at Beau again. "Tell her everything, Beau."

Beau shrugged again. "We'll see. We're going to talk this weekend. I'm going to see how it goes." Meeting Ace's look, he frowned. "Don't give me that look. She'll know everything before I marry her, but I'm not about to dump my issues on her. She's got enough on her plate."

Ace laughed softly. "Your accent is more pronounced when you get pissed off."

"Kiss my ass, Sheriff." Blowing out a breath, he grinned at Ace's laughter, and shook his head. "Does Hope know what an ass you are?"

Ace chuckled. "She must. She calls me one often enough, usually when she's not getting her way."

"Smart girl."

Ace raised a brow. "I think so. She married me. She's stubborn, though, and spoiled. She knows how I am, and still tries to get around me."

Beau laughed, some of his tension easing. "She can't help it. Both of them have always been headstrong."

"Their daddies should have turned them over their knees once in a while. If they had, I wouldn't have to spank Hope so often now." The laughter and possessiveness in Ace's tone told Beau his friend didn't mind disciplining his wife a bit.

Beau couldn't help it. He burst out laughing. "Yeah, it's their daddies' fault. That has nothing to do with it. You spank Hope because she goads you into it, and you enjoy every minute of it."

Ace smiled, saying nothing.

Wishing he had the same closeness with Charity, Beau made himself more comfortable, enjoying the quiet as they drove down the streets of Desire. As they passed his store, he reminded himself that he'd have to check on some things earlier than he had planned. "I'm going to go check out the warehouse tomorrow morning, but I'll be back. You need help with anything in getting ready for the storm?"

"And to check on Anna?"

Beau's stomach knotted. "Yeah. Jeffrey probably hasn't given a thought to the blizzard. Fucking asshole." He took a deep breath and blew it out, hoping to loosen some of the tension inside him. "So what do you need help with?"

Ace's smile fell, and in a blink of an eye, he was all business. "I'm probably going to need some help if we get cars stuck in this. Dillon and Ryder aren't going to be able to do it all alone."

Beau nodded, thinking of his friends who owned the town's only garage and gas station, and how busy they'd be out towing once the storm started. "Hopefully, everyone will be smart enough to stay off the road."

Ace grimaced. "You never know. With all the new stores, traffic's been increasing, especially on the weekend. It seems like we're seeing new people in town every day. Our small town's growing." His face hardened. "It just better stay peaceful. Troublemakers piss me off."

Beau couldn't help but smile. The men in Desire were very protective of their women, and didn't want them bothered by ridicule. Ménage relationships were prevalent in town. Many men who lived here also liked to dominate their women, and it infuriated them when assholes from out of town came to Desire thinking that the women were fair game.

Troublemakers in Desire got thrown out of town, by word, and if that didn't work, by deed. Beau had even done it himself a few times, but no one outshone Ace when it came to getting rid of trouble.

"I heard you'd got the funding for some new men. Any candidates?"

"Yeah. Met with them a couple of weeks ago. Good men. Best friends since they met in the service. They'll be here in another month or so."

Beau stiffened, something in Ace's tone alerting him. "Problem? If they have issues with the way we live around here—"

Glancing at him, Ace shook his head. "No, it's not that at all. It'll be hard for them, but not in the way you think." Blowing out a breath, he waited until he turned another corner before glancing at Beau again. "Look, Beau, we're close enough to being brothers-in-law for me to know that I can confide in you. Their business is their business, but they're hard. Cold. I don't want people here to think they disapprove. In fact, the opposite is true. They shared a woman."

Beau blinked. "That's good. Are they bringing her with them?"

"No." Ace's jaw clenched in anger, his eyes going hard. "They sound like they really loved her. They apparently liked the arrangement they had, at least for a while. She couldn't live with the disapproval. The names. The looks. They tried to keep it a secret for her sake, and they were all miserable. She went out one night and got drunk and drove off a bridge."

Beau's stomach did a nosedive. "Jesus."

"Yeah." Ace stopped at a stop sign and turned to him. "They mentioned it, but didn't go into details. I found it when I did a background check. I read the police report. It appears they don't know if it was an accident or suicide. Finally settled on accident, but if I was in their shoes, I would always wonder."

Shaking his head, Beau cursed. He couldn't even imagine the pain they must have gone through. "I don't know how they got through it."

Ace hit the gas again. "Like I said. They're hard. Cold. Said they wish they'd known about Desire a long time ago. They seem like the type of men who'd do anything to keep that kind of thing from happening here. Just the kind of men I was looking for, don't you think? They're sure as hell not going to pass judgment here, and I don't think they'd have any patience for anyone causing trouble for the women here."

Pleased that Ace seemed to have the perfect candidates for more deputies, Beau smiled. "I didn't doubt you for a minute." They drove for a few minutes in silence, going past the bar again. "I'm sure you'll be glad to have more nights off. I doubt that Hope likes sleeping alone."

Ace grinned. "I make it up to her. She suspects, you know."

Beau shrugged, knowing that Ace was talking about his relationship with Charity. "Does she? I don't care. I'm getting sick and tired of sneaking around. It's starting to piss me off."

Ace inclined his head. "I can imagine. I'm a little surprised you've put up with it this long. I figured we would have been related by now."

Beau laughed humorlessly. "Your wife has a very different temperament than her sister. Charity's too serious and doesn't appreciate my efforts to get her to relax and have some fun."

A few minutes later, Ace pulled into Beau's driveway. Shifting into park, he turned to Beau. "Charity loves you."

"I know." Beau sighed and rubbed his stomach where the knot began to form again. "That's not the problem. She fights my efforts to get her to relax, and thinks that life is nothing but a series of fun and games to me, *but* as soon as I bring up anything serious or start talking about a future, it scares her off. I want to take care of her. She looks so damned tired."

"Yeah. Both of them have been busting their asses to get the club open again, but Charity wasn't ready to go when Hope left today. My wife called her sister a damned machine." Ace smiled, his affection for his wife's sister apparent. "Said she was on the phone arguing with some poor unsuspecting salesman earlier."

Beau chuckled, imagining her pacing back and forth in front of her desk as she chewed someone a new asshole. "I've been on the receiving end of that enough times to feel sorry for him."

Reaching for his door handle, Beau paused. "I've gotta do something. We can't go on like this anymore. I'm sick of the charade. I'll tell her everything tomorrow when she leaves that damned club. You're going to be best man at the wedding, aren't you?"

"Wouldn't miss it. Good luck."

Beau watched Ace drive away, knowing luck wouldn't have anything to do with it.

He'd explain about his childhood, and his family, and hope it would make a difference.

No matter what it took, Beau wanted Charity in his life, and he wanted the world to know it.

Chapter Three

Beau walked into Lady Desire, the club Charity and Hope owned, closing the new door behind him. Rubbing his hands together against the chill, he couldn't help but smile when he thought about where he could warm them up in a hurry, and Charity's reaction to that.

The thought of her beaded nipples against his palms made his cock stir, but it was the thought of overcoming her struggles to get away and her squeals of laughter and cursing that excited him the most.

He paused just inside the door to look around, and caught sight of Boone and Chase installing ceiling tiles. As he made his way toward them, he looked around, impressed by the amount of work that had been done, and the women's understated elegant style.

It infuriated him that they'd had to redo the place so soon after opening, especially for something so unnecessary, and just plain evil.

Several weeks earlier, a man, crazed by the fact that he couldn't have the woman he wanted, a woman now married to his friends Royce and King, threw a Molotov cocktail through the front window in a fit of rage. The subsequent fire and water did just enough damage to make Charity and Hope close the club for repairs, but thankfully, no one had been hurt.

An attack on the women was just the kind of thing that the men of Desire feared most.

Walking toward his friends, Beau heard the sound of Charity's voice raised in anger coming from her office. Fearing that someone was in there with her, and she might be in danger, he started to race in that direction, coming to a halt when Boone called out to him.

"She's okay, Beau." Wiping his hands, Boone strolled toward him, nodding toward Charity's office. "She's been on the phone arguing with salesman and suppliers all day."

As Beau got closer, he could see into Charity's office, and blew out a breath of relief when he saw her pacing back and forth in front of her desk.

Boone slapped his back. "You didn't really think Chase and I would just be standing here if she was in trouble, do you?"

Scraping a hand over his face, Beau shook his head, the tension easing. "Hell, I wasn't even thinking about anything except getting to her."

Shaking his head, Boone started back to where his brother stood on a ladder. "I know that feeling well."

From the top of the ladder, Chase grinned down at Beau as he reached out a hand for another tile. "Your woman's got a nice head of steam on her today. She's been chewing people out for hours and doesn't seem to be running out of mad. You two have a fight or something?"

Beau shrugged, looking toward Charity's office door and watching her pace back and forth as she argued with someone about carpet. "Or something."

Looking back at his friends, he watched Chase slide in another tile. "Don't let her hear you say that she's my woman. She's still under the illusion that no one knows."

Straightening after retrieving another tile, Boone blinked. "She was born and raised in this town. You'd think she would understand the way things work here."

Beau nodded, forcing a smile. "I think it's a matter of believing what she wants to believe." Glancing toward Charity's office, he blinked at her inventive cursing. "I'm gonna have to rip those blinders off of her real soon."

Chase finished installing the tile, glancing at Beau as he accepted another one from Boone. "I can't believe you've put up with it for this long."

Beau grimaced, his anger at himself, and his frustration with Charity mounting. "Yeah, there's a lot of that going around." Looking toward the doorway again, he clenched his jaw, determined that he'd have it out with Charity once and for all.

"It won't be much longer." Beau winced when Charity slammed the phone down and kicked her desk.

Turning back to his friends, he smiled, wanting to change the subject. "So, how are Rachel and Theresa?"

As he'd expected, both men grinned, and seemed more than happy to talk about their wife and daughter. Boone handed another tile to his brother. "Rachel's great, and Theresa has to be the cutest baby that ever lived."

Chase laughed. "Theresa says 'dada' now. Man, I'll tell you. I never get enough of it. There's nothing on earth like being a daddy."

The pride and love on their faces and in their voices made Beau more aware of the emptiness inside him.

He'd totally renovated his house years ago, and loved it, but ever since Charity came into his life, the house seemed cold and empty. He'd built a home for a family, and couldn't wait to fill it.

Still grinning, Boone shook his head. "She's gonna break hearts one day."

Chase paused, grimacing. "I can't say I'm looking forward to that. I want her to be daddies' girl as long as possible."

Beau couldn't resist ribbing Chase, who used to be somewhat of a playboy. "And then some man, just like you, is going to come along and want her."

Chase paled. "Don't say that. I hear enough of that. Hell, I don't know what the hell I'm gonna do."

Taking pity on his friend, Beau gestured toward Charity's office. "I wouldn't worry about it too much. Hope and Charity are still their daddies' girls."

Chase nodded. "Yeah, well I'm sure their fathers are relieved to have men like you and Ace to take care of them. I know I'd feel better if men like you two came along for Theresa."

Beau shrugged. "Yeah, well, now I just need to convince Charity."

"Stubborn, huh?" Boone broke open another box of tiles. "She'll come around. She's always been the type of woman who weighs things carefully. She'll see that you're the right man for her."

"You son of a bitch! Why the hell didn't you tell me that before? I just spent an hour on the phone with that asshole salesman and he didn't say a word. Fine! Yes, I will. I just said I will, didn't I?" Charity cursed and slammed the phone down, kicking a box in the corner as she turned.

Beau grimaced as more cursing followed. "I'd better go see if she broke anything."

Boone gestured toward the ceiling. "We only have two more tiles to put up and then we'll get out of here. We have some things to take care of at home before the snow starts. Rachel gave us a grocery list and we have to go buy a sled for Theresa."

Beau grinned, anticipation flowing through his veins at the thought of being alone with Charity. "Have fun with that sled." He headed toward Charity's office, frustrated that she picked up the phone again. Leaning against the doorway, he watched as she rifled through papers on her usually immaculate desk, taking the time just savor the sight of her.

Her quick, angry movements irritated him, and made him think of the languorous way she'd moved against him the night before.

She carried so much stress, stress that he could alleviate in small segments, but it wasn't enough.

He tuned out her conversation and just watched her, wondering if she had any idea just how much he loved her. The attraction between them had started the night of the party her parents had thrown shortly after she and Hope came home from college.

Her long, dark, shiny hair and chocolate brown eyes gave her an exotic look, even more pronounced by her olive skin. Curvy, but with a tiny waist, she had a body that screamed *sex*.

Her smile stole his breath, her dimples giving her the appearance of an imp. She had the perseverance and attention to detail, though, of a four-star general.

She liked everything in order, and lived on lists.

Even while talking on the phone, she sorted papers into piles. Every pencil had a place in one holder, while pens went into another. Everything had been ruthlessly organized, even the notes she'd stuck to her bulletin board, which had been lined up perfectly.

She kept every aspect of her life in scrupulous order, and he'd found out right from the start that she didn't want any complications in her life.

That included getting involved with him.

It had taken over a year to get her to go out with him, and she would only see him if he'd agree to keep it a secret. He'd been so in love with her by then that he would have agreed to anything, confident that it wouldn't remain a secret for long.

He thought he'd just begun to make headway when tragedy struck, and the club she and her sister had spent their life savings to open was nearly destroyed.

Since then, he hadn't wanted to pressure her, especially with the stress already on her, but he'd had enough.

He wanted to teach her how to have fun—to throw the lists away once in a while and do something spontaneous.

He wanted the chance to love her the way she deserved to be loved—and that didn't include hiding their relationship from the rest of the world.

He heard Boone and Chase leave just as Charity hung up the phone, and he straightened in an effort to seek a more comfortable position, but with his cock pressing against his zipper, it wasn't easy.

Meeting Charity's glare, he grinned and hoped he could tease her out of her bad mood.

He gestured toward the foot she kept rubbing. "Hey, beautiful. You hurt yourself? Wanna play doctor?"

* * * *

Charity shook her head, smiling despite her effort not to. Restacking the papers on her desk, she craned her neck to look past him. "Be quiet. Boone or Chase might hear you."

"Boone and Chase left." Beau wagged his brows, his mischievous smile pebbling her nipples. "So, you wanna play doctor, beautiful? I promise, I'll look you over real good, and even kiss all your boo-boos." His smile fell, his expression becoming somber, but his eyes still danced with mischief. "It's my duty."

Sitting back in her chair, Charity let her eyes feast on him, relieved that he didn't mention their disagreement of the night before. Biting the inside of her cheek, she struggled to keep a straight face. "I have a feeling that if I play doctor with you, you wouldn't get anywhere near my foot."

Beau's attempt to look insulted might have been more successful if the amusement in his eyes hadn't given him away. "I resent that. Of course I would look at your foot." He grinned, his eyes narrowing. "Eventually."

Enjoying their banter, Charity narrowed her eyes, mimicking his look. "Let me guess. You'd have to check out my breasts to make sure that they didn't somehow have something to do with my foot hurting. Then, you'd have to get my pants off because you couldn't quite see what you need to see with my pants in the way."

Beau nodded soberly. "I'd have to be thorough."

Another giggle escaped before she could prevent it, and it struck her how quickly Beau had dispelled her bad mood. "Uh-huh. Thorough. Is that what you call it?"

Watching him, she leaned back, her pulse leaping at his slow smile, and it took every ounce of self-control Charity possessed not to burst into laughter.

God, she loved him.

He could make her laugh with just a look, make her happy just by walking through the door.

He made her feel *good.*

She found his playfulness contagious, and made her worries feel small and insignificant. The stress of her day seemed to melt away whenever she was with him.

But, she didn't want just a playmate.

She wanted someone who would be with her through thick and thin. She wanted someone who wouldn't get bored when dealing with bills and the responsibility of children.

She wanted a lover who would also be her partner—a man who wouldn't leave her to deal with all the problems and responsibilities while he played.

She wanted forever—and she couldn't imagine forever with anyone but Beau.

Hope knew how she felt about Beau, and was constantly trying to play matchmaker, no matter how many times Charity explained it to her.

Her sister had married someone solid. Responsible.

A man she could lean on, a man like her fathers.

Inwardly wincing at the twinge of guilt she felt at hiding the fact that she and Beau were lovers from her family, Charity looked away from his smiling face, straightening the pile of receipts on her desk.

Hope would be furious when—if—she ever found out.

If her sister knew she was sleeping with Beau, she'd be planning the wedding. Her parents loved Beau and if they knew she and Beau were having an affair, they'd do everything in their power to get her to marry him.

Opening the drawer to her left, she dropped the receipts she'd already sorted inside to deal with later. Suddenly aware of the lengthy silence, she glanced up at him, unsurprised to find him watching her. Forcing a smile, she shook her head. "It's hard to believe that you're older than I am."

Beau clicked his tongue. "So young to have forgotten how to play."

Charity snorted and sat up, folding her hands in front of her on her desk, mentally rescheduling her day. "You play enough for both of us."

Beau straightened and came into the room, circling her desk, and settled himself on the corner, his thigh dangling very close to her own, his nearness making her heart race. Reaching out, he ran the backs of his fingers down her cheek, his touch and the tenderness in his eyes doing strange things to her stomach while awakening every erogenous zone. "I want to come over tonight. I want to seduce you. Slowly."

Her pulse tripped, the immediate surge of lust making the inner walls of her pussy clench and tingle with anticipation. "Damn it, Beau. You know I can't resist when you say things like that."

She could already imagine it. She could almost feel the slow slide of his hands and lips moving over her.

Bending low, he brushed his lips over hers, reaching out to cup her breast as he did, his slow, seductive movements enthralling her. "I know." He brushed his lips with hers again. "With you, I need every advantage I can get."

Charity shivered at the feel of his warm breath on hers, her nipples beading tightly in a demand for attention. "You have too much of an advantage as it is."

Beau smiled against her lips, lifting a hand to tease the ends of her hair. "I love playing with you. Teasing you. Tormenting you. I need to keep you coming back for more. I'll do whatever it takes to keep you."

Her body tingled with an awareness that had her shifting uncomfortably in her seat. She leaned into him, unable to help herself. Turning her head and lifting it slightly, she brushed her lips against his, breathing in the scent of him like an addict. "You have a way of playing that's a little hard to resist."

"Good. Does that mean you're going to let me come over to play with you tonight?"

Charity leaned closer, breathing in the exotic clean scent that was uniquely him. "Hmm. I bought a roast."

Nibbling on her bottom lip, Beau ran his finger back and forth over her beaded nipple. "Is that an invitation to dinner?"

The knowledge that each night she and Beau spent together could be their last made every minute they spent together even more precious.

This thing between them couldn't last forever, and she dreaded the moment it ended.

Dreaded it more every day.

The tension between them couldn't be ignored much longer, and knowing that she caused most of it made her feel even worse.

Charity let her lips slide lower to brush against his jaw, careful to keep her tone playful, while inside her heart ached. "Gotta keep your energy up."

Cupping the back of her head, he wordlessly encouraged her, sliding his hand inside her shirt and unhooked the front closure of her cotton bra. "That's not all you keep up."

Giggling, Charity pushed him away, hurriedly fastening her bra again. "Cute. Now go away and let me finish." She missed his touch already, and the dark gleam in his eyes almost had her giving in to temptation to close the door and let him take her right on top of her desk.

With a combination of a groan and a chuckle, Beau got to his feet. "Fine. I'll get out of here so you can finish up. I'll be over around six." His narrowed gaze sharpened. "You'd better be there."

Charity waved her hand negligently, knowing that if she didn't finish in time, he would understand. "Don't you have to close up the store?"

Pausing just inside the door, Beau shrugged, his eyes unreadable. "That's why I hire employees—so I can spend time with you."

Shaking her head, Charity blew out a breath, wondering if she'd ever get through to him. "Beau, you can't just hire people so you can play."

"Sure I can."

"There's more to life than play."

"I know that. There's also more to life than work." Leaning against the doorway, he crossed his arms over his wide chest, his eyes hooded. "When are you going to marry me?"

Charity groaned, dropping her head on her hand. "Beau, don't ruin it. You'd hate marriage. Too much responsibility for a man like you."

"You can't keep avoiding the subject."

Straightening in her seat, she picked up a pencil and tapped it on the desk, nervous now. "We've already *covered* this subject. Damn it, Beau. I love you. You know that. We're lovers. Why can't that be enough for you?" It appeared they'd arrived at a stalemate, and it scared her. Her stomach knotted and churned.

She didn't want to lose him, but it would be even worse if they stayed together and he got bored with her or considered her a burden.

He wanted fun and adventure, and she was willing to go along with that, but if she married him, she'd expect more, something that was bound to drive Beau crazy and have him looking for a way to escape.

Beau stepped toward her, leaning over her desk. He took the pencil from her hand and tossed it aside. "Because I love you, Charity. Just because I like to have fun, and play, doesn't mean I don't know how to take care of you. It doesn't mean I don't take care of my responsibilities, something I thought I'd made clear. I run a successful business, don't I?"

Charity stiffened, her stomach knotting. "You run a business that's all about play, a business you started with the money left to you by your grandfather. You don't know what it's like to struggle."

She jumped to her feet, too nervous to sit still. "I don't care about the money, Beau, it's the attitude that drives me crazy. Hard work is all I know. My dads have always been there whenever one of us needed them. Marriage and children are a hell of a responsibility."

Beau ran a hand through his hair, his expression one of frustration. "I damned well *will* be there for you, and my children, but that doesn't mean I can't enjoy life! There's not a damned thing wrong with enjoying your work. *You* don't know how to play. To relax. To have fun."

She gestured toward the papers on her desk, while mentally running through the list of things she still had to do before the grand reopening. She could feel her neck tighten up almost immediately, the stress of worrying about getting everything done on time giving her the beginning of a headache. "I don't have time to play."

Beau's expression softened, his voice dropping to an intimate drawl as he closed the distance between them. "Yes, you do. You play with me."

Charity moaned at the feel of his warm lips against her neck, sighing at the feel of being enveloped in his warmth. "You're corrupting me. Damn it, Beau, I've got work to do. I don't have time for this. Please go."

She'd made the mistake of falling in love with a man she could never live with, and it hurt. Afraid that she would start crying in front of him, she swallowed the lump in her throat and pushed him away. "Please. I don't want to talk about this anymore. I can't take any more today. Please."

Beau released her, his face hardening as he stepped away from her. "Fine. I've had enough of this conversation myself. I'm tired of wasting my time with a woman who doesn't love me enough to believe in me—a woman who's so embarrassed about loving me that she doesn't even want her family to know."

Shaking his head, he smiled sadly. "It's funny. Our relationship is the only thing in this world you don't take seriously. I'm just a man who knows how to satisfy you. When you do decide to take what I feel for you seriously, you know where to find me."

Sucking in a breath at the sharp stab of pain and fear, she stared up at him, chilled by the distance he'd put between them, both physically and emotionally. "What are you saying?"

Beau eyes narrowed, becoming hard and cold. "I'm saying that *I'm* tired of playing *your* games. You know how I feel about you. You know that I want to marry you. I'm not going to let you keep putting me through this emotional wringer, Charity."

The lump in Charity's throat threatened to choke her. Even though she swallowed heavily, her voice didn't come out as more than a ragged whisper. "Are you saying that you don't want to be with me anymore?"

God, it hurt!

It hurt even more than she'd expected—more than she thought she could bear.

Beau's sad smile made her stomach hurt even more. "No, Charity. I'm saying I want to spend my life with you. You say you don't want to play games—then commit. To this. To us. When you're ready to do that, I'll be waiting. I don't want to hide what we have anymore. I don't want to wonder if I'm going to see you, and wonder what you're going to do when people find out about us. I love you, Charity, and because I do, I can't live this way anymore." Turning, he started out the door.

Charity stared after him, stunned. Jumping to her feet, she held on to her desk, her knees turning to rubber. "Beau! You can't do this. You like to play. We play. Why the hell do you have to want more?"

Pausing, he braced a hand on the doorframe, sighing as he half turned. "I told you. Because I love you, cher, and I want a life with you. I want it all. I'm tired of trying to convince you of that. You're just going to have to figure it out on your own."

Stunned, she watched him turn and walk away.

She stood for several heart-pounding seconds, her breath coming out in rapid gulps as she tried to comprehend what had just happened. Panicked that she'd ruined everything and just lost the man she loved, she leapt forward, hitting her leg on the corner as she raced to the doorway of her office just in time to see him close the front door behind him.

What had she done?

Furious at him, and at herself, and more scared than she'd ever been in her life, she moved on shaky legs around her desk and dropped into her seat.

What the hell had she done?

She'd ruined everything. She couldn't let it end. She just couldn't.

The phone rang, startling her so badly she jumped, a sob escaping. Whipping her head around to look at it, and surprised that her vision blurred, she waited for it to ring again before she reached for it with hands that shook.

Picking up the receiver, she swallowed a sob and cleared her throat. "Hello?"

"Miss Sanderson?"

Disappointed—devastated—that it wasn't Beau's voice, she swallowed again, fresh tears blurring her vision.

"Yes. Who's calling?" She hoped whoever it was didn't notice that her voice cracked.

"This is Joe, the manager of Carpet Mart. I wanted to apologize again for the misunderstanding, and I just wondered if you were still going to be able to come in today."

Taking a shaky breath, and then another, she stared toward the doorway as if Beau would magically appear again, and struggled to focus on the conversation.

Blowing out a breath, she forced a calmness into her voice, while her insides shook. "Yes, I'm leaving now. Thank you, Joe." She looked at the clock. With the snowstorm expected the next day, she didn't want to be stuck, unable to get to Tulsa. "I'll be there in about an hour."

"Are you sure?"

Reaching for a tissue from the box on her desk, Charity attempted to keep the anguish from her voice at the realization that her plans with Beau tonight had been cancelled. "Yes."

She hung up on whatever Joe said to her, finding it impossible to focus.

Taking several deep breaths, she dropped her head in her hands and struggled to stop shaking.

She couldn't believe it was over. Doubling over, she squeezed her eyes closed, unsurprised that tears ran down her face.

God, it hurt.

Suddenly finding it hard to breathe in the confines of her office, she got to her feet and wiped her eyes, grabbed the checkbook for the club, and shoved it in her purse.

She needed some air, and hoped that a drive would help her calm down. Maybe if she had some time to think, she could figure out what to do about fixing the mess she'd made of things with Beau.

She had to fix it. She didn't have to rely on someone to take care of her. She didn't care if he wanted to play all the time. She had to have him in her life.

The alternative was inconceivable.

Chapter Four

Shivering against the cold that seemed to go all the way to her bones, Charity turned the heat up a little higher as she turned on to the road leading out of town.

She couldn't seem to stop shaking, and suspected it had as much to do with nerves and her fear of losing Beau as it did the weather.

The sky seemed darker than she'd expected, especially since the blizzard wasn't due to hit until the following morning, but the darkened sky fit her mood.

Everything seemed distant, as though nothing could penetrate the dark cloud of shock and sense of loss that surrounded her.

She stayed on the back roads as much as possible, too distracted to deal with traffic, and hopeful that the drive would help clear her head.

The image of the way Beau looked right before he turned away from her played over and over in her mind. His eyes, usually dancing and playful had been hard, the glint of hurt in them slicing through her like a knife.

The image wouldn't go away, making the knot in her stomach tighten more each time she thought about it.

She couldn't believe he'd given her an ultimatum like that.

In hindsight, she realized that, if not for his patience with her, he would have done it sooner.

Blowing out a breath did nothing to relieve any of her tension.

Nothing would, until she fixed things with Beau.

He'd never given her any reason to doubt him. Her own insecurities fed her need to keep him at an emotional distance.

She'd always felt so bland and boring next to her outgoing and charming sister, and couldn't believe a man as incredible as Beau would want her. She'd used his playful nature as an excuse to reinforce her belief that he could never want more than just fun with her.

A bitter sob escaped.

"Why the hell would a man like Beau pick someone like me for fun? Oh, Beau. I must have been such a trial for you. You could have any woman you wanted, and you picked someone like me."

She looked in her rearview mirror to see the sign for Desire, slowing slightly as the need to turn back to town became nearly overwhelming. "Damn it, Beau. You've got me so mixed up."

Thankful that no one was on the road to see her talking to herself, she wiped another tear, noticing for the first time that it had started to snow.

Flipping through her mental calendar, she confirmed that it was Friday. Frowning, she thought about the weather forecast she'd seen the other day, she remembered that they'd predicted that the storm would arrive on Saturday afternoon.

She remembered it well.

She'd been in Beau's bed at the time, wrapped in his arms and still trembling from his lovemaking.

He'd been nuzzling her neck during most of the weather report, so she'd missed some of it, but could clearly remember Beau mentioning something about the storm starting on Saturday afternoon. He'd been particularly playful that night and she'd forgotten all about everything else.

Smiling, she thought about how much they'd laughed that night.

She had to get him back.

Or, would it be better for both of them if she let it end now?

"No. Not happening. You and I are going to have this out, Beau. I'm not letting you walk away from me."

Swallowing a sob, Charity reached down to turn the wipers on high.

The snow continued to fall, becoming heavier by the minute. When the wind began to pick up, she started to curse, tightening her grip on the wheel, fighting to keep her car in the center of the lane.

She should have stayed home. She should be back in Desire right now, in bed with Beau, instead of driving on a slippery road.

Damned weather forecasters.

Seeing the brake lights on the car on front of her, Charity tapped her own brakes, a little shaken when she lost traction. It only lasted a second or two, but it made her even more nervous.

Putting a little more distance between her and the car in front of her, Charity slowed even more. Surprised by the amount of snow that had already fallen, she sat up straighter, shifting her shoulders in an effort to ease the tight muscles there.

The snow seemed to be coming down harder by the minute. With a curse, she turned on the radio, trying to push thoughts of Beau out of her mind and concentrate on her driving.

She wished Beau was here. She had to admit that with him at the wheel, she wouldn't have been concerned at all. She would have felt completely safe with him—just as she would have with any of the other men in Desire.

They were a strange breed, liberal in many ways and totally old-fashioned in others.

She was probably prejudiced, but Charity considered the men of Desire perfect, and just what a man should be.

Frowning, she realized she'd included Beau part of that group.

Her thoughts went back to the night he'd taken her virginity, something she thought about often.

He'd been so patient with her, and had made love to her with a gentleness that brought tears to her eyes each time she thought about it. He'd teased her fears away, making her laugh when she got too nervous. He'd been the most magnificent lover, drawing out their lovemaking until every inch of her body tingled with awareness and she'd wanted him so much that all fear fled and most of her inhibitions melted away.

She'd been so aroused that even the slight sting of pain as he entered her didn't quite register at first, but Beau had paused, holding her and murmuring to her soothingly until it eased.

He'd told her over and over how much it meant to him to be her first lover, and had eased her fears with a playfulness and affection that made the experience special—a memory she would never forget.

She hadn't given her virginity lightly, and he'd made it clear that he hadn't taken it lightly, either.

Since that night, Beau had become possessive, and even more protective than ever.

Beau made her feel special. He made her feel beautiful and desired. She felt good when she was with him.

If she was honest with herself, she'd started to fall in love with him before she slept with him. She'd been falling harder ever since. In bed, he was loving, caring, teasing, and so incredibly wonderful.

She should have stayed home.

If she and Beau had been snowed in together, she knew they'd spend the entire day making love.

The epitome of tall, dark, and handsome, Beau somehow managed to be both elegant and masculine—and the kindest, most patient man she'd ever known.

He'd pulled her away from work more times than she could count, teasing her out of her bad moods, and making her laugh when she'd been knee deep in problems.

He handled her without seeming to handle her at all.

Her car slid again, startling her out of her musings. She gripped the steering wheel even tighter, shocked at how hard it was snowing and that several inches of it had already coated the road. It crunched under her tires, making her lose tractions several times, forcing her to slow down even more. The slight traffic had lightened considerably, so much so that she hardly saw another car now. It had gotten even darker, much darker than it should have been in the middle of the afternoon.

She realized she hadn't paid any attention to the radio at all, and annoyed with the static, reached over to turn it off.

As she drove, she saw fewer and fewer cars, and the snow just kept piling up, increasing the sense of isolation.

Shivering, she turned the heat up as high as she could, wishing Beau was there to keep her warm. She wouldn't have worried much at all if she'd been with him.

He would have made it an adventure.

Life with him would always be fun. Exciting.

Damn it, Charity, stop thinking about him and just concentrate on driving.

Tense and alarmed at the number of times she skidded, Charity leaned forward, and with a white-knuckled grip on the steering wheel, inched her way toward Tulsa.

She breathed a sigh of relief when she finally reached the city, and smiled when she saw several plow trucks passing her as they went in the opposite direction.

Knowing the roads would be cleared, she wanted to hurry so she could get back on the road before the snow accumulated all over again, and get home.

She couldn't wait to get back to Beau.

She didn't know yet what she would say, but she loved him too much to let what they had end.

Not until he'd walked away from her did she realize how much he'd endured for her, and just how much he had to love her.

"Jesus, Charity. How could you have been so stupid?" Grimacing, she watched for traffic. "Great. Talking to yourself again."

With the roads nearly deserted, it didn't surprise her to find plenty of parking in front of the carpet store.

The parking lot hadn't yet been plowed, so she had to drive slowly, and got stuck twice. Once she got her small car moving again, she pulled in close to the building, out of the wind and where the snow hadn't accumulated as much. Getting out of the car, she sucked in a breath at the shock of cold air and hurriedly pulled her coat closer, and pulled her scarf higher to cover her mouth and nose.

Wishing she'd worn her boots, Charity ducked her head against the icy wind and snow, and made her way around the corner of the building and into the store.

Her sneakers were soaked before she got to the door of the store, but at least they provided traction.

Looking forward to a hot shower, and Beau, she pulled the door open and walked into the store, wincing at the squishing sound her shoes made on the tile floor.

A man approached her at once, the man she recognized from dealing with him before. "Hello, Miss Sanderson. I've got the samples all set aside for you."

"Thanks, Joe." Following him to the counter, she grimaced as the cold seeped through her socks. "I want to get out of here as soon as possible. I can't believe the snow started already. If that inept salesman had taken the order right the first time, I wouldn't have had to come out in this."

The older man frowned and rubbed his protruding stomach, looking more than a little nervous. "Yes, well, he doesn't work here anymore. I'm sorry for the mix-up, and I'm *really* sorry that you had to come out in this. I heard they'd changed the forecast and predicted that the storm would come a day early, but I didn't realize it would start this soon. I tried to call you back, but you'd already left."

In the process of writing her check, Charity stilled. "You're kidding, right?"

"No." Joe gestured toward the wall of windows and outside to where the snowstorm seemed to have gotten even more intense. "I wish I was. I stayed open just to wait for you. As soon as you leave, I'm closing and going home."

Charity finished writing the check and accepted her receipt, folding it and putting it in the compartment of her purse for just that purpose. "If I had known, I wouldn't have come out. I missed the news. I was halfway here before it started snowing, and I really thought it would only be an inch or two before the storm."

"Maybe you should stay in town until this blows over."

Shaking her head, Charity grabbed her keys from the counter and started out, consumed by a sense of urgency. "No. Several snowplows passed me on the way here. Hopefully, I can just follow one of them. Call me and let me know what day the carpet's going to be delivered."

As soon as she stepped outside, the cold air stole her breath. Hurrying to her car, she cursed when she saw all the snow that had piled on it while she'd been inside. "Damned stupid snowstorm."

Moving as fast as she could, she cleaned off the car, her anger at herself allowing her to make short work of the task. When the light of the store went off, leaving her feeling even more isolated, she paused and looked around, unable to hear much of anything above the blowing wind.

Joe came outside just as she'd finished and giving her a quick wave, started toward his own car—the only other car in the large parking lot. "You need help?"

Charity shook her head. "No, I'm done." She wanted to call Hope before she left to let her know where she was.

Joe nodded. "I have to clean my car off. I'll watch to make sure you get out of the parking lot all right."

Seeing a snowplow, Charity nodded and jumped in her car, pushing thoughts of calling her sister aside in her race to follow the plow. Not even taking the time to let her car warm up, she hurried as fast as she could to follow the big plow. Relieved to see that he took the same road she would be taking, she stayed behind him, careful to keep enough distance between them, but not falling too far back.

The wind picked up, coming in harder gusts, and blowing her small car all over the road. The heavy, blowing snow blocked out a lot of the light from the streetlights, making the deserted road seem even darker. The wind and the snow seemed to pick up from one minute to the next, and within only a few minutes, Charity found herself struggling to see the plow. The snow came down even harder, and soon became just about all she could see in her headlights.

Several minutes later, she realized with a sinking heart that she'd lost sight of the snowplow completely. Easing her foot from the gas pedal, she slowed even more, fighting the gusts of wind to stay in the tracks made by the plow.

She didn't see any approaching lights, and couldn't see anyone behind her.

It appeared she and the snowplow that she could no longer see on the dark, snowy road were alone.

She'd never felt so isolated, or wished for Beau more.

Shivering with both cold and nerves, but not wanting to take her eyes off of the road, she felt for the controls and turned the heat and defroster on high. Sneaking a glance at the side of the road, and surprised by the amount of snow that had already accumulated, she swallowed heavily and focused on staying in her lane.

The snowplow had pushed the snow to the side, creating a wall about three feet high of snow that she used to judge her position in the lane.

Alarmed at how much snow had already fallen, she wondered how much more would fall before she could get back home.

Cursing, she gripped the steering wheel tight and focused on driving straight. Sliding several times, she had to slow even more, alarmed at how fast the snow covered the road again.

She wished Beau was here.

He'd be a hell of a lot calmer than she was. Hell, he'd probably pull over and start a snowball fight.

The snow had started coming down so fast that it stuck to her windshield wipers, slowing them to almost a crawl. Wincing at the sound they made as they jerked over her windshield, she moved her head from side to side in search of a clear spot.

Minutes later, she knew she had no choice but to pull over and clear the wipers before she could go any farther.

Slowing, she eased her car to the side as far as she could without getting stuck in the pile of snow created by the plow. Putting the hazard lights on, she reached for her cell phone.

She didn't want her parents or sister to find her missing and panic.

She knew that if she called her parents, they would just worry, so she dialed Hope's home phone number.

Hope answered on the first ring. "Where the hell are you?"

Charity couldn't help but smile at her hotheaded sister's demand. "Don't yell at me. I drove into Tulsa to order the carpet."

"Drove into Tulsa? Are you out of your fucking mind?"

Charity sighed and grabbed the scraper. "Look, the other salesmen messed up. They needed me to pick out the color today and they needed a check. Their computer's down so I had to do it in person."

"There's a blizzard and you drove almost a hundred miles to order carpet?" Charity had to hold the phone away from her ear, wincing at her sister's inventive cursing. "Didn't you watch the news? What did you think—that the storm wouldn't dare mess with your fucking plans?"

Charity sighed again, looking around at the deserted road. "I don't have time to argue with you. I pulled over because my wipers are stuck. I was following a snowplow, but now I've lost him. I just called because I want you to know where I am and that I'm okay. Figure out something to tell Mom and the dads so they don't worry. I'll call you as soon as—"

"Would you mind telling me just what the hell you thought you were doing?"

Charity shivered at the ice in Ace's tone. "Ace, listen, I—"

Ace growled, a sure sign of trouble. "I swear, your fathers should have beaten both of you—and often. Where are you? And don't tell me you're on your way home, or I just might beat you myself. Where—*exactly*—are you?"

Swallowing heavily, Charity looked around, shivering against the cold, and at Ace's tone. "Hell, Ace, nothing looks the same. It's pitch dark out here and everything's covered with snow. Wait a minute." Squinting, she studied her surroundings. "I think I'm closer to home than I thought. I'm close to that grove of trees about two miles away from the turnoff to town."

"Stay there." His tone brooked no argument, making her bristle.

"Ace, I'm halfway into the road. I couldn't pull off all the way because the snow's piled up on the shoulder from the plow."

She didn't know how anyone could out-curse her sister, but Ace managed it.

"Stay put, damn it! I'll come and get you. I can't believe Beau let you go out in this. I'm going to beat the hell out of him as soon as I see him."

Rushing to Beau's defense, Charity tightened her hold on the phone. "Beau doesn't know, and don't bother coming after me. As soon as I get these wipers clean—shit." Charity's heart pounded furiously with a sense of dread.

"What's wrong?" The panic in Ace's tone matched her own as she stared into the rearview mirror.

She had to swallow again before speaking, but still her voice shook, something Ace would pick up on. "Ace, some asshole is coming up behind me and driving way too fast, he's skidding all over the road. I have my hazard lights on, but I don't know if he even sees me."

Absently aware of Ace cursing in her ear, Charity braced herself and watched in horror as the driver closed in on her. She saw the truck and knew she couldn't do anything to avoid the collision. "Shit, Ace, he's gonna hit me!"

It happened so fast that Charity didn't have time to do anything except scream. The truck turned at the last second, but it wasn't enough.

He hit her left back bumper hard enough to send her car flying through the snow bank, spinning out of control. She screamed again when the car became airborne and headed right for a tree, holding on tightly to the wheel as it hit the trunk at a sharp angle and slammed down hard on the driver's side.

A deafening silence followed as Charity's mind screamed that this couldn't be happening.

The left side of her head hurt almost immediately, and she realized that she'd hit it hard on the window.

She felt trapped, almost smothered, and panicked until she realized that the airbags had deployed.

She lay there on her left side as they deflated, pushing them out of the way, aware of no other sounds but a ticking noise, the howling wind, and her own harsh breathing. Shaking, and scared to move, she listened for sounds of the other driver, but couldn't hear any movements.

Mesmerized by the faint glow of a blinking light, she thought at first that the car had caught fire until she recognized it as her hazard lights, which also explained the ticking sound.

Shaking, she struggled to move, slowly becoming increasingly aware that she hurt everywhere.

Her uncoordinated movements and shaking forced her to move slowly as she tried to straighten from her uncomfortable position, gasping at the pain in her shoulder and chest. It took several attempts, but she finally managed to undo the seat belt, breathing a sigh of relief as the pressure against her chest eased.

Slumping back with a groan, she tried to move to a comfortable position, crying out at the pain, which now included her left hip and the left side of her head. Because her left arm hurt and she couldn't move herself off of it, she lifted her right one to her left temple, and probed where it hurt, wincing at the pain. Finding it wet, she rubbed her fingers against her thumb, hoping it was water, but fearing that what she felt was blood.

She felt around for her cell phone, whimpering in pain, and inwardly wincing as she imagined Ace's reaction to hearing the horrifying sounds of her accident.

He would be frantic.

And he would tell Beau—who would be crazy with worry.

She wanted his arms around her, his solid strength holding her against him. She'd be warm and safe in his arms.

She didn't know how much time had passed as she sat there watching the light from the blinker. It didn't seem to matter. She lay there, hoping that if she rested a few minutes, she'd be able to move.

Without the heater, it got cold in the car fast. Shivering, she gingerly stuck her hands in her coat and tried to imagine Beau's warm arms around her.

His body, like a furnace, would warm her in no time.

She'd love to call him, to tell him what happened and that she was all right, but she had no idea where her phone had landed.

Stretching as far as she could in all directions, she felt around for it, each movement slow and painful.

Her neck hurt and moving at all became a herculean effort. Disoriented and weak, she thought about trying to climb out of the car, but since she didn't smell smoke, she figured it would be safer to stay inside than to get out. She didn't relish being out in the elements at night in the middle of a blizzard.

Ace knew where to find her, and she hoped her hazard lights would lead him to her.

If the snow didn't bury her car before they could get there.

Thankful that she'd had time to tell him her location, she felt confident that he would find her.

He had to.

She could imagine both Ace and Beau searching for her. They wouldn't give up. She knew that.

She could only hope they wouldn't tell her mom or dads.

They'd tell them.

Damn.

The wind seemed to have picked up even more, and she could just imagine her parents trying to drive in this.

God, she was cold. She just wanted to curl into a ball and go to sleep, but she knew she had to stay alert.

She hoped her decision to stay in the car had been a good one, but she kept sniffing for gasoline, and checking around for any sign of a fire. If she had to get out quickly, she figured she'd do it somehow.

Right now, though, she had no plans to do anything except wait, thinking about the blanket and flashlights in her trunk.

Her own side window had shattered, allowing the cold in, but the windshield, although badly cracked, remained intact enough to keep the snow and wind out.

Her feet burned with the cold, and she couldn't stop shaking, the movements painful and making her ache all over.

She wanted Beau.

Beau would come.

She knew it as well as she knew her own name.

Ace would call him, and when Ace found her, Beau would be with him.

She didn't bother to blink back the tears that burned her eyes.

She loved Beau.

She didn't care if he played, as long as he was in her life.

If she had to be the one doing the worrying, so be it.

It would be worth it, if she could only have him.

As soon as she saw him, she'd tell him she'd marry him. Nothing else mattered. She loved him and would hold on to him as long as she could.

He was everything to her, and she couldn't live without him.

Cold, hurting, and getting scared, she wrapped her arms around herself the best that she could and lowered her head carefully back to the broken side window.

And waited.

Chapter Five

Tightening his hands on the steering wheel, Beau inwardly cursed the weather that made the ride to find Charity painstakingly slow. Scared out of his mind, he hadn't drawn a steady breath since Ace called him.

The closest he'd come to feeling this way had been the day the Molotov cocktail went through the window of the club.

He'd raced with the others toward the fire, anxious to get the women out of the building, but for several heart-pounding minutes, he hadn't known if Charity was hurt, or even alive. He'd been able to get to her within a minute or two, but it had been the longest two minutes of his life.

This time, the terror seemed to last forever.

He didn't even know if she was still alive. They couldn't get through to her on her cell phone, an ominous sign that made the drive even more tension-filled.

She had to be alive.

He couldn't bear to think of the alternative.

The eerie silence only seemed to emphasize the tension in the air, but everyone stayed off the radios Ace had handed out unless they had something important to say.

Beau had lived in Desire for years, and knew how everyone stuck together, but the number of men who'd joined the search staggered him.

Word of Charity's accident, and the fact that they had to search for her in a blizzard, swept quickly through town, and the town of Desire came together in a way Beau had never seen before.

Ace drove in the lead, with Hope and one of her fathers, Drew.

Beau and another one of their fathers, Garrett, followed, while Finn, the youngest of Hope and Charity's fathers stayed home with their mother, Gracie, trying to keep her calm.

John Dalton and Michael Keegan had closed the bar in town without hesitation and joined the search.

Another truck held Lucas Hart, Devlin Monroe, and Caleb Ward from Desire Securities, who'd shown up with their SUV loaded with boxes of who knew what.

Jared Preston and his brother, Duncan, had left their younger brother, Reese, with their pregnant wife, Erin, and drove behind them.

King Taylor drove his truck, with Royce Harley, Ethan Sullivan, and Brandon Weston inside.

Boone Jackson left his brother, Chase, home with Rachel and their daughter, and rode with Jake Langley, and Clay and Rio Erickson, who'd dropped their wife, Jesse, to stay with Blade and his very pregnant wife, Kelly.

The three men who worked with Boone and Chase—Sloane, Cole, and Brett Madison, newcomers to Desire—had also joined the search.

Hunter and Remington Ross brought up the rear.

Dillon and Ryder, who owned the garage in town, were on their way with their tow truck.

A woman from their town was hurt and in trouble, and everyone rushed to help.

Beau appreciated the support and help more than he could ever repay.

Floodlights of all sizes shone brightly from every vehicle window, illuminating both sides of the road, but with the snow still blowing hard, it was difficult to see.

The thought that Charity could freeze to death in this before they got to her weighed heavily on his mind.

They'd left in a hurry, within minutes of her accident, and Beau prayed they would find her in time.

The crunch of the snow under his tires and his own heartbeat were the only sounds as the line of SUVs and pickup trucks slowly made their way to where Charity claimed to be, and Beau hoped like hell she'd been right.

As they approached the spot, Ace, in the lead, slowed his truck to a crawl.

Beau slowed behind him, knowing the fear Ace felt. He'd heard it in his voice when Ace had called him, but the sheriff of Desire, known for the ice in his veins and take-charge attitude hid his fear to comfort his wife.

Hope had been nearly hysterical.

As the storm raged on around them, Beau and the others continued to shine high-powered flashlights out their windows, searching for any sign of Charity's white car.

Beau divided his attention between driving and scanning the sides of the road, glancing periodically toward a stone-faced Garrett, who shone another flashlight from the passenger side.

Beau turned back to search for her, not wanting to miss anything. "We'll find her soon. She'll be all right."

"You tryin' to convince me, or yourself?" The worry in Garrett's low growl had Beau glancing back with a sigh.

"Both of us, I guess." Swallowing heavily, Beau turned back, slowing even more, his hands tightening on the wheel as he swept the area with his light. "I suppose you and the others are blaming me for this. I want you to know that I blame myself. We had an argument this afternoon and I walked out. If I had known she would do something like this, I never would have left."

He'd been kicking himself for leaving, and had planned to use the storm as an excuse to check on her. Ever since Ace called him, he'd blamed himself for her accident.

"I would have stopped her, or driven her in my truck. She wouldn't have been alone in this in that tiny car of hers."

Garrett sighed. "I don't blame you, and neither do my brothers. We know you love her and we know what kind of man you are. We spoiled them too much, and ended up raising two very stubborn daughters."

Beau clenched his jaw. "It was my fault. I want you to know that this kind of thing won't happen again. I'm going to convince her to marry me, and I'm not going to take no for an answer this time." He wouldn't allow himself to believe that he wouldn't have the chance.

"Good. She needs you." The tension and fear in Garrett's voice seemed to grow worse by the minute.

Beau didn't turn, keeping his attention focused on their surroundings, and squinting against the snow blowing in his window as he searched for the woman he loved. "I need her, too." His voice broke, surprising him.

She had to be all right.

As the minutes dragged on, terror for her gripped him by the throat, nearly choking him. "Where the hell is she? It's pitch black, and we're in the middle of a blizzard. What if the snow's already covered her? She's got to be freezing."

It had already been over an hour since her accident, and there was no sign of her.

"Just tree after fucking tree, and everything's covered with snow." Hearing the desperation in his voice, Beau swallowed heavily as he realized that he would upset Charity's father, and forced himself to remain silent.

Garrett looked like he'd aged five years since he'd heard the news, and Beau didn't want to scare him even more.

"Look. Oh, my God! Is that her? Look to the left! It's her! It's Charity's car." Hope's voice, filled with relief and excitement, came over the radio, making Beau stiffen and slam on the brakes, his heart pounding nearly out of his chest when he saw the faint glow of flashing lights.

"I see it!" Thinking at first that it was a fire, Beau stopped breathing, dimly aware of Garrett answering Hope on the radio.

Ace's voice followed as he brought his truck to a stop. "Shine your lights to the left. Over there by that tree."

Beau struggled to see through the snow, his door already open as he threw his SUV into park. Holding his breath, he scrambled out of the truck and raced toward the faint glow, which he realized with no small amount of relief, to be her flashers reflected in the snow. Moving faster, he tried to figure out why the glow seemed to be coming from such an odd angle. As soon as the other floodlights pointed in that direction, he realized why when he saw what appeared to be the underside of her car.

"Christ, her car flipped!" Boone's voice came from Beau's left and slightly behind him, the horror in it matching his own.

Beau raced across the uneven and snowy ground toward Charity's car, whipping his head from side to side in search of her.

When he didn't find her, the fear that she'd been hurt and unable to get out of the car threatened to strangle him.

He was the first one there, skidding to his knees in front of the windshield. "Charity!" Brushing away the snow, he screamed her name again, his heart in his throat.

Hardly daring to breathe, he shone his light in the window, his gut clenching in fear.

Huddled in a ball with her eyes closed, she lay unmoving. White. Fragile. So small and defenseless.

Hurt.

Please, God! No!

She blinked, holding her hand up against the light, her movements slow and sluggish.

Moving the light from her eyes, Beau swallowed heavily, dizzy with relief. Filled with a sense of urgency, he jumped to his feet and began throwing aside tree branches that stood in his way. "Don't move, baby. I'm gonna get you out of there."

Blocking out the sounds of the voices and barked orders around him, Beau made his way around the base of the tree she'd crashed in to, thinking about nothing but getting to her.

Holding her.

By the time he'd made it around and climbed up onto the passenger side of her car, his friends had surrounded the car, throwing away more branches. He knew they'd all have looks of concern on their faces, but he didn't take the time to look.

Lucas knelt in the deep snow near the windshield, talking to Charity. "Don't move, Charity. You just stay put and let us do all the work. Where does it hurt, honey?"

Ace came running toward them, handing a crowbar up to Beau, his face, all hard lines and concern. "No ambulance for at least an hour. I told them we could handle this on our own. Lucas, Devlin, Caleb and I all know first aid and have kits in our trucks. Jake, can you and the others get them for us?"

"We packed an emergency kit with extra supplies," Lucas yelled over his shoulder. "And somebody put out some flares!"

Using one of the branches of the tree for support, Beau pulled at the car door, but couldn't open it. He pushed several inches of snow from it and fought to get the crowbar into the small crack. Little by little, he managed to bend the metal door, cursing the entire time.

Caleb hoisted himself up and appeared beside him with another crowbar. Between the two of them, they managed to pop the door open enough to get their hands inside.

Curling his fingers around the metal, Beau started to pull, cursing when Caleb yelled for him to stop and shoved his hands away.

"What? Move, damn it." Impatient, Beau brushed him off and reached for the door again. "Get outta my way."

Caleb handed him a pair of thick work gloves. "Use these. If you cut all your fingers off, you're going to be no use to her."

Beau grabbed the gloves from Caleb, nodding once in thanks, the fear in his throat making it impossible to speak.

Every second seemed to last forever in his quest to get to her.

He couldn't stand the thought of her getting colder by the moment, or being in pain any longer than necessary.

He shoved his hands into the gloves and reached for the door again, pulling with every ounce of strength he possessed.

"Need any help up there?" Jake's voice came from behind him.

Relieved that the door gave way, Beau repositioned himself and shoved for all he was worth, desperate to get to his woman. Fury and fear fueled him, and with a hard jerk, the door of the car broke free.

As the door hit the ground, Caleb yelled down to Jake. "Uh, not with that."

Beau didn't even glance at the detached door as he turned to Caleb, or thought anything of it, focused on getting to Charity. "Shine your light in here. I don't want to step on her." With all the lights being shined inside, Beau could see a little of the interior of the car, but not enough.

He was just too damned big, and her car was so fucking small. One slip and he could fall on her and hurt her even more.

Lowering himself into the car, he felt another surge of panic at the sight of blood on Charity's white face as she turned to him. "Baby? Where are you hurt? I'm coming in for you." He struggled to keep the fear out of his voice, and inject into it a confidence he hoped would relieve her fear.

Charity smiled weakly. "You don't fit. You're always saying my car's too little for you."

Scared at the shakiness in her voice, and worried that she'd gone into shock, Beau fought his panic and smiled back, careful to keep his tone calm. "I'll fit."

Standing on the console, Beau eased his way into the car, forcing another smile, while searching for any sign of more injuries. "See? Tell me where you're hurt so we can get you the hell out of here without hurting you any more."

Charity groaned, a sound that tightened the already-tight knot in his stomach. "Shoulder and arm a little, I think. So cold. My hip hurt before, but it doesn't anymore. I think I hit my head. There's some blood there." The nonchalance in her voice worried him even more. "My feet. Wet and cold, and now they hurt. Forgot my boots."

Standing with one leg behind her seat, and the other braced on the console, Beau reached around her and under her legs to ease the seat back. "I know, baby. I'm gonna get you out of here and we'll get you nice and warm. You hurt anywhere else?"

He couldn't wait to have her in his arms.

He ran his hands over her, searching for broken bones and using the flashlight handed down to him to search for any more signs of blood. Hiding a wince at the bleeding at her temple, he felt around her head until he found a huge knot.

"Where's she hurt?" Ace's voice came from the other side of the windshield.

Because the other men remained quiet, all of their attention apparently focused on what was going on inside the car, Beau didn't have to raise his voice much.

"Big knot on the left side of the head, but not much bleeding, probably because of the cold. She said her hip hurt before, but not now, probably because of the cold, too. She says her left shoulder and arm hurt—not sure if they're broken or not. Said her feet are wet and cold."

He just hoped like hell she didn't have frostbite.

Turning her head, Charity smiled at him. "I knew you'd come with Ace."

Now that he'd checked her out, he struggled out of his shearling coat, wishing he'd thought to take it off before he crawled into the confines of her tiny car. "Of course I came. I'll always be there when you need me, cher." Covering her with the coat, he tucked it around her the best he could without hurting her, and dropped a quick kiss on her icy lips. "Always."

Lucas tapped on the windshield. "You got enough room to get her out?"

Beau shook his head. "Not much room at all, but I can do it." He'd do whatever it took.

Ace squatted next to Lucas. "I think it'll be easier on her if we bring her out the windshield. We'll pry it out. Clay, get some blankets in there."

Ace met Beau's gaze, a hundred messages passing between them at their shared horror. "Cover yourselves in case the glass shatters. It's already cracked in several places."

A blanket fell from above, hitting his shoulder. Beau wrapped it around Charity making sure to cover her face. "Throw me another one."

Making a cocoon for them with the blankets Clay threw down, Beau continued to run his hands over her, still looking for injuries and hoping to warm her up some. He half listened to the voices surrounding them, and the sounds of the men trying to pop the windshield out in one piece.

When he attempted to tuck the blanket more firmly around her, Charity moaned. "God, I'm so cold. Beau, I'm sorry about earlier."

"No, I'm the one who's sorry. We'll talk later, and I'll apologize all you want. Just a few more minutes and we'll get you out of here and get you nice and warm." Reaching under the front of her seat again, he reclined the seat as far as it would go, holding her and easing her back. With one foot planted behind her seat and kneeling on the console, he tried his best to surround her without hurting her, wincing when she reached out with her left arm to touch him and moaned.

"Your shoulder, baby?" The blankets surrounding them blocked out the light and kept him from seeing her face.

"Yeah. I thought about trying to get out, but my shoulder hurt. Figured it would be better to stay inside. Didn't want to be out there in the wind." Her words seemed more slurred than before, alarming Beau.

Lucas had just finished prying the window free. "That was smart, honey. It gave you some shelter, and made it easier for us to find you."

Beau cuddled her as best he could, hoping to warm her. Over the sounds of the windshield being lifted and tossed aside, he kept talking, hoping to keep her awake. "I'm gonna have to make sure you have a blanket and flashlight in your car from now on, huh?"

Charity's soft laugh ended in a groan. "They're in the trunk."

Ace pulled the blanket from their faces, studying Charity's features. "We're ready now." He glanced at Beau. "Can you hand her out to us? We'll check her over here before we start for the hospital. We'll wrap that shoulder and splint that arm just in case. There's no point in letting her hurt any more than she does."

Nodding, Beau focused on Charity's face as he lowered the blanket and slid his hands under her. "Be real still. I'm gonna move slow. If anything hurts, tell me."

It seemed to take forever, but between him, Lucas, and Ace, they eased her out through the windshield and onto a blanket they had waiting for her.

Beau forced his way out, feeling helpless as he watched Ace splint her arm and bandage her shoulder while Lucas dealt with the gash on her head.

With a lethal-looking knife, Caleb sliced her pants at the hip and checked for injuries. "It looks like she got slammed hard against the door. There are no lacerations, and I don't think anything's broken, but she's gonna be black and blue."

Devlin checked her eyes. "She's probably got a concussion." While Ace kept up a running conversation with Charity, Devlin pressed at her stomach. Turning his head, he spoke to Beau in a low voice over his shoulder. "I don't think she's got any internal bleeding, but I can't be sure. As soon as Ace has that arm stabilized, we've got to get her to the hospital. Want me to drive your truck?"

Beau nodded. "Thanks." His arms ached to hold her.

Once they finished, Ace got to his feet. "She's all yours."

"She certainly is." Bending, Beau gathered her in his arms, cradling her against his chest as he painstakingly made his way across the snow-covered ground.

Someone threw a blanket across his shoulders, and with Clay steadying him on one side and Ace on the other, they made their way across the deep snow to his SUV.

Gathering blankets, first aid kits, and tools, the others made their way back to their vehicles, each pausing to see Charity and say something to her.

Hope walked next to him in front of her husband. "Jeez, Charity. All this for carpet?" Despite her teasing, Beau could see Hope's concern. Her eyes were brimming with unshed tears and she kept trying to touch Charity, pulling her hand back at the last second, as if afraid to hurt her.

The atmosphere had lightened quite a bit since finding her, but tensions remained high due to the storm that showed no signs of letting up.

Amid low conversation, it was decided that Garrett and Drew would go to the hospital with Ace, while Hope rode with Beau and Charity in Beau's truck, with Devlin at the wheel.

Everyone else would go back to Desire and their families, and would check in with Linc and Rafe to see if they needed help since the two Desire deputies would be working around the clock through the storm.

Beau listened with half an ear as they talked about plowing, his attention focused on the woman in his arms. He bent over her the best he could to protect her from the wind, grimacing at how badly she shivered.

When they got to his SUV, he got into the back seat to give Charity more room, while Hope, talking nonstop to her sister, slid into the front passenger seat next to Devlin.

Hope reached back to touch Charity's hand. "The dads are going to ride in with Ace. They're probably on the phone with Mom already. You gave everybody quite a scare."

Charity cuddled closer to Beau as he slipped off her wet sneakers and socks and rubbed her icy feet with the blanket. "Sorry. Didn't mean to. So cold."

Listening to Hope and Charity talk, Beau shared a look with Devlin in the rearview mirror. "At least I had a chance to hook the plow to the front. We should make it to the hospital okay."

Devlin grinned. "We'll be fine. I already told Ace that I'd take the lead. We'll get there faster. Hang on, Charity. We'll get you to the hospital before you know it." He shared another look with Beau. "Don't worry. I've got this. Just do your best to get her warm. I've got the heat on high."

Looking down at Charity in his arms, Beau could see the bruises starting on her temple, and thanked God she was alive. Bending over her, he touched his lips to the bruising. "I may never let you out of my sight again."

With a weak smile, Charity let her eyes flutter close, her voice so low he had to strain to hear her. "I knew you would come. I knew Ace and Hope would come looking for me, but I knew you would come, too. Even though you were mad at me, I knew you would come. I'm sorry. I've been acting stupid. I can't live without you."

Despite the weariness in her voice, something inside Beau settled. "You won't ever have to live without me. I need you too much. You're mine, Charity, and you're staying that way."

Chapter Six

He could have lost her tonight.

The thought kept playing over and over in his head, torturing him.

After spending hours in the bustling emergency room, Charity had finally been taken to a private room, one that he'd arranged for when he'd filled out the paperwork and taken responsibility for the bill.

Garrett had objected, but once Beau made it clear that he blamed himself for the accident and that he had every intention of talking Charity into marrying him, he'd backed off.

Accidents and heart attacks from the storm seemed to be rampant, but thankfully, the floor where they'd taken Charity was much quieter.

She looked so tired. So frail.

It seemed to take forever, but the nurses finally finished settling her for the night.

Beau sat in a dark corner in her room, his arms aching to hold her, wincing every time Charity did. Thankful that they'd given her pain medicine, he watched her, meeting her gaze several times as her eyelids seemed to get heavier and heavier.

Once the nurse realized that no one would be leaving until everyone had a chance to see Charity and assure themselves that she was all right, she allowed everyone in for a few minutes before hustling them out.

Beau wouldn't budge.

He could have lost her tonight.

He couldn't stop shaking.

Charity's injuries, although not serious, scared him more than he wanted her to see.

She had a cracked collarbone, a cracked sternum, a seriously bruised hip and arm, and a minor concussion, along with several cuts on her face from her broken window.

Her eyes looked too big for her pale face, and she looked exhausted. She seemed determined to thank everyone for finding her, smiling when Ace bent to kiss her head. "I'm sorry. I can only imagine how you felt—hearing the crash, but then nothing else. Did you find my cell phone?"

"Didn't look for it. Dillon and Ryder already have your car."

Charity looked toward the window, trying to hide a wince at the movement, and dropped it back on the pillow. "Isn't it still snowing?"

Ace straightened, putting an arm around his wife, silently encouraging her to lean on him. "It sure is. They didn't want to leave your car out there, though. I heard they had a bunch of help, with the snowplow leading the way."

Charity laughed softly, wincing again. "I can just imagine. I'm so sorry to put everyone to so much trouble." Her voice slurred, probably a result of the pain medication they'd given her, and exhaustion.

Ace leaned over her again. "As soon as you're feeling better, you've got a nice lecture coming to you."

Garrett, standing protectively at her side, reached out to touch her hair. "Get in line. It took me an hour to calm her mother down."

Consumed by guilt, Beau bent, resting his elbows on his knees and stared at his hands.

He should have been with her.

He should have known what she would be doing. He should have known when his own woman was leaving town, especially in the middle of a blizzard.

He blamed himself.

He'd thought he'd made some headway into loosening her up, and had managed to carve time out of the busy schedule she forced herself to keep and get to relax.

He'd hoped she felt closer to him, and would confide in him.

He'd tried to show her that he loved her, but he'd failed.

Miserably.

He could have lost her tonight.

The thought of how close he'd come to losing her made him cold inside, an icy fear that went all the way to his bones.

He couldn't bear the thought of something like this happening again.

Something had to change.

It had to be him.

* * * *

Charity couldn't stop looking at Beau, shaken at the change in him.

She'd met his eyes several times and smiled, hoping to ease some of the tension that kept him stiff, and wipe some of the misery from his eyes, , but Beau seemed lost in his own thoughts.

Hope fussed with the blankets that she'd already straightened several times. "Are you in any pain? Are you comfortable? Do you want some more water?"

Charity turned away from Beau to meet Hope's worried gaze, carefully lowering her head back to the pillow. "I'm fine. Just tired. The weather's awful. How the hell are you going to get back home?"

Hope blinked. "What are you talking about? I'm not going anywhere until they release you. The doctor said you should be able to leave tomorrow. They just want to watch you overnight. Ace and Beau will get us home all right."

Charity sighed. "At least Mom settled down a little. I didn't mean to scare anyone." It got harder and harder to keep her eyes open, the combination of fatigue and pain medicine making her drowsy.

Her father, Garrett, pulled the covers higher. "Your mother won't settle until she sees you and has a chance to fuss."

Blinking back tears, Charity smiled. "That's true. She's such a worrier."

Hope straightened the blanket over Charity again, and unfolded another. "Look who's talking. If you hadn't been so obsessed with getting the club ready, this wouldn't have happened. The damned carpet could have waited a few days, Charity."

Charity glanced at Beau again, narrowing her eyes to silently question him about what she could see bothered him, but he merely shook his head. "If I'd known the storm was going to hit, I never would have left town. I can't believe so many people came to look for me." Charity blinked back tears, grateful once again to be part of such an amazing town.

Ace shared a look with Beau before turning back to her, bending to kiss her hair again. "I'm going out to the waiting room to make some phone calls. I already set up the cot for Hope. Get some sleep, honey."

Her fathers left soon afterward with the intention of getting a few hours of sleep in the chairs in the waiting room, leaving Charity alone with Hope and Beau.

Charity followed her sister's movements, glancing at Beau again as Hope turned off the overhead light.

Leaving just the small light over her bed on, Hope adjusted the blankets again before moving to the foldaway bed the hospital had provided and crawled under the blanket.

Lying against the pillows, Charity looked to where Beau shifted to a more comfortable position, his expression hard as he propped his feet on the foot of her bed.

The look in his eyes was terrible to see, but she didn't know what to do to ease the terror she still saw in them. Settling back in his seat, he crossed his arms over his chest. "Go to sleep, cher. We'll watch over you."

She glanced toward where Hope lay several feet away, careful to keep her voice low. "Beau, we need to talk." Other than a few whispered words on the way to the hospital, she hadn't had a chance to speak to him alone since the accident, and wanted very much to talk to him.

She wanted very much for him to hold her again.

Beau sighed, his jaw clenching. "We'll talk tomorrow. Go to sleep."

It surprised her that her fathers and sister hadn't said anything about Beau being present, or the fact that he'd stayed behind in her hospital room. She wanted to ask him about it, but her eyelids became too heavy to keep her eyes open, and her words slurred so much, she didn't think a conversation would even be possible.

Frustrated, she focused on speaking clearly, wanting to erase the look of horror from Beau's features. "I'm okay, Beau. Just groggy."

Beau's features tightened. "You're far from okay. Just go to sleep, Charity."

The nurse came into the room, glancing at Hope before giving Beau a hard look.

He met it steadily and leaned back in the chair again, folding his arms over his chest and resting his head against the wall, clearly not about to go anywhere.

With a shake of her head and disapproving look, the nurse went about her business, checking Charity's vital signs under Beau's watchful stare.

When the nurse left the room, Charity glanced at Hope to see that her sister had fallen asleep.

The pain medicine they'd given her made it hard to focus, but she had things to say to Beau that couldn't wait.

"You know how much I love you, don't you?"

Beau grimaced. "Yes, enough to sleep with me, but not enough to marry me. Go to sleep, Charity. This isn't the time to get into this conversation."

"But, Beau—"

"Tomorrow, Charity. Go to sleep." Leaning his head back again, he closed his eyes, clearly ending the discussion.

With a sigh, Charity let her eyes close, unable to keep them open any longer. She loved Beau, and wanted to spend the rest of her life with him.

She had to tell him that their differences didn't matter.

Love hadn't seemed like enough before, but lying in the car, aching for Beau, she realized that love was everything.

Nothing else mattered.

* * * *

Beau opened his eyes again as Charity's breathing evened out. He knew the combination of the pain medicine and the release from the adrenaline rush would leave her exhausted.

Confident that she would sleep for hours, he watched her, knowing it would be quite a while before he slept—if he slept at all. Each time he closed his eyes, he found himself haunted by the image of her lying pale and injured in her wrecked car.

"You *are* going to marry her, aren't you?"

Smiling faintly at the indignation in Hope's whispered question, Beau glanced in her direction. "Yes. I'm going to get it settled with her before we get back to town."

Rolling to her side, Hope braced herself on her elbow to stare at him, her eyes narrowed. "It seems that everyone in Desire knew that the two of you were seeing each other except me."

Beau shrugged. "Ace and I talked about it many times, and I told your dads months ago that I intended to marry her. You believed your sister. That's to be expected."

Hope frowned. "I'm usually not so gullible, and Charity never lies. This one was a doozy. How the hell did she manage to fool me all this time?"

For the first time since Charity's accident, Beau felt a flicker of amusement. "She can be pretty convincing." Swallowing heavily, he rubbed the knot in his stomach and slid his gaze to where Charity slept. "She thinks I play too much."

Hope snorted. "She thinks *everyone* plays too much. When we were in school together, she didn't even want to go to parties. Beau, if you can't teach her to have fun, I don't know who can."

Beau didn't reply to that. He sure as hell didn't feel like having fun or playing games, especially since it had caused such a rift between him and the woman he loved.

After a few minutes of companionable silence, in which both he and Hope stared at a sleeping Charity, Beau glanced at Hope again. "Do you think you can make sure she and I are alone together on the ride home?"

Hope met his gaze, and smiled impishly. "Of course, especially if I can tell them that you're proposing."

"That's what I'll be doing." Beau settled back again to watch Charity sleep, his gaze lingering on the brace Charity wore to keep her from moving her shoulder.

"Hopefully, this time she'll accept. If not, I may just have to kidnap her."

She'd accept.

He wouldn't take her home until she did.

Chapter Seven

Although Charity appeared momentarily surprised that the others piled into Ace's SUV for the ride home, she didn't ask about it, much to Beau's relief.

He lifted her from the wheelchair, careful not to jostle her any more than necessary, and set her gently on the passenger seat before tucking the blanket he had waiting around her.

Light snow still fell, but the wind had died down, and it appeared that the worst of the storm was over.

Following Ace, they rode in silence for several minutes as he navigated his way to the main road, and around piles of snow and cars that had gotten stuck. Pleased to see that the road had been cleared, Beau looked over to see that Charity seemed to be going to sleep. He hated to wake her, but they had a few things to work out before they got back home. "Can we talk, chéri?"

She jerked upright, wincing. "Sure." Glancing around as though getting her bearings, she blinked several times, shading her eyes against the bright sunlight reflected off of the snow. "I'm glad the roads are clear. I saw on the news that we had over three feet." Turning, she frowned. "It was a hell of a storm, wasn't it? I was only inside the carpet store for a few minutes, and by the time I got back out to my car, it was already covered in snow."

Beau glanced at her, noticing she seemed even paler. Clenching his jaw, he tightened his hands on the wheel, the need to hold her almost overwhelming. "Yes, it was a hell of a storm, and the thought of you out in it still makes me shake."

He wanted to pull her tightly against him, burying his face in her hair, and just breathe her in until he could get the cold knot of fear in his stomach to unravel.

Glancing at her again, he gritted his teeth, alarmed at her paleness, a paleness that emphasized the discoloration that marred the left side of her beautiful face.

"How bad's the pain?"

With her head against the headrest, she turned her face toward him, the circles under her eyes even more pronounced in the bright light. "I'm fine, Beau."

Beau wanted to hit something. He could never remember feeling so helpless. Once she agreed to marry him, he hoped he'd feel more in control of the situation, but even having the right to care for her wouldn't make seeing her in pain any easier. Forcing himself to keep the rage from his voice, he took several deep breaths before speaking. "You're white as a sheet, and you had a dose of pain medicine before you left the hospital. How bad is it?"

"Not bad." Shrugging, she winced. "Except when I move my shoulder." She smiled, wincing again. "I'm fine, Beau. Just tired. I promise. I was very lucky, but it's over now. I hate that look in your eyes."

"Then marry me."

With slow deliberation, Charity lifted her head and turned toward him. "What did you say?"

Tired and irritable himself, Beau divided his attention between driving and Charity, wanting this settled before they got back to Desire. "You heard me, cher. Marry me. I want the right to take care of you. When we get back to Desire, I want to tell your parents that we're engaged. I want this settled here and now."

"Take care of me? I don't need anyone to take care of me." If possible, she sounded even weaker.

"I beg to differ." Clenching his jaw again, he forced himself to stay calm, knowing that he'd have to use logic in order to get through to her.

Charity thrived on logic.

Attempting a nonchalance he was far from feeling, he kept his voice calm. "You and I both know that we're going to get married, and I don't see the point in waiting. Whatever has to be worked out can be worked out."

He paused, looking over to find her frowning. He continued, not giving her the chance to speak until he'd pled his case. "You need someone to stay with you for the next couple of days, at least until you heal. Hope would run herself ragged between taking care of you and trying to get the club ready for the Grand Reopening. Your mother and fathers will run up and down the stairs all day to check on you, and your mother will come up to your apartment and stay up half the night watching you after working all day in the diner. All of them are going to be wondering what I'm doing there since I have no intention of going anywhere."

Charity sighed. "Once I explain to them that I can be alone—"

Beau blinked, whipping his head around to her. "You're kidding, right? You can't take care of yourself, and the doctor gave explicit instructions about your care. Do you really think your parents and sister are just going to leave you there by yourself? Do you think I will?"

Blowing out a breath, Charity rubbed her forehead. "Yeah, you're right." Her grimace of pain and the fact that she slumped to the side as if too weak to hold herself upright made Beau even more determined to keep a sharp eye on her.

Pressing his advantage, and wanting to make everything crystal clear before they got back to Desire, Beau lowered his voice. "We'll announce our engagement, and then there'll be no questions about me staying with you."

"But, there'll be questions about us that I don't feel like dealing with right now. Maybe we should wait until—"

"No." Inwardly cursing himself for snapping at her and making her jump, he sighed. "I don't want to wait. We both know this is going to happen eventually, don't we, chéri?"

Smiling, she grimaced again and put a hand to her swollen and discolored cheek. "It's not the most romantic proposal."

"Romance doesn't seem to work with you." Cursing himself for putting that flash of hurt in her eyes, he blew out a breath and slid a hand over her hair.

"I'm sorry. That was uncalled for. I'm tired, frustrated, and you scared years off my life. Look, let's just get home and get you well. The most important thing is that we get married. I want the right to take care of you, and my patience has run out."

"Beau, you don't need to stay with me. Don't you have a store to run?"

Pushing his frustration aside, Beau forced a smile. "You forget. I hired several new employees so I didn't have to work so many hours. I believe you called it *frivolous*."

He tightened his hands on the wheel as he looked over to where her car had been run off the road, bile rising up in his throat. Clenching his jaw, he shook off the image of her lying pale and broken in a wrecked car, an image that just wouldn't go away.

"Just say yes."

"Yes, Beau. I love you. I realized while I was lying there in the car that I don't want to live without you. I think I told you that on the way to the hospital. I just don't want to be a burden to you, and taking care of me now is going to be a hell of a burden." Charity gave him an odd look, frowning. "Are you okay?"

Forcing a smile, he patted her thigh, scared to touch her for fear of hurting her. "I'm fine. You're not a burden. You couldn't be if you tried. Now that we have things settled between us, won't don't you try to sleep a little?"

"Beau?"

"What is it, cher?" Some of the tension eased, but he knew he wouldn't settle completely until she'd recovered and carried his name.

"I probably should have called you when I was going to leave town, but I didn't know about the blizzard. I thought it was coming in today. I thought I could get there and back before—"

Beau sighed at her admission, more of his tension easing. "Don't worry about it. It won't happen again." Turning to her, he smiled. "I'm glad you agreed to marry me. I told Hope I'd kidnap you if you didn't."

Charity smiled, flashing her dimples, a smile that ended abruptly with a wince. "I'd rather just go home now, but will you promise to kidnap me at a later date?"

For the first time since he'd left her office the day before, Beau breathed a little easier. "That's a promise."

Chapter Eight

Charity tried to roll to her side, frowning when something that had been wedged against her prevented it. Half-asleep, she tried to shove the obstruction out of the way, her hand closing on what she recognized as a pillow. Without opening her eyes, she tugged at it, wincing at the pain that radiated through her shoulder.

A large, warm hand closed over hers, a hand she recognized at once. Sliding his fingers against her palm, Beau eased her grip on the pillow and took her hand in his, his lips warm as they brushed over her fingers. "No, cher. Leave the pillows where they are. They're keeping you from rolling onto your sore side. Just tell me what you need. I'll help you get comfortable."

Smiling at the low voice, husky with sleep coming from directly above her, Charity forced her eyes open. Surprised to find the room dark except for a small stream of light coming in from the partially open bathroom door, Charity lifted her eyes to his.

She reached up with her right arm to touch his cheek, and for the first time since she'd met him, found him unshaven. If possible, he looked even more exhausted. She looked toward the chair positioned close to the side of her bed, and the blanket he'd tossed aside. "You need a shave. Why are you sleeping in that chair instead of sleeping next to me?"

Beau's eyes narrowed, his gaze searching. Moving the blanket aside, he studied her arm. "Your bed's too small and I didn't want to accidentally bump you in your sleep."

His eyes, full of concern as he leaned over her, narrowed as he gently straightened her brace. "You keep trying to roll to your side.

You'd hurt like hell if you did, so I put the pillows there." He lifted her slightly with a hand pressed between her shoulder blades, his hands gentle as he adjusted the pillows around her again.

Struck by the distance in his tone, Charity searched his features for any sign of anger, but found nothing but concern and caring.

She knew her accident had upset him, but she'd expected him to be back to his usual teasing self by now, especially with his pattern of teasing her out of bad moods. She figured he would have been just as determined to tease her in an effort to make her forget about her pain.

The fact that he didn't worried her.

"I want to sit up." Before she could move, Beau's hands slid to her back, the warmth and solidness of them against her body easing some of her soreness. "Just relax. Let me do the work." His touch remained tender, but with a solid strength that felt incredible as he helped her into a sitting position, holding her there while he slid pillows behind her to prop her up.

"I figured you'd be waking up soon. It's time for another pain pill." His gaze sharpened on her face, his eyes filled with concern. He must not have liked what he saw because he clenched his jaw.

Turning away, he picked up the prescription bottle from the nightstand, watching her steadily as he shook out a pill. Holding out his palm, he offered it to her, along with the glass of water that he'd apparently refilled. "Take this and we'll get you more comfortable."

Struck by his flat tone, she watched him warily as she took the pain pill from his palm and accepted the glass, never taking her eyes from his as she swallowed the tablet.

Not wanting to bother him any more than necessary so he could get some sleep, Charity braced herself to get up. "Thank you."

Nodding, Beau accepted the glass from her and placed it back on her nightstand. "I'll ease you down. Just let me—"

She looked away, her face burning. "I have to use the bathroom."

"Okay, cher. There's no reason to look so embarrassed. I've seen and touched every part of you." He threw back the covers and reached for her. "I swear, you worry way too much about things."

Her breath caught when he slid his arms under her and lifted her against his chest in a show of strength that never failed to warm her and make her feel safe. Because he looked so tired, she felt compelled to protest. "I can walk."

Cradling her gently, he straightened. "And I can carry you a hell of a lot easier. Be still. I don't want to jostle you."

Leaning against him, she noticed for the first time that she wore one of her most comfortable cotton nightgowns, one that had thinned from wear in several places, but that she couldn't bear to part with. Frowning, she tried to remember arriving back at her apartment and putting it on, but couldn't.

"I don't remember putting this on." Knowing that Beau would see her in it, she probably would have put on something else.

He pushed the bathroom door open, and turning to the side, eased through the doorway and into the small bathroom. "You didn't."

Blinking against the light, she tried to focus on his features, her face burning at the thought of Beau undressing her when she'd been asleep. Having a sexual relationship was one thing, but she considered being undressed and put to bed when she'd been unaware of it something entirely different.

Once inside the bathroom, he paused, searching her features as though looking for something. "Your mom and Hope undressed you and put it on you after I carried you in. Hope said it was one of your *comfort* nightgowns—whatever the hell that is."

Her relief that he hadn't been the one to dress her diminished at the sense of loss in his voice that he'd desperately wanted to.

Charity yawned, fighting to lift her head. "It's something I wear when I don't feel well. It's very comfortable." Frowning, and aware of his gaze moving over her, she shrugged, regretting it immediately as pain shot from her shoulder. "It's not very attractive, though. Not exactly like the lacy stuff you keep buying me, is it?"

Beau shook his head without a trace of the smile she'd expected. "No. I'll call Rachel tomorrow and ask her to send over some more like this." He eased her down, setting it on her feet. Straightening, he held out his hands in an obvious attempt to steady her if she needed it, frowning. "Do you feel dizzy?"

Holding on to the small vanity, she shook her head carefully. "I'm fine. Just give me some privacy." Her legs shook, her knees felt like rubber, and she had to use the bathroom. Badly.

Beau frowned again, clearly reluctant to leave her. "Fine. I'll be right outside the door. Call me when you're done." His tone hardened, the threat in his eyes undeniable. "I don't want you trying to walk by yourself."

Charity nodded and gripped the small countertop, breathing a sigh of relief when he left. She moved as fast as she could to use the bathroom, and then made her way on shaky legs back to the sink.

Washing her hands, the brace making her movements clumsy, she looked up into the mirror, inwardly wincing.

The dark bruise above her cheek drew her attention first. On the left side of her face, it went from her temple down to her cheekbone, and explained why the left side of her face ached.

Still studying her reflection, she dried her hands and probed her cheek, unsurprised to find it slightly swollen.

She pulled the neckline of her nightgown aside to see her shoulder, pushing the brace aside and wincing at the bruise under it. She had another bruise on her chest from the seat belt, which had also cracked her sternum.

She'd already gotten good a good look at her hip, and had been shocked by the size of the bruise there, but felt pretty lucky that it hadn't been worse.

Running her tongue over her teeth, she grimaced and reached for her toothbrush, wishing she could take a shower. By the time she'd finished brushing her teeth and running a comb through her hair, she was exhausted. Holding on to the bathroom sink, she shivered at the cold, her knees rubbery, all thoughts of taking a shower dissipating.

She thought about trying to make it back to the bedroom on her own, but trembled so badly, she feared she'd fall down before she got there. Wincing as she imagined how much that would hurt, and cursing her own weakness, she called out for Beau, hating the fact that she had to bother him yet again.

* * * *

Beau closed the door behind Charity and went to the bed to straighten the rumpled covers, listening for her as he moved around the room.

Charity had been moving restlessly in the bed for the last hour, and she'd managed to kick the covers off several times.

He'd kept covering her, not liking how cool it had gotten in the small apartment.

She lived above the diner in an older building that didn't have the insulation it should have, and he'd had to turn the heat up several times in the last few hours in an effort to get it warm enough.

On the way home, he'd tried to convince her that she'd be more comfortable at his house, but she'd dug in her heels and insisted that he bring her home. When he'd persisted, she'd gotten upset, so he'd relented, wanting her to be as comfortable as possible.

He finished with the bed and straightened, turning when he heard his cell phone vibrating. Crossing the room to her dresser, he picked it up and looked at the display, unsurprised to see that the call came from Ace.

"Hello, Ace. You on duty tonight?"

"Getting ready to go home in a bit. I saw the light on upstairs. Is everything okay?"

Beau sighed and moved to the window, pushing the curtain aside and frowning at the amount of cold air that came in. "Charity woke up. It was time for another pain pill. I'm waiting for her to finish in the bathroom so I can tuck her back in. This fucking apartment's freezing."

"Yeah. I remember those days. There's extra blankets in the hall closet. Is it too cold in there for her?"

Beau glanced on the bed with the pile of covers. "I turned the heat way up, which I'm sure she'll complain about in the morning. I found the blankets and have most of them on her bed."

"How's the pain?"

Beau rubbed his gritty eyes, and knew he'd have to get a couple more hours of sleep in order to stay as alert as he needed to be for Charity, but he woke up each time she moved. "She winces every time she moves, but tries to pretend it doesn't hurt. She's white as a sheet, and I know that some of it's from the pain." Running a hand through his hair, Beau sighed. "She's getting some sleep, though."

"You sound like you haven't gotten much. You need us to come over there and give you a break?"

"No. I'll doze again when she goes back to sleep." He knew he wouldn't get any sleep at all if he wasn't with her.

Ace sighed. "We'll be over tomorrow to see her. Hope would have come over to spend the night tonight, but she thought the two of you could use some time alone together."

Hearing the sound of running water, Beau stepped away from the window and moved toward the bathroom. "Tell Hope that Charity's fine. The doctor just wants her to take it easy until she has a chance to heal. Dillon stopped by earlier with Charity's purse and cell phone. The cell phone's destroyed. I'll get her a new one when I get out."

"I'll get Hope to do it. She's going crazy, trying to figure out ways she can help Charity." Ace chuckled. "If I know my wife, she'll get her something pink and girly just to tease her sister. It'll make them both feel better."

Beau could hear Charity moving around and wondered what the hell she was up to. He hated to barge in and embarrass her, but listening for the sound of her falling stretched his nerves to the breaking point. "That's fine."

Hearing her call his name, he hurried toward the bathroom. "Charity's calling me. See you tomorrow." He disconnected and tossed the phone onto her dresser, never slowing his stride. Anxious to get to her in case she'd fallen, he burst through the door, catching it in case she'd fallen behind it.

Seeing her holding on to the sink and shivering, his stomach lurched, and gritting his teeth, he rushed toward her, scared she would fall. "You're so fucking pale. You look like you're about to fall on your face." He took the towel from her hands and tossed it into the sink. "You feel sick?"

"No. Just so damned weak."

He lifted her, her pitiful attempt to slap at him angering him even more. "Stop fighting me. You're mine, and I have every right in the world to take care of you."

"Just help steady me. You're too tired to be carrying me. Christ, I hate being such a burden."

"Then stop arguing and let me tuck you in and we can both get some sleep."

He strode to the bed, and tucked her in, trying not to jar her any more than necessary. "I'm sick and tired of this game we've been playing. It's over. Besides, you're too weak to fight me." He adjusted the pillows that would keep her shoulder in place, fighting the urge to gather her against him.

Charity frowned at him. "Since when do you get tired of games? You live for them."

Leaning over her, he fisted his hands on either side of her head, fighting the almost overwhelming urge to yank her against him, and hold her until he reassured himself that she was safe. "Not anymore. Go back to sleep."

"My feet are cold."

Beau moved the end of the bed and reached under the covers to take her feet in his hands. "Cold? They're like ice!" Remembering how cold and wet her feet had been when they'd found her, he hurriedly adjusted the covers around them. Holding first one, then the other between his hands, he warmed them, watching her battle to keep her eyes open.

"Beau, what did you mean—not anymore? Why don't you ever smile? Are you sorry you talked me into marrying you?"

Beau couldn't believe she would even think such a thing. "That's the most ridiculous thing I've ever heard you say. I love you, Charity. Nothing's more important than keeping you safe." Her feet felt warmer, but still not warm enough to suit him. They seemed so small in his hands, and seeing her looking so tiny amidst the piles of blankets and pillows hit him hard.

He loved her so much, more than she would probably believe, and nothing seemed as important as caring for her and keeping her safe.

"Beau, I feel like something's wrong." Her voice had become so weak, it barely reached him.

"You scared the hell out of me. You could have been killed, Charity, or seriously injured. My stomach's still tied up in knots."

That was putting it mildly.

Tucking the blankets around her feet, he smiled to ease the concern in her eyes. "Go to sleep, Charity. Your eyes are unfocused and you can't even keep them open."

"But—"

"Everything's going to be fine now. We're going to get married, and I'm going to be able to keep a closer eye on you. Go to sleep. You're slurring, and not even making sense."

He waited, watching her as her eyes closed, only to open, before closing again. He didn't move as it happened over and over, cursing her stubbornness, and not wanting to do anything that would wake her up again. Satisfied when her eyes closed and stayed closed, he remained motionless, listening to her breathe.

Once her breathing evened out, he got to his feet and made his way to the bathroom, closing the door almost all the way, leaving just enough light coming into the room to enable him to watch over her.

Moving back to the chair, he propped his feet on the foot of the bed, moving them close to hers so he would feel her move if he happened to fall asleep.

Settling back, he thought about her concern that something was wrong.

Relieved that she'd agreed to marry him, he didn't feel as tense as he had before, but he still worried about her injuries.

Playing just didn't seem as important to him as it had before. He couldn't explain it, but his thinking had changed dramatically since Charity's accident.

After the scare she'd given him, he doubted that he would ever be the same again.

Chapter Nine

Dropping her fork, Charity leaned back against the pillows with a sigh. She just didn't feel like eating anymore. Frustrated that everything seemed to take such an enormous amount of effort, and tired of being tired, she cursed and looked toward the doorway, waiting for Beau to reappear.

Warm and comfortable, she listened to Beau moving around in the kitchen, impatient for him to get back to her. She missed him, but more than that, she missed the Beau she'd known before the accident.

It had been three days since she'd come home from the hospital, and she wanted to get back to normal.

She missed Beau's grin.

She couldn't deny that it had been nice being alone with him, but she'd been asleep most of the time, thanks to the pain medicine he kept doling out.

Bored with herself, she knew being stuck in her small apartment must be boring Beau out of his mind.

Sighing, she looked at her plate and then toward the doorway again. She hated the achiness, and the weakness still lingering, and wanted to get back to having Beau look at her with desire in his eyes, instead of guilt and concern.

Since her accident, he'd watched over her like a hawk, and hadn't left her for more than a few minutes at a time.

He'd been loving, patient, solicitous, and understanding. He'd fixed her meals, given her pain medication, helped her shower and dress, carried her to the living room to watch television when she got bored, and basically waited on her hand and foot.

The playful man she'd fallen in love with, and criticized for his playfulness had been conspicuously absent since her accident. He'd been replaced by a thoughtful, serious man with watchful eyes—a man who didn't laugh or tease her at all.

A man who looked like he'd been kicked in the gut.

And it was all her fault.

If she'd only known about the snowstorm, or taken the time to mention to him that she would be going out of town, none of this would have happened.

Beau appeared in the doorway, wiping his hands on a dish towel. "You finished, cher?" Tossing the towel over his shoulder, he strode into the room and to her bedside, his graceful movements stirring a hunger inside her, but she knew she didn't have the strength to see it through. Glancing at her plate, he frowned down at her. "You only ate half of your breakfast."

Hoping for a smile from him, she reached out and tugged his sleeve, smiling easier now that the swelling in her cheek had gone down. "I keep telling you that I can't eat as much as you do."

Beau didn't smile back as she'd hoped. Instead, he stared down at her steadily, his eyes hard, and with a glimmer concern. "You're going to eat every bite of your lunch, even if I have to feed you myself."

She waited until he removed the tray before throwing the covers aside, wincing at the abrupt movement. Lifting her chin, she smiled faintly, hoping to get a reaction from him. "I'm eating lunch downstairs at the diner."

Beau half turned, his smile cool. "And you think I won't force feed you in front of your parents?"

Determined to get him to smile, and possibly play a little, she laughed softly. "You wouldn't dare."

He threw the covers back over her legs and started out of the room. "That's where you're wrong. Stay where you are. I'll be right back to help you shower and dress. Figure out what you want to wear that's warm and comfortable. The wind's picked up again."

Disappointed that she couldn't seem to get a rise out of him, Charity frowned at his back. "Beau?"

He paused in the doorway and turned back abruptly, glancing from the tray to her. "You didn't take your pain pill."

Meeting his gaze, she shook her head, trying to understand what had changed. "I don't need it." Not trusting the look of intention in his eyes, Charity lifted her chin, bracing herself for the confrontation that was long overdue, and one that would hopefully end this distance between them.

Holding up her hand, she threw the covers aside again, her patience at an end. "I don't want them, damn it! They make me groggy and keep putting me to sleep."

Beau paused beside her, a muscle working in his jaw. "In this instance, I don't particularly care what you want. The pain medicine keeps you comfortable and lets you get the sleep you need in order to heal."

Charity narrowed her eyes at his solicitous tone, wishing she could read his mind. Ever since the accident, he'd been almost like a stranger to her. She wanted the man she'd fallen in love with, the smiling, playful man who'd stolen her heart.

"They keep me unconscious!" Smiling, she crossed her arms over her chest. "I guess that makes me easier to deal with, huh?"

A flash of impatience flashed in Beau's eyes, but disappeared almost immediately. "Calm down. I know you're just upset because you're in pain and tired of lying in bed. The pills just let you sleep, and the doctor said he wants you to take them and get the rest you need at least for a week. Now, stop getting yourself all worked up and take your pill."

Charity gritted her teeth. "I'm. Not. Taking. It."

Remembering all the times she'd criticized him for playing too much, she wanted to kick herself. With a sigh, she held her hand out to him, delighted at how quickly he took it. "Beau, I want everything back the way it was. I'm really sorry for the things I said to you before. I didn't really mean them."

"Yes, you did."

"Are you mad at me?"

Beau frowned. "Of course not. If you want to go down to the diner to eat, why don't you lie back and rest a little."

Hoping to get a reaction from him, Charity smiled playfully, wrinkling her nose at him. "I'm surprised you're not trying to prevent me from leaving the apartment."

Instead of the teasing comment she'd hoped for, Beau shrugged. "Your mom and dads have been worried about you, and almost every time one of them comes up to see you, you've been asleep. This will give you a chance to visit with them, and I know they'll watch over you and make you eat while I run some errands and check on some things."

Her smile fell. He probably had a million things to do, and instead, hadn't left the apartment. If she was going stir crazy, he had to be bored out of his mind. "What kind of errands?" Maybe she could talk him into taking her with him.

His smile didn't even come close to reaching his eyes. "I need to check on the store." His eyes narrowed. "And to pick up your engagement ring. Jake called this morning to tell me it's ready." Turning, he left the room.

Charity frowned as several things hit her at once. Raising her voice to be heard in the kitchen, she fisted her hands on her lap. "Those pain pills you keep shoving down my throat have made me stupid. Damn it, Beau. You've ignored your business to take care of me."

Beau came back into the room, carrying a stack of her clothing, already folded. "Contrary to popular belief, it took years and a lot of work to get my business to a point that it practically runs by itself. I didn't lose a dime by being here." In the process of putting her clothes away, he met her reflection in the mirror over her dresser. "But, even if it had cost me every cent I have, I wouldn't have left you. Clear enough? Have you decided what you want to wear?"

Her gaze went to his shoulders, which seemed wider than ever, smiling at the images that raced through her mind.

Gripping his shoulders as he took her.

Resting her head on his warm, muscular shoulder as he held her after sex and talked to her in a low intimate tone in the darkness.

She let her gaze linger on his arms, arms gentle enough to carry her across a snow-covered field without hurting her, and strong enough to rip a car door from its hinges to get to her.

Arms that wrapped around her and made her feel safe, loved, and very desired.

She'd needed him, and he'd been there.

He'd been strong when she'd needed his strength, and gentle when she needed his tenderness.

She loved him more than ever, and wanted to understand how such a playful man could have hidden this part of himself from her.

Determined to dig deeper, Charity watched him move around the room, planning her strategy.

Now that most of the pain medicine had worn off, she could think again, and she wanted nothing more than to get to the bottom of what made Beau Parrish tick.

Nothing she said seemed to make any difference in his demeanor. She had to find a way to get him to talk. Really talk. "Beau, I really appreciate all that you've done."

Beau nodded, frowning as he exchanged the pair of socks he'd picked out for her for a thicker pair. "You're welcome. Get back into bed and go to sleep. You'll need your energy for going out later, and you sure as hell won't get it from the little you eat."

Bristling at his distant tone, she ran a hand over her hair, embarrassed at how grungy she felt. "I want to take a shower and wash my hair."

She also needed to brush her teeth, which felt as if they all had little sweaters on them.

She also wanted to smell a hell of a lot better.

Placing the bra, panties, and socks he'd picked out for her on the bed, he appeared to consider that. "Okay. You'd probably sleep better, and it'll give me a chance to change your sheets."

When he bent as though to carry her again, Charity waved him away, not wanting him near her until she cleaned up. "I can walk. I need to move. I'm stiff all over."

Beau frowned. "Lie down and I'll give you a massage. Jesse brought a basket over for you and I think there's some massage oil in there."

Grinning, she jumped on the opportunity to tease him. "I can only imagine what a massage from you would be like."

To her surprise, Beau frowned. "I hope you don't mean that I would try to fuck you when you can barely move. Hell, you're black and blue all over."

Pulling her nightgown down from where it had slid high on her thigh, Charity covered the ugly bruise. "That's not what I meant."

"Don't." Beau seemed to regret his harsh tone, and blew out a breath. "Don't insult me by covering your bruise as if you think anything would make you unattractive to me." Bending and gathering her close, he kissed the top of her hair. "I've always thought you're the most beautiful woman in the world." Lifting her chin, he dropped a soft kiss on her lips. "Nothing will ever change that. How about that massage?"

Touched, and humbled by his loving words, Charity swallowed heavily, blinking back tears. "Oh, Beau. That has to be the sweetest thing anyone's ever said to me."

She started to cuddle against him, and then remembered how badly she needed a shower. Leaning back, she smiled. "Would you mind if I took a rain check? I really want to take a shower and wash my hair." She'd definitely take a rain check and get the massage he promised when it would do her the most good. She already had plans for the next several minutes.

He rubbed her lower back, always cautious of her injuries as he removed her brace. "Of course, cher. Anytime you want it."

He took his time undressing her, working her nightgown off and over her head and leaving her naked except for a pair of cotton panties. Sliding his hands over her skin with a familiar tenderness that made her skin tingle with awareness, he bent to kiss her temple. "You are so incredibly beautiful."

Careful not to move her left arm and hurt her shoulder, Charity cuddled against him. "Beau, this feels so good. I've missed you so much."

Lifting his head, Beau stared down at her and smiled, a real smile that made his beautiful dark eyes twinkle. "I've been right here, cher."

Her heart lurched at his smile, the butterflies in her stomach reminding her of the night they'd first become lovers.

Cupping his cheek, she urged him to lower his head and reached up to kiss his chin. "Yes, you have. You've taken such good care of me. Beau, I'm so sorry for all the things I said to you. I was just so scared."

Gently cupping her breast, Beau ran his thumb back and forth over her nipple. "Scared of what, Charity?"

Moaning at the rush of pleasure to her slit, Charity gripped his forearm to steady herself. "I was scared that this was all just a game to you. I love you too much, Beau. I couldn't stand it if none of this meant anything to you."

Running his other hand down to caress her bottom, Beau nodded, his eyes flat. "I know that, Charity, and I have to admit that it hurts. I think it's ironic that I've spent years building my business into something that doesn't require a great deal of my time so that when I fell in love with a woman, I could spend as much time with her as I could, only to fall in love with a woman who thinks working his fingers to the bone is the only way to show that he cares for her."

Charity frowned. "That makes me sound awful. Oh, Beau, I swear I didn't mean it that way."

To her relief, Beau smiled. "I know you didn't. It's just that we never really talked about it. I'm not blameless in this, Charity. I've kept things from you, too."

Something in his tone sent a chill through her. "You've kept things from me? I know we never really talked about you. You turned every conversation around." Straightening, she crossed her other arm in front of her, grasping her injured one. "What kind of things have you kept from me?"

Lifting her chin, he frowned. "Don't look like that. It's nothing bad, just a problem I have to deal with. As soon as you're feeling better, we'll talk about it. Now, come on and take your shower. It's too cold for you to stand here in just a pair of panties. This damned apartment's like a refrigerator."

Nervous now, and wondering about Beau's secrets, Charity allowed him to lead her into the bathroom, holding his shoulder as he bent and removed her panties. "Beau, you're scaring me."

Careful of her injured arm, Beau gathered her close and ran his hands down her back, his hands warm and firm against her skin. "There's nothing to be afraid of. We'll talk about it, but it's not going to change the fact that we're getting married."

"So tell me now."

"I will." Frowning slightly, he patted her bottom. "But, not until you get better. That should be motivation enough for you to eat and get enough rest."

Slapping his back as he bent to turn on the water, Charity glared at a spot between his shoulder blades. "You know damned well that the suspense will drive me crazy."

Beau finished adjusting the water temperature and straightened. Turning, he grabbed a towel and dried his hands, grinning in a way so much like the Beau she knew that she could only stare up at him, her heart pounding furiously as a rush of desire washed over her.

"I know, chéri." Wrapping an arm around her, he helped her into the shower. "Take your shower. I'll be right out here. Let me know if you feel dizzy."

Shaking her head as he closed the curtain, Charity pulled the lever to start the shower, raising her voice to be heard above the spray. "I never realized how devious you are."

"I didn't want to scare you off. I brought in the basket that Jesse, Nat, and Kelly brought. Would you like me to open it for you?"

"Sure." Standing under the spray, Charity let the warm water wash over her. Like most of the women she knew, she already had several of the products from Jesse and Kelly's shop, Indulgences. The products were fabulous, and she just couldn't get enough of them.

She hoped Jesse included something that smelled good enough to entice Beau. "I don't remember them coming over." Stepping out of the spray, she heard the rustle of plastic wrap. "Is there any shampoo in there?"

"You were sound asleep. A lot of people have been here. And yes, there are two shampoos. One is the unscented one you use and the other is vanilla fig. Damn, that smells good."

Charity stilled. "Give it to me." With her good hand, she pushed the curtain aside and reached out a hand for the shampoo. "Any more vanilla fig bottles in there?"

If not, she'd go down to Indulgencies and get everything she could find in that scent. Seeing that Beau had opened the bottle for her, she smiled and lifted the bottle to her nose. "That *does* smell good." Careful not to move her left arm any more than necessary, she poured a dollop of shampoo into her right hand, and struggled to wash her hair one-handed.

Beau moved the curtain aside and poked his head in, his eyes raking over her body as he took the shampoo bottle from her, making her skin tingle. "Yeah, cher, it does, and you have more. Bodywash, body lotion, even some massage oil. I think I remember this from

Jesse's store. I went in there one day to meet Rio, and they were making it. The whole place smelled like it and I didn't want to leave."

God bless Jesse.

Charity grinned. Jesse or Nat must have remembered how much Beau liked the scent. She rinsed her hair and held out her hand for more. "Thanks."

Beau closed the curtain again. "Do you want the bodywash, too?"

"Sure, I might as well use all the same scent."

If Beau liked it, she'd wallow in the stuff.

Careful not to make him suspicious, Charity sighed loudly enough to be heard over the shower, and injected a touch of weariness into her voice. "Forget it. My arm's too tired." Reaching for the conditioner, she hid a smile when Beau poked his head through the curtain again, and made a show of struggling to pour some out. "You don't think you could come in here and—no. Forget it."

As she'd expected, Beau rushed to help her.

"Sure, I can come in and help you. It's probably better. That way I can make sure you don't fall."

He left the shower curtain partially open, and over the sound of the shower, she could hear him hurriedly throwing off his clothes.

Smiling with anticipation, Charity held the bottle to her chest and waited.

Her breath caught at the sight of him stepping into the shower, all lean muscle and hard lines taking up most of the room in the small stall.

The thrill of having him naked and close enough to reach out and touch proved irresistible. Holding the bottle against her chest with her left arm, she reached out her good one, laying her hand on his chest, and smiling at his sharp intake of breath.

Meeting his speculative gaze, Charity bent forward to kiss his chest, looking up at him through her lashes. "I've missed you."

Smiling when his cock jumped against her belly, she reached down and wrapped her hand around it, her smile widening when it grew longer and thicker under her touch. "It looks like you've missed me, too."

With a faint smile, Beau unwrapped her hand from around his cock and placed it back on his chest. "No."

Charity couldn't help but run her hands over him, the sight of his sleek, wet body enticing her to explore. "We can, if you take me slowly." Lifting her eyes to his again, she leaned into him, smiling when he set the conditioner and shower gel aside and took her gently by the shoulders. "Remember the night you took my virginity?"

Beau's eyes flared with heat. "That's a night I'll never forget."

Reaching up, she ran her fingers through the ends of his damp hair. "Take me like that again."

Beau's body shuddered, his eyes closing briefly as his cock jumped against her belly. "Baby, I'd love nothing more." Bending low, he touched his lips to hers, pushing her wet hair back from her temple. "As soon as you've healed. You're sore and injured. It won't be long. Now, behave yourself so I can wash you."

"Then can I wash you?"

Beau's lips twitched. "I already had a shower. Let's just get you washed and out of here before you fall."

Charity held her breath as he poured a dollop of shower gel into his hand, her skin tingling with anticipation. Wanting his hands on her as much as possible, she sighed. "Since I'm hurt, you should probably do it slowly. *Real* slow." She wanted it to last as long as possible.

She met his suspicious gaze with what she hoped to be a look of innocence, pushing her bottom lip out just a little, the way Hope did when confronted with Ace's temper.

Beau's eyes narrowed, and he watched her for several long seconds, his eyes searching. Finally, he smiled faintly and nodded once. "Of course. I planned to be gentle with you. You should know that. What's wrong with you?" His eyes narrowed again. "If I didn't know you better, I'd think you were up to something."

Charity gasped at the feel of his hands closing over her breasts. "I could ask you the same thing. Ever since my accident, you're different. Oh, that feels good."

"Don't wiggle so much. Your chest has to be sore." His hands moved lower to wash her belly. "What makes you think there's something wrong with me?"

Stiffening, she sucked in a breath when he moved toward her sore hip, but relaxed again under his gentle touch. "Beau, that feels so good. I think I'm going to take you up on that massage."

Straightening, he braced her with a hand at her back as he moved the other in a circular motion over her bruised hip. "Feel good, cher?"

Keeping her sore arm between them, she wrapped the other around his waist and leaned into him. "Heaven." The feel of his cock pressing hard against her belly caused a stirring between her thighs and had her pussy clenching with need.

His touch both soothed and aroused her, and within minutes, she found herself giving in and going wherever he took her.

Beau rubbed her back, the slow side of his hand over her wet skin relaxing her sore muscles even more. "Why did you ask if there's something wrong with me?"

Charity couldn't hold back a moan as Beau focused on a particularly tight muscle. "You don't laugh anymore."

"You're hurt. There hasn't been much to laugh about, has there?"

Alarmed at his flat tone, Charity pushed against him, lifting her face to his. "Beau, I'm fine. I'm just a little sore, but I feel better every day."

He nodded once, not looking convinced. "Good. Now be still so I can wash the rest of you."

She shivered as he poured more of the gel into his hand and knelt in front of her. Bracing herself with a hand on his shoulder, she spread her legs as he began to wash her. "I never thought I'd have to say this, but I miss playing with you."

Beau glanced up at her as he finished her legs and moved his hand higher. "I don't think either one of us has been in the mood to play." He washed her slit with a speed that left her frustrated and yearning for more. "Don't look at me that way. When I get you back to bed, I'll make you come if you need relief, but I'll be damned if I'll do it in here where you can fall."

"If I wasn't hurt, I'd make you change your mind."

Beau glanced up at her again, lifting a brow. "If you weren't hurt, it wouldn't be an issue. Can you turn around?"

Charity glared at him and turned, rubbing her thighs together as she did. "Yes, I can turn around. You're being mean. Touching me just enough to arouse me, and then—"

"You were aroused when I stepped in here. You get even more aroused when I touch you, which gives me a great deal of satisfaction. In case you haven't noticed, you have the same effect on me, cher." The hint of laughter in his voice warmed her all the way through, relieving some of the tension tightening her muscles. Biting her lip as his hands ran over her bottom, Charity swallowed a moan. "Beau?"

Thinking about the number of times he'd talked about taking her there, and the smooth slide of his hands over her cheeks, Charity found herself clenching her buttocks against the slight tingling of her puckered opening.

"Were you serious about what you said about...you know. Or, were you just teasing me?" Cursing the fact that her face burned and her inhibitions kept her from finishing the question, she stopped abruptly.

Beau chuckled, a sound that vibrated over her skin. "About me taking your bottom?" Straightening, he turned her in his arms and, with a tenderness she'd come to rely on, began to wash her injured shoulder and her arm.

Charity nodded, lifting her arm slightly at his urging. "Yes." Careful to keep her gaze averted, she watched his soapy hand move over her, sneaking glances at his cock, and trying to imagine how something so large could fit inside her. Her bottom clenched again, the tingling there driving her crazy.

"Don't worry about it. You're too delicate for something like that."

Charity stiffened, insulted. "Too delicate?" Turning, she fought a wave of dizziness, frustrated that she had to reach for him to keep her balance, and even more irritated that he caught her against him before she could—as if he'd known.

"Look, Beau. I got hurt, but that's it. You didn't seem to think I was delicate before the accident."

Setting the gel aside, Beau pushed her gently under the shower spray. "You are the most contrary woman I've ever met. Every time I ever mentioned taking that tight ass, you got skittish, but then when I touch you there, you come hard and fast. Now that you're injured, and can barely move, you want me to fuck your ass."

Charity sputtered, wiping the water out of her eyes so she could see him. "I didn't say that. I just want you to be the way you were before, damn it."

Beau reached behind her and turned off the water. "You didn't like the way I was before. It kept you from marrying me, didn't it?"

When he reached for a towel, Charity laid a hand on his chest, desperate to make him understand something she didn't quite understand herself.

"Beau, I need you to listen to me."

He wrapped the towel around her and with gentle hands, helped her from the shower. "I always listen to you, cher. Stand still so I can dry you."

Still naked and dripping, Beau ran the towel over her before wrapping her in a dry one and drying himself. "How do you feel? You're swaying."

"I feel better." Grabbing the comb from the countertop, she started to run it through her hair. "I really want to talk to you."

"So talk." He tossed the towel aside and lifted her in his arms. "I'm going to put you in the chair while I change the sheets."

Charity made herself comfortable, feeling guilty because she didn't have the energy to help him. "I hate being waited on, and that's all you seem to do lately."

"Don't worry about it. I haven't done much. If you want to talk, you'd better hurry before you fall asleep."

Cursing the weakness that pervaded her, Charity blew out a breath, fearing he was right. "Beau, you have to understand that you have quite a reputation in town. You always have."

Looking up from where he tucked in the sheets, he frowned. "What kind of reputation?"

Remembering the jealousy she felt every time she heard another woman talk about him, Charity forced a smile. "You've always been known as a playboy—as a man who could never be pinned down. You liked to play and made no apologies for it. You rarely dated a woman more than a few times, and made it plain that having fun was your first priority."

Beau frowned as he moved around the bed. "The women I went out with knew the score. I didn't hurt anyone, Charity."

Charity sat forward and pulled the top sheet to straighten it. "Well, I felt like I was playing the same game with you and I didn't know the *score*. I thought you would assume I did. I tried to pretend like I did so you wouldn't think I was unsophisticated, but I didn't know what the hell I was doing."

Lifting her gaze to his, she forgot about her shoulder and shrugged, instantly regretting it. "I couldn't resist you. Stupid, huh?"

Beau came toward her and knelt at her feet, taking her hands in his. "And I sure as hell couldn't resist you." His smile made him even more gorgeous. "I knew you were unsophisticated, cher. You were a virgin, remember? I never would have taken your virginity if I hadn't planned to marry you."

Stunned, Charity could only stare up at him. "But, Beau, that was months ago. You couldn't have known you wanted to marry me then."

His lips curved. "And yet I did. Let's get you into bed and under the covers before your feet get cold again."

Charity couldn't hold back a moan as he lowered her to the bed, propping her into a sitting position, and pulled the blankets over her. "God, I feel good. I haven't felt this good in days."

"Good."

Lulled even more by the feel of a comb going through her hair, and the warm air of the dryer, Charity closed her eyes and started to droop, leaning more heavily against Beau.

A few minutes later, he turned the dryer off, setting it and the comb aside. His hands went to her waist, holding her steady as he dropped the softest of kisses on her shoulder. "Sit up just a minute so I can get the brace back on you."

"Do I have to wear it while I'm sleeping? I'm tired of it."

"I don't want you to move your arm the wrong way in your sleep."

Turning her head toward his, Charity smiled. "Why don't you lie down with me and make sure? You look exhausted."

If she could get him to lie down with her, maybe she could get him to get some of the sleep he so desperately needed. Real sleep, not the kind he got in the chair.

Beau smiled faintly. "I'm fine, but if you think you can lie on your right side, I'll slide in behind you. It's been a long time since I held you, and never when you were sleeping."

Charity moaned in pleasure as Beau lowered her to the bed and stretched out behind her. "I was stupid. I don't deserve you."

Pulling the covers up, Beau kissed her bare shoulder before tucking the blankets around it. "We deserve each other. Now, stop moving around and go to sleep."

Warmed by the heat of his body against her back, and by the hint of laughter in his gruff tone, Charity smiled. She knew Beau hadn't had a lot of sleep since staying with her, sleeping either in the chair next to her bed, or short naps on her sofa while she watched television.

"This feels good. Will you stay here with me? You won't leave?"

"Hmm. I won't leave." He sounded half asleep already, his Cajun accent even thicker and sexier. "You sure you don't need a pain pill, chéri?"

"I'm sure. You give off a lot of heat, and it's making me feel good already." She hadn't felt this good in days. "Just don't leave me."

Beau wrapped his arm around her waist, holding her left hand in his, effectively keeping her from moving it. "I'm not going anywhere, cher. Neither are you."

Smiling, Charity let herself drift to sleep, amazed at how wonderful it felt to fall asleep in the arms of the man she loved.

Now that they'd talked and she'd explained herself, she was confident that everything would be back to normal.

He just needed some sleep.

Chapter Ten

She shivered with the cold, a cold that went all the way to her bones. She didn't think it was possible to be this cold.

She tried to move, and gasped at the pain in her side, a pain that went from her shoulder all the way to her hip. Her entire left side hurt, and each small movement, even a deep breath, made her whimper.

Beau!

She wanted Beau.

He would get her warm. He would make the pain go away.

They would come. He would come. She knew they would come— but what if they couldn't find her?

How long could she last in this cold?

So cold. She couldn't stop shaking. So scared.

Beau!

Her head hurt, but the headache accompanying it hurt even more. It pounded with every click of the flashers. The constant blinking of her hazard lights reflecting off the snow, and on her dashboard made her headache worse. She couldn't turn them off, though, or Beau may never find her.

So dark.

Closing her eyes, an image formed, one of Beau smiling at her.

The surge of love that swelled up inside her brought tears to her eyes.

She wanted Beau. She needed Beau.

When he found her, everything would be all right.

She had to make everything all right with him again. She couldn't stand the thought of losing him. She opened her eyes again, hoping to see his face.

So dark.

The snow came down harder and faster, building up outside the window and partially blocking her vision.

If the snow covered her car, he'd never find her in time.

So cold. Freezing.

She would die out here and he'd never know that she'd made a mistake.

He'd never know that nothing was as important as being with him.

He'd never know how much she loved him.

So cold. So tired.

The snow continued to pile up, covering her car until she couldn't even see the glow of the blinking lights anymore.

She was going to die in here, and Beau would never know how sorry she was.

Where was he? Beau!

* * * *

"Beau!"

Beau jerked upright, Charity's tortured cry scaring the hell out of him. Cursing, he tightened his hand on hers to keep her from thrashing. "Charity, wake up, cher."

"Beau! I'm so sorry."

Beau stilled when she began to sob, his heart pounding as she called to him over and over. Gathering her closer, he pressed his lips against her ear, anxious to wake her. "I'm here, cher. Wake up. Open those beautiful eyes for me."

"So cold."

"No, cher." He pulled the covers higher, his heart breaking at her choked cries. He struggled to keep his tone calm and soothing, but raised his voice to wake her from the nightmare that held her in its grip. "You're nice and warm in bed with me. Wake up for me. Come on. You can do it."

She stilled briefly and then the tension left her body in a rush, and he knew she'd finally woken up. "Beau?"

The lump in his throat nearly choked him, but he forced a smile to reassure her. "Of course. Who else would it be? You had a bad dream. You're still shaking." Nuzzling her neck, he kissed her hair. "Tell me about it."

She gripped his forearm, her breath coming out in short pants. "Oh, Beau. I dreamed that I was trapped in the car. The snow piled up so you wouldn't have been able to see the lights and I would have died in there without telling you how sorry I am for doubting you."

Thinking about his own nightmares of not finding her in time, Beau gathered her close. "I've had that same nightmare quite a few times. We found you, and thank God you weren't hurt worse."

Keeping one arm around her, he bent to see her face, rubbing a hand up and down her back in an effort to get her to stop shaking. Concerned that she looked so pale again, he kept an arm around her to steady her. "I was afraid you would have nightmares. The painkillers knocked you out and probably kept you from having them until now."

When she struggled to get into a sitting position, he wrapped his arm around her waist and sat up, using his own strength to pull her with him instead of making her use her sore muscles.

Breathing in the scent of the bodywash she'd used, a scent mingling with her own tantalizing sweet scent, Beau ran his hands over her soft skin. "Let's get you dressed in something warm and get out of here."

Hoping that getting her out of the small apartment would be good for her, he started to rise, pausing when she caught his arm, his stomach clenching when she looked up at him with tear-filled eyes. "Cher, don't!" Bending to bury his face in her hair, he groaned. "Please, Charity. Try not to think about it."

"Beau, it's not that. I'm just so sorry. Please forgive me."

Lifting his head, he smiled down at her, tucking her hair behind her ear, and wondering if she knew just how much she meant to him. "There's nothing to forgive. You were scared but you were honest with me. I just hope you can forgive me when you see that I wasn't entirely honest with you."

As he'd hoped, she narrowed her eyes, all remnants of fear gone. "You're driving me crazy. If you don't tell me what you're hiding—"

He tapped her nose, relieved to see the terror in her eyes dimming. "I will. Let's just get you better first."

* * * *

Giggling, Charity pushed at his shoulder despite the fact that it felt so good to be in his arms. "Beau, you don't have to do this. I *can* walk, you know?"

Beau nuzzled her ear. "Maybe I just like carrying you."

Secure in his arms, Charity rested her head against his shoulder as he carried her down the stairs from her apartment, and through the back door of the diner. "Beau, I love you so much. Would it sound stupid if I said that it irritates me to be so weak that you feel as if you have to carry me, but that I love how it feels to be in your arms?"

"Not stupid at all, cher." Beau smiled and paused just inside the back door to the diner. "I feel the same way. I hate that you're hurt, but I love carrying you." Shaking his head, he started to move again. "Sometimes I wish I could just put you in my pocket so you'll be safe."

Disturbed by the worry in his voice, Charity cursed the fact that the brace on her arm kept her from reaching up to cup his jaw. "Beau, don't. I'm the same as I was before. I can take care of myself. Don't let things change between us."

Disappointed when he set her on her feet, she leaned into him another few seconds, reluctantly straightening when her fathers rushed to her side.

"How are you feeling, honey?" Her oldest father came forward, dropping a kiss on her forehead. Gripping her chin, he lifted her head, studying her critically. "You're looking a hell of a lot better than the last time I saw you. Beau must be taking good care of you."

She accepted kisses from her other two fathers, who darted out to check on her before rushing back to the busy kitchen.

Beau bent, his lips brushing her ear. "The restaurant's packed. Let's get you out of the way and settled out front. Everyone wants to see you."

A shout went up when Beau ushered her through the swinging door to the seating area as several of the residents of Desire called out to her. Blinking back tears, she smiled at everyone, touched and once again thankful to be part of such a town. When Hunter and Remington dropped their forks and rushed to her side, Beau stepped back to give them room, but stayed at her back, his hands warm at her waist.

Looking from Hunter to Remington, she smiled, hoping to relieve some of the concern in their eyes. "Thank you both so much for coming out to look for me."

Remington grinned, the rare softening of his features lasting only an instant before his eyes narrowed at the bruise on her cheek. "We would have found you first if Beau and Ace had gotten out of the way. I hear congratulations are in order."

Charity slid her gaze toward Beau, who stood talking to Clay and Rio. "Thank you." Meeting Remington's gaze again, she couldn't resist teasing him. "So when are the two of you going to finally settle down?"

Hunter unbuttoned her thick jacket and helped her out of it, easing it away from her shoulder. "Now that you're off the market, we're doomed to stay single."

Intrigued and concerned by the haunted look in his eyes, Charity frowned. "Is something wrong?"

Remington shot a look at his brother and smiled. "Not at all. We're just too picky. I'm glad to see you looking a little better. Your progress is pretty much *the* topic of conversation."

Charity groaned, but smiled, warmed by their concern. "That doesn't surprise me. That's what happens when you live in a small town." Touching first Hunter's arm, and then Remington's, Charity looked from one to the other. "It also means that everyone comes to help when you need it. I can't thank you enough."

Hunter kissed her forehead. "Just don't ever scare us like that again."

"Here. Here!"

Charity grinned, blinking back more tears, and turned to find Beau watching her.

Smiling at the indulgence and love in his eyes, she moved slowly from table to table to thank her friends for coming to her rescue, and accepting congratulations on her upcoming marriage.

After a few minutes, Beau appeared at her side, his hand warm on her back. "You've been standing long enough. Your mom's anxious for you to sit down. She's got your lunch ready."

Knowing that Beau would be just as anxious for her to sit as her mother, Charity went willingly. "*My* lunch? What about you? Aren't you eating?"

Beau looked out the window, clearly distracted. "I'll grab something later. Jake's waiting for me and I have a couple of errands to run."

Her mother came up behind him and tugged his arm until he turned toward her and hugged him. "Hi, Beau." Leaning back to look up at him, she frowned. "You look exhausted. I'll come up tonight and watch over her."

Beau smiled, laying a hand on her shoulder. "She's fine now. There's no need to sit in the chair and watch over her anymore. I'm just there to make sure she doesn't try to do anything she's not supposed to do, and to make sure she doesn't get dizzy and fall. She's getting better and it's all thanks to that delicious food you keep sending up."

Amused at her mother's blush, Charity settled back in the booth and met Beau's gaze. "You flirting with my mother?"

Beau smiled down at her mother. "Of course." He lifted his gaze to meet Charity's again, his tone much cooler. "Since you didn't eat the breakfast I fixed, you'd better eat all of your lunch."

Aware of her mother's searching look, Charity carefully kept her smile in place. "Beau thinks I can eat as much as he does." She lifted her gaze to Beau's again. "Are you sure you can't stay and eat with me, and then I can come with you to run your errands?"

Shaking his head, Beau straightened. "No. It's too cold out, and you'd be worn out in just a couple of minutes. I can get everything done faster while you're here. You stay in here where it's warm and have someone looking over you. You're still too weak to be running around."

Gracie looked up at Beau, her eyes narrowing in a way Charity had come to know well. Her mother knew that something wasn't right. "We'll take care of her—just as you have. Get your things done, and when you get back, I'll have a nice meal waiting for you."

In the hope of keeping her mother from worrying, Charity forced a smile. "He's probably dying to get out a little. Sitting in my apartment day after day, he's probably bored out of his mind. Beau, I can't tell you how much I apprec—"

Beau nodded once. "So you've said. Several times. If you really want to thank me, eat your lunch, cher. I'll be back in a couple of hours."

As soon as he walked away, Charity's mother slid into the booth across from her. "Reminds me a lot of your fathers. You picked a good man, honey." She followed Charity's gaze, watching Beau as he crossed the street. "That's a fine man. Impressed the hell out of your fathers. I didn't think anyone could ever impress them as much as Ace, but Beau sure has."

Her oldest father came to the table, placing a cup of coffee in front of her mother. "Sure has. He's been worried about you, and took it upon himself to take care of you, hardly ever leaving your side. Good man."

He touched Charity's hair before turning and walking away, leaving Charity and her mother alone to talk.

Charity turned to smile her thanks to her father, and then turned back to watch Beau through the front window of the diner. She hadn't wanted to say anything to her mother, but figured that since her mother had three husbands of her own, she would be something of an expert.

Turning back, she reached for her mother's hand, blurting out her concern. "He hasn't been the same since the accident. He never really smiles anymore." Frustrated at her inability to put it into words, she blew out a breath. "Well, he smiles. It's nothing that I can put my finger on, but he's not the same. No playing. No teasing. I mean, he's been there for me. Helpful. Caring. Protective. I couldn't ask for anything more."

Pulling her hand back, she ran it through her hair, remembering how Beau had dried it for her. "I shouldn't be complaining. There's nothing to complain about. He's just...different."

Lifting her gaze to her mother's again, she swallowed the lump in her throat. "It scares me. I think I changed him—that he changed for me. I don't want that."

Despite the concern in her eyes, her mother smiled and patted her hand. "He's probably just anxious. I know he didn't care for the fact that you didn't want anyone to know you were seeing him. He's relieved that he doesn't have to hide it anymore."

Charity stilled at something in her mother's tone. Whipping her head around to face her, she winced at the pull to her shoulder. "You knew?"

Her mother frowned. "Of course. It was a relief to him that you finally agreed to marry him. He's been telling everyone who stopped by."

Her mother sighed. "Everyone's been so worried. Some people didn't want to bother you, and came in here to see if you and Beau needed anything. That man didn't leave your side except to come down to shovel the snow while Hope and I stayed with you. Even when we went up to visit, he left the bedroom door open so he could hear you if you called out for him."

Smiling, she looked down at her hands. "I was there one night when you did. You should have seen his face when you woke up moaning, calling for him."

Meeting Charity's gaze again, she shook her head. "Jesus. If I didn't already know that man loved you, just the look on his face as he ran to you would have convinced me."

Charity stilled. "What do you mean 'if' you hadn't already known?"

Wrapping her arm around Charity, Gracie led her to the table. "I know my daughters, and I sure as hell know when they're in love. I didn't want your heart broken, and I knew you were lovers—"

"What?"

Her mother chuckled. "Charity Sanderson, I'm surprised at you. You were born and raised in this town. Everybody in Desire knows everybody else's business. Did you really think you could have a lover and nobody would know about it?"

Her oldest father, Garrett, came up to the table again, nodding as he placed a glass of sweet tea in front of Charity. "Beau came to us right up front. He didn't want us thinking he was using our girl. He's been in this town long enough to know how it's done. Told us he wanted to marry you, but that you were being stubborn."

He bent to kiss her forehead. "Since I know you well, I believed him, and wished him luck."

Straightening, he ran a hand over her hair. "You wanna tell me why it took so long?"

Grinning, Charity shrugged. "Just wanted to be sure I was getting a man as good as my daddies."

Her youngest father, Finn, came up behind her mother, tickling her as he leaned over her shoulder. Grinning at Charity, he ignored her mother's efforts to slap him away. "Baby, your daddies are in a class by themselves."

Gracie sighed, bending her head and rubbing her eyes. "Good Lord. Now, you've done it." Lifting her head, she sent him a look of exasperation tinged with love. "I'll go get your lunch while your daddy piles it on."

As soon as her oldest father and her mother left the table, her youngest father slid into the booth across from her, his smile falling and his eyes narrowing in concern. "Now that we're alone, do you want to tell me what's going on between you and Beau that's putting that sad look in your eyes?"

Charity sighed, propping her chin in her hand. She started to speak, surprised when her voice broke, and had to swallow before she could try again. Voicing her fears proved more difficult than she'd thought. "Oh, Daddy! I've made such a mess of things."

"Tell me."

With a sigh, Charity sat back, blinking back tears and smiling her thanks when her mother set a plate piled high with chicken and dumplings in front of her.

Her parents' thoughtfulness didn't surprise her. They'd served her one of her favorites, and thankfully something she could eat with one hand. When her mother shared a look with her father before leaving to help a customer, Charity began hesitantly, and between bites of the succulent food, told her father the entire story.

When she finished, she sighed and took a sip of her sweet tea, feeling much better. "I start the arguments we have. I know that. I've just been nervous about marrying him. He teases about everything and won't really talk much about himself. How was I supposed to know that he took things between us as seriously as I do? I want someone for forever, like you have with Mom."

Her father frowned, turning his head to watch the movements of his wife. "I play a lot, and like to tease your mother and my brothers. Have you ever seen me shirk my responsibilities, or known me not to be there for any of you if you needed me?"

Charity's stomach clenched and she felt even worse. Blinking, she stilled, surprised that she'd never thought about it that way before. "No, Daddy. You've always been there for us."

His handsome features hardened. "Did you, your sister, or your mother ever have any doubt about how much I love you?"

Struck by how upset her father looked, she could only imagine Beau feeling the same thing. "Of course not. We always knew. I just didn't know with Beau. I needed to make sure."

Sitting back, he eyed her thoughtfully. "Do you still have any doubts?"

Charity smiled and blinked away tears, a sense of relief washing over her. "Not a one. Not about that, anyway. I just know how much work it takes to raise a family and I don't know if Beau's sure of what he'd be getting into."

Sitting back, she pushed the plate away and wiped away a tear. "You worked so hard. You and the other dads always did what needed to be done."

Pushing her plate to the side, her father took her hand in his. "Oh, honey. Do you really think we would have worked so hard if we didn't have to? We would have loved to spend more time with our girls. We would have given anything to be able to take you on vacations."

Scraping a hand over his face, he sighed, his soft curse surprising her. "Between the three of us, we tried to make sure we spent as much time with all of you as we could. I didn't realize you felt this way."

Feeling even worse, Charity tightened her hands on her father's. "Daddy, no! Please don't think I didn't appreciate everything all of you did for us. I did. That's just the point. I grew up with three wonderful fathers who were always there for us. That's what I want. For me, and for my children. I see the way the three of you always try to keep Mom from worrying, and try to take care of everything—and there are *three* of you. How can I expect *one* man, one who seems to want to play more than he wants to take care of his business, to be able to deal with that?"

Her father raised a brow, his eyes hard and searching. "And now?"

Running her finger down the side of her glass, Charity shrugged, instantly regretting it as pain radiated down her left arm. Wincing, she reached for her shoulder with the other hand, thankful that the pain faded almost as quickly as it came. "When I was lying there, all that other stuff seemed stupid. I realized that I love Beau even more than I thought. I can't live without him. Whatever it takes, I want him in my life."

Her dad smiled, the tension leaving his features. "He's a good man. His circumstances make it even easier for him to have free time for you and your children. He's been a rock through all of this, taking care of you, dealing with the insurance company, and he even came down to shovel snow while your mother and sister sat with you. If I'm not mistaken, he even ordered you a new car. Yours was totaled. He'll be there for you, honey."

"Oh, Dad. I've got to find a way to fix this. He's been so wonderful." Her stomach hurt at the thought of not being able to make things right between her and Beau. She couldn't stand it if what she'd done had changed their relationship forever.

"You will, baby. You will. You've always been a worrier. It'll be fine." His gaze followed her mother as she refilled coffee cups around the diner, his eyes filled with love for her. "Your mother's been worried. It's a relief to all of us that you're marrying Beau, but your mother especially. She's always had a soft spot for him."

Her mother must have heard him because she made her way to the table. "You can thank your lucky stars that I've got a soft spot for *you*. Now, get out of here so I can talk to my daughter alone. You've hogged her long enough."

Watching her father slide from the booth, Charity giggled as she watched the play between him and her mother.

He managed to tickle her as he dropped a hard kiss on her lips, deftly avoiding her efforts to push him away. "Stop nagging me, woman." Turning his head, he winked at Charity. "She's just mad because every time she went up to see you, you were asleep. She's been chomping at the bit to spoil her little chick and talk about your wedding."

Her mother slapped at him, but her smile, the twinkle in her eyes, and the flush on her cheeks told Charity that her mother delighted in her father's teasing. "Get out of here."

Charity's own smile fell as memories assailed her—memories of her mom and dads laughing.

When she thought about it, she realized that her home had always been filled with laughter. Fun. Teasing.

It seemed so long since she'd moved out to go to college that she'd forgotten.

How could she have forgotten?

Many times, her fathers had chased her mother around the house. Laughing, she and Hope had joined in, running with their mother as her fathers made a game of it, coming close, only to pretend to miss them at the last moment. Eventually, her fathers had each caught one of them, tickling them and demanding a kiss.

They'd teased each other as they played card games and board games.

All three of her fathers hadn't always been present, and her youngest father had played more than her other two, but she could remember good times with all of them.

She and Hope used to sit on their laps, watching animated movies, and eating the popcorn they'd made. She smiled when she remembered that at those times, her mother had been doing something with her other father.

At the time, she and Hope hadn't paid any attention. They'd been thrilled to be spending time with their daddies.

Staring down at her tea, she waited until her father left and her mother slid into the booth. "The dads sure did have a lot of patience. I'm sure they hated all those animated movies Hope and I used to watch."

Her mother smiled. "They might not have liked the movies, but they loved spending time with you and your sister."

Charity grinned. "I just realized that two of the dads stayed with us, while you were off with the other."

To her delight, her mother laughed and turned a becoming shade of pink. "With three husbands, it's important to spend time alone with each of them." Her laughter faded, but she smiled as she patted Charity's hand. "And your daddies always felt bad because they couldn't spend as much time with you as they wanted to."

Shaking her head, she blew out a breath. "They were scared to death when they heard you were in that accident. I haven't seen any of them ever look like that before."

Charity stared down into her cup again. "I didn't mean to scare anyone. If I could have found my phone, I would have called to let you know I was okay. The damned thing flew out of my hand."

She couldn't get the images of laughing with her dads out of her mind. "We had so much fun growing up." She looked up at her mother's burst of laughter, a little surprised to see that the diner had pretty much cleared out.

Still laughing, her mother turned to where her oldest father stood, leaning on the counter and watching them. "Garrett, do you remember the time we played hide-and-seek with the girls, and Charity fell asleep?"

Her father smiled faintly, his eyes still dark with concern as they lingered on her face. "Scared the hell out of all of us. Finally found you curled up in a basket of laundry your mother had just taken out of the dryer."

Charity smiled. "You and the dads had a lot to deal with. Hope and I must have been quite a handful."

He walked around the counter and to the table, eying her critically. "You were, but we loved every minute of it. Are you feeling all right? Beau will be happy to hear that you had a big lunch, but you're looking a little pale."

"I feel fine—better without all the pain medicine." Blowing out a breath, she sat back, her stiff muscles making it difficult to get comfortable. "I made a mistake with Beau, and I don't know how to fix it."

Seeing a movement out of the corner of her eye, Charity turned her head to look out the window.

Her breath caught at the sight of Beau coming toward the diner, the powerful grace in his stride stirring something warm and feminine inside her.

It had been too long since they'd made love, and she was impatient to heal and get back to it. She wanted that special tenderness, the soft words in the dark.

The connection that only lovemaking could bring.

Her mother patted her hand, drawing her attention back to her parents. With a small smile, her mother leaned against her father, a familiar sight that never failed to make Charity smile.

"You should see the way your face lights up when you see him. Whatever it is, you'll fix it. You both love each other too much not to."

Chapter Eleven

Cuddling against Beau, Charity enjoyed the ride back up the stairs, loving the feel of being held securely in his arms. Studying his profile, she smiled, sliding her hand into the front of his thick jacket and running the backs of her fingers over his chest. "You know, it's kind of sexy when you carry me."

Without slowing, Beau glanced down at her, his eyes narrowed. "Is it?" When he reached the top of the stairs, his breathing hadn't changed at all. "It won't be if you wiggle and we fall down the stairs. Just be still so I can open the door."

Charity didn't bother trying to hide her smile. "It's not going to work, you know."

He glanced down at her as he opened the door and carried her inside. "What's not going to work?" He lowered her to her feet and worked her jacket off of her, careful to ease it from her shoulder.

Grinning up at him, she tossed her hair over her shoulder, and crossed the room to sit on the sofa. "Trying to be serious all the time. It's not you."

Beau knelt in front of her, holding her gaze while he removed her shoes. "Like this playful act that you've adopted since your accident? That's not *you*, either."

Tossing her shoes aside, he rose to his feet, his expression grim. "Don't try to be what you're not to please me. It pisses me off."

Charity lifted a brow, settling back. "Ditto, darling."

With a sigh, Beau dropped to the sofa beside her. He stared at the door for several long moments, the tension emanating from him keeping her silent as well.

After several long seconds, he turned to her, his eyes dark and thoughtful. "My father was a workaholic." His lips twisted. "That's putting it mildly, I guess. All he ever thought about was work. It's all he ever did."

Sitting back, Beau stared at his hands. "He took his role as a provider very seriously. He became obsessed with it. He didn't enjoy life at all. I can't ever remember even seeing him smile." He took a deep breath, and blew it out slowly. "My grandfather, on the other hand, made a killing in the liquor business and enjoyed himself immensely. He made and lost fortunes his entire life. He enjoyed every day. He laughed. He played, and he was happy every day of his life."

Glancing at her, Beau shrugged. "My father hated the cavalier way his father did business—called it luck—and vowed never to be like him. He worked hard every day of his life. He made a fortune, but guarded each dollar like it was his last. He paid the bills and made sure we had a nice home, good clothing, and that I went to nice schools, but nothing frivolous was ever allowed."

Sitting forward, he looked at his hands. "He had several companies. Several investments. A hotel that my mother couldn't even stay in. She had nice things. No jewelry or anything like that, but she had all the comforts she could want. She had everything except my father."

Struck by the desolation and sadness in his voice, Charity sat up, taking his hand in hers. "Oh, Beau."

Beau stared at his hands and continued as if he hadn't heard her. "As far as I know, they never even took a vacation together. He died of a heart attack while sitting at his desk. He was only forty-seven years old."

"Dear God!" Charity squeezed his hand. "That's terrible."

Beau disentangled her hand from his and got to his feet as if too restless to sit still. Going to the window, he looked out, but Charity doubted very much he saw anything on the street below. "My mother was left with plenty of money and businesses she didn't know how to run. My grandfather tried to help her, but my mother remarried, and her new husband took over. He ran the businesses down to the ground. He cheated on her. My mother died a broken woman."

"Oh, Beau."

She couldn't imagine what it must have been like for him. "I'm so sorry. Were you and your father close?"

Beau's lips twisted. "I hardly knew the man. My mother and I were close until she remarried. After that, her husband didn't want me around, and I spent more and more time with my grandfather."

She heard the love for his grandfather in his voice, and saw it in the softening of his expression. "Tell me about your grandfather."

Some of the tension in Beau's body eased. "He was a character." He smiled, and glanced at her. "Every day was an adventure. I used to spend my summer vacations with him and my grandmother, and then moved in with him when my mother remarried. I was still in high school. He taught me not to take life too seriously. To have fun, and to enjoy every day. He and my grandmother were still going strong into their eighties. You could see how much they loved each other."

Turning from the window, he met Charity's gaze. "They died within months of each other, and were happy until the end. My grandfather told me many times about my father, trying to ease my bitterness. He said that I could learn something from him. He wasn't a bad man. He wanted to provide for his family."

Moving closer, he knelt at her feet again, his eyes dark with turmoil. "He provided financially, but ignored the rest. Life is to be enjoyed, Charity. I have plenty of money. My grandfather made sure of that. I invested quite a bit of it, and more than doubled it."

Shaking his head, he smiled, his eyes begging her to understand. "I have a huge warehouse where I sell everything that I sell in the store, and much more, online. I like Desire, and opened a store just for something to do. That store's more of a hobby than anything.

Something to do and a way to be part of the town. I enjoy it. I enjoy meeting people."

He got to his feet again, running a hand through his hair. "I made up my mind a long time ago that I wouldn't be like my father. I always knew I wanted to get married one day. I want a family. I organized my life in a way that would allow me to have the kind of marriage my grandparents had. Fun. Exciting. Filled with love."

Beau sighed. "And then there's Jeffrey."

Charity stilled, shocked at the anger in his voice. "Who's Jeffrey?"

Beau scrubbed a hand over his face and moved away, once again putting distance between them. "Jeffrey is my stepfather's illegitimate son. He seems to think that he got cheated because I got my grandfather's money and he didn't. He likes to make trouble every chance he gets, and instead of working to make a good living, he tries to take the easy way out. All he wants to do is play and have fun, not giving a damn about the wife he has at home who depends on him."

Beau turned, meeting her gaze again. "And then there's Anna?"

Charity's stomach clenched at the affection in his voice. "Who's Anna, or shouldn't I ask?"

Beau blew out a breath. "Anna's his wife and she needs me. That's one of the errands I had to take care of today. I give her money to survive, and I'm paying the lawyer so she can divorce Jeffrey. She's not like you, Charity. She's helpless and dependent, and Jeffrey doesn't even give her enough money to pay the bills. She wants to leave him, but she's scared of being on her own. I've been trying to help her."

Falling deeper in love with every word, Charity stood and wrapped her good arm around him, surprised at how tense he'd become. "Christ, every time I think I can't love you any more than I do, you make me love you more."

Breathing in the scent of him, she cuddled closer. "I didn't understand you at all, did I?"

To her relief, Beau pulled her close and kissed the top of her head. "Just like I didn't understand that you thought my teasing meant that I didn't take my love for you seriously."

Leaning back, Charity searched his features, relieved to find the love shining in his eyes she'd come to rely on. As always, her pulse tripped, her heart beating faster. "I understand now, Beau. I do. I'm so sorry. You're nothing like Jeffrey. I was so afraid that I was falling more and more in love, and you were just playing a game."

Gripping her chin, he lifted her face to his, grinning. "And still you came back for more?"

Charity shrugged, careful to use only her good shoulder. "You're handsome and good in bed."

One of Beau's dark brows went up. "And all it takes is good looks and the ability to make you come for you to fall in love?"

Relieved to see him smile again, Charity faked a glare and pushed at his chest. "Shut up."

Beau caught her before she could escape. "You can't resist me, can you?"

Bubbling with happiness, Charity sighed and hid a smile. "Don't get cocky."

A smile, one so much like the ones she remembered, lit his features as he pressed his cock against her belly. "I can't help it, chéri." Lifting a hand to cup her breast, he searched her features. "Do you know what it does to a man to know that the woman he loves can't resist him?"

Curious, Charity cocked her head, more than willing to help lighten the atmosphere. "What?"

"It makes him feel about ten feet tall." Wrapping an arm around her, he guided her toward the bedroom. "Come on. Let's get you to bed. I'll give you your ring and you can go to sleep."

Charity tried to pause, but he didn't let her. "I want my ring now."

"No." Beau smiled faintly. "You have to get into bed first and promise to take a nap. I want you to recover as fast as possible."

"That's blackmail."

Beau seemed to consider that before nodding once. "So it is. It seems I have a penchant for it. Interesting."

Thrilled at the amusement in his voice, Charity decided she wasn't above a little blackmail herself. She'd always thought the way her sister pouted to get her way with Ace ridiculous, but had to admit, she didn't mind the results at all.

Hiding a smile, she took several calming breaths and worked up a pout before turning to look up at him. "I don't think I can sleep."

Beau stopped by the bed and started undressing her, his eyes narrowed. "Why not?"

Staring down at his hands as he worked her sling free and removed her shirt, Charity found herself arching toward him. "Well, I'm achy and I don't want to take any of those pills."

Beau's eyes glittered with suspicion, making it even more difficult to maintain her pout. After several seconds, he nodded once. "Where do you hurt? I'll massage the kinks out so you can sleep."

"Can I have my ring first?"

Glancing up at her as he removed her sweat pants, Beau nodded toward the bed. "Once you're in bed. Leave your socks on. I don't want your feet to get cold again."

Charity allowed him to help her into bed, and with her good hand, pulled up the covers. "I'm in. Gimme."

Beau's lips twitched. "Greedy little thing, aren't you?"

Lifting her chin, Charity smiled. "I just want something to flash in front of your face whenever you think about changing your mind."

Reaching into his pocket, he produced a ring box. "I won't be changing my mind, cher, and neither will you." He opened the box and pulled out a ring, one even more stunning by its simplicity.

The large, square-cut diamond took her breath away.

Charity gasped, unable to look away from it. "Dear God, Beau. It's beautiful. Beau, it's so big."

Lifting her gaze to his, she shook her head, holding her hand out as if to ward him off. "Take it back and get something smaller."

"No." With a gentle hand, he held her left one, not moving it as he placed the ring on her finger. "I want everyone to be able to see it. That way they'll know that you're taken."

Putting a finger over her lips to cut off her protest, he shook his head. "This was the diamond from my grandmother's ring. She wore it every day and never worried about it. She enjoyed it. I want you to do the same."

Bending, he touched his lips to the ring before lifting his head. "I had it set in a durable setting. Jake made sure it's secure. My grandmother would want you to relax and enjoy it. So do I."

With her heart in her throat, Charity blinked back tears. "I'm going to be scared to lose it. I can't believe you gave me your grandmother's ring."

Shaking his head, Beau adjusted her on the pillows. "No. I gave you the diamond she wore. The ring I had made special for you."

Incredibly moved that he'd given her something that belonged to someone special to him, Charity wiped away a tear. "Beau, this is so thoughtful, and the most beautiful thing I ever saw."

With a smile, Beau bent forward and brushed her lips with his as he ran his fingers down her cheek, catching another tear. "And this is the most beautiful thing I ever saw."

Blinking back more tears, Charity sucked in a breath, and then another. "You never talked to me this way before. Well, except—"

"Except for the night I took your virginity."

Using the massage oil Jesse and the others had given her, Beau worked the muscles in her back loose. "Feeling better?"

Charity groaned, every slide of his hands over her skin easing the tension in her tight muscles. "Much. You know, I feel closer to you now. Beau, why didn't we ever talk like this before?"

Beau sighed, and slid his fingers in a gentle caress around the muscles of her injured shoulder. "Every time I tried to talk about something more permanent, you got skittish, and I didn't want to scare you off. I knew that I couldn't tell you about Anna and Jeffrey until you were more secure in our relationship, but I didn't know what to do to get you there. I hated having secrets from you, and didn't know if you'd understand how much Anna needs me."

Charity sighed, relaxing even more under his expert hands. "I knew your reputation and figured you were playing a game with me. I didn't think you were really serious."

Rolling her gently to her back, Beau lifted her left hand slightly and kissed the ring he'd placed there. "Now you know I am." He slid into bed next to her, his oil-coated hand covering her belly. "You're mine, Charity, and you'll stay that way."

Her stomach muscles tensed under his hand, her breath quickening. Unable to look away from the intensity in his eyes, Charity arched into his touch as need built inside her. Wincing at the pull to her shoulder and chest, Charity reached for him. "I need you."

Beau smiled. "You're in no shape to have sex. It would only hurt you." Touching his lips to her, he slid his hand lower and into her panties. "Spread your legs for me."

The feel of his oil-coated finger sliding over her clit drew another moan from her. "Beau, it feels so good. But, what about you?"

"Don't worry about me. This is about you. Besides, it excites me to watch you come. Just stay still. I don't want you hurting yourself by thrashing around."

He covered her mouth with his, cutting off her protest as he parted her folds and slid his oiled finger over her clit. Swallowing her cry, he deepened his kiss, taking her mouth with a fierce possessiveness that made her forget everything else except the pleasure.

His hand felt so big and hot pressed against her abdomen, holding her still while his fingers worked their magic.

The wave hit her hard, the new closeness between them making her orgasm stronger than ever. Amazed that he could send her senses reeling with such ease, Charity whimpered in her throat as the pleasure peaked, digging her heels into the mattress in an effort to lift into his touch.

Frustrated that the pressure against her abdomen prevented it, she fisted her hand on his shoulder and tugged at him to pull him closer.

Beau lifted his head, staring down at her with glittering eyes. "You're so beautiful. So incredibly sweet." He moved his finger once more before withdrawing it from her panties, the surge of sensation earning another cry from her.

Settling his hand at her waist, he dropped his head onto the pillow beside her. "Go to sleep, cher."

"Beau, I don't want to sleep." Her trip to the diner and her orgasm had worn her out more than she wanted to admit. "I want to talk. Tell me more about your grandparents."

"No. Sleep."

She turned her head toward him, frowning to see that he'd closed his eyes. "Beau?"

"You promised to take a nap. I thought you prided yourself on being reliable. Are you breaking your promise to me?"

Frustrated at her own weakness, she stifled a yawn, and poked him in the stomach. "That's not fair."

One dark eye opened. "You agreed to it."

After several minutes of silence, she opened her eyes again. "Can I ask you something?"

Although he'd relaxed, she knew he hadn't yet gone to sleep.

"What is it, chéri?"

"Are you mad at me for something?"

"No. Why would you think that?"

"We talked and got everything cleared up between us, didn't we?"

"I'm sure there are issues we haven't ironed out, but for the most part, I think we understand each other."

Closing her eyes, she dropped her head back on the pillow. "I hate when you do that. I can't tell what you're thinking. If you're still mad, just say so."

Lifting his head, Beau pulled the covers higher over her shoulders. "I told you that I'm not mad, Charity. If I was, I would tell you. I don't want any more secrets between us."

Keeping her voice low, she reached out to touch his arm. "Okay. No secrets. Then tell me why you don't want to play anymore. I already know how much it means to you."

Beau sighed. "It did."

"And it doesn't anymore?"

"Not as much as it used to. I'm never going to be like my father. I know that, but since the night of your accident, I haven't felt much like playing. You scared the hell out of me, Charity."

"But I'm fine."

"I know, cher, and I'm eternally grateful. Everything's fine. Just leave it alone."

"But—"

"Go to sleep, cher."

When his voice slurred, Charity thought about all the nights that he'd slept sitting in the chair, or squeezed into the bed beside her. With a sigh, Charity shifted to a more comfortable position, careful not to take up any more room than necessary.

Lifting her hand as far as she could, she admired the ring he'd given her.

The sentiment behind it meant more than its monetary value— something she didn't want to think about.

She found it so endearing that he wanted a marriage like his grandparents. She'd completely misunderstood him, but now that she did understand him a little better, she wanted the old Beau back more than ever.

She'd do whatever it took to do it.

Chapter Twelve

Charity looked up from where she'd signed another woman in, her breath catching at the sight of Beau approaching with a petite blonde woman.

The woman smiled up at Beau in a way that made Charity bristle, the possessive hold she had on Beau's arm making her grit her teeth.

Keeping his arm protectively around her, Beau smiled. "Charity, this is Anna. I hope you don't mind that I brought her to the Grand Reopening, but I thought she could use some time away from the house."

Remembering what a rough time the other woman had, Charity forced a smile, fighting back jealousy. "Of course. There's always room for one more. Hello, Anna. It's so nice to finally meet you. Let me just get you a name tag."

Anna smiled up at Beau adoringly, fluttering her heavily mascaraed lashes. "Thank you so much. Wasn't Beau sweet to bring me here?"

Forcing a smile, Charity reminded herself that Beau loved her. They were going to be married. This woman meant nothing to him. "Of course. Beau is always *sweet*."

Ignoring Beau's searching gaze, she gestured for Anna to go inside. "Help yourself to refreshments. We'll be starting soon."

Holding Anna's arm, Beau frowned. "Is everything okay?"

"Everything's fine. Quite a turnout, huh?"

"Yes." He didn't appear convinced. "I'm just going to introduce Anna to—"

"No." Embarrassed by her jealousy and rude behavior, Charity smiled wider. "I'll introduce her around. I think Ace wants to talk to you."

She hated her jealousy, but couldn't resist the chance to get Anna away from Beau.

Once she introduced her to Hope, Charity made her way to the table where Jesse sat with her sister, Nat, along with Rachel Jackson, and her sister, Erin Preston. Smiling at the way Erin rubbed her swollen abdomen, Charity nodded to each of them.

"Hi. This is Anna, a friend of Beau's." Aware of the women's looks of interest, Charity introduced each of them to Anna.

"Anna doesn't know anyone, and the four of you know just about everyone here. Would it be all right if she sat with you?"

Nat smiled, a smile that didn't quite reach her eyes. "Sure. Have a seat, Anna. Charity, you go back to what you were doing. I know you're busy. We'll take care of her."

Charity left the table on shaking legs, her gaze automatically going to Beau's as she crossed back to the table set up in the front to greet people.

Beau grinned from across the room, winking at her as he listened to whatever Ace said to him.

Reminding herself that she had nothing to worry about, she greeted several more women, gave them name tags and schedules of upcoming events before inviting them to help themselves to refreshments.

When she finally got to the end of the line, she looked up, smiling to see Beau striding toward her. "Quite a turnout, huh?"

Taking her hand in his, Beau rounded the table. "I didn't expect anything less." Kissing her hair, he moved in behind her.

Charity moaned at the warmth of his hands on her shoulders. "Most of the people from the last opening showed up again, along with several more. I hope they didn't come looking for the excitement we had last time."

"God forbid. Hell, honey, you're tight."

Smiling at the concern in his voice as he began to rub her shoulders, Charity turned to look at him. "You've said that before."

Beau blinked, a slow smile curving his lips. "Are you by any chance flirting with me?"

Charity shrugged and turned back as Hope stepped on to the small stage, stiffening when she saw Anna watching them. "Could be. Would you mind?"

Moving in close behind her, Beau bent to nuzzle her neck in that spot he exploited at every opportunity. "I like when you flirt with me. It makes me weak in the knees."

Charity laughed at that. "Liar." Turning her head, she looked up at him over her shoulder. "Nothing makes you weak in the knees."

"You do, cher. Every day."

"Excuse me, Beau, but I don't feel very well."

Gritting her teeth, Charity turned her head again, her hands fisting at her sides to see Anna standing in front of the table, looking up at Beau through her lashes.

Her pout made Charity see red.

Beau released Charity and hurried around the table. "What's wrong, Anna? Do you need a doctor?"

Anna leaned into Beau, pressing her face against his chest. "No. It's just one of those headaches. You know how bad they get ever since we started the divorce proceedings. I'm just so tense."

Straightening, she wiped at her eye as if there'd been a tear there, but Charity could see clearly that there hadn't been one. "Is there anything I can do? Perhaps you'd like to sit in my office where it's quiet."

"No, thank you. I need to go home and lie down." Turning, she pressed against Beau's chest, laying her hand on what Charity considered *hers*. "Beau, I wouldn't want to take you away from your little friend's party. Maybe you could call me a cab…"

"Of course not. I'll take you home." Wrapping an arm around her shoulder, Beau led her toward the door. "I'm sorry, Charity. I'll be back as soon as I can."

Charity smiled, but inside she was seething. "Of course."

Fisting her hands at her sides, she watched Beau leave with Anna.

"If she didn't wear such high heels, she wouldn't have to hold on to him to walk."

Charity smiled at Nat's comment, and turned to find her friend watching Beau and Anna leave. "When Beau told me about her, I pictured someone a little younger—you know needy and naïve."

Nat's lips thinned. "All that makeup she wears might be designed to make her *look* younger, but it doesn't. As for needy, she is that, but that woman's not the least bit naïve. She knows exactly what she's doing. All we heard at the table was how wonderful Beau is, how he's helping with her divorce, and how much more of a man he is than her own husband."

After the door closed behind Beau and Anna, Nat turned to face the stage, leaning back against the table. "She kept saying that it was *real sweet* of Beau to watch over you, and to help you after your accident, and kept insinuating that Beau wants her to get divorced so he could marry her himself. I asked her if she knew that Beau already had a fiancée, and she told me that I must be mistaken."

Charity blinked, lifting her left hand. "She didn't see this?"

Nat grinned. "Honey, a man on the moon could see that." Her smile fell. "Be careful. She's out to get Beau, and as you can see, she's not above playing dirty to do it. She didn't have a headache until she saw Beau rubbing your shoulders."

Charity looked toward the doorway, and then at the clock, wondering how long Beau would be gone. "How can Beau not see what she's doing?"

Nat snorted. "Honey, when it comes to women, men can be remarkably stupid."

* * * *

Charity kept a smile plastered on her face until the door closed behind the last of the women. Leaning back against it, she let her smile fall, meeting Hope's furious gaze.

"He's been gone for *four hours*, Charity. Four fucking hours."

Charity straightened, and began cleaning up. "Four hours and twelve minutes."

She didn't want to think about what Beau had been doing all that time. She only knew that she was so mad, she didn't want to see him. "Let's get this cleaned up. I want to go home."

Hope shook her head. "You're not going home alone. I have a plan."

"Oh, hell." Charity dropped into one of the padded chairs. "I always get nervous when you have a plan. I want to go home, take a nice long bubble bath, and talk with Beau when he gets back. That's it."

"My plan's better."

"Your plans always get someone in trouble."

Hope grinned. "Oh, I think the men in Desire can handle a little trouble. Let's see. Who should I call?"

Charity sighed, rubbing her temple where she had the start of a headache of her own. "Hope, I don't know what you're talking about, but—"

"You're rubbing your head. Great! You have a headache, and I'll bet your shoulder's bothering you, too. Too much lifting and cleaning up. Yeah. That's it. We had to clean up alone and it was too much for you. I'll bet you're exhausted. Who knows? You may have a relapse!"

Charity frowned at her sister, knowing that whatever Hope had planned would cause trouble. "You don't have to sound so happy about it."

Hope waved a hand negligently. "You'll be fine. Just as soon as we get you back to the hospital."

Charity jumped to her feet, holding on to the table as her head spun. "I don't need to go back to the damned hospital."

Rushing forward, Hope frowned, her gaze full of concern. "You really *don't* feel well, do you?"

Charity gritted her teeth. "I'm fine. Just tired. I have a headache, and want to go home."

Kneeling beside her, Hope shook her head. "No. We're going to rush you back to the hospital, but we need a couple of strong men to take us."

Blinking, Charity wondered if Hope wasn't what made her dizzy. "Since when do we need help driving to the hospital? Why don't I just call Doc—"

"Nope. Stay put."

Hope turned away to dial her cell phone, putting several feet of distance between them as she started cleaning off the tables, throwing things in the garbage with a speed that stunned Charity.

"Oh, Hunter! Thank God, you're home. This is Hope. I need your help."

Charity's mouth dropped open. "What the hell are you doing?"

Waving away Charity's objection, Hope moved farther away. "It's Charity. You know we had the Grand Reopening tonight. Well, we were cleaning up, and Charity doesn't feel well. Ace has the shift tonight and I can't bother him, and Beau isn't around. He had to take a sick friend home. He never even came back to help us clean up, and I think it was too much for Charity. Her head and shoulders hurt and she's dizzy. I'm so upset, I can't drive her to the hospital. Can you and Remington take us? Please? I'm so scared something's wrong with her."

Jabbing a fist in the air, Hope grinned, but kept her voice shaky. "Oh, thank you! We're at the club."

She hung up and raced around, throwing cups, plates and napkins away. "They're on their way."

Charity sighed and dropped her head on the table. "Sometimes I can't believe we have the same parents." Lifting her head, she propped it on her fist, watching her sister clean up. "I've never seen you move that fast. Have you thought about the consequences of this? What's Ace going to say? What happens when Mom and the dads find out?"

Hope shrugged. "I'll call them when we get there. They'll blame it on my over imagination, praise me for taking such good care of you, and chew Beau a new asshole. See? It'll work out well for everyone."

"Except Beau."

Hope grinned. "Except Beau. Maybe he'll think twice before he abandons you for his lady friend again."

Hunter strode into the club a few minutes later, his face dark with fury and concern. Rushing to where Charity sat, he knelt at her feet, his expression softening. "How are you, honey?"

Charity slid a glance at where Hope stood wringing her hands. "I'm fine. Really. Hope shouldn't have called you."

Remington came around to kneel at her other side. "Of course she should have. We take care of each other in this town, or have you forgotten?"

Hunter's jaw clenched. "Especially if your man isn't around to do it."

Remington slid one arm under her legs and another at her back, lifting her against his chest. "Hope said your head hurt and that you're dizzy."

Pushing against his chest, Charity shot another glare at her smirking sister. "You don't have to do this. I'm sure it's just a headache."

"So your head *does* hurt. How about the dizziness? Do you feel dizzy?"

Charity wanted to lie to him, but her nature prevented it. Resigned, she blew out a breath. "Just a little. Look, I'm sure it's because of the stress of getting the club ready. I haven't slept much."

Remington slid into the back seat of the car while Hunter helped Hope into the front. Settling her on his lap, Remington turned her face to his, frowning as he looked into her eyes. "I can see you have a headache. How about the shoulders? Hope said that your shoulders were hurting. You're probably not healed all the way."

Hope turned in her seat, her expression full of concern. "I *told* her that she shouldn't be doing all that lifting. Then when we went to clean up…"

Hunter started the truck. "Where's Ace?"

Hope sighed pitifully. "He helped all night and then only got a few hours sleep before he had to go to work. He's on patrol now, and since Linc and Rafe went out of town this afternoon, he can't take off. I didn't want to bother my parents. Oh, I hope you're not upset that I called you. I should have just driven her, but Ace doesn't like me driving out of town at night by myself, especially since there are still patches of ice on the road."

Hunter turned to frown at her. "Ace is right. You'd better not be out driving at night. You did the right thing, calling us."

Hope turned in her seat to look at Charity again, waiting until Remington stared down at Charity before winking.

Meeting Charity's gaze in the rearview mirror, Hunter smiled, a smile that people in Desire knew meant trouble. "And where did you say Beau is?"

* * * *

Beau scrubbed a hand over his face, glancing at the clock on the dashboard again.

He'd missed Charity's Grand Reopening, and he was mad as hell about it.

But, what could he have done?

With a curse, he pushed a button on his dashboard and dialed her cell phone with the intention of telling her to leave the cleaning for the night. He'd go in the morning to take care of everything.

"Hello?"

Hearing a man's voice, Beau frowned, wondering if he'd dialed the wrong number. He'd thought that Hope had gotten the same number, but now he wasn't so sure. "Hello. This is Beau. Where's Charity?"

"Well, it's about fucking time you called. I swear, if I thought you were fucking that other woman, I'd kick your ass."

Beau's stomach clenched at the sensation that something was very wrong. "Who is this, and why the hell are you answering Charity's phone?"

"This is Hunter. Hope called us about an hour ago because Charity wasn't feeling well. Remington and I brought her to the hospital. Hope's back there now. Ace knows we're here and is waiting for us at home. Charity's going to stay there tonight—if they don't admit her."

Beau's heart pounded furiously. "Oh, God. What's wrong with her?" He pressed on the gas pedal, once again cursing himself for not being there when she needed him.

"She had a bad headache and was dizzy. They're x-raying her head and her shoulder. It seems her shoulders have been bothering her for hours and she never said anything. Hope called when Charity got dizzy while they were cleaning up. Ace was patrolling and Hope was smart enough not to drive out of town at night, and not when there are still icy patches on the road."

He paused meaningfully. "I'm just glad Charity wasn't alone."

Beau gritted his teeth. "I already feel like shit, Hunter. How the fuck is she?"

"I don't know. Wait. Hope's coming out now."

Running a hand through his hair, Beau listened to the sound of the phone brushing against something and the low sounds of voices in the background. Frustrated that he couldn't understand anything being said, he tightened his hands on the wheel.

Charity. Christ, he'd never survive if something happened to her.

"Beau?"

Beau stiffened. "Hope? How is she? What's going on? I'm on my way."

"Don't bother. She's been checked out, was given a strong muscle relaxer, and is being discharged. I'm taking her home with me."

"She's okay? What did the doctor say?" Beau wanted to kick himself in the ass for not being there.

"He said that she's probably been doing too much, which is no surprise. Damn it, Beau, where the hell were you? I thought you were going to keep her from overdoing things. Apparently, you're too busy taking care of another woman to take care of your own!"

Beau didn't think he could feel any worse. "Damn it, Hope! If I'd known, I never would have left. Anna needed me and—"

"*Charity* needed you! She's being released now. I'm taking her home with me."

"I'm on my way. Tell Charity that I'm on my way, damn it. I'll take her home with me."

"No. Anna might call you in the middle of the night, and you'll have to run over to help a woman who's trying to get into your pants, but you're too stupid to realize it. I'm taking her home with me, and you'd have to get through Ace to get to her. Just go home, Beau."

The sound of the phone disconnecting stunned Beau. "What the hell?"

"Fuck!" Slamming the steering wheel, Beau threw himself back in his seat, pressing the gas pedal even harder in his race to get to Charity.

He'd known her shoulders were tight, and had already blamed himself for letting her push herself too hard again.

He knew she'd been sore, and had planned to take her back to his house, open a bottle of wine, and give her a long, slow massage until every knot in her back and shoulders melted.

The thought of her being hurt and needing him ripped his heart to shreds.

Hunter and Remington were with her instead of him.

Clenching his jaw, he sped down the road to Desire, anxious to get to Charity.

He pulled up in front of Ace's house, unsurprised to find Ace sitting on the porch waiting for him. "Where is she?"

Ace, still dressed in his uniform, gestured toward the chair next to him. "They're on their way. The emergency room was busy and it took them longer to get her signed out than she'd planned."

Ace smiled, but his eyes remained hard and filled with concern. "Apparently, Charity hasn't eaten much today, and the muscle relaxers they gave her knocked her out."

Beau's stomach knotted even tighter. "I'm taking her home with me." His tone dared his friend to argue.

Ace turned to him, nodding once. "I expect so."

Beau shook his head. "I didn't expect it to be so easy. Hope told me that I'd have to go through you to get to Charity."

Pursing his lips, Ace stared thoughtfully toward the street. "My wife says a lot of things. She also likes to meddle, something I thought I'd gotten under control. She and I are going to have a nice talk when she gets home."

Beau blinked. "I don't think it's meddling to take her sister to the hospital when she needs it. I owe her."

Ace turned his head, smiling faintly. "Yeah, she took Charity, and I'm glad she did. Don't you think it's a bit odd that she didn't call me until she was already at the hospital? That no one called you? I'll be willing to bet my next paycheck that she reamed you a new one about leaving Charity and going off with Anna."

Frowning, Beau got to his feet. "She did and I deserved it. But, Anna needed me, and I didn't want to leave her like that."

"What happened?"

Beau shrugged, trying to ease some of the tension in his shoulders. "I brought Anna to the club because I thought it would do her some good to get out. She's been really down about the divorce. I also wanted her to meet Charity."

Cursing the fact that his face burned, he stared out into the night. "Anna's made a few comments about wanting a man like me, and she's tried to flirt a couple of times. I told her that I was engaged, but it didn't seem to make a difference. I thought that if she met Charity, she would realize that I'm in love with someone else. I'd hoped she and Charity could be friends."

"Does Charity know you've been giving her money?"

Nodding, Beau took his seat again, anxious for Charity to get back. "Yes. I told her that Jeffrey didn't leave any money for the bills and that Anna was broke. I've been honest about everything."

"Except that Anna wants to get her claws in you?"

Beau got to his feet again, to restless to sit still. "I'd hoped that after today, it wouldn't be an issue anymore."

Ace's brow went up. "So why did you stay so long?"

With a sigh, Beau leaned against the railing. "Anna wanted to leave because she had another migraine. She's been getting them ever since she started the divorce proceedings. By the time I got her back to her house, it was worse. She couldn't even open her eyes. I helped her into bed, and was just about to leave when Jeffrey showed up. He didn't appreciate that I was there, and started screaming, waking Anna up. She came out and fainted. I tried to get Jeffrey to leave, but he wouldn't. Christ, I've been so stupid."

Ace raised a brow, saying nothing.

Amused at his friend, Beau shook his head. "It turns out that Anna's been playing me all along. Jeffrey showed me receipts and bank statements. He's been paying the bills all along. *She's* the one who wanted more money. She married him, thinking he was rich, and when she found out that I was the one with the money, she set her sights on me."

Straightening, he went back to his seat again, suddenly weary. "She's been spending the money I gave her on new clothes and tucking some away for a rainy day. Jeffrey showed me her bank book, with Anna screaming at him the entire time to get out, and begging me not to believe him. But, it was all there in black and white."

Clenching his jaw, he met Ace's gaze. "I can forgive her for the money, but I can't forgive her for causing this rift between Jeffrey and me, and I sure as hell can't forgive her for keeping me away from Charity when she needed me."

Ace got to his feet as Hunter's truck pulled up, catching Beau's arm as he started to race forward.

"Charity needed you, but I have a feeling Hope made it out to be worse than it was. She wanted you to feel guilty because she absolutely despises Anna, and knew what she was up to. She wanted to shake you up. She loves her sister, and in her own way, tried to protect her. I'll deal with her, but don't let yourself feel too bad. Charity knows that if she needed you, she could have called you. She didn't. If I were you, I'd be pretty upset about that."

Beau forced a smile. "I'll be upset tomorrow. Right now, I just want to take care of her. Hunter and Remington look furious."

"I'll explain things to them. Just get Charity home."

Chapter Thirteen

"Good morning."

Charity blinked against the bright sunlight pouring in from the window, trying to focus on Beau. "Good morning." Her pulse tripped at the sight of him. "We're at your house." Frowning, she looked around as she realized she was naked. "I don't remember getting here."

Sitting up, she rubbed her forehead where the remnants of her headache still lingered, unnerved by the way Beau stared at her. "This is getting to be a habit. That stuff they gave me last night really must have knocked me out."

Beau shrugged and handed her the cup of coffee he held. "It did. It probably wouldn't have if you'd eaten something yesterday like you promised me you would."

"I tried." She fell back against the pillows, wondering if he'd bring up the subject of Anna. "Hope brought a bunch of little sandwiches. She eats like crazy when she's nervous, but I couldn't eat a thing. I promised myself that I'd get something as soon as everyone left."

Beau's expression never changed. "Hmm. Didn't quite make it, did you?"

"No, but—"

Beau got to his feet, his expression so cool that it sent a chill through her. "Your breakfast is almost ready. Do you need help getting dressed?"

"No, I—"

"Good. Come out when you're ready. I have a few things to talk to you about."

Charity watched him go, her stomach fluttering with nerves. Wondering if he'd decided to call their engagement off because of Anna, she eased herself from the bed, surprised that her muscles didn't protest.

By the time she got to the kitchen, she was shaking. Standing in the doorway, she crossed her arms over her chest to hide it as she watched Beau fill a plate with scrambled eggs, bacon and sliced strawberries, lifting his gaze to hers as he set it on the table.

"Come sit down, Charity. I won't bite. Yet."

"Just say whatever it is you want to say."

Beau's brow went up. "I will. As soon as you sit down and start eating."

Feeling as if anything she ate would come right back up again, Charity plopped into the chair and reached for her orange juice while Beau refilled her coffee. "Fine. Say it so I can go."

"Excuse me?" Beau set her coffee in front of her and gripped her chin, lifting her face to his. "The only place you're going is the doctor. You have an appointment in about an hour, so get going on that breakfast."

Charity blinked up at him. "But I thought...you and Anna—"

Beau lifted her left hand, running his finger over the huge diamond. "I'm engaged to you. Or have you forgotten?"

Yanking her hand away, Charity started to jump up from her chair, but Beau pressed a hand to her thigh, effectively stopping her. "I didn't forget! You're the one who disappeared on a day that you knew was important to me. You were gone for *hours*. With *her*."

Dropping into his seat, he kept his hand on her thigh. "Is that why you didn't call me when you weren't feeling well?"

Uneasy at the unfamiliar edge of steel in his tone, Charity went on the offense. "Don't you dare turn this around! I wasn't going to call anyone. I had a headache and got dizzy when I got up too fast."

"Perhaps because you hadn't eaten, like you promised me you would?" Leaning back, he sipped his coffee. "I don't like that you didn't call me, Charity, and before you get your panties in a bunch, let me tell you what happened last night."

Charity listened as Beau told her about Anna and Jeffrey, stunned that he'd suspected Anna's intentions. She picked at her breakfast, her jaw dropping when he told her about Jeffrey and what he'd told Beau about Anna.

"Oh, Beau. What a night you had!" She'd been busy feeling sorry for herself and mad at him while he'd been dealing with something that must have been a very painful experience. "Is she still going to divorce him?"

Beau shrugged and got up to refill their cups before she got a chance to get up to sit on his lap. "She and Jeffrey have a lot to work out, but she won't be calling me anymore."

"Holy shit. I can't believe she was so conniving. Nat knew it after five minutes with her."

Beau nodded. "Yeah. It was a very revealing night." He came up behind her, rubbing her shoulders, his touch both comforting and exciting, warming her through and sending little sizzles of electricity through her. "If you'd called me, I would have come home right away. I should have watched the time better, but Jeffrey and I started talking and I lost track of time. We haven't talked like that in years."

Struck by Beau's pensive tone, Charity tilted her head back to look up at him, smiling apologetically. "And then you called to find that Hope had taken me to the hospital."

Taking his hand in hers, she turned to face him. "Hope kind of hustled me along, and my head hurt so much that I didn't put up the fight that I should have. Part of it was because I was mad at you and hurt, too. Nat told me how Anna went on and on about you, and I was afraid you were falling for that giggle, and the way she kept clinging to you made me want to hit her."

Bending, he touched his lips to hers, pausing to brush them back and forth. "I'm always here for you, cher." Straightening again, he gripped her chin when she would have turned away. "But you play games like that with me again, and I'm going to turn you over my knee. Understood?"

Unconcerned by his threat, Charity waved her hand and reached for her fork again, frowning to realize that she'd eaten everything. "Yeah, yeah, yeah." Picking up her glass of orange juice, she rose from the table with her plate. "Why did you make an appointment with the doctor? I just got checked out last night."

Raising a brow again, he crossed his arms over his chest and gave her the arrogant look he'd adopted since her accident. "I wasn't there. I want to ask the questions I want to ask, and I want to make sure your own doctor sees you. This isn't up for negotiation, Charity."

Feeling bad about what a rough night he'd had, and her part in it, Charity nodded. "Okay. I'm sorry about last night." She smiled as Beau gathered her close.

Rubbing his hands up and down her back, he buried his face against her throat. "So am I, cher. So am I. I hate that I wasn't there for you."

"And I'm sorry I didn't call." She rubbed against him, lifting her face for his kiss. "I love you. I should have known better."

"Yes, you should have. Maybe one day you'll believe that what I feel for you is real. Until then, I'll just have to keep trying to convince you."

* * * *

"Told ya." Charity grinned at Beau, as they walked out of the doctor's office. She'd just gotten the all clear from her doctor, who fielded all of Beau's questions about her recovery.

Beau, who'd shortened his steps for her, moved the hand he held at her back in a gentle caress. "I still want you to be careful. Now that you've had the Grand Reopening, you can settle down a little."

"I'm just fine." She moved to stand in front of him, effectively forcing him to stop. Smiling up at him, she slid her hand inside his open jacket and ran it over his chest, loving that everything had started to get back to normal again. She missed the intimacy, and she couldn't wait to get back to it. "You heard the doctor. I can have sex and everything."

Beau grinned, his eyes dancing. "I can't believe you asked him that. You're just not the type, cher."

"And you're the type who would have asked him right off the bat." Sliding her hand higher, she stroked his nipple, thrilling at his sharp intake of breath. "Don't you want me anymore?"

Wrapping his arms around her, he bent to brush her lips with his. "Don't be ridiculous. I always want you." Stepping aside, he began walking again, the hand at her back urging her forward. "I'm just in a mood. I'll pick you up for dinner tonight, and then we'll go back to my house."

A thrill went through her at the thought of making love again, and she couldn't resist teasing him. "You don't want to make love in *my* bed?"

Beau opened the door of his SUV and helped her inside. "There isn't enough room to move in your damned bed." He helped her fasten her seat belt and paused, lifting his gaze to hers. "Now that you're healed, there's no reason for me to stay with you any longer. Your fathers have already voiced their opinion about us living together, or I would have asked you to move in with me already. It looks like we sleep in separate beds until we're married, but that doesn't mean I'm not making love to you. I won't, however, be doing it in *your* small bed."

Gripping the front of his jacket, she pulled him closer. "As long as you make love to me, I don't care where we do it."

They drove back to Desire, both looking toward the place where she had her accident as they passed it. Since most of the snow had melted, with only small patches remaining, the area looked nothing like it did that night.

She'd never forget that spot, though, and judging by the way Beau's jaw clenched and his white-knuckled grip on the steering wheel, he wouldn't either.

"Beau, don't look that way. It's over and I'm fine."

"Yeah."

He didn't sound too convinced, and Charity didn't know what else to say, so they made the rest of the trip back to Desire in silence.

After he dropped her off, Charity stared at the back of his SUV as he drove away, hoping that after they made love tonight, Beau would relax.

A hand touched her arm, startling her. "So what did the doctor say?"

Charity turned her head at Hope's question and smiled, her thoughts still on Beau. "He said I'm good as new."

"Great. You have to call Mom. She keeps calling to see if you're back yet. She wasn't real happy that we went to the hospital last night without telling her."

Nodding, Charity turned back in time to see Beau turn the corner. "I'll call her now." She turned back to Hope, noticing that a small smile played at her sister's lips. "Okay. What happened?"

Hope shrugged. "Ace figured out what I did." Frowning, she shifted her feet. "I don't quite know how he does that. Scary. He decided to teach me a lesson." Her grin turned into a yawn. "He kept me up half the night. By the way, he told me what happened with Beau. Made me feel like crap. I'll apologize when I see him."

"Good." She stared down the road toward where she'd last seen Beau. "He's really still upset about not being there, and he blames himself enough. I don't want him to think that you blame him, too."

Hope touched her arm, waiting until Charity turned to her. "You don't sound too happy. What's wrong?"

Charity sighed, feeling the muscles in her neck and shoulders tightening again. "Beau. I told you that he's changed since the accident. He doesn't play anymore. He's too serious. He's too careful. It's like he's afraid I'm going to break or something."

"Isn't that what you wanted—someone as much a killjoy as you are? They always say to be careful what you wish for." Hope grinned at Charity's glare. "Don't look at me like that. You got exactly what you asked for." Taking her arm, Hope led Charity up the stairs to the club. "Beau was fun, wasn't he? I'll bet he used all those toys he sells in his shop, didn't he?"

"I told you to stop asking me. I'm *not* telling you about our sex life."

"You owe me."

Charity paused, blinking at her sister. "How the hell do you figure that?"

Hope grinned again and put a hand at her back to urge her up the steps and into the club. "Because you lied to me about seeing him. I'm your sister so you're supposed to tell me the truth, *and* you're supposed to give me all the juicy details when you have an affair. You didn't, so you owe me."

Turning as Hope closed the door behind her, Charity smiled at the smug look on her sister's face and shook her head. "You're unbelievable."

Hope leaned back against the door. "So, what toys did he bring home?"

Charity sighed. "A bunch. I have no idea how many there are, but Beau seemed to know how to play with all of them." She went behind the bar and opened the small refrigerator there. "You want something?"

Hope looked up from where she sorted through the mail. "No, I'm good."

Reaching in for a bottle of water, Charity watched her sister. "Does Ace ever get upset with you for playing too much?"

Hope looked up again, and smiled. "Upset—no. Amused at my attempts is more like it. I egg him on until I cross the line and earn the appropriate punishment." Grinning, she winked. "Then we play—his way, which is fine with me, because it happens to be my way, too."

After kicking the refrigerator door closed, Charity twisted the top from her bottle of water. Taking several sips, she made her way to the new window. "I think I ruined Beau. He doesn't want to play anymore." Turning her head, she met her sister's knowing grin. "What the hell are you smiling about?"

Tossing the mail aside, Hope sauntered toward her in that easy stride Charity had never been able to duplicate. "People don't change, Charity. They might try, but people don't change. Hell, I've been trying to change you for years. People. Don't. Change. That's how I knew Ace was right for me. He tried to change, too. Tried to pretend he didn't need to be so dominant, but I knew he couldn't change. I just hung in there and kept pushing him."

Charity felt a stirring of hope. "Daring him, more likely."

"You'll have to use the same tactic with Beau. You're so impatient."

"Impatient? You're the one who always goes hell-bent into situations without thinking them through."

"And you think *too* much. Just go with the flow, Charity. If you want Beau to play, then *play*. Beau loves having fun. He won't be able to resist you for long."

Chapter Fourteen

Charity jumped at the knock on her door, her heart pounding with excitement. She crossed to it on shaky legs and flung the door open, sucking in a breath at the impact Beau had on her senses. Amazed that even after being with Beau all this time, she could still be startled by his amazing good looks, she leaned against the doorway and drank in the sight of him.

The black dress slacks and gray dress shirt did nothing to tone down the aura of wicked sensuality surrounding him.

Eyeing him hungrily, she straightened and swung the door wide. "I didn't expect you to knock. Don't you still have your key?"

Stepping into the room, he whipped an arm out and around her waist when she would have stepped back, his smile thrilling her. "I still have my key, but this is a date."

Flattening his hands on her back, he pulled her close, bending to take her mouth with his. Pressing his lips against hers, he forced her mouth open, taking it in a sensual kiss that sent her senses reeling. As one hand slid in her hair to hold her in place, the other tightened on her back, pulling her even closer.

Charity melted under his kiss, her pussy clenching at the feel of his hard cock pressed against her belly. She'd missed this so much. She'd missed the erotic feel of his body, hard and hungry against hers. She'd missed the seduction in his kiss, and the demand in his much more forceful hold when he wanted her too much to be gentle.

His kiss—his hold—had an element of arrogance to it now that hadn't been there before. Instead of teasing or cajoling a response from her, he swept in and smashed through her defenses and took, silently demanding a response from her that she found herself helpless to deny.

Her breasts felt swollen against his chest, her nipples tight and aching for his touch. Pressing herself against him, she gasped at the feel of his cock pressing against her, now even harder than before.

The hand at her back lowered to her bottom as Beau lifted his head. "A real date. We're going out in public where everyone can see that you belong to me."

Threading her hands into his silky hair, Charity nodded, swallowing heavily as desire flowed through her veins. "Yes." Rubbing against him, she moaned. "I can't wait until we're alone, though."

With a smile, Beau ran his hand over her hip. "Neither can I, cher. I've been thinking about it all day." Putting only a few inches between them, Beau slid a hand over her bottom. "You look beautiful. I don't think I've ever seen you in a dress before."

She knew she looked good, but the appreciation in Beau's eyes made her feel even more beautiful. "Thank you. I haven't worn a dress in years. You told me to dress up, but I don't know where we're going."

She knew the teal dress showed off her olive skin to perfection, and that it hugged her curves in all the right places. She wouldn't have chosen the low, revealing neckline for herself, but she was glad now that Hope talked her into it.

She also had a new appreciation for the lingerie Hope had talked her into buying.

She couldn't wear a bra with the dress, and the sensation of the material sliding over her nipples with every movement made her feel decadent and very, very sexy.

The way Beau's gaze lingered there made her feel even sexier.

Hope had talked her into forgoing the panties, and instead of her usual pantyhose, Charity wore a black garter and stockings.

Unused to going without panties, Charity fidgeted restlessly in Beau's arms, enjoying the feel of the slippery material sliding over her bottom. Feeling naughty and confident, Charity looked forward to the evening ahead with Beau, determined to get back the man she'd first fallen in love with.

Beau's smile sent a thrill of anticipation racing through her, a smile that fell, his eyes going wide. "You're not wearing panties."

His hand moved again, the warm of his touch penetrating the material and making her pussy clench again. His entire body tensed, his groan rumbling in his chest and vibrating against her nipples. "You're wearing a garter belt."

Thrilled with his response, and that she'd managed to surprise him, Charity ran a hand down his chest, anxious to surprise him more. "A black one with stockings." It had been so long—too long—since she'd felt so free and uninhibited, and she wanted to make it last, and tease both of them as long as possible.

Walking carefully in her heels, she grinned and turned to retrieve her purse from the sofa. Her breath caught when Beau came up behind her, holding the only dress coat she owned to help her into it.

Once she had it on, she turned her head to smile her thanks, her breath catching when he jerked the edges of her coat wide, preventing her from buttoning it.

With another groan, he buried her face against the side of her neck and slid his hands over her breasts. "No bra, either. Do you have any idea what you're doing to me?" The rough growl in his voice thrilled her, and made her heart beat faster.

With a gasp, she dropped her head back against his shoulder, a moan escaping when Beau slid his warm hands inside the low neckline of her dress to cup her breasts. "Hopefully, tempting you. I want you to want me again."

Groaning, he rubbed his cock against her belly. "You always tempt me. I always want you."

Sliding his hands from her dress, he pulled it back into place, nuzzling her neck as he buttoned her coat. "It's cold outside." Once he finished, he slid his hand lower and caressed her mound. "That cold air's going to blow right up your dress and you're not even wearing panties to keep your pussy warm." With a grin, he ran a hand over her hair. "I guess I'm going to have to make sure it stays warm."

She couldn't resist the playfulness in his tone, delighted to have everything back to normal. Lifting her arms to wrap them around his neck, and thankful that it only caught a slight pang to her left shoulder, Charity tilted her hips into his touch. The rush of need his words inspired dampened her inner thighs, his teasing exciting her like never before. She felt the desperation she hadn't felt before, so attuned to him that the slightest movement of his body against hers made her heart beat faster. Because of it, her words came out breathless as she leaned into him. "I wouldn't worry about that. It feels pretty warm down there."

"You don't mind if I check for myself, do you?"

"Oh, God." Her clit tingled in anticipation. She could almost feel him touching her, her imagination running wild. She shivered at the feel of his breath against her neck, her knees turning to rubber at the slow slide of his fingers up her inner thigh. Her breath became harsher and more labored with every inch he gained, her stomach muscles tightening in expectation.

He moved slowly, intensifying the anticipation, his other hand pressing against her abdomen, effectively holding her in place. "We wouldn't want this pussy getting cold now, would we? What the hell?"

Charity smiled at his incredulous tone, a tone filled with sexual tension. "I made another stop today after I shopped for the clothes."

Smoothing his fingers over her bare mound, he turned her face to his. "Apparently." With a harsh groan, he turned her in his arms, lifting her face to his again, his eyes hooded and darker than usual. "Do you have any more surprises for me?"

Flattening her hands on his chest, she leaned closer, breathing in the clean, exotic scent of him, a scent she could recognize with her eyes closed, a scent that never failed to ignite her senses. Sucking in another breath, she smiled, her voice catching at the hunger building inside her, a hunger fueled by his. "I haven't surprised you enough?"

Adjusting the collar of her coat to cover her neck, Beau smiled, his eyes dark and hooded. "You've given me quite a few surprises tonight. I planned for us to talk more at dinner, but now I'm going to have trouble focusing on the conversation."

Bending low, he brushed her lips with his, frustrating her by straightening before she could entice him to deepen his kiss. He ran a hand over her hair before pressing it at the small of her back to urge her toward the door.

"I'm going to sit through dinner, anxiously anticipating the time when we get back to my house, I strip you out of that dress, spread your thighs, and have my dessert."

If not for Beau's hold, Charity would have stumbled.

Instead of the teasing that always made her heart race, his tone had an urgency to it that emphasized his need for her. The raw huskiness in his voice ignited a primitive hunger that erased all thoughts of play.

She wanted heat. She wanted passion. She didn't want him to hold back anymore. She wanted everything Beau had to give.

Knowing how he felt increased her sense of sexual awareness so strongly, she trembled with it.

Halfway down the steps, he ran a hand over her bottom, a touch that had become more possessive since her accident, but seemed even more possessive now. "You'd better keep those legs closed as much as possible, chéri. I wouldn't want that bare pussy to get cold. I want a nice warm dessert."

Charity shivered at the gust of wind, smiling when he pulled her closer and rubbed her back. "The things you say sometimes make me crazy. Where are we going?"

Beau took her hand as they went through the alley between the buildings. "We're going to the hotel. I want everyone to see that we're together." As they approached his SUV, he pressed the button to unlock it and glanced at her. "Our dinner is probably going to be interrupted several times, but I want for us to be out in public together." He opened the door and lifted her by the waist to help her inside, once again surprising her with his strength.

Bending, he brushed his lips over hers, nibbling at her bottom lip before straightening and fastening her seat belt. "I want everyone to see that you're mine. It's about time, don't you think? Is this okay on your hip?"

Charity nodded. "It's fine. I'm okay now, Beau. If you baby me tonight, I swear I'm going to hit you." She met his glare with a steady look, watching as he rounded the front of his SUV and got in. "Beau, not that I mind going to the restaurant in the hotel, but people have seen us together all over town for weeks."

Glancing at her, Beau started the SUV and put it in gear. "Walking around town to exercise that hip, going to the doctor's, the drug store, and the grocery store isn't exactly the same thing as going out on a date."

Grinning at his indignant tone, Charity laughed softly. "I would think that doing things like grocery shopping together would signify that we were together more than going out on a date."

Beau smiled and reached over to pat her hand. "Still, we're not getting married without even dating *once*."

It took only a few minutes to get to the hotel, and as they pulled into the parking lot, Charity turned to Beau. "It looks busy. Are you sure they're going to have a table for us?"

"Of course. I told Brandon we were coming."

She couldn't take her eyes off of him as he got out and rounded the front of the SUV, once again struck by the fact that he would soon be her husband. Bubbling with excitement, she reached for him when he opened her door. "Are we going to sit in one of the privacy booths?"

The privacy booths had to be reserved in advance, and there had always been a waiting list for them. People who wanted to participate in a little—or a lot—of naughtiness while they ate could reserve them, and the waiter only went inside when he'd been summoned.

She could only imagine what went on inside. Curious, she'd asked her sister, but as much as Hope wanted to eat in one of the privacy booths with her husband, Ace refused, saying that it wasn't appropriate behavior for the sheriff.

As much as she wanted to tempt Beau to be his playful self again, she could already feel her face burn at the thought of everyone in the restaurant speculating on what they were doing behind the heavy curtain.

Beau helped her down, steadying her before closing the door. "No. It would only embarrass your parents. Anything we can do in there, we can do back at my place—and with a hell of a lot more privacy."

Relieved, and oddly disappointed, Charity walked across the parking lot with him. Unused to walking in heels, she appreciated Beau's steadying hold and the fact that he slowed his steps to match hers.

Beau kept hold of her hand as they made their way through the hotel lobby, and into the restaurant. "Between shopping with your sister and going to the spa, you sound like you did a lot of running around today. Did you eat anything?"

Smiling at Brandon, who came around the desk to greet them, she glanced up at Beau. "I had a slice of pizza while we were shopping. Hi, Brandon. I see the restaurant's as busy as usual." She started forward, but Beau wrapped a hand around her upper arm and pulled her back.

Frowning, he held up a finger to signal Brandon to wait. "Pizza? That's all you had today?"

Grinning, Brandon moved closer. "Uh-oh. It looks like you'd better eat your dinner tonight." His eyes narrowed as they raked over her face. "You look beautiful. Beau must be taking good care of you."

Charity smiled. "He is, but I've recently noticed that he can be somewhat of a nag."

Brandon threw back his head and laughed, the handsome owner of the restaurant earning several admiring looks from women sitting nearby. "Give him a break. He's been hovering over you for weeks."

He led them to a table off to the side. "I saved this one for you. I figured you'd want a little more privacy. Anyone who hasn't seen Charity for a while is going to be coming over to see how she is, and to congratulate both of you on your upcoming marriage."

Once they were seated, he braced himself on the back of the chair across from her and nodded toward one of the waiters, who rushed over with two menus. "I got the invitation the other day. I'm going to have to find me a sweet thing to bring as my date."

Knowing Brandon shared women with his friend and business partner, Ethan, Charity smiled. "You mean you and Ethan?"

Brandon's smile dimmed, as did the light of amusement in his eyes. "Ethan's bringing his own date." Blowing out a breath, he straightened. "So what did the doctor say?"

Amused at the fact that he knew she'd had an appointment, Charity still worried about Brandon's obvious unhappiness, and shared a look with Beau, who shook his head imperceptibly before meeting Brandon's gaze again. "The doctor said that I'm as good as new."

Beau finished buttering the piece of warm bread from the basket and placed it on Charity's bread plate. "Charity thinks she's indestructible."

Brandon chuckled, he and Beau sharing one of those looks of male communication she'd come to recognize. "That seems to be one of the female traits that drive the men around here crazy the most. They just don't realize how small and fragile they really are."

Turning, Brandon gave her a considering look. "Don't look at me that way. You know damned well that it's a man's job to protect you. If you don't believe me, ask your daddies. The waiter's on his way over with a complimentary bottle of champagne to celebrate your engagement."

He gestured toward her ring and grinned. "It's about time." Turning to Beau, he inclined his head. "You're a lucky man. Having a woman of your own must be incredible."

Something about his demeanor bothered Charity. Leaning forward, she opened her mouth to ask him about it, but a look from Beau kept her silent.

Beau, who'd seemed inclined to sit back and watch her, his gaze indulgent, sat forward. "Thanks for the champagne, and thank Ethan for us."

Curious about the strange look on Brandon's face, Charity watched him walk away, waiting until she could no longer see him before turning to Beau. "What's wrong with Brandon? Don't tell me you don't know because everyone talks in Desire, especially you men."

Beau's brow went up. "Oh, and the women don't talk?" Leaning back, he watched the waiter open the champagne and pour each of them a glass. "The men have to know what's going on with all the women. Some of them get half-cocked ideas about doing crazy things—like driving in a blizzard. We have to know what's going on in order to protect them."

Once the waiter left, Beau handed her one of the glasses, lifting the other. "To my beautiful bride-to-be." Taking her hand in his, he held it to his lips before taking a sip of the champagne. The love shining in his eyes, and the possessiveness of his gaze as it moved over her face stunned her with its intensity. When he leaned forward, she did the same, hardly able to believe that this was the same man who'd tied her to the bed, who'd used feathers to ignite every nerve ending in her body with passion, and who'd used flavored paints to tease her senses.

The sincerity in his eyes couldn't be mistaken, and she wondered how she could have missed so much. Beau had layers to him that she hadn't seen—maybe hadn't wanted to see, or been ready to see—and she found this side of him as fascinating and compelling as the playful lover she'd known.

Blinking back tears, Charity gripped his hand. "Beau, sometimes I feel as if I never knew you."

With a smile, he brought her hand to his cheek, interlacing his fingers with hers. "I've been here all along, cher. My need to play in no way diminished what I felt for you."

The waiter's appearance kept her from answering, but she didn't know what she would have said anyway. Realizing that her own fears had caused the wedge that had been between him, she knew she had to do something in order to make him see that she didn't mind his playfulness at all.

She didn't know how she would go about it yet, but she knew she had to find a way.

Setting the menu aside, Charity took another sip of champagne. "I think I'll have the chicken with the mushroom sauce."

"Good. You need your protein."

Slipping her shoe off, she ran her bare foot up his leg. "You mean to keep my energy up for tonight?"

Beau's lips twitched as he set his own menu aside. "That, too. Despite my best efforts, you've lost some weight. You need to put it back on."

Reaching down, he took her foot in his hand and began to massage it. "Those heels must be killers on your feet. You probably should have worn something with a lower heel, especially with that hip." Frowning, he glanced toward her hip. "Does it bother your hip to walk in them?"

Insulted that he didn't seem as bowled over as she'd hoped by the look she'd worked so hard to achieve, Charity blew out a breath. "So much for looking sexy."

Shaking his head, Beau took her hand in his again. "I think you look sexy as hell, but that doesn't mean I can't be concerned about you."

His gaze slid to her breasts. "Your nipples poking at the front of your dress have been teasing me ever since we sat down. That low neckline is driving me crazy. No, put your hands back down."

Feeling self-conscious, Charity had automatically reached to cover herself, but the disappointment in his eyes had her dropping her hands back into her lap. Her nipples tingled under his appreciative gaze, becoming even tighter.

The flare of heat in his eyes before they lowered to her breasts again had her shifting restlessly in her seat and sitting up straighter.

Taking another sip of his champagne, he bent closer, keeping his voice low and intimate. "The curves of your breasts make my fingers itch to touch you. I already know that your breasts are as firm and soft as they look, and as your lover, I know how incredibly sensitive they are, too. I know how delicious you are. I can't stop thinking about that soft pussy, or how wet and needy you'll be once I spread those thighs and get my mouth on you."

Lifting her left hand to his lips, he kissed the ring he'd placed there and lowered his gaze to her lap before lifting it to hers again. "*Le mien.*"

Hardly able to breathe, Charity leaned closer as if being pulled by a magnet. "I love when you speak French, and I love when you speak in that low, deep tone. What did you say?" Her stomach muscles tightened, her breath hitching at the seductive quality in his voice.

Beau leaned closer, answering her in the same tone, his eyes filled with possessiveness. "Mine."

Charity remained silent as the waiter came over and Beau gave him their order, her mind reeling as she remembered the number of times she'd heard him say the same thing to her when he'd taken her virginity.

Once the waiter left, Beau turned back to her, regarding her intently. "I've said that to you many times. This is the first time you've ever asked me about it."

Nodding, Charity took another sip of her champagne. "I guess I figured you'd be embarrassed if I asked you what it meant, like something you might say in the throes of passion and regret."

Beau grinned. "I never regret anything I say to you in the throes of passion, cher. Usually, I can't manage more than a string of groans and grunts."

"And a lot of cursing."

To her delight, Beau threw his head back and laughed, his throaty chuckle more potent to her senses than the champagne she drank.

Sitting back as the waiter brought their food, Beau shared an intimate look with her, waiting until the man left before speaking again. "When my cock's inside that tight pussy, my baser instincts take over."

Sitting back, he gestured toward her plate. "Eat your dinner."

Despite Brandon's warning, most of the people they knew in the restaurant had already congratulated them on their engagement, and only stopped by the table to see how she was doing.

Jared, Duncan, and Reese Preston hovered over their pregnant wife, Erin, as she approached the table. Beau jumped to his feet to pull out a chair for her, but Duncan beat him to it.

Erin waved her hand toward the chair and shook her head. "No, thanks. I need to stand a few minutes. Damn it, Jared."

Jared guided her to the chair, and with gentle firmness, forced her into it. "You don't want your ankles swelling again, do you?"

Erin looked at Charity and rolled her eyes. "They're driving me crazy. They act like I'm the only woman who's ever had a baby before."

"You're the only one who's ever had *our* baby." Reese ran a hand over her hair. "Something you've heard often enough in the last six months."

Beau gestured toward the other chair, and offered to get more, but the other men shook their head.

Duncan braced his hands on Erin's chair and leaned over her. "We're going to get Erin home. She's tired, but doesn't want to admit it."

Erin waved her hand negligently in the air. "According to you three, I'm always tired or hungry." She smiled at Charity. "So how are you feeling? I heard you had a checkup today."

Charity couldn't help but smile. "Small town, isn't it? It went fine." She raised a brow. "How did yours go?"

Erin's eyes widened before she burst out laughing. "Touché. It went great." Glancing at her husbands, she smiled. "They worry too much. Still, they're kinda cute." She yawned, leaning more heavily against Duncan.

Reese took her hand and helped her to her feet. "You just never give up do you, baby?"

With the help of her husband, Erin got to her feet, rubbing her stomach. "Yeah, yeah, yeah. Charity, you take care of yourself. I can't wait to dance at your wedding."

Duncan took her hand in his. "Slow dancing."

As Duncan and Reese led Erin out, Jared paused beside the table, the love and concern in his eyes obvious as he stared after his wife. Turning back, he smiled. "We'll be there. We're all really happy for both of you."

Watching Jared walk away, Charity sipped her champagne, and started to turn away, hesitating when Jared paused and looked toward the doorway before changing direction. Sitting straighter, she watched him say something to Brandon, whose answering smile seemed forced.

"I'm going to get jealous if you keep staring at other men."

Charity turned to Beau. "No, you're not. You know damned well you're the handsomest man in Desire and that I love you madly." Leaning closer, she snuck another glance toward the other men just in time to see Jared walk away.

"Okay. Spill it. What's going on with Brandon?"

Beau cut into his steak. "It's just something he and Ethan are going to have to deal with. It seems that the women they meet aren't interested in having a ménage relationship. It's making them reassess what they want, and I don't think either one of them is really happy."

Shrugging, he gestured toward her plate. "Eat."

Charity winced, hurting for her friends. "Damn. I was young, but I can still remember people talking about Clay and Rio. They knew they wanted a woman to share, but they ended up marrying different women, and both of them were miserable. I hope Brandon and Ethan don't make the same mistake."

"I'm sure they'll work it out." Sitting back, Beau eyed her steadily. "It's funny that you and Hope were both raised in a ménage household, and yet neither one of you chose a ménage marriage."

Grinning, Charity stabbed another mushroom. "You're more than enough for me. Besides, you can't help who you fall in love with, and I fell in love with you. My mom fell in love with all three of my fathers, and always told us to follow our hearts." Grinning, she touched his forearm, her stomach muscles quivering at the feel of hard muscle shifting under her hand. "I did, and so did my sister."

Beau's slow smile took her breath away. "My grandfather said the same thing. I looked across the diner at your college graduation party and finally knew what he was talking about. Knocked me for a loop."

Charity's breath caught at the love shining in his eyes, her heart melting. "I didn't expect you, either. I was so scared that you would want someone more sophisticated." Laughter bubbled free as she thought of her friend.

"I guess the same thing happened to Erin. She came to town to talk Rachel out of marrying *two* men, thinking that an arrangement like that would never work."

Beau laughed. "We all enjoyed watching that play out. She came to talk her pregnant little sister out of marrying the two men she'd fallen in love with, and who both claimed responsibility for the baby—"

Giggling, Charity had to swallow before she choked. "And then she ends up married to *three* men and now they're having a baby of their own."

"And they couldn't be happier." Taking her hand in his, he leaned close. "I'm going to make sure you're just as happy."

Charity stabbed another piece of chicken. "I just hope you're happy." Her body tightened with anticipation as she thought about the evening ahead. "What kind of toy did you get for tonight?"

Taking the fork from her hand, he slid the piece of chicken past her lips. "Just you, chéri. You're my toy tonight." Gesturing toward her plate, he reached for his glass again. "Finish eating. I want my dessert."

Chapter Fifteen

As soon as they walked through the front door of Beau's house, he shut and locked it behind them, tossed his keys onto the table in the entryway, and wrapped his arms around her from behind. Burying his face against her neck, he breathed deeply. "You smell delicious. Warm and sweet. That pussy didn't get cold on the way in here, did it?"

Dropping her head back against his shoulder, Charity let her eyes flutter closed, only to open them again as his hands started moving. Her body tightened as need slammed into her. "Not a chance."

He untied the belt of her coat, and made quick work of unbuttoning it. "I'll have to check it out for myself."

With his big body behind hers, he nudged her forward. "I want my dessert." He took the purse from her hand and tossed it on the sofa before removing her coat. He tossed the coat to land on top of her purse, and without slowing, lifted her into his arms, making her feel small and ultra feminine. "I'm dying to see you in just a garter and stockings." He strode into the bedroom, not pausing until he reached the bed, and with slow deliberation, slid her body against his as he lowered her to her feet.

The moonlight streaming in from the large window provided enough light for her to see the hunger in Beau's eyes, a hunger that always stoked the fire inside her. Her clit swelled with anticipation, her nipples beaded tight against the silky material.

Trembling with an excitement that made her giddy, and grateful for Beau's steadying hold, Charity stood on rubbery legs as he worked her out of her dress. Her breath came out in a rush as the dress fell to the floor to puddle at her feet. "God, I want you. It's been so long."

Pressing her thighs together did nothing to ease the ache there, and when she leaned into him, rubbing her nipples against his warm skin made the ache even worse.

"Step out of the dress." Beau's deep voice washed over her, his accent more prominent and seductive than ever, came from right next to her ear. His hot hands closed around her waist to steady her as she stepped out of the puddle the dress had made at her feet.

When she started to kick off her shoes, Beau slid his hands to her breasts, cupping them and rubbing his thumbs over her nipples.

"No. Leave those shoes on. I want to see you just the way you are."

Bereft of the warmth at her back, Charity forced herself to remain still as he moved slowly to stand in front of her. Without taking his eyes from hers, he bent to turn on the light.

His eyes widened, the awe in them making her feel like the most desired woman on earth. Taking her hands in his, he held them away from her body, his gaze filled with heat as it raked over her. "Beautiful."

Charity felt beautiful. Desired. Seductive.

Confident.

Wearing nothing more than her black, lacy garter belt and stockings, and a pair of ridiculously high heels, Charity lifted her chin to face him squarely. Running her fingers over her stomach, she bit back a moan when he smiled and took a step closer.

"Very sexy, cher. Turn around. I want to see that pretty ass, too."

Overwhelmed by the aura of male sexuality and hunger surrounding him, Charity did as he demanded without hesitation, stunned at the change taking place inside her.

It was as if a mask had been ripped away, revealing a sexual primitiveness in Beau that he'd never allowed her to see before.

Turning, she whipped her head around to watch his face, never looking away from him as she completed her circle. "Beau, you've never been this way before." Gulping as he dropped to his knees in front of her, she sucked in a breath at the slide of his fingers over her newly bared flesh.

"I was afraid of scaring you off." The shock of his touch on her overly sensitive mound made her jolt, but his hands went to her hips and tightened, holding her in place. "How does it feel to be bare?"

Her knees weakened at the demand in his voice, a masculine need in it that she'd never heard from him before. "Naked. Exposed. Sexy."

His touch—his voice—so familiar, and yet with a difference that seemed so erotic, stroked her senses with an intensity that made her shake all over. His hands clenched on her hips as his lips touched her abdomen. "Good. I like you this way. Very much." Leaning back, he held her with one hand while sliding the backs of his fingers of the other over her mound, drawing another gasp from her and sending a riot of tingling sensation racing through her.

Lifting his hooded gaze to hers, he watched her intently. "Why did you do this?"

Surprised at the question, and finding it hard to form a coherent reply when his fingers moved lower. "Uh." She hissed in a breath at the slow caress of his fingertips back and forth over her folds. "It's, uh…"

Chuckling softly, Beau rose slightly and slid a hand to her bottom, pulling her closer. "Why did you get waxed, cher?"

His warm mouth hovered over her nipple. "Why, cher? After all this time, why would you wax yourself now?"

Threading her fingers through his hair, she tried to pull him closer, but Beau held firm. "Because I wanted to please you. I wanted to excite you. Damn it, Beau. What are you doing?"

He seemed so tense, a tenseness that she'd never noticed before. His hands tightened against her bottom a split second before his lips closed over her breasts, as if he anticipated her jolt.

The sharp tug shocked her, the pull to her clit so sharp she couldn't hold still. It ended almost as soon as it began as he lifted his head, but the heat and pinpricks of pleasure lingered.

"I'm making love to you." Straightening, he brushed her hair back, and ran his fingertips over her collarbone to her shoulders. His eyes seemed lit from within as he stared down at her, his fingertips tracing a slow pattern from her shoulders down to her breasts. "You did. You do."

Sucking in a breath, Charity lifted her hands to his shoulders, arching her back to give him better access. Her breath quickened when he slid his fingers over the upper curve of her breasts, catching again when he circled her nipples. "I d–did what? I d–do w–what?"

His fingertips closed over her nipples, applying just enough pressure to bring her to her toes. "You did please me. You did excite me. You still do. You're a constant source of pleasure and excitement that I just can't get enough of. Thank you for waxing your pussy for me. I'm going to show you just how much I appreciate it."

Fisting her hands in the material of his shirt, Charity lifted her face to his as another rush of moisture coated her thighs. "Beau, please!"

"Please, what? Does that clit need my attention?" Releasing her nipples, he gently lowered her to the edge of the bed, his body covering hers and forcing her back. "My mouth's watering for my dessert. Stay just like this. I want to look at you."

Charity's skin tingled everywhere, the heightened awareness so intense, it made her dizzy. Her veins bubbled with excitement and combined with the warm flow of love and desire poured over her, filling her with a sense of well-being and hunger that somehow went hand in hand.

It didn't matter how he touched her, as long as he touched her. She wanted his hands and lips everywhere, and she wanted to touch him just as badly. Wrapping her arms and legs around him wasn't enough. She pulled him closer, rubbing against him. Her hands moved over his shoulders and back and into his hair. She kissed him everywhere she could reach, and it still wasn't enough.

She whimpered when he started to rise, needing his closeness more than she needed her next breath. Tightening her arms and legs around him, she wrapped her arms around his neck and held on tight. "No. Please don't go."

Rubbing her slit and breasts against him, she rained kisses over his cheek. "Take me, Beau. Please. I need you so much."

She'd never needed quite this way before, a physical and emotional neediness to be as close to him as possible.

Beau lifted his head, pushing her hair back from her forehead. "Shh. It's okay, cher. I've got you. I'm not going anywhere. I just want to taste you. I want my mouth on you."

He nuzzled her jaw, disentangling himself from her hold as he worked his way down her body, leaving a trail of sizzling heat all the way to her slit.

Standing between her thighs, he prevented her from closing them as he unbuttoned his shirt and shrugged out of it. "I find I have a weakness for garter belts and stockings, especially when they frame a soft, bare pussy."

Charity's breath caught at the sight of his bare chest, the moonlight creating mysterious shadows her fingers itched to explore. Her stomach clenched when he reached for the fastening of his dress pants as he toed off his shoes. "Beau, I want to be exciting for you."

Seconds later, he stood naked in front of her, his cock already hard and thick. "You're everything to me."

He reached into the drawer beside the bed and retrieved a condom. Fisting his cock in his hand, he rolled it on, his eyes never leaving hers. "All mine." Once he'd rolled on the condom, he reached for her leg, lifting it high. Bending to touch his lips to her calf, he slipped her shoe off and tossed it aside. "Every gorgeous inch."

By the time he did the same to her other leg, she shook uncontrollably, a whimper escaping as he went to his knees between her thighs. "Beau." Her stomach clenched in excitement, her thighs shaking so hard she wouldn't have been able to hold them up on her own.

Smiling, he bent to touch his lips to her sensitive mound. "I love the way you say my name when you're aroused. It has this little catch in it that drives me crazy. Underneath all that brass and bossiness, you're a temptress."

Charity's breathing became so ragged, she had to focus in order to hear him. "I'm—oh, God!"

The first slide of his tongue over her clit sent a jolt of erotic electricity through her slit that made her forget what she'd been about to say. She felt so wanton and free. Seeing the raw hunger he'd kept hidden from her, she'd never felt as desirable as she did in that moment.

Crying out, she lifted into his touch for more, even as the intensity of it had her trying to dig her heels into his back to push herself away.

With his shoulders beneath her thighs, Beau wrapped his arms around her hips, holding her high and firmly in place as his mouth worked its magic, the demand and hunger in his touch and low groans driving her insane.

Unable to remain still, she bucked and kicked her feet, thankful that his strong hold kept her firmly in place for the delicious torment. Gripping his forearms, she cried his name, her moans and cries mingling and becoming one tortured sound after another.

Humming his approval, he arched her hips higher and slid his tongue into her pussy, fucking her with it as he slid a hand lower to cover her abdomen and mound, his thumb stroking slowly back and forth over her clit.

The combination drove her wild and had her writhing beneath him, crying out her pleasure as she gripped the covers of his bed to ground herself. "Beau! Oh, God. So good. I'm gonna come."

Beau lifted his head slightly, readjusting his hold. With a hand over her belly, he held her still, staring up at her. Still using his shoulders to hold her hips high, he cupped her bottom with his other hand and slid a thumb into her pussy. "You're nice and wet, *mon petit. Doux.* Sweet. So sweet."

Charity kicked her feet as the need for friction on her clit became overwhelming. "Beau! Damn it, when you talk like that it makes me crazy."

Sliding his thumb slowly in and out of her pussy, he rose slightly. "Look at me, cher." He waited until she met his gaze, the slow strokes to her pussy never faltering. "That's it. Hmm, look at you. That glazed look in your eyes makes me just as crazy. It's the look you get when you're ready to come. Needy, helpless, and yet with a spark of attitude. It gets me every time."

Clenching on his thumb, Charity kicked at him and used the pressure of the backs of her knees on his shoulders for leverage to rock her hips. She wanted more. She wanted him to move, but even though his need for her shone clearly in his eyes, he continued to stare down at her, turning his head to brush his lips over her inner thigh while stroking her pussy.

The pressure inside her became so intense she bowed, thrashing her head from side to side in frustration. So close. The warning tingles started, simmering just below the surface and driving her wild. Her inhibitions had long since deserted her, and in the confines of the dimly lit room, she didn't feel the least bit shy about voicing her demands. "Beau. I need to come. Take me, damn you! I want you inside me."

Beau chuckled, a deep, throaty sound filled with satisfaction. "I'm not finished with my dessert yet." Raising a brow, he smiled, a dark, devious smile that sent a thrill of erotic anticipation racing through her.

Whimpering in frustration when he slid his thumb free, Charity struggled to sit up, crying out in shock when the tip of his thumb, wet with her juices, pressed against her puckered opening. "Beau!"

"I love the way you respond. Let's go a little farther, cher." He pushed into her bottom at the same time his lips closed over her clit.

The dual sensation stunned her so much that it took her several heart-stopping seconds before her mind could process the pleasure that had already taken over her body. The shower of sparks that radiated from her clit outward astounded her, as did the realization that her bottom clamped down on his finger, milking it as though trying to suck it in deeper.

"Dear God!" Her orgasm slammed into her so hard and fast, it took her mind several seconds to catch up. The slow slide of his devious tongue over her clit wouldn't let her down, holding her at the peak with an expertise that she couldn't fight.

She didn't want to fight it. She wanted it to last forever.

The hot tingling spread and rolled through her, wave after wave of delicious heat that held her in its grip as Beau continued to work his tongue over her clit and move his thumb inside her.

Paralyzed by the ecstatic pleasure, she had no choice but to endure it, and the swells of bliss rolling through her.

She cried out, but nothing emerged except a throaty gasp.

Every nerve ending in her body felt as if it shimmered, the warm swells of erotic pleasure seeming to consume her everywhere.

The intense pleasure made her body jerk once, and then again, as if touched by an electric cord.

"No!" Whimpering as the pleasure began to subside, she writhed on the covers, reaching for Beau as the stimulation of her clit became too sharp and more than she could bear. "No more. No more. Oh, Beau. Please, I can't take it." She couldn't stop clamping down on the thumb inside her, rocking her hips to take it deeper.

Tears stung her eyes. She wanted the warmth and steadiness of his arms around her. She wanted him to hold her. She wanted him inside her.

Beau seemed to know just what she needed. With a low murmur of approval, a rumble of caring that danced over her senses, he lifted his head and withdrew his thumb to gather her against him.

Her ass and pussy still clenched at the rippling waves of pleasure that just wouldn't stop. Trembling, she reached for him as he rose over her, gasping at the full, delicious feeling of his hard, hot cock thrusting deep inside her pussy.

He filled her completely, his steely, thick heat stretching her inner walls and warming her from within. Holding himself deep, he slid a hand under her bottom, and slid impossibly deeper while raining kisses over her cheek, her jaw, and even her now-healed shoulder.

Holding her to him, he murmured in French, the silky cadence of his words a sharp contrast to his harsh, deep, almost tortured tone.

So weak, and trembling so hard she could barely move, she finally managed to thread her fingers into his hair, moaning softly with each decadent stroke. Thrilling at the feel of solid muscles bunching and shifting against her, she lowered her hands to his shoulders, tilting her head to the side as he nuzzled her neck in a particularly sensitive spot.

Beau groaned, his teeth scraping over her neck. "Your pussy's so tight. So hot. So wet. Yes, cher, move with me. Yes. So fucking good. If I had my way, I'd spend the rest of my life inside you."

The hand at her bottom clenched tight, his finger moving with every thrust as he worked his way closer and closer to her bottom. "This tight little hole is begging for my attention, isn't it, cher? Now that I've touched you there, that tight little ass of yours wants more."

Charity's toes curled as Beau pressed against her puckered opening again, her whimpered cries growing louder. Her pussy clenched repeatedly on his cock, which seemed to get thicker and harder with every thrust.

Hard. Hot. Thick.

The pressure against her bottom hole drove her mad, the wicked threat of being breached there creating a primitive hunger that made her wild and wanton.

She didn't know how he knew that her bottom tingled with anticipation, but the fact that he did know both excited her and filled her with a sense of sexual vulnerability that had her gripping him even tighter. "Beau. I don't know how you make me feel like this, but with you, I want it all. It's so wicked."

"Yes, it is." Lifting his head to stare down at her, he slipped the tip of his finger past the tight ring of muscle and inside her. "Don't you want to be wicked with me?"

Digging her heels into his tight butt, she lifted into his thrusts, every muscle in her body tightening as the pleasure mounted. "God, yes!"

Having both her pussy and ass penetrated was a feeling unlike any other, and one that she found hard to adapt to.

She liked it far too much for her own peace of mind, becoming almost animalistic in her need to come. "Fuck me harder. Harder. More. Oh, God. I want more."

Beau groaned, his movements becoming rougher. "You want my finger deeper, cher? You want me to fuck your ass with my finger?"

"Yes, damn you!" She wanted it deep. "I want to feel it."

She rocked harder, fucking herself on his cock and finger, her cries becoming louder and more desperate with every stroke.

With a hand at her back, Beau lifted her higher. "Yes." His short breaths became harsher, his words guttural and deep. "Come. Yes. Clamp down on me. Give it to me."

Charity had no choice.

Trusting him implicitly, and loving him with every fiber of her being, she let herself go completely, clamping down on him and screaming his name.

* * * *

Her cry of completion was like music to Beau's ears.

Sitting back on his heels, he gathered her against him, holding his finger deep inside her ass, not willing to give up any part of her yet. Knowing how completely she lost herself when she came, he held her for several long minutes as his breathing slowed and his pulse went back to normal.

She excited him on so many levels, and each time he made love to her, she stole a little more of his heart.

Her own insecurities and inhibitions made her shy and unsure at first, but as soon as he took her past the point of no return, she let loose with a passion that never failed to astound and delight him.

God, he loved her, and each time he took her was better than the last.

He'd missed making love to her even more than he could have imagined, but now that she was fully healed from her accident, the need to play with his lover resurfaced.

Holding her close, he felt the shiver that went through her as she clenched on his cock and his finger again.

Almost immediately, she stiffened, and he knew it was out of embarrassment that he still had his finger inside her bottom.

If she thought she would get away with keeping any parts of herself from him, his darling bride-to-be had a lot yet to learn about him.

With slow deliberation, he moved his finger, stoking the inner walls of her bottom, hiding a smile when she moaned softly and instinctively clamped down on it.

Now that he'd calmed some, and could think, a plan formed in his mind, one that made his cock jump inside her, drawing another whimpered moan from her.

God, he adored her.

Ever since her accident, things had changed between them.

His need, stronger than it had ever been, now held a hint of desperation, a need to possess that had sharpened since her accident.

After having her again, he knew he'd never be happy with a life without laughter and playfulness in it.

He wanted to play again, but realized that it wouldn't be any good until Charity wanted it, too.

He needed her to see just how much more they could have—could *be* to each other.

He didn't want her to play just because she knew he wanted it. He wanted to teach her the joy they could have with each other, a joy she'd never allowed herself.

He'd wait until *she* made the first step.

And she would.

He didn't doubt it at all.

Her stubbornness would demand that he return to his former playfulness, but to do so, she'd have to initiate it.

Anticipation bubbled in his veins.

Hiding a smile, he leaned back slightly, kissing her cheek. "You okay, chéri?"

He had to bite the inside of his mouth to keep from smiling when she buried her face against his chest and refused to look up at him.

"Yes."

Fisting his free hand in her hair, he tilted her face back, his cock jumping at her blush.

Showing nothing but concern, he frowned down at her. "Is something wrong?"

Charity groaned, glaring up at him. "Beau, your finger…"

It took every ounce of willpower he possessed not to laugh. Narrowing his eyes, he moved his finger, sliding it almost all the way out of her and angled it to stretch the tight ring of muscle, his stomach clenching at the thought of how it would feel closing over his cock.

"My finger is in your ass, something that gave you a great deal of pleasure." Keeping a straight face, he forced it deep again, marveling at her shudder, and the glazed, unfocused look in her eyes.

Her bottom lip trembled, an invitation he couldn't ignore.

Taking her lips with his, he sank deep, keeping her hair fisted in his hand to hold her exactly the way he wanted.

Her soft lips opened immediately, her tongue tangling with his and drawing him deeper.

Taking control, he nipped at her lips and sank in again, his head spinning at the taste of her. The softness. The need for him that had her short nails sinking into his shoulders.

He moved his finger again, stroking her hot inner walls, his entire body tightening when she whimpered and began to rock. With a groan, he lifted his head, breaking off their kiss, holding her head in place to stare down at her.

"Like that, do you, cher?"

As he'd expected, Charity blinked and he could almost hear her inhibitions snap firmly back into place.

She looked up at him as though trying to judge his mood, which made it even harder to keep his expression stern. Sliding her soft hands over his chest, she looked up at him through her lashes—a look that he'd never been able to resist and almost promised she'd get whatever she asked for.

God help him when she figured *that* out.

"Beau?"

"Yes, cher?"

Not about to let her get the upper hand, he moved his finger again, stretching the tight ring of muscle, his cock stirring again at her soft, whimpered cry—a cry of passion and vulnerability—a sound that made his body clench with hunger for her.

It made his chest swell, and made his need to possess her even stronger. He wanted to pleasure her and comfort her at the same time—to simultaneously protect her and fuck her senseless.

She brought out his baser instincts, something he still struggled to understand, but that he embraced enthusiastically.

"I, um, oh, God."

Staring down at her, and moving his finger inside her, he knew he'd never seen anything as beautiful in his life as the way Charity looked at him now. With love and lust shining in her eyes, and a vulnerability caused by her own passions, she stared up at him for guidance, stoking his primitive instincts even higher.

"You're not scared now, are you?" Not wanting to miss anything—pleasure, or signs of distress—Beau kept her head pulled back to see her face.

"You've always been nervous and tightened up whenever I've tried to touch you here. When you relax and enjoy it, it feels good, doesn't it?"

Fisting her hands on his chest, Charity gulped, and tried to glare at him again, but her parted lips and the fact that her voice remained at a husky whisper, made her glare almost comical.

"I'm not like that."

Beau allowed a smile. "Oh, chéri, you're exactly like that. You're a passionate woman. There's no reason to be embarrassed." Sliding his cock free, he released her hair to touch her clit again. With her straddled on his lap, she couldn't close against him, allowing him free access to her clit and ass.

He didn't take it slow or easy, determined to prove to her without a doubt that she had desires that hadn't yet been tapped.

Using her slick juices to lubricate her sensitized clit, he worked his fingers over it with a speed designed to send her over quickly. At her stunned cry, he moved the finger in her ass just enough to keep her focused on it.

Gripping his shoulders, she threw her head back with a hoarse cry, her tight ass clamping down on his finger hard as she came.

He slowed his fingers, drenched with her juices, withdrawing the other from her ass. He dropped a kiss on her swollen pink lips as he rose from the bed and eased her down to the mattress. "That should be the end of any arguments on the subject."

Dropping her head on the pillow, Charity grinned. "You playing with me, Beau?"

Pausing beside the bed, he smiled at the picture she made. Her hair was a mess of tangles from his fingers, her lips swollen from his kisses. She had the look of a woman who'd been well and truly tumbled, and he was the only man on the face of the earth who'd ever seen her like this.

"No, cher." He let his smile fall, raising a brow when she opened her eyes and frowned. "I'm not playing with you. I'm just showing you the way it is."

Turning, he headed for the bathroom, pausing again when she called his name. He would swear he could almost hear her mind spinning. Turning, he raised a brow, careful not to show any sign of amusement. "Yes?"

"Why don't you want to play anymore?"

Taking a deep breath, he let it out slowly, ready with his answer. "After that foolish stunt you pulled by going out in a blizzard, protecting you seems more important."

Turning back, he headed for the bathroom, closing the door behind him before he allowed himself another smile.

That oughta do it.

Chapter Sixteen

"He's driving me crazy!"

In the small kitchen of her apartment, Charity reached into the dryer for another towel and straightened, folding it as she glanced back at her sister. "I think he's doing it on purpose. Then again, I just don't know."

Hope frowned as she dried a plate. "Okay, I don't understand. You went home with him last night and had sex. Was it awkward? Did he seem as if he wasn't into it? Didn't you like it?"

"No. No. No. Damn it." Reaching in for another towel, Charity shook her head, her frustration growing. "It was wonderful." Straightening, she leaned back against the small dryer. "He wouldn't make love to me until the doctor said that my shoulder and sternum were completely healed."

Hope frowned again. "And you went to the doctor yesterday, found out everything was healed, Beau took you out to dinner and then back to his place and had sex with you?"

"Exactly." Frustrated with herself, and with Beau, Charity folded the towel with movements so jerky, she almost dropped it. "Damn it."

"I'm sorry. I just don't get it. Was the sex bad?"

"It was incredible. He was so intense, and..." Blowing out a breath of frustration, Charity ran a hand through her hair. "Something's different. I told you what he told me about his reasons for being so playful. Now, he doesn't consider it as important as *protecting* me. I don't need protection. He says that after going out in a blizzard, I need someone to look after me. Damn it, Hope! I'm not a child, and I'm not stupid. I wouldn't have gone out in the damned thing if I'd known. The reason I hadn't watched the news was because I was busy. How was I supposed to know the damned thing would get here a day early?"

Leaning back against the counter, Hope grinned. "He's really got you ruffled, doesn't he? Good. You need a little ruffling."

"You're not helping."

Hope folded the towel she'd been using and set it aside. "I don't see the problem. You've got a gorgeous man madly in love with you, a man you also happen to love. You're getting married in a few weeks. The sex is great between you and you're perfect for each other." She ticked each item off on her fingers.

"Mom and the dads love him, and he makes you happy." Dropping her hand, Hope leaned forward. "I repeat—what is the fucking problem?"

Charity dropped the last towel into the basket. "I know it sounds crazy. Beau's wonderful." Raking a hand through her hair, she went to the table and dropped into a chair. "Before the accident, Beau was always playing. Teasing. Bringing toys into the bedroom. He hasn't done that since. He's loving, attentive, and so caring, but he doesn't play the way he used to. I mean, he plays, I guess. It's just not like before. Christ, I sound like an idiot."

"Have you asked him about it?"

"Of course. He says that since the accident, he's realized that it's more important to take care of me. I told you that." Unable to sit still, she jumped up again. "But, he explained to me why he liked to play. I told you about his grandparents' marriage. He wants to enjoy life and I'm afraid he's not doing something that's so important to him because of me."

Pacing back and forth in her small kitchen, Charity chewed on a thumbnail. "How can I just let that go?"

Hope sipped at her coffee. "Charity, you're such a worrier. I already told you that it would probably get better in time. You haven't had sex in weeks because of your injury, and you're all upset because the first time you make love with him, he didn't bring any toys. Jesus, did you use toys every time?"

Charity shrugged. "No, of course not. But, he always had this playfulness in bed."

"So last night he was boring?"

Her bottom still tingled from his attention there, and after coming three times in rapid succession, she'd come again when he'd taken her once more before driving her home. She couldn't stop thinking about the look in his eyes as he'd stared down at her newly waxed pussy.

She couldn't stop thinking about the way he touched her, a firm gentleness that seemed far more intense than it ever had before.

The way he held her.

The look in his eyes as he entered her.

Pausing, she glanced at her sister. "No. Beau's never boring."

He made her heart race with just a look.

Hope got to her feet and reached for her coat. "I think, as always, you're thinking into this too much. Give Beau some time." She shrugged on her coat and came forward, touching Charity's arm. "Ace said that your accident really shook Beau. He said Beau used to just sit there and stare at you while you slept, because every time he went to sleep, he had nightmares that he couldn't find you. Beau blames himself for your accident."

Charity blinked. "That's ridiculous. He didn't force me to drive to the carpet store."

"No, but he didn't stop you."

Charity gaped at her sister. "Do you hear yourself?" Shaking her head, she sat back at the table. "Ace must have spanked the spunk right out of you."

"Wait a minute! I'm trying to help you and you insult me?" Hope plopped into the chair across from her. "You grew up in this town. You know damned well how the men are. If Beau considered you his and you got hurt, he would blame himself." Getting to her feet again, she grabbed her small purse and grinned at Charity over her shoulder.

"You're damned lucky he didn't turn you over his knee and paddle your ass. I know that's what Ace would have done to me."

Swinging the door open, Hope paused. "Just for the record, when my husband spanks me, it doesn't make me meek. It riles me up and makes me horny. If you had a man who spanked you, you'd know that." After sticking her tongue out at her sister, she went out the door, closing it behind her.

Shaking her head, Charity laughed softly and got to her feet with the intention of going down to the diner for lunch. Shocked when the door opened again, she spun toward it, surprised to see Hope poking her head through.

"Forget something?"

Hope frowned. "Yeah. How the hell did Beau get you to play?"

Charity had to think about it. "I don't know. I didn't really have a choice. He just pulled out the toys and we played."

Hope grinned. "There you go. Just play. I know a great place where you can buy some toys. Beau won't be able to resist."

* * * *

Two nights later, Charity thought about her sister's advice as she made her way to Beau's house. She'd thought about it several times since then, and the more she thought about it, the more she realized her sister was right.

If she played, Beau would have no choice but to join in.

He'd been out of town all day, checking out his warehouse, so Charity had decided to surprise him with dinner. She'd picked up some groceries and drove her new compact to his house with the intention of letting herself in with the key he'd given her, and making the fried chicken she knew he liked.

After a long drive, and being out all day, she figured he'd appreciate spending an evening at home with his feet up.

She just wanted to see him.

She hadn't seen or heard from him since they'd had dinner together in her apartment with Hope and Ace the night before.

She couldn't believe how much she missed him.

It gave her an inordinate amount of pleasure to use his key for the first time. Pausing at the threshold, she paused, inhaling deeply, smiling when she caught the lingering scent of him.

After unpacking the groceries, she checked out the contents of his cabinets, struck by the realization that although she'd been here many times, she didn't know where he kept anything. Finding the plates and glasses, she set the table, and then went in search of the pans she'd need to cook dinner.

She frowned at the limited supply, and at the fact that he didn't seem to have a salad bowl. Thankful that she'd brought the spices and staples she needed, she began to reorganize to make a convenient place for them.

Her cell phone rang just as she'd put the potatoes on to boil. Her heart raced as she rushed to answer it. "Hello?"

"Hey, cher. I'm on my way home."

Charity grinned, a rush of desire warming her at the sound of Beau's voice. "That's good news. How did it go?" Frowning to realize she didn't even know what he'd gone to do, she leaned back against the counter.

"It went fine. Better than I expected. I had to fire a manager for stealing, and hired two more, and seven more employees. Business is picking up, and they were having trouble keeping up."

Charity blinked. "The online business is doing that well?"

Beau's soft chuckle sent another rush of warmth through her, this one making her nipples bead, and awakening a surge of awareness in her clit. "In case you haven't heard, Charity, sex sells."

Tracing a finger over the cold granite, Charity smiled, lowering her voice to a whisper. "What else does sex do, darling?" She had to slap a hand over her mouth to hold back a giggle at the stunned silence that followed.

When Beau finally spoke, his low, silky tone caused a flutter in her stomach, one that had her shifting restlessly in her seat. "Are you flirting with me, cher?"

Charity couldn't hold back a giggle. "If you have to ask, I'm obviously not doing it right."

"You're doing it just fine."

Trembling, Charity drew in a shaky breath, more nervous than she would have expected to be. "Did you bring any toys home with you?"

After another pregnant pause, Beau sighed. "No, cher. We don't need toys. Look, when I get back home, I'll get showered and changed and I'll come get you. I won't be home for another hour or so, though. If you're hungry, don't wait for me. Eat a little something and I'll take you out to dinner when I get back. Did you eat anything today?"

Frowning, Charity straightened. "Beau, I'm not a child. Of course I ate. There's no need to pick me up. I'm at your house."

"You are?"

Taken aback at the surprise in his voice, she realized that she'd never come over to surprise him like this before. She'd had the key for months, but hadn't used it.

"That's okay, isn't it?"

"It's great, Charity. I gave you the key to use."

Too restless to stay still, she made her way to the living room. "I figured that after being gone all day and the long drive, you would rather sit back with your feet up tonight. I'm making fried chicken for dinner."

"Sounds great. Are you sure it's not going to be too much trouble? I know you've been working at the club all day. I don't want you to overdo it."

Charity sighed. "Beau, ever since my accident, you've treated me as if I might break. Please stop it. I'm tough. I'm fine. Stop babying me and treat me like an adult."

"I'm fully aware of the fact that you're an adult, Charity." His cold tone sent a chill up her spine. "You're all woman, a fact that gives me a great deal of pleasure, and at times scares the hell out of me. You're delightfully feminine, but you're also small and fragile. It's up to me to protect you, and I don't take my responsibility lightly. I'm running into some traffic, so I'm going to get off the phone. I'll see you as soon as I can get there."

Not wanting to distract him from his driving, Charity had no choice but to let it go. "Okay. Drive safely."

"I will. Just stay put. I don't want you driving home at night, and I'm very much looking forward to that chicken."

When he disconnected, Charity got to her feet again with the intention of starting dinner, stilling when she heard a knock at the front door. Wondering who it could be, Charity moved to the large front window to look out, smiling when she saw Ace's SUV parked behind her car in the driveway.

With a smile, she flung her door open. "So, Sheriff, you like my new car?"

Ace grinned. "I thought it had to be you, but I ran the plates anyway. What are you doing here?"

Charity stepped back, opening the door wider and walking back to the kitchen, knowing Ace would follow her. "Beau had to go to the warehouse today, and I thought I'd have a nice dinner waiting for him." She glanced over at Ace as he took a seat at the table, opening the cabinet where she'd found the coffee cups earlier.

Pouring him a cup, she glanced at him, once again shocked by how small a room looked when he was in it. "I figured he'd be tired and wouldn't feel like going out."

Accepting the cup of coffee with a smile of thanks, Ace settled back in his chair, appearing to relax, but Charity knew Desire's sheriff seldom relaxed, especially when on duty.

"They say the way to a man's heart is through his stomach."

Amused, Charity started making a salad, using a large pot to put it together. "Hope doesn't cook. She's terrible at it." Washing the lettuce, she turned to smile at Ace.

Although his expression never changed, his eyes glimmered with amusement. "Let's just say that your sister found a shortcut, and leave it at that."

She finished washing the lettuce and began to work on the tomatoes. "Hope is madly in love with you. She loves as fiercely as she does everything else."

Ace inclined his head, his lips twitching. "She does, and I love her just as fiercely." He took another sip of his coffee, his pose relaxed. "Beau loves you, too."

Charity shrugged. "I know." Working on the vegetable, she glanced at Ace again, getting a strange feeling in the pit of her stomach. "You didn't just happen to stop by. What's Hope up to now? She must have sent you over for something."

Ace shrugged, his deceptively mild expression not fooling her for an instant. "Nothing. She just worries about you."

"Well, there's nothing to worry about."

Ace inclined his head. "I'm glad to hear it."

Knowing his sharp gaze missed nothing, Charity struggled not to show any sign of nerves, at the same time wondering why the conversation even made her nervous. "Hope makes too much of things."

"She does get wound up at times."

Chopping the cucumber with more force than necessary, Charity glanced at Ace again. "I told her about something that was bothering me. She acts like it's nothing, and then she sends you to grill me about it."

Ace took another sip of coffee. "Yeah, your sister has a lot of brass."

"She probably figured that since she's the same as Beau, that I'm the one who's in the wrong."

"Could be."

"They play around all the time—at least Beau used to. You and I are the serious ones."

"That's true."

Charity threw the cucumbers into the pot with the other vegetables. "I'll bet she thought you would tell me that I made a big deal out of nothing, and that it's *my* fault that Beau doesn't want to play anymore."

"She'd be wrong."

"I ruined him." Charity threw the knife into the sink and slumped against the counter. "It *is* all my fault."

"Takes two to tango."

Charity blinked back tears, her stomach knotting. "I criticized him over and over for not taking things seriously, and it was just because I thought he was playing with *me*. I didn't think a man like Beau could ever be really interested in a woman as plain and ordinary as I am."

"If that were true, he never would have touched you—a woman who didn't know the score."

"Hell, Hope's always telling me that I'm no fun."

"She tells me the same thing."

Straightening, Charity wiped the water from the counter. "I was wrong. Beau loves me, but I've made him into something he isn't. He's never going to be happy like this." The thought of it scared the hell out of her.

Ace got up and helped himself to another cup of coffee. "Charity, Beau is—"

"Hope's right. It could be just because of the accident. I'll give it some more time. If things don't change, I already have a plan. I'll just do that."

"It sounds like you've got everything figured out." Taking a sip of his coffee, Ace moved back to the table.

Nodding, she opened the refrigerator to put the salad inside and grabbed the chicken. "I know. You're right. I probably shouldn't wait too long. The longer it goes on, the more likely that it'll be permanent."

Ace's lips twitched. "And you're too impatient to wait for anything. That's something you and your sister have in common, but you're always trying to fix things."

She unwrapped the chicken pieces, her movements jerky. "What am I supposed to do? Just let it go on this way forever. It's driving me crazy!"

"I see that it is."

"Well, I can handle it myself. I appreciate that you cared enough to come over here, but I can handle it on my own."

Ace's lips twitched. "I have no doubt."

She washed her hands and began dumping flour and spices into a plastic bag, her movements automatic. She measured everything by eye, having done it too many times to count.

She dried the pieces of chicken, one by one, the repetition of it calming her and settling some of her nerves. Aware of Ace's watchful gaze, and admiring his patience, she glanced at him as she reached back into the refrigerator for the buttermilk. "Did you ever think Hope was playing games with you?"

"Yes."

Charity blinked and turned to him, still patting a chicken leg dry with a paper towel. "Really?"

Ace smiled. "Really. That's what took us so long to get together. I thought it was all a game to her."

"But you loved her." She began coating the chicken, the action so familiar, she didn't even have to think about it.

Ace shrugged. "Thought for sure she was going to break my heart." He eyed her meaningfully. "Scary as hell, isn't it?"

Charity checked the flame under the pan she'd readied for frying. Straightening, she glanced at him again as she began to transfer the chicken she'd coated into the frying pan.

"Yeah. I tried my best to keep my distance, but I didn't have much luck with that."

"I know how that feels. They're a pain in the ass, but they're worth it."

"I resent that."

Charity gasped, spinning at the sound of Beau's deep voice coming from just inside the kitchen. "You're back!"

Dropping the plate back onto the counter, she ran to Beau, jumping as she reached him, secure in the knowledge that he would catch her.

He did. Holding her close and dropping a kiss on her lips as he turned to Ace, who'd stood and had started for the door. "You don't have to go. Stay and eat with us."

Beau met her gaze again, the look in his eyes holding a promise for later. "I'm sure there's plenty."

Charity smiled, reaching up to kiss his jaw as he lowered her to her feet. "Absolutely." She turned to Ace. "You have your cell phone with you and you have to eat anyway. It might as well be here. You like my fried chicken."

Shaking hands with Beau, Ace took his seat again. "Don't tell your mother or fathers, but yours is better. It drives your sister crazy."

Giggling, Charity turned back to check on her chicken and to get another place setting for Ace. "Good to know." She could use it against her sister when the opportunity arose.

Charity enjoyed watching the camaraderie between Ace and Beau as they ate their dinner, ogling Beau every chance she got.

She couldn't stop looking at his hands, and couldn't help thinking about how well they knew their way around her body.

His shirt pulled taut over his shoulders and biceps as he reached for another piece of chicken, outlining the hard muscle she couldn't wait to sink her finger into again. His dark eyes narrowed as he turned to her, the heat in them banked, but still visible. "You're not eating."

Charity took another bite of mashed potatoes. "Stop nagging."

Beau's eyes narrowed even more, promising retribution, before he turned back to his meal, and his conversation with Ace, a conversation that had shifted to the man who'd been stealing from Beau.

Ace frowned. "I don't see why the hell you won't press charges."

Beau paused with a forkful of mashed potatoes halfway to his mouth. "Because his wife is pregnant, and if I press charges, she won't have anyone to support her. I'd already given him a second chance. If not for her, he wouldn't even have had that."

Beau and Ace talked about Beau's business and the new employees, and it struck Charity that Ace knew more about Beau's business than she did.

She also realized that Beau had a soft spot for women in distress.

He worried about his employee's wife so much that he'd kept him on so he could provide for his wife. He'd worried about Anna and had rushed to take care of her.

Ever since her accident, he'd been loving and gentle, and hadn't played like he had before.

He also felt guilty about the accident.

Charity's stomach clenched. She didn't want Beau because he thought she was weak and needed to be taken care of. She wanted him to see her as strong and capable.

It appeared she'd have to prove to him that she wasn't one of the needy women he felt compelled to take care of. She needed him to see her as an equal.

After a few more minutes, Ace wiped his mouth and pushed back from the table. "I appreciate the meal and the company, but I've got to get back—"

His cell phone rang, interrupting him. Ace was already on his feet when he answered. "Tyler."

Beau turned to Charity and touched her arm. "You have a good day, cher?"

"I missed you." Charity squeezed his hand. "You look tired."

"I'm fine."

Ace sighed, rubbing his jaw. "I'm on my way. For God's sake, don't let them kill anyone." Disconnecting, he started for the door. "Bar fight. Thanks again."

Beau shot to his feet. "You need help?"

Ace shrugged on his coat and grabbed his hat, his face set in grim lines. "No, thanks. Hunter and Remington are at it. Again. Christ, those two get riled up at the drop of a hat lately."

Standing at the door with Beau's arm around her shoulders, Charity watched Ace shoot out of the driveway, his tires squealing as he left.

Beau sighed and pulled Charity back inside. "Come on in out of the cold and finish your dinner."

"I'm done." Charity began collecting her plate and Ace's, watching Beau as he bit into another piece of chicken. "What's all that about Hunter and Remington?"

Beau finished chewing before answering. "They're getting out of hand. I think the number of marriages in town are depressing them. They want their own woman, but neither one will admit it. They both feel that they'd only end up hurting her and won't let themselves get involved with anyone except the woman at the club only looking for a good time."

Charity dropped to the seat Ace had just recently vacated. "That's ridiculous. They'd make great husbands."

Beau shrugged. "You know how they are. After their father killed their mother, they're both afraid they're just like him. They won't take a chance. They won't even have sex with another woman unless it's in the club in full view of everyone. They know someone would rush in to stop them if they hurt her."

Shocked, Charity got to her feet. "Neither one of them would ever hurt a woman."

Beau nodded. "I know that. You know that. Hell, everyone in town knows that—except for Hunter and Remington. They're just going to have to figure it out for themselves."

"I hope they find someone." Charity took the dishes to the sink. "I can't bear to see them spend the rest of their lives alone for something they didn't do. It's so sad."

"It is." Beau finished and pushed back his plate. "Come here."

Charity went to him, smiling as he turned his chair and patted his lap. Dropping on to it, she threaded her fingers into his hair. "You know, it occurred to me while you were talking to Ace, that he knows more about your business than I do."

Bending his head, Beau nibbled at her lips. "We had other things on our minds. Right now, I'm more interested in getting you out of these clothes than I am in talking about my business."

He slid his hand inside her sweater, unclasping the front closure of her bra with an expertise and speed that made her gasp. Closing his hand over her breast, he brushed his lips over hers, swallowing her moan. "I want you naked and under me. Now."

Charity arched, pressing her breast more firmly against his palm, the friction and warm feel of his hand on her breast sending delicious sizzles of excitement through her.

Lifting the edges of her sweater, he bared her breasts. Adjusting her to lean back over his arm, he stared down at them, running his finger lightly back and forth over her nipple as he watched her face. "I've been thinking about this all day."

Beau's phone rang, shattering the erotically charged atmosphere.

With a curse, he wrapped his hands around her waist and stood, dropping a kiss on her forehead as he set her on her feet. "I'm sorry, cher."

Retrieving his phone from the countertop, he frowned as he looked down at the display. Clenching his jaw, he answered. "Hello?"

Pulling her sweater back down to cover herself, Charity frowned at his cold tone.

"No, Anna. I'm not coming over. You and Jeffrey are going to have to work things out for yourself." With a small smile, Beau snaked an arm around Charity's waist and pulled her against him. "No, Anna. Yes, Charity and I are really getting married."

Smiling at the warmth in his gaze, Charity snuggled closer, relieved that he no longer considered Anna his responsibility.

Using his shoulder to hold the phone to his ear, he lifted Charity's sweater again, running his hands over her breasts as he stared into her eyes. "Of course I love her. Good-bye, Anna."

He hung up and tossed the phone back to the countertop. "Now, where were we?"

Chapter Seventeen

Naked and sprawled on Beau's bed, Charity watched him undress in the waning light, her pussy clenching in anticipation.

She saw him bend, and heard the drawer of his nightstand open and close. Her entire body flushed with need as the bed dipped and she felt the warmth of his body against hers.

"Beau."

She breathed his name on a sigh as his hand slid over her breast, sucking in a sharp breath when his fingers closed over her nipple.

"Come here." He didn't wait for her to move, picking her up, flipping her to her belly, and positioning her on all fours with a speed that made her dizzy. With a hand in her hair, he turned her face toward him, the head of his cock pressing against her cheek.

Opening her mouth, she shivered with delight, and took his cock into it eagerly, the hard, thick length of it forcing her to open her mouth wide to accommodate him.

Delighted at his aggressiveness, and his obvious hunger, Charity began to suck him, hoping she was doing it right.

Holding her head, Beau began to move, fucking her mouth with short, shallow strokes. "I've been thinking about this all day. Fucking this hot mouth. You don't want me to baby you. Isn't that what you said?"

Charity nodded, her mouth too full to speak as she fought to please him. Her nipples beaded tight and began to tingle, moisture running down her inner thigh, her entire body trembling at Beau's sexual arrogance.

The firmness in his touch and his demeanor thrilled her as he drew her deeper into an erotic world of sexuality she'd only begun to explore.

Fisting his hand in her hair, he held her steady for his slow thrusts, while reaching under her to caress her breast. "You think I don't consider you all woman when you're in my bed?"

Charity gasped, losing her concentration when he rolled her nipple between his thumb and forefinger, the pressure sending a jolt of heat from her nipple to her slit.

Beau had never spoken this way to her before. He'd never touched her with such firm intent.

She loved it.

He tightened the hand in her hair, the tension in his voice more prominent with every word. "You know now that I'm serious in the way I feel about you. You were right. I should never have brought toys to the bedroom. I should have just taken you this way before, but I was too afraid of scaring you. I want you too much sometimes to be easy with you."

Charity moaned around his cock, rocking her hips as the heat and awareness there became unbearable. She tried to pull her mouth away to answer, but Beau tightened his grip on her hair and thrust again, keeping her mouth too full to speak.

"No. I think you've said enough." His voice held a silky decadence that sent a thrill of delight through her, one that danced over her skin and heightened the awareness in every erogenous zone. "Everyone knows about us now, Charity. Everyone knows you're mine. You want me to stop babying you. You won't be babied tonight, cher. You want to know how much I want you? After tonight, there should be no doubt that I'm not playing games."

Beau's hand left her hair and breast, as he slowly withdrew with a groan. "Damn, that mouth feels good."

Charity fisted her hands in the pillows as he moved in behind her, another rush of moisture escaping at the feel of his hard thighs touching the backs of hers.

His hands closed around her waist as he used his knees to push hers apart. "I've been thinking about this all day."

She heard the rip of foil, gasping at the feel of his cock brushing against her ass as he rolled on a condom. "So have I. Beau, I don't mind the toys. I like them."

Beau chuckled softly, a low rumbling sound that made her clit tingle. "I was in the warehouse checking out all the new toys and thinking about you." With one swift thrust, he plunged into her. "But playing that way gave you the wrong idea. We don't need toys, do we, cher? It feels so good without them."

Charity cried out at the pleasure, gripping the headboard to push back against him. "Yes. Oh, Beau, that feels so good."

His hands tightened on her waist as he thrust harder. "Yes, it does. There's nothing like having my cock inside you. Warm. Tight. Gripping me."

When he moved his left hand, sliding it back to her hip, Charity's puckered opening tingled with anticipation, but he only got a firmer grip. Slipping his other hand lower, he parted her folds and delved between them with a firm possessiveness that left her reeling.

Charity's hoarse cry filled the room at the first touch of Beau's fingers against her clit. "Beau, oh, God!"

His forceful thrusts and the slide of his fingers over her swollen and needy clit sent her soaring. "No. Too soon. Damn it. Ahhh!"

The rush of pleasure stunned her, but she didn't seem to have any defenses against him.

When Beau wanted to send her over, he did, and when he wanted to drag it out, he did, and there didn't seem to be anything she could do about it.

Her body hummed with delicious pleasure, her pussy gripping his cock as her orgasm washed over her.

Beau thrust deep, his hand tightening on her hip as his cock pulsed inside her. "Too good to wait. Next time." He groaned, slowing his fingers on her clit. "Next time we'll go slower."

Still trembling, Charity struggled to catch her breath, moaning when Beau slowly withdrew. Her pussy clenched as if trying to hold him inside, drawing another low chuckle from Beau.

"My cock will be back inside you again real soon, cher." Wrapping a strong forearm around her waist, he lifted her against him and into his arms. "Time for a shower."

Once in the shower, Beau pulled her back against him, his hold demanding, and began nuzzling her neck. "I want your ass."

Charity shivered, the feel of his cock pressing against lower back reigniting her passion. Struck by the forcefulness in his growled tone, she couldn't help rubbing against him. "Beau, I don't know how to."

"I'll show you." His hands came around to cup her breasts, his fingers teasing her nipples. "I don't want to hurt you, though. Will you trust me?"

"Yes." She didn't have any choice. She loved and wanted him too badly not to.

He released her only long enough to fill his hand with bodywash, and began to wash her, starting with her breasts. Teasing her slippery nipples, he scraped his teeth over her neck. "I would have used butt plugs to stretch you, but since we're not using toys, I'm going to have to use my fingers."

Charity moaned, her ass clenching in response. "Hope told me about anal sex. She told me that dominant men demanded it. You're not like that. Why do you want to take me there?"

Beau slid a hand upward, holding her by the neck and jaw and pressing her head back against him, while the other hand slid lower to rub her clit. "Because it's going to feel fantastic. Because I want to take your virginity there the same way I took your virginity in your pussy. Because I want you to realize that all of you belongs to me. Because it's going to be so hot, so fucking tight."

He thrust a finger into her pussy and began to fuck her with it, raising his voice to be heard above her moans. "And because I want to start as I mean to continue. I don't want you to have any insecurities about how much I want you, how much I need you, how much I love you. I don't want anything to keep us from exploring our limits."

"Oh, God." She knew his reputation, and had already experienced his erotic brand of lovemaking, but now realized that she'd only begun to scratch the surface layers of Beau's desires.

Parting her thighs wider, she clenched on his finger, crying out when he used a thumb to manipulate her clit. "How much more can there be?"

She wanted to explore all of them.

The warm water spraying over her made it impossible to open her eyes, keeping her in a dark world that seemed even more erotic.

Beau's throaty chuckle sent a shiver of fear up her spine, one of the unknown, and that sent her senses soaring. "There's a lot more, cher. There's a lot more that I want to explore with you. No matter what we do, no matter what I do to you, I want you to remember that you're the most important thing in the world to me. I love you, Charity, more than I ever thought it was possible to love a woman. Everything I do to you is done with love."

The combination of his words and his hand at her slit sent her soaring. She came hard, gripping his forearms as her knees weakened. Trembling at the sharp burst of pleasure radiating from her clit and pussy, Charity screamed his name, jolting as he continued to fuck her with his finger. "Beau. Oh, God. Oh, God."

He stroked her through her orgasm, touching his lips to her ear. "So passionate. So hot. So sweet."

Stunned at how quickly she'd come, Charity struggled to hold on to his slippery arm, moaning again when the firm hand at her slit slid up to her waist and flattened, plastering her against him.

"Damn it, Beau. You don't even give me time to catch my breath."

She wanted to give him the kind of pleasure he gave her, but as soon as he touched her, she fell apart in his arms.

Cupping her breast, he tightened his arm around her waist to steady her. "You don't need to play, cher. One touch and you go up in flames. Very sexy. Makes me want to keep touching you. Makes me curious to see how many times I can make you come."

Instead of tickling her and playing in the shower as he'd done in the past, Beau washed her with slow, deliberate intent, making every inch of her skin tingle with heightened awareness.

Weak and trembling, she laid her hands on his chest, finding it hard to believe that just by washing her, he'd managed to arouse her again. "You'd kill me."

Sucking in a breath, she blinked against the spray. "Now I want to get my hands on you."

Beau held out his arms, his slow, wicked smile stealing her breath. "Help yourself, cher."

The chance to explore the gorgeous masculinity in front of her excited Charity even more. Nervous, but eager to touch her lover and give him pleasure, Charity smiled playfully and reached for the bottle of bodywash.

Hoping she didn't make a fool of herself, she poured some of the soap in her hand and set out to seduce him.

Avoiding his gaze, she rubbed her hands together to warm the soap the way he'd done with her before flattening them on his wet upper chest. Marveling at the texture, the softness of his skin layered over the hard muscle underneath, Charity blinked against the spray and slid her hands up to his shoulders.

Using her thumbs to trace his collarbone, she slid her hands lower again, using her fingertips to press into the muscle of his shoulders and upper arms, the soap and the water making it easy to slide her hands over him.

All thoughts of playing fled as she slid her hands over the sleek muscle of his biceps and forearms. Fascinated by the bunch and shift of muscle under her hands, she moved her hands back up his arms, pausing to press her fingertips into the hard muscle as she worked her way back to his chest.

The heat inside her continued to build as she explored his leanly muscled physique, her body so sensitized that even the spray of the shower had her shifting restlessly.

Her hands began to tremble as they moved over him, the sharp difference in their bodies so intriguing, she wondered why she hadn't had the courage to do this before.

She had the chance to explore, and didn't want to miss anything.

* * * *

Beau gritted his teeth, his body tightening under Charity's soft exploring hands.

Her smile had fallen almost as soon as she'd touched him, her expression becoming one of desire and fascination as she slid her hands over his body.

He didn't know if he'd survive it.

His cock stirred to life as her hands moved lower, his stomach muscles quivering beneath her touch. He fisted his hands at his sides to keep from reaching for her, the need to yank her against him almost more than he could stand.

For a woman who didn't know how to play, she was driving him out of his mind.

He realized a moment later, that she wasn't playing at all.

She just wanted to touch him.

He swallowed a groan when she bit her lip, the need to take her mouth with his making his own lips tingle. With another rush of pleasure, his cock twitched, the head of it brushing against her soft belly.

A soft groan escaped, and he had to fist his hands tighter when she glanced up at him through her lashes, her eyes dark with hunger and fascination, the silent question in them making his cock throb as a bead of moisture escaped.

"Be my guest."

His voice sounded harsh and ragged to his own ears, even though he'd kept it low so as not to startle her.

Bracing himself for her touch, he lifted his hands, holding on to the wall and the top of the frame for the shower door as the need to reach for her became unbearable.

Fascinated by the beads of water that ran down her body, the drops that teased him by clinging to the tips of her nipples, Beau held his breath as Charity flattened her hand beneath his cock and lifted it to brush as lightly as butterfly wings along the underside.

Drawing in a sharp breath, he threw his head back at the jolt of sharp pleasure that shot through him, inwardly cursing when she jerked her hand away.

"Did I hurt you?"

Beau gritted his teeth and fought to breathe. "You're killing me." Glancing down at her, he forced a smile, his head spinning with the thought of bending her over and fucking her hard and deep. "Don't stop."

Charity had always been too inhibited to touch him very often, and he'd hoped that eventually, she would loosen up.

It appeared his patience had begun to pay off.

God help him when she realized the effect she had on him.

To his delight, she smiled, a smile that held a small amount of smugness as she reached for him again.

"I like touching you this way." She wrapped her hand around his cock, her light squeezing driving Beau insane. "My fingers don't even touch."

She squeezed again and every muscle in Beau's body tightened in reaction. "It's hard to believe this fits inside me. No wonder it feels as if it goes all the way to my stomach."

Beau couldn't stand much more. His control had never been so shaken. He had to swallow heavily before speaking, his throat too tight to talk. "It's snug when I fuck you. It's going to be even tighter when I work it into your tight ass."

Because he'd watched for it, he saw her buttocks clench in response to his words.

Good. If he was going down, he was taking her with him.

Knowing how well his lover responded to mental stimulation, Beau continued to speak, despite the effort it cost him. The more she aroused him, the more guttural his speech, but at this point, he didn't care.

"Little by little, I'll work my cock into you. Your tight ass is going to have to stretch. It's going to sting at first, and then it's going to burn. Still, you'll want more." His cock jumped again in her hands, the light pressure from her grip adding to his fantasy.

Unable to stand not touching her any longer, he reached for her breasts, cupping them as he ran his thumbs over her pebbled nipples.

He almost swallowed his tongue when she reached under him to cup his sac. Not about to be outdone, he pinched her nipples, careful to keep his touch light. "And it's gonna be so tight, I'll feel like I'm dying."

Charity threw her head back, arching her back and giving him better access. Her nipples were so sensitive that he always made sure to be careful, increasing the pressure a little here and there to see how she reacted.

Her passion astounded him.

He groaned in frustration when she released him, another groan escaping when she poured more of the soap in her hand. Beau hissed when she wrapped her hand around him again, this time without warming the soap.

"You keep it up, cher, and I'm gonna come in your hand."

To his surprised delight, Charity smiled up at him and began to move her hand on his cock, the soap making it an easy slide from the base of his cock to the head and back again. "I'd like that."

Her slow caress threatened his sanity, his thighs shaking when she reached under him to cup his sac, her other hand moving faster. "I want to make you come. I want you to feel the way I feel when you touch me."

"You're driving me crazy." Beau groaned, his balls tightening.

"Good. I'll have to do it more often. Come for me."

Her soft whispered plea and the slide of her hand on his cock proved to be his undoing.

With a low groan, he came, a strong surge of pleasure that seemed to come from his soul, his cock pulsing and shooting his seed to splash on her stomach. "Slow down, cher. Slow down. Yes. That's it. Nice and easy." Trembling, he fought to keep his voice low and even, but it came out much harsher than he'd meant it to.

Covering her hand with his, he stroked his cock a few more times before pulling her hands away and gathering her close. His legs shook, and he found he had to brace himself with a hand flattened against the tile wall as he held her with the other.

"Um, Beau."

Running a hand up and down her back to her bottom, which kept clenching under his palm, he smiled into her wet hair.

"Yes, cher."

"Did you mean it when you said that you had to stretch my ass, or were you just teasing me?"

Dropping an openmouthed kiss on her shoulder, Beau squeezed the firm cheek of her soft, wet bottom. "No, I wasn't teasing you. I'm going to have to stretch you a little before I take you there. It's not something you can just jump into. I've got to get you ready."

"Tonight?"

Beau wanted to say yes, but decided that letting the anticipation build might be better for her. When he took her ass, he wanted her to want it so much that she wouldn't tighten up in fear.

"No. Not tonight."

She stiffened in his arms, and then slumped, her disappointment apparent. "Oh."

Beau bit the inside of his mouth to keep from laughing. Schooling his features, he straightened. "Be patient, cher. I don't want to hurt you. The next time you come over, you can drape yourself over my lap and let me start to pl—stretch you."

He hoped she didn't catch his slip. He wanted to make it clear to her that playing was off the table.

At least until she talked him into it.

She'd made a good start tonight, but he knew his impatient bride-to-be wouldn't be happy until they played again.

Knowing Charity, it would be soon. Very soon.

He'd make her wait just a little while longer, and see how far he could push her into playing.

If she went into it with the same determination with which she did everything else, he had a feeling he might be in big trouble.

Keeping his expression cool, he ran a hand over her hair. "Easy, cher. You're not ready yet."

He hugged her again, hiding his smile of anticipation when she stiffened. "Shh, baby. Be patient."

Patience was not Charity's strong suit.

He was counting on it.

Chapter Eighteen

"I've been thinking about that tight ass all day."

Charity's buttocks clenched in anticipation at Beau's admission. She slid a glance at him as they walked up the sidewalk to his house. "Sometimes, I can't believe what comes out of your mouth." It never ceased to amaze her that he could arouse her with words. With just a look.

They'd just returned from a steak restaurant out of town, and she knew that within a matter of minutes, they would both be naked. The thought of what he planned to do to her tonight had consumed her imagination all day, keeping her aroused and needy as she worked in the club.

Beau's hand slid to her bottom as he unlocked the door, as if to remind her about his intentions. "There's no need to be nervous. If you're that upset, it can wait."

Charity stepped into the foyer and turned to look at him. "It can wait? I thought you wanted—"

A dark brow went up. "Your ass. Oh, yes. Very much."

Walking into the living room, she heard Beau close and lock the door behind them. "It doesn't seem like it." Hating her petulant tone, she looked up at Beau as he dropped his keys onto the table and shrugged out of his coat.

Beau frowned. "What do you mean by that? I've told you and shown you often enough how much I want you."

Charity sighed. "I know." She forced a smile, frustrated that every time she voiced her concerns, it sounded silly. "I just want to make sure you're having fun."

"Fun?" Beau frowned, looking at her as if she'd lost her mind. "Nothing gives me more pleasure than being with you."

Charity eyed him suspiciously, something about his tone not quite right. Before she had a chance to get a good look at his expression, he moved behind her and removed her coat. "Take your boots off. I'll be right back."

Watching his tight, denim-covered butt as he walked down the hallway, she dropped into a nearby chair and began to remove her boots.

She'd just finished when Beau walked back into the room, carrying a tube.

He didn't stop until he reached her, something in his eyes arousing her suspicions, but she couldn't quite put her finger on it. "Ready?"

Charity's bottom clenched, her gaze going to the tube, the rush of pure lust striking her hard and fast and making her dizzy. "Ready for what?"

* * * *

Beau hid a smile. Normally, he would have looked forward to chasing her, and would have her giggling before he stripped her out of her clothes.

Instead, he remained serious, forcing her to contribute to her own seduction, curious to see how far she'd go.

"You know what, Charity. We're going to start stretching your ass and getting you accustomed to my touch there. Have you changed your mind?"

Her eyes flashed and he wondered how she'd handle having to admit that she wanted this.

To his incredulous delight, Charity nodded, saying nothing, her face a fiery red.

The thought of doing this to her had kept him hard as a rock all day. To get back at her, he would play with her, tease her, without appearing to.

He wouldn't be happy until her ass wanted his cock as badly as her pussy did.

Setting the lube on the table next to him, he gestured toward his lap. "Over my lap, cher. Let's get started."

He knew she'd expected more foreplay before they got to this, and he loved keeping her off guard. Knowing that she didn't realize the game he played with her now, he kept his tone cool and controlled, while he was anything but.

Charity's eyes widened. After several heartbeats, she nodded again, her hands twisting in front of her.

Beau reached for the fastening of her jeans, unbuttoned the button, and pulled down the zipper, hiding a smile when her breath caught. With slow, deliberate intent, he lowered her jeans and panties to just below the cheeks of her bottom before taking her arm and urging her over his lap.

Pretending not to notice how badly she shook, Beau ran his hand over her firm, smooth bottom, careful to keep her sweater pulled down to cover the small of her back.

He knew that by exposing just her ass, she would be more conscious of her nakedness exactly where he wanted her to be. Her ass would feel more exposed than if he'd pulled her jeans and panties all the way off.

Caressing her bottom with his right hand, Beau placed his left forearm over her back in anticipation of her jolt.

She would thrash quite a bit in the next several minutes and he didn't want her to be able to escape.

Before he started, however, he slid a finger between her folds, smiling to himself when he found her wet. "You're already wet. It seems you like attention to your ass as much as I want to give it."

"I'm always aroused when I'm with you."

Beau grinned at her shy, but disgruntled tone, and struggled to keep the laughter out of his own. "That's true. I guess only the next few minutes will tell if it's the attention to your ass that gets you aroused." He slapped her lightly, the sound of it, and the bounce of the firm, rounded flesh, making his cock jump.

As anticipated, she jolted and would have jumped up if not for his hold. "What did you do that for? Are you going to do what you said, or not?"

Beau's continuous caress to her bottom made it impossible for her to hide the fact that her ass clenched incessantly. Amused at her anger, he decided that this would be the perfect time to turn up the heat. "There's another matter that has to be dealt with first."

Charity tried to lift up again, turning her head toward him, but he held her down, preventing her from looking at his face.

He knew that if she saw his grin, it would be over.

Apparently realizing that her struggles got her nowhere, she stopped and blew out a breath. "What other matter?"

Careful to keep his tone low, and making sure she couldn't possibly miss the threat in it, Beau covered her ass with his hand. "The matter of you scaring the hell out of me and almost getting yourself killed. You didn't really think I'd forgotten that, did you?"

Charity stilled, her entire body tensing. "Ace and my fathers already lectured me."

Beau smiled at the trepidation in her soft voice, and firmed his touch on her tight buttocks. "A lecture wasn't what I had in mind." He slapped her ass, careful to keep it light enough to warm.

His cock jumped at her answering cry, her wiggling forcing him to bite back a groan.

"You can't spank me, damn it!"

Beau chuckled, knowing it would piss her off. He didn't want her limp and uninvolved. He wanted her in this with him every step of the way. The warmth he would create in her bottom would heighten her awareness there and make her even more prepared for him to stretch her tight ass.

He slapped her ass again, this time adding a little more sting to it. "It appears, cher, that I can."

* * * *

Charity fisted her hands in the material of his jeans, hardly able to believe he would do this.

The heat spread, making her more aware of how exposed her bottom felt with her jeans and panties pulled only low enough to frame it.

She wondered if he knew what it did to her.

As another slap landed, she tried to writhe away from him, but Beau's hold proved even stronger than she'd anticipated. "Damn it, Beau. I've never been spanked in my life!"

"That's obvious."

Another sharp slap landed, making her bottom even hotter. To her mortification, a rush of moisture escaped to coat her inner thighs. His arrogance both infuriated and aroused her, which angered her even more. "Damn it, Beau. I didn't do it on purpose!"

He slapped her ass again, making it hotter. "I want your promise—right now—that you won't ever, under any circumstances, or for any reason, leave town again without telling me about it."

Not about to make this easy for him, Charity turned as far as she could and growled at him. "What are you, my mother?"

A thick finger slid into her pussy. "No, my little wet bride-to-be. I'm your fiancé, soon to be your husband, and you're my responsibility. You'll have to answer to me when you do something careless. We might as well get that established right here, right now."

Having grown up in this town, Charity knew the rules well, and she also knew there was no way around them. She also knew Beau to be much like the other men who lived here, knew that he meant well, and that he took his responsibility seriously.

She also knew there would be ways to circumvent all but the most serious infractions.

Understanding his intention to protect her eased some of her anger, and she couldn't deny she looked forward to outmaneuvering him in the future. Blowing out a breath, she tried to relax. "Okay. I know. I know. I promise."

She tightened up when Beau withdrew his finger from her pussy, anticipating another slap.

Instead, he smoothed his hand over her ass again, spreading the heat and making her puckered opening tingle. He continued to caress her, his slow massage loosening her muscles, but building the anticipation.

She stiffened again when she felt him move, her heart pounding nearly out of her chest when she heard him squirt lube onto his finger. "Beau, I'm scared. Oh, God. I didn't mean to say that." She heard the tube hit the table again.

Beau repositioned his arm, still holding her down with a forearm pressed to the center of her back, sliding his hand down to the cheeks of her bottom. "You're not as scared as you are aroused—or didn't you think I noticed that your pussy's soaked? I'll go slow. I won't hurt you, cher. I wouldn't hurt you for the world."

Charity jolted as he used his fingers to pull the cheeks of her bottom high and wide, shocked at the firm touch exposing her forbidden opening. She couldn't help but cry out at the first touch of his finger against the outer rim, the cold lube startling her, and making her realize just how exposed she was.

Beau chuckled again, a low sound filled with devious intent, and a hunger she found irresistible. "I know it's cold. It'll be warm real soon."

Charity clenched her teeth to keep from crying out again as he continued to circle her opening. She tried to tighten her bottom, but couldn't close against him. To her embarrassment, she found herself lifting her ass, the tingling awareness inside driving her mad. "Just do it, damn you!"

His soft chuckle made her want to hit him. "You're always so impatient for everything. Just relax, Charity. Let yourself feel. Just enjoy your arousal. We're not in any hurry, are we, cher?"

Another rush of moisture escaped to coat her inner thighs. She knew he could see her ass clenching, but couldn't stop it.

She didn't even want to think about what she looked like, draped over his lap with her bottom sticking up in the air, her ass probably as pink as her face felt.

Beau's words came back to her.

Everything I do to you is done with love.

Under his hypnotic caress, she found herself loosening again, but the finger he kept moving over her puckered opening in slow, deliberate circles kept her tense and on edge.

A whimper escaped when he pressed, her position and the slick lube making her instinctive tightening against his invasion useless.

With his firm fingers holding her buttocks high and spread, it made clenching her buttocks even more difficult, and left her feeling more exposed. The feel of his cock pressing against her through his jeans told her that this excited him as much as it did her.

She couldn't stay still, a shiver going up her spine when he pushed the tip of his finger a little deeper inside her and began to move it.

The intensity of it stunned her, the helpless feeling of having his finger inside such an intimate place making her tremble even harder. The sensation seemed even stronger since she had nothing else to focus on. In the past, he'd always touched her somewhere else at the same time, but this time, he didn't touch her anywhere else.

"That's it. Relax your muscles there."

Charity sucked in a breath, soothed by his silky voice, stiffening again when he pushed his finger deeper. "Beau, I don't know if I can do this. Oh, God."

How could something so intimate feel so good?

"You're doing just fine, cher. The way you're gripping my finger has my cock throbbing. I know how tight it's going to be inside you. Your ass is gonna grip my cock the way it's gripping my finger. Do you know what that's going to do to both of us?"

She wished she could see his face.

A moan escaped when he withdrew slightly, but she sucked in a breath when he pushed his finger deeper. It felt so tight, she couldn't even imagine how his cock would feel. She drew in one ragged breath after another, each one ending in a moan. "It'll never fit."

Beau groaned, his cock jumping against her hip. "It'll fit, cher. Nice and slow, we'll make it fit, won't we?" He stroked her bottom hole, pulling his finger almost all the way out before sliding it a little deeper than before, setting off a riot of sensation against the inner walls of her ass. "That's why I have to stretch you a little before, and get you used to loosening up these muscles for me. You trust me, don't you?"

"Yes. Oh, God." Charity's toes curled as Beau slid deeper, the decadence of having her ass impaled overwhelming her senses. The too-intense feel of it made her insides flutter, as every nerve ending in her ass tingled with awareness and a hunger for more.

Whimpering with need, she pressed her face against his leg, tightening her fists in the material of his jeans. "Beau. Oh, God."

She found herself trying to part her thighs to give him even more access, but Beau appeared to have all he needed, thrusting the length of his finger inside her.

"That's it. See? You can take it. Yes, cher. Very nice. You have no idea how much it excites me to see you this way." He slid his finger free, drawing another whimper from her and leaving her ass grasping at emptiness.

Another rush of moisture coated her thighs, her pussy clenching and her clit feeling so swollen and heavy that it throbbed. Biting her lip to keep from begging for more, she gasped when Beau released the cheeks of her ass and she heard the scrape of the tube on the table.

Beau rubbed her bottom. "Relax that ass, cher. I'm getting some more lube, and then I'm going to work two fingers into you."

His words caused a restlessness and slight panic inside her that had her wiggling on his lap. She tried to lift up, the thought of having two fingers inside her making her ass clench and tingle even hotter. "Beau, I don't know if—"

He caught her when she started to slip, a strong hand around her hip yanking her back into position again. "None of that. Be still." His fingers, firmer and more demanding than before, lifted and spread her ass cheeks again. He didn't even give her time to adapt, pressing the tips of two fingers against her puckered opening with enough pressure to force the tight ring of muscle to give way.

Crying out with shock, Charity jolted at a sensation much stronger than before. "Beau! It stings. Oooohhh! It burns." The tight ring of muscle burned as he stretched it, and to her utter mortification, intensified her need to have him fill her deep.

"Yes. Oh, God. Please. More, Beau."

The words slipped out before she could stop them, but the need to have more proved too strong to deny.

"A butt plug would help prepare you for my cock. My store sells dozens of styles. And sizes." His usually silky tone had become so harsh and filled with tension that she barely recognized it.

Charity shivered as he began to stroke her ass again. "Yes." She wanted his cock inside her. She wanted her ass to burn even hotter. She wanted to be stretched there, to be filled in the most intimate way by the man she loved.

She wanted Beau to take her ass, to bend her over and hold her with his firm hands. She wanted to hear him growl with pleasure, and to lose himself in her.

"Please, Beau. I want you to take me there. Oh, God."

"No, cher. You're too tight. I don't want to hurt you." He slid his fingers deeper, stroking her inner walls and sending sharp sizzles of sensation up her spine. "I'm going to stretch you a little tonight, but I won't take you there until you're ready."

Charity gritted her teeth, knowing that he rarely changed his mind about anything. "I'm fucking ready." She kicked her legs, frantic to get more.

She wanted him there. She wanted the friction against her inner walls, wanted the feeling of being filled in the most intimate way possible by the man who excited her like no other man ever had.

She wanted the man who filled every erotic desire, and who took her places she'd never have imagined going—and making her love every step of the journey.

Shivers raced through her, the hunger she felt like nothing she'd ever experienced as her bottom clenched on him, the wicked feel of being stretched in her most intimate opening sending warm waves of sizzling delight through her, even as it sent erotic chills up and down her spine. "Please. I don't know what to do. I can't stand it."

"Yes, you can."

Her juices ran down her inner thighs, the need she felt becoming so sharp, it brought tears to her eyes. "Please, Beau. Take me there. I need it now."

* * * *

Beau gritted his teeth, his cock so hard it hurt. Pressing his fingers deeper inside her, he tried to scissor them, but her ass was too tight for it. The need to sink his cock into her tight ass made him dizzy, but he'd already promised himself that he wouldn't do it tonight. He wouldn't do it until she was ready.

Mentally *and* physically.

He worked his fingers as deep as they would go, delighted that she pushed back against him. She fucked herself on his fingers in a way that spoke of experience, but knew she had none.

To think that he could turn someone as straightforward and no-nonsense as Charity into a creature of need, who begged him to fuck her ass, made his chest swell, his cock throbbing to give her all that she asked for.

A future of fulfilling erotic fantasies and creating even more loomed ahead of him.

Her cries of pleasure and the way she kept clenching on him warned him that her orgasm was fast approaching.

In a deliberate move, he yanked his fingers free, watching in fascination as her little hole, shiny with lube, clenched as she cried out in frustration. Her hoarse throaty cries, begging him not to stop nearly made him come in his pants like a fucking teenager.

"No." His own voice, much harsher than usual, made her still. "That's it for tonight."

Since the heightened awareness he'd created in her ass wouldn't be satisfied, he held her steady, prepared to deal with her temper. "Easy, Charity. I'll make sure you're satisfied before we're done here, but I'm not taking your ass."

"Bastard!"

He smiled, knowing his lover well. Because he denied her, she'd want it even more now, something he could use to his advantage in the near future.

Lifting her from his lap to stand in front of him, he held her waist until she steadied herself. The sight of her bare pussy and the shine of her juices on her inner thighs nearly sent him over the edge.

Her eyes had a glazed look to them, so dark with passion they appeared almost black. She swayed slightly, her small hands reaching out to grip his shoulders. "Beau, please."

"No."

Sliding his hands up her sweater, he teased her nipples through her bra, hiding a smile when she arched toward him and moaned. "You look like a little girl who's been punished. I should make you stand in the corner like this while you think about what you did wrong."

Her face flushed even more. "You wouldn't dare."

Smiling, he got to his feet. "No, but it's fun to imagine." Taking her hands in his, he prevented her from pulling her jeans and panties back up. "By the way, if you ever do anything so stupid again, I'll shove a butt plug up your ass before I spank you."

Knowing that her hunger had reached a level unlike any before, becoming a primitive hunger that would make her want it hard and rough, Beau deliberately softened his expression, determined to make sweet, slow love to her.

Even if it killed him.

"Come on, cher." Lifting her in his arms, he held her high against his chest and kissed her. Keeping his kiss soft and romantic, he carried her into the bedroom, pretending to ignore the way she pressed up against him and fought to get him to take her mouth harder.

Once in the bedroom, he placed her on the bed, and with slow deliberation, began to strip her. "No games, cher." He smiled, pretending not to notice her look of shock and frustration. "We'll go nice and slow."

He'd satisfy her, but on *his* terms. He'd give her the loving without the play, and drive her straight up the wall.

Once he'd stripped both of them and donned a condom, he turned off the light, not wanting her to witness his own torment.

Making a space for himself between her damp thighs, he gathered her close. "Slow and sweet."

* * * *

Charity couldn't believe it.

The son of a bitch she'd promised to marry seemed determined to torture her.

On top of that, he made it so that she couldn't even complain.

Gripping his wide shoulders as he covered her body with his, Charity spread her thighs eagerly. Sucking in a breath when his cock brushed against her mound, she moaned in frustration and lifted against him when he settled over her instead without entering her.

His position prevented her from touching him, which frustrated her further.

He *had* to know she wanted it hard and fast, but he seemed determined to drive her crazy.

Gripping his hair, she rocked her hips in invitation, need clawing at her.

The swipe of his tongue on her nipple sent even more heat through her, but it wasn't enough. "Beau, you're killing me." Gritting her teeth, she threw back her head and groaned, tightening her hands in his hair when he chuckled against her breast as his mouth closed over it again, and began to suck.

Hard.

Finally.

Using his teeth to scrape over her nipple, he slid his hands under her and gathered her closer. He held her nipple between his teeth for several heart-pounding seconds, the pressure more intense than it had ever been before.

Her pussy and ass clenched, the need to have him inside her a living, breathing hunger that clawed at her, the primitive demands of her body destroying all inhibitions. She tried to dig her heels into the mattress for leverage, but his hold prevented it, leaving her sliding her heels on the soft sheets. "Fuck me, damn you!"

The awareness he'd created in her ass threatened to drive her wild, a raw purely sexual need that had her writhing against him in the need to get his cock inside her. The warmth from his spanking seemed to get worse and spread, the friction against the soft sheets reigniting the heat.

Releasing her nipple, Beau ran his tongue over it, easing the slight sting. "With pleasure."

Beau thrust into her, threading his fingers with hers and raising them over her head. "You're soaking wet, cher."

Pressing his body against hers, he held in her place, effectively subduing her struggles with ease, and making it impossible for her to touch him the way she wanted to. "Do you know what it does to me to know that your tight little bottom is lubed and desperate for attention?"

Tightening her hands on his, Charity moaned, her pussy clenching on his cock. Now that the nerve endings in her ass had been awakened, the lack of his attention there drove her crazy.

By his own admission, he knew it.

With a growl, she fought his hold, bucking her hips to get him to move faster, and frustrated that she couldn't budge him. Throwing her head back, she dug her heels into his tight butt and rocked against him. "You son of a bitch! You knew what that would do to me!"

Beau's lips touched her hair. "Of course I knew what it would do to you. I know your body, cher, as well as I know my own. You want it fast and hard. You think you need it that way. Your ass wants attention. You don't think you can come without it."

Bracing most of his weight on his elbows, he bent to nuzzle her ear. "You can. You're close now. That velvety pussy is gripping me, trying to suck me in."

Charity gasped as he changed the angle of his thrust. "Beau!" The feel of his warm hand covering her breast sent her higher, her breath catching as his fingers closed over her nipple. Her body tightened, the pleasure magnified by the awareness still lingering in her ass.

"Come for me."

The hunger in his soft demand sent a thrill through her, sending her over in a shower of inner sparks.

"Ahhh! Oh, God! Yes. Yes." Arching, she cried out as the pleasure washed over her in wave after wave of sizzling heat. Her toes curled as she dug her heels harder into his butt, lifting into him to prolong the pleasure.

He kept moving, creating a delicious friction against her nipples, his cock filling her over and over with heat. Murmuring to her in guttural tones, he fucked her faster, his need for her fulfilling a need for feminine power that she hadn't realized she'd needed. Gripping her hands tighter when she fought to get them free, Beau bent low, his voice a deep rumble in her ear. "Not escaping this, cher. You're not getting away from me. Ever."

Beau groaned, thrusting deep and hard, sending another thick wave of bliss through her, and making her tingle all the way to her toes.

Thrilled at the way his big body shuddered over hers, Charity tightened her legs around him, turning her head to kiss his neck. With her face buried in his hair, she breathed in his scent, tightening her legs around him to hold him as close as possible.

Charity reveled in his warmth and the closeness she felt with him. As soon as he released her hands, she wrapped her arms around his shoulders, smiling against his neck as she caught her breath. "I love you, Beau."

"And I love you. Very much." He bent to touch his lips to hers. "Hmm. Nice and slow just might kill me." He rolled to his back, taking her with him. "You okay, cher?" He reached out to turn on the light at the bedside.

Draped over his chest, Charity ran her hands over his upper arms, struggling to catch her breath. "Peachy." Her bottom still clenched, but her orgasm had left her completely sated.

Beau traced his fingertips up and down her spine, pulling the covers over her when she shivered. "That didn't sound *peachy*. Something wrong?"

Lifting her head, she tried to glare at him, but didn't have the energy. "You did that on purpose."

Beau closed his eyes, his lips twitching. "Of course I did."

"You're sneaky." Running a fingertip over his chest, she circled his nipple.

Beau pursed his lips as though considering that. "Hmm. Possibly."

Charity tried to work up anger at the smugness underneath the lethargy and satisfaction in his tone, but she was too lethargic and satisfied herself to make the effort.

"I really do love you, you know."

Beau lifted his head, opening his eyes to meet hers. "I know. I love you, too."

"Why didn't I ever see this side to you before?"

His smile held a tender affection that warmed her heart. "You did, cher. It just made you nervous, and I wanted to keep it light until you were ready."

She tapped his nipple. "I'm ready."

"I know." He wrapped his hand around her fingers and brought them to his lips.

"I loved when you played."

"It kept us apart."

"It won't ever do that. I understand you now."

"Hmm."

Charity cuddled closer, smiling against his chest. "You enjoyed spanking me, didn't you?"

"It had to be done."

Bristling at his tone, she lifted her head to tell him off, stopping when she saw the look of renewed hunger in his eyes. Dropping her head again to hide her smile, she nearly purred when his hand slid lower to caress her still warm bottom.

"You'd better not do it again."

Please do it again. Soon.

Now she understood why her sister smiled every time she talked about Ace spanking her.

Beau squeezed her ass. "You'll get one when you earn one."

Charity smiled as his cock stirred inside her.

Thrilled at the knowledge that Beau still had that playful streak inside him, and knowing just how much both of them would enjoy another spanking, Charity snorted inelegantly for show, but she was determined to earn another one.

And soon.

She wouldn't stop until she got him to love playing again.

Chapter Nineteen

Charity wiped her damp palms on her jeans as she made her way to Beau's store, her heart pounding.

It had been almost three weeks since she and Beau had started making love again, and she still couldn't get him to play the way he used to.

Each day, her wedding day got a little closer, and each day, she became a little more desperate.

It was time to put her plan into action.

When her cell phone rang, she paused, looking down at the display. Recognizing her sister's number, she grinned and took the call.

"Hey, Hope."

"Where are you? I thought we were going to pick up our dresses and to have lunch."

"We are. I told you that I'd pick you up at two. I have something to do first."

"What?"

Charity smiled at her sister's nosiness. "I'm going to do a little shopping here in town."

"Where? I'll meet you."

Saturday's meant a lot of foot traffic in Desire, and Charity stepped to the side to avoid it while she spoke to her sister. "No. This is something I have to do alone."

"You're doing it? You're going to Beau's store?"

"Yep." Charity turned and walked in the other direction, taking the longer trek around the block so she didn't approach Beau's store while she was still on the phone. "He's in there today working. I want to go in while he's there."

"Have you told him that you're going out of town yet?"

Charity grinned, her bottom tightening in anticipation. "No. Not going to either. That's part two of my plan."

Hope giggled. "There you go. It's about time. Maybe now you'll understand a little better when I purposely get under Ace's skin."

Charity couldn't hold back a smile. "Did you tell Ace that you were going out of town?"

"No way. Mom and the dads know, but I didn't tell my darling, dominant husband. I want some action, too, and it never hurts to keep him on his toes."

"Need any toys while I'm there?"

Hope snorted. "You've got to be kidding. Ace has an entire room filled with toys. He's always bringing home something new."

Charity sighed. "I wish Beau would again. I was so stupid, Hope."

"You weren't stupid. Just self-conscious and scared that it was all a game to him. Now that you know why he likes to play, and that it doesn't diminish what he feels for you, only intensifies it, you understand. Do you really think I would let Ace use a fucking whip on me if I didn't trust him, and know how much he loves me?"

Frowning, Charity smiled at King and Jake as she passed them, returning their wave. Both King and Jake were Dominants, and she knew for a fact that both men were madly in love with their wives.

Both men carried bags from Beau's store.

Charity grimaced, her steps slowing. "I guess I never thought about that before. It's a good thing you called. King and Jake just left Beau's store. I can only imagine what it would have been like if I'd walked in while they were still there. I wonder if the store's busy." Biting her lip, she looked around at the number of people who carried bags from different stores in town. Surprised at the number of dark blue bags from Beau's store, Charity sighed. "Judging by the number of dark blue bags I'm seeing, Beau's store must be busy."

"Charity, everyone in town goes to that store. Look, I'm going to the diner to spend some time with Mom and the dads. I'll wait for you there."

"Okay." Charity approached the store. "I'm almost there. Talk to you in a bit. Wish me luck."

"Stop worrying, and just have fun." Hope giggled. "I'd love to see the look on Beau's face when you start shopping. I'm going to want to hear every detail."

With a laugh, Charity disconnected. Seconds later, she paused outside of Beau's adult toy store, and took a deep breath before reaching for the door.

Jolting at the sound of the bell on the door chiming, Charity paused, letting her eyes adjust from the bright sunlight to the interior of the store. Once her eyes began to adjust, she realized that the interior wasn't as dark as she'd first expected.

Her eyes widened at the vast displays, and the sheer number of items filling the shelves, and occupying every wall.

"Holy shit."

A soft, familiar chuckle came from her right. "It's nice to see you, too. You've never been in here before. To what do I owe the honor? Did you come to have lunch with me?"

Turning toward where Beau leaned over the counter, obviously in the middle of some paperwork, Charity glanced at him, shaking her head and staring openmouthed at the large inventory. "Uh, no. I'm meeting Hope in a bit. Beau, I didn't realize you carried all this stuff."

Grinning, Beau closed the notebook he'd been working in and came around the counter. "This is just a small portion. You should see the warehouse."

Turning to him again, Charity nodded. "I'd like to."

A dark brow went up. "If you're not busy the next time I go, I'll take you with me." Wrapping his arm around her, he hugged her close, dropping a kiss on her lips just hard enough to make them warm. "So, is this just a friendly visit?"

Thankful that they were alone in the store, Charity cupped the bulge at the front of his jeans, thrilling when his eyes narrowed and he stiffened. "We're not friends." Stepping out of his arms, she began to stroll around the store. "I'm here to shop."

"Excuse me?"

Hiding a smile, she picked up the first thing she came across. "I'm shopping. Is there something wrong with a woman coming in to buy some toys for herself and her lover?"

"Not a thing." With a faint smile, Beau went to the door and locked it, turned the sign to closed, and pulled down the shade. "Not a damned thing, especially when my help is out to lunch. Women come in here all the time, either to buy something to satisfy themselves, or spark their sex lives. Which are you shopping for—and let me tell you up front, if it's to buy something to use to masturbate, I'm going to insist on watching."

Realizing that she'd picked up a butt plug, Charity struggled not to blush. "I've decided to buy some toys to entice my lover to play. He doesn't seem interested anymore. What do you suggest?"

Beau's expression never changed, but a combination of heat and amusement glittered in his eyes, making his delight in the game obvious. "What you have in your hand is a butt plug. Does your lover play with your ass?"

Charity sighed, pouting slightly as she shook her head. "Not as much as I'd like him to. He tried before but I was always too scared. He got me over it and made me want more, and then seemed to forget all about it. I really don't know why and I'd like him to know that I'm interested."

Beau hadn't touched her there since the night he'd spanked her, frustrating her to no end.

Nodding solemnly, Beau pursed his lips, his eyes narrowed. "Have you told him that you want him to?"

Charity's cheeks burned, but she wouldn't let herself back away from her mission. Looking up into his eyes, she shrugged, inwardly cursing her own sudden shyness. "That's what I'm here for. I don't know how to ask him." Sucking in a breath, she fought her unease, and forced herself to continue. "I figured that if I brought the right things to the bedroom, he would get the hint."

After several long seconds, Beau smiled faintly and inclined his head toward the package in her hand. "That should do it. Do you think it's the right size for your needs?"

For the first time, Charity really studied the butt plug, her bottom clenching at the size. Swallowing heavily, Charity shrugged. "It does look big. I mean, how do I know what size I need?" Shifting restlessly at the tingling in her bottom, she looked up at him through her lashes.

Beau didn't let her get away with that, lifting her chin and forcing her to meet his gaze squarely. His eyes danced with mirth as he glanced down at the package she held before meeting her gaze again. "The size you're holding is about the size of two fingers. Do you want him to stretch you for anal sex?"

Warmed by his playfulness, and the fact that her role-playing obviously delighted him, Charity shrugged, fighting not to giggle as nerves overtook her. "I hope so."

"Then he will." He gestured toward a large display. "There are all sorts of sizes. If you're going to have anal sex, then it might be a good idea for him to gradually increase the size. You mentioned that your lover likes to play?"

Charity looked up at him through her lashes. "He loves to, but he stopped because of me. It's all my fault and I don't know how to fix it."

Beau's eyes narrowed. "He probably thinks you don't want to play, and that you're suggesting it to please him."

Charity gasped. "But, that's not true!" Desperate to get him to believe her, she gripped his hand. "It just made me nervous because I thought he did it to keep me at a distance. I thought it was just fun and games for him. I told him that."

"And now you've decided that *you* want to play in the bedroom?"

Nodding, Charity grinned. "Very much."

Beau held out a hand, gesturing toward another rack of adult toys. "I'm sure that'll make him very happy. Let me show you some other things."

Gripping his arm, Charity waited until he looked at her again, searching for any signs of what he was thinking. "Do you think so?"

Grinning, he winked. "I do." His smile fell, and he became all business once again. "Now, ma'am, let me show you a few items that I would suggest."

Playing the part of a customer in Beau's store proved more fun than she could have imagined. Eyeing the basket Beau held and the contents, Charity crossed her arms over her chest to hide her beaded nipples, and then decided against it.

Playing this way with him aroused her and she wanted him to know it. Smiling when Beau's gaze lowered to her breasts, Charity sucked in a breath at the renewed awareness that made her breasts feel swollen and warm. "I'd like to see some other things. We've played before, and I don't want to get anything that we've already done. I want it to be new and fresh—a new beginning."

Beau smiled, reaching out to run his fingertips through her hair. "That sounds wonderful. Your lover is a very lucky man."

Charity moved closer and placed a hand on his chest, lifting to her toes. "I hope he thinks so. I'm so lucky to have him."

As she'd hoped, Beau accepted her invitation and kissed her, a warm loving kiss she felt all the way to her toes. Lifting his head, he held her chin in a gentle grip, running his thumb back and forth over her swollen and damp lips. "I'm sure he loves you with everything he is."

Charity flashed him a grin. "I wanna shop some more."

"Of course." Beau adopted a professional smile once again. "There are a few things over here that I think your lover would appreciate."

He led her to another display. "Here we have some nipple clips." Lifting one, he held it up to her. "See? There's a clip on each end and a chain between them. The chain's heavy enough to tug at your nipples each time you move—something both you and your lover would appreciate—and the chain gives your lover the opportunity to use one hand to tease both of your nipples at the same time, leaving his other hand free for something else."

Swallowing heavily, Charity eyed the item in his hand, automatically tensing and taking a step back. "Um, we don't do pain." She hoped he didn't plan to do anything more painful than the light spanking he'd given her weeks earlier. Scared that there was another side to him he hadn't shown her, Charity eyed him, anxiously searching his features.

To her relief, Beau smiled, bending close to kiss her nose. "These are adjustable and can be used just to apply enough pressure to thrill both of you." Straightening, he ran his fingertips over her hair again, his eyes dark and hooded. "Trust me." His body tensed, his eyes becoming guarded and searching.

Warmed by his concern, and touched at his apparent anxiety at the thought of scaring her, Charity smiled and nodded. "Why wouldn't I trust someone who takes such good care of me?"

Beau's answering smile lit up his face. "I adore you."

Taking her hand, he led her to another part of the store. "I think your lover would like this."

Charity blinked as he turned, her eyes widening at the sight of the vibrator he held. Frowning, she remembered that Hope had bought one to rile her husband, and that Ace had taken it away from her.

Hope had told her that Ace made it clear that if she wanted an orgasm, she would get it from him or not at all.

Wondering if Beau meant for her to use it on herself, Charity met his gaze, surprised at the heat in them. "Isn't that something a woman would buy for herself?"

"It can be, but I think your lover would like it. You said he liked to tease you and play. I think he would love to tease you with this." His playful grin sent her heart racing. "Would you like me to demonstrate?"

Charity gulped, eyeing the vibrator and nodding. "Please." The breathless plea in her voice surprised her, her pulse racing when Beau set the basket aside.

"Of course." Beau's eyes glittered with devilish intent. "I'll be glad to show you how it works." Holding the vibrator in front of him, and almost at eye level to her, Beau turned it on.

The sound it made sent a thrill of erotic heat through her, making the nerve endings in every erogenous zone dance with excitement.

With slow deliberation, he pushed the edges of her jacket aside and reached for the hem of her sweater. Raising it slightly, Beau touched the tip of the vibrator to her belly, his eyes narrowed and watchful.

Shocked at how good it felt, Charity sucked in a breath, her stomach muscles quivering under the vibrations. Unsettled, she looked instinctively to Beau, shocked at the pleasure in his eyes.

Lifting her sweater in slow increments, Beau ran the vibrator over her belly in increasingly wider circles. "I'll bet he would like to tease you with this. I'll bet he would know that doing something like this will make your nipples bead and ache for the feel of the vibrator on them."

Reaching out for support, Charity gripped his forearms, a moan of delight escaping before she could prevent it. "That feels so good."

Beau stepped closer, wrapping an arm around her waist and pressing a hand at her back, effectively keeping her from stepping back. "I know it does. I can see it in your eyes."

She missed the feel of the vibrator against her skin when Beau switched it to the hand at her back, holding it there while he pushed her sweater higher and unclasped the front closure of her bra. Excited at having her breasts exposed to his gaze, Charity arched toward him, lifting her face to his. "Can you?"

Switching the vibrator to his free hand again, Beau touched it to her belly, his eyes hooded. "Hmm. I can. Imagine what it would feel like on your breasts."

At the feel of the vibrator moving higher to the sensitive underside of her breast, Charity tried to slump against him but the hand at her back fisted in her hair and prevented it. Crying out as the need to have it on her nipple sharpened, Charity let her head fall back and closed her eyes, struggling to get the delicious vibrations where she needed them most.

Once again, Beau thwarted her.

His grip tightened, his arm firming against her back to support her as he circled the vibrator around her nipple without touching it.

Need had her struggling for air, her pussy clenching and her juices soaking her panties. Her cry of frustration became a gasp at the sharp pleasure when Beau touched the vibrator to her nipple. Fire raced through her, the need at her slit so intense it brought tears to her eyes.

Dancing it lightly back and forth over her nipple, Beau groaned. "I have an assortment of vibrators—some that can go inside you."

Just the thought of it weakened Charity's knees. "Oh, God."

"In your pussy. In your ass." Leaning closer, he brushed her lips with his. "Can you imagine your lover filling your ass and pussy with vibrators and using another on your clit?"

Charity gasped, parting her lips eagerly for his kiss as the pleasure exploded.

Her knees buckled, and she would have fallen if not for Beau's strong hold. Tingling everywhere, she cried out as the heat engulfed her, whimpering as it spread in massive waves to consume every inch of her body.

Beau's tongue slid against hers as the vibrator went quiet.

She heard the light thud of it hitting the floor just a second before he caught her up in his arms, pulling her firmly against his chest.

Sliding her hands to his hair, she held him close, matching him kiss for kiss, pressing against the hard bulge at the front of his jeans.

As he straightened, she wrapped her arms around his neck and her legs around his waist, desperate to get as close to him as she could.

She wanted him deep inside her. Hard. Fast.

Wrenching her mouth from his, she fisted her hands in his hair, her breathing ragged. "Take me."

Beau was already moving.

With movements much rougher than usual, Beau took her mouth again and headed for a room in the back. Lifting his mouth from hers, he reached out to a nearby shelf and retrieved a strip of condoms. Ripping one off, he tossed it on an empty table and with quick movements, undid her pants, yanked them down to her knees, and bent her over the smooth, flat surface.

"You make me crazy to have you. You're so fucking responsive. Fuck. Damned short table. Don't move."

Amused at his evident frustration, Charity straightened slightly as Beau cursed. Watching as he pulled something from another shelf, she giggled as more cursing ensued as he struggled with the plastic covering what looked like a huge pillow.

"What's that?"

"A wedge. I'm taking it home with me, too. I've got big plans for this thing."

Wrapping an arm around her waist, he lifted her and put the leather-covered wedge at the edge of the table. He settled her over it and shoved her thighs apart, his movements hurried.

Surprised that her feet no longer touched the floor, Charity gripped the far edge of the table as Beau cursed again while rolling on the condom, his impatience thrilling her.

His hands closed over her hips, his hold secure as he thrust into her, filling her with his cock with one smooth stroke. "Big plans."

Crying out, Charity held on as Beau began to thrust hard and fast into her, the angle of his thrusts driving her quickly to the edge again. "Yes. Harder."

Beau's thrusts came harder and faster, making her come with a speed that stunned her. He tightened his hold when she jolted, holding her for his deep strokes, which kept her orgasm rolling through her. "So wet. So fucking hot." With something between a growl and a groan, he thrust deep, his body covering hers. The feel of his cock jumping as he came inside her thrilled her even more. "Jesus, cher."

Moving her hair aside, he scraped his teeth over her shoulder. "I hope you got what the hell you came here for."

Spent and still trembling, she reached down to touch his hand, smiling when he released her hip to take it in his. "I sure as hell did. More than I planned, in fact. My knees are shaking."

Turning to look at him over her shoulder, she narrowed her eyes. "You'd better not give this kind of service to other customers."

He'd make a damned fortune if he did.

Slipping his cock free, Beau chuckled, a raw, throaty sound filled with satisfaction and amusement. "Just one impudent customer." Pulling her back against him, he nuzzled a particularly sensitive spot between her neck and shoulder, finding it with an ease that only a lover familiar with her body could. "She's a handful, and more than enough for me. Besides, my lover has quite a temper."

Holding on to the table as he set her on her feet, Charity leaned back against him. "Don't you forget it." Her voice sounded so weak and pitiful that she couldn't force the indignation and threat into it that she'd wanted to, but she was too sated and happy to care. Trembling, she appreciated his help in getting dressed again.

After he'd righted her clothing, he rid himself of the condom and refastened his jeans. "Not a chance."

Sliding her hands over his chest, Charity smiled up at him. "That was quite a demonstration. I think I'll take it all."

Beau grinned. "I'll put it on your tab. I'll even deliver it. Are you eating with me tonight, or do you have plans with your sister?"

Dropping her forehead against his chest, she rubbed against him, weak with satisfaction. "Don't know yet. Can I get back to you?"

"Of course." Wrapping an arm around her, he led her back out to the front. "I'll be waiting to hear from you."

"Okay." Looking up at him, she cuddled closer. "I can't believe you closed the shop. I hate the thought of you losing customers because of me."

Beau grinned. "Nothing's more important than you. Besides, you didn't seem to mind at all a few minutes ago. You weren't thinking about anything except playing with me." Bending, he kissed her nose. "I'd say we were making progress. I'll corrupt you yet."

He gave her a lingering kiss before lifting the shade, turning the sign and unlocking the door again. Patting her ass, he grinned. "See you later, cher."

"I'm counting on it."

Unable to wipe away her grin, Charity headed back down the sidewalk and toward the diner to meet her sister.

If everything went according to plan, she and Beau would be playing with her new toys tonight—after he'd thoroughly punished her for what she was about to do next.

Chapter Twenty

Hearing the bell, Beau looked up from his paperwork, grinning when he saw Ace walk into the shop and toward him.

Amused at the awe on the face of the young man who worked for him, Beau chuckled. "Easy, Tim."

Ace's brow went up, his eyes hard. "Problem?"

Chuckling, Beau straightened. "More of a case of hero worship. He thinks you're the greatest thing since sliced bread, and as indestructible as a superhero."

Ace's eyes tingled with amusement. "Smart kid."

Beau chuckled. "He's twenty-two, Ace."

Shaking his head, Ace scrubbed a hand over his face. "Hell, that seems like such a long time ago. Can we talk?"

Beau frowned, straightening. "Sure. I just finished up the order for next week."

"You talk to Charity?"

Beau's cock stirred at the memory. He looked at his watch. "Yeah. A couple of hours ago." Uneasy at the look on Ace's face, Beau tensed, his stomach clenching. "Why? What's wrong?"

The hard, jagged ice that formed in his stomach, much like the night he'd heard about Charity's accident, numbed his brain for several heart-stopping moments.

Ace shook his head, smiling faintly. "No. Nothing like that. Calm down. I figured Charity would have told you that she and Hope were going out of town."

"Out of town?" Beau frowned, and thought back to his conversation with Charity. Struggling to shake off his panic, Beau looked up at his friend, and soon-to-be brother-in-law. "No, she didn't tell me. Where are they?"

Ace lifted his cell phone, allowing Beau to see the display. "They took Hope's car, thank God. I told you to get that chip installed in Charity's new one. They went to pick up their dresses for the wedding."

"But they're okay?"

"As far as I can tell, they're fine." Ace gestured for Beau to follow him outside, waiting until Beau came around the counter and they were both out of range for Tim to hear them.

Ace chuckled, but his eyes remained hard. "Hope knows better than to leave town without telling me, so I can only assume that my darling wife is challenging me. You didn't know Charity was leaving, either?"

Remembering Charity's playfulness, Beau breathed a sigh of relief. "No. I think she's trying to make a point." Anticipation flowed through his veins. "She knows the consequences for that."

Ace nodded. "Good. I was hoping you'd made that clear. Charity's not the type to do something so irresponsible. I'm sure my impudent wife had something to do with this, and urged her sister to do this. Knowing what the consequences would be, she didn't want to be left out. That'll be taken care of."

Thinking about the items Charity had already picked out, Beau folded his arms across his chest, unable to hold back a grin. "Charity's decided that she wants to play, and has been tempting me for weeks, trying to get me to play with her again. It's been hard as hell to resist her, but I wanted her to initiate it and see how much fun it can be."

He'd already made up his mind to add a few things to the large bag of items from his store, but after her daring, decided to add a few more.

Ace sighed, but Beau could see the light of anticipation in his friend's eyes. "These women are going to drive us crazy. I'd say they'd better learn their place—"

Beau grinned. "Oh, they know their place, all right."

"Yeah." Ace slapped his back. "Under our protection, and browbeating us. They've got to test the limits from time to time. It's to be expected. They have to find out just how far they can push us." Grinning, he started back toward his SUV parked at the curb, turning as he rounded the hood. "Mine's going to give me gray hair. I'll make myself clear on the issue later on tonight. Good luck getting the point across to yours."

Beau grinned. "Luck has nothing to do with it."

* * * *

Charity checked her phone again, her stomach clenching. "Beau hasn't called. He has to know I'm not in Desire. Ace has already called *you*."

Hope grinned. "Yeah. I'm in for it tonight. That reminds me—I want to go get some new panties for him to rip off of me."

Distracted by thoughts of Beau, and his indifference, Charity frowned. "Why don't you just buy them from Erin and Rachel's store in Desire?"

Hope giggled, her eyes bright with eagerness. "If I know my husband, he'll have plans for me as soon as I get to town. I doubt if I'll have time to run over there."

Thinking about Beau's apparent indifference, Charity wanted to cry. "Maybe I pissed Beau off by leaving without telling him." The meal she'd just eaten soured in her stomach. "I've done it again, haven't I? I've ruined everything. Damn it, Hope. *This* is why I never wanted to get involved with Beau. I'm not like you. I don't know how to play the games you play. I tried. Evidently, I failed. I'm too boring to keep a man like Beau."

Hope grinned and tucked her arm through Charity's. "You're always so intense—and such a worrier. You need Beau, and he needs you. Come on. We'll get you some fancy panties, too. I'm sure Beau's gonna love ripping them off of you."

Allowing Hope to lead her to the lingerie store in the mall, Charity stared at her phone again, unable to stop thinking about Beau.

"Maybe I should call him."

Hope sighed. "Whatever he says to you is just going to make you even crazier than you are now."

Charity paused outside the lingerie store. "I'm not crazy. I'm worried."

Scared all the way to her toes.

Waving Hope to go ahead, she dialed Beau's number, taking a deep breath and blowing it out in a rush while she waited for him to answer.

"Hello, cher."

Shivering at the edge in his voice, Charity wrapped an arm around herself. "Beau? Is everything okay?"

"Of course. Why wouldn't it be? Are you okay?"

Charity's heart pounded, a cold knot forming in her stomach at his distant tone. "I'm fine. I, um, forget to tell you that I was picking up my wedding dress today."

"Did you?"

Charity cleared her throat and forced a laugh. "Well, we were busy with something else."

Beau's tone didn't warm the way she'd expected. "There was time. I asked you specifically what you were doing. Don't you think I deserve the courtesy of knowing where you are?"

Uneasy now, Charity gulped. "Of course."

"Didn't I tell you specifically that I want to know when you leave town?"

Shifting restlessly, she shrugged. "Um, yes. But, Beau—"

"I take it you're going to be busy all night?"

The butterflies in her stomach took flight. "No. We got something to eat, and came to the mall. Hope needed to pick up a few things." Tired of being on the defense, Charity went on the offense. "Damn it, Beau. Don't you take that attitude with me!"

"What attitude, cher?"

Not wanting to be overheard, she moved away from the crowd. "You know damned well what attitude. You're giving me the cold shoulder. I didn't mean to hurt you or make you mad."

"So what *did* you mean to do?"

She opened her mouth to tell him, snapping it shut again. She wouldn't give him the satisfaction of revealing her stupidity. "Nothing."

A tense silence followed.

Regretting her childishness in defying him, Charity gulped. "Are you busy tonight?"

"No. I finished getting my order together this afternoon. Should I expect you tonight?"

"Do you want to see me tonight?"

"I always want to see you, cher. What time can I expect you?"

Charity checked the time. "I want to get a shower and change first." She wanted to join her sister and find something special. "Is eight okay?"

"I'll expect you then. Charity?"

"Yes?"

"Don't be late."

Chapter Twenty-One

Charity wiped her damp palms on her sweatpants before reaching out to knock on Beau's door. Shivering against the cold, she was glad that she'd taken the time to buy a nice sweat suit to wear tonight, in addition to the sexy panties and bra she wore, and the lacy nightgown stuffed in her purse.

She hoped to be spending the night.

As she waited for Beau to answer, she thought about Hope's parting comment. She'd told her sister that she hoped the evening was everything she wanted, and that she hadn't bitten off more than she could chew.

Hope had grinned at her, her eyes dancing. "I know what to expect from my husband, and know how to handle him. You'd better figure out how to handle yours in a hurry."

The door opened, and she looked up into the handsome face of her soon-to-be husband, and forced a smile, wondering if she'd ever learn to *handle* such a man. "Hi."

Beau stepped aside and gestured for her to enter, reaching out to take her arm when she would have passed him. "You lose your key?"

Charity frowned, the glitter in his eyes making her uneasy. "Of course not. I never lose my keys."

"Of course not. You're too *responsible* to do something like that." He removed her coat, tossing it over the back of a chair, and turning back to watch her.

His expression gave nothing away, making her even more nervous.

"Uh, yeah." Turning away from his searching look, she made her way into the living room, kicking her shoes off and nudging them aside, out of the way.

She paused in the doorway, some of her tension easing when she saw that he'd lit a fire, and that he'd already opened a bottle of wine. The fire danced, casting shadows on the walls, and reflecting off of the wineglasses on the heavy, wooden coffee table.

Turning to look at him over her shoulder, she smiled, holding her hands out to the fire to warm them. "This is wonderful. It's so cold outside."

With a warm hand at her back, Beau urged her forward. "I'll get you nice and warm."

Unnerved by his monotone, she eyed him warily and took a seat on the sofa, accepting the glass of wine he poured, trying desperately to read his mood.

The possessiveness and hunger in his eyes was a sharp contrast to the distance in both his tone and body language, and she didn't know quite what to make of it. Unable to judge his mood, she made herself more comfortable on the sofa and waited for him to make the first move.

Dressed in a casual sweater and jeans, Beau leaned back against the sofa and sipped his wine, watching her over the rim. "Did you have a nice day?"

Leery, and feeling foolish for defying him, Charity nodded, searching his features for any sign of what he was thinking. "I picked up my dress. It's so beautiful. I can't wait for you to see me in it."

Beau smiled and reached out to toy with the ends of her hair. "I can't wait, either. Three weeks from today. Everything has already been arranged. All you have to do is relax and show up in your new dress."

Warmed and slightly relieved that he reached out to touch her, Charity leaned closer, hoping to soften him up. "Thank you so much for taking care of it. You always take such good care of me." Shifting uncomfortably, she shrugged. "I had a nice day with my sister. I probably should have told you my plans."

Beau smiled faintly, the knowledge of what she did shining in his eyes. "I wondered how long it would take you to try to bring it up. Guilty conscious getting to you?"

Once again taken aback that he seemed to read her so easily, she took a sip of her wine, using it as a delay tactic while she studied him. Seeing the light of anticipation in his eyes, she hid a smile and looked away, weighing her options.

She already felt bad about what she'd done and didn't want to get into an argument with him, but she certainly didn't plan to let him think he could get away with his arrogance. Smiling, she turned back to him. "You really don't expect me to report to you all the time, do you?"

Beau pursed his lips, looking so damned sexy, she wanted to jump him. "Yes, as a matter of fact, I do. I need to know where you are. I don't want to have to try to find you again in a fucking snowstorm. I need to know where you are, and if you're going out of town, I expect you to let me know. When I went out of town, didn't I tell you about it?"

Charity didn't know how he did it, but Beau had somehow turned the tables on her, something that no one else ever did. Setting her wine glass on the table, she jumped to her feet. "Damn it, Beau. You're making me feel like the irresponsible one."

Beau's arrogant smile set her teeth on edge. "Not a pleasant feeling, is it, cher?"

She wanted to stamp her foot, but didn't want to do anything so childish in front of him. Stepping over his feet and around him, she moved away. "You've been playing me all along, haven't you?"

Beau sat forward, set his glass on the table next to hers and got to his feet, his movements slow and deliberate. "I wouldn't call it playing you, cher. You made a lot of assumptions about me. That was on you."

He took a step closer, and in a panic, Charity stepped back. "I tried to tell you that your assumptions were wrong."

Another step.

"You didn't want to listen."

Another step.

"You're so used to being the responsible one—the one always running the show—that you have a hard time accepting that I'll be the one taking care of *you*."

Another step.

Unnerved at the way he seemed to be stalking her, Charity took a step back for every step he moved closer, but he still seemed to be gaining. "Beau, it's not that."

Another step, his eyes narrowed, and darker than she'd ever seen them before. "Oh, it's exactly *that*. You think you can get away with defying me—"

Not trusting the look of intent in his eyes, Charity took another step back, swallowing heavily. "Defying you?"

"—because you figure that you can take care of yourself." He finished as if she hadn't spoken and took another step. "It doesn't work like that anymore, Charity. You had to push it, didn't you? You had to see if I would react, or just let it go. Why? To get me to play, to get my attention, or just to see if I would let you get away with it?"

Taking another step back, and then another, Charity held out a hand, as if that could hold him off, and tried to get him to understand why she'd done something so defiant on purpose. "You're twisting everything around. I just wanted you to play. I did it for you. For us. I couldn't bear it if I ruined something that was so important to you." She backed up again, her heart pounding when her back hit the wall behind her.

His eyes glittered, his smile filled with devious intent. "You didn't, and I've already told you so. Your accident scared the hell out of me, and I sure as hell didn't feel like playing. Did you think I would get over the scare you gave me so easily?" He took another step closer. "You've got to learn that you're not on your own anymore. Whether you want to hear it or not, you're my responsibility, and I don't give a damn how independent you *think* you are. It's my job to protect you, and I can't do that if you're going to run around defying me just because you want to play. Why didn't you just play?" He kept moving closer, his eyes dark and hooded, his body tense as if poised to catch her if she made a run for it.

Lifting her chin, she glared at him. "I don't know if I can do that."

Beau moved closer, bracing a hand on either side of her head and bending toward her. "You're going to have to learn, or find another way of getting your point across without doing something so stupid again."

Blinking at the insult, she fisted her hands on her hips. "Stupid?"

Leaning closer, Beau inclined his head. "And stubborn. You think you can do things your own way and not pay the consequences of leaving town without telling me where you were going?"

"Uh. Yes." Charity grinned, hoping he would laugh and carry her to the bedroom.

Beau frowned and appeared to consider that. "What would you do if you found out that I left town and didn't tell you about it? What if you needed me? What if you had to hear from someone else that I left town without telling you?"

Charity had to admit to herself that she wouldn't have liked that at all. She would have felt as if he hadn't cared enough to tell her. Instead of admitting it, she shrugged. "Point taken. It won't happen again."

Beau straightened and smiled, a smile filled with wicked intent. "I think the only *responsible* thing for me to do is make sure of that— and we all know just how much importance you place on being responsible."

Panicked, Charity bolted, shrieking when a hard arm snaked out and caught her by the waist, stopping her before she could even take a step. "Beau!" She cried out in surprise and alarm when he tossed her over his shoulder, leaving her hanging upside down and hanging on for dear life as he headed for the bedroom.

Beau's hand landed hard on her bottom, startling her, and filling her with a sense that she was about to be in over her head. "Since I'm excellent at multitasking, I can discourage that kind of behavior, satisfy your obvious need for attention, and give you the playtime you've been angling for—all at the same time."

Charity's struggling stopped when she saw the items laid out on the nightstand—items she'd picked out with Beau this afternoon, and if she wasn't mistaken—a few more. "Beau, we need to talk about this."

"I think we've done enough talking."

Finding herself on her feet again, Charity automatically grabbed for his shoulders, fighting to steady herself while Beau quickly stripped her out of her clothes.

Her jeans and sweater disappeared with surprising speed, leaving her in only her new bra and panties.

When Beau reached for the fastening of her bra, Charity slapped at him and tried to jump out of reach. "Wait!"

A dark brow went up. "For what? Change your mind? Lose your nerve?"

Sucking in a breath at the insult, Charity slapped at him again. "Of course not!" Growling, she stamped her foot. "Look what you're doing to me! I'm not like this."

Beau laughed. "Sure you are—temper and all." He reached for her again, frowning when she danced away to evade him. "Is there a problem?"

"Yes, there's a damned problem." Gesturing toward herself, she posed. "It took me almost an hour to pick out a new bra and matching panties for tonight, and you haven't even noticed."

Beau grinned, his eyes moving over her from head to toe and back again. "Oh, cher, I noticed." The silky cadence in his voice sent a sharp stab of lust through her, one that made her feel flushed and warm all over. "You look amazing in red lace."

Charity barely had a glimpse of appreciation and hunger in his eyes before he moved again, catching her by the waist and yanking her against him.

Cupping her jaw, Beau tightened the hand at her waist and pulled her closer, pressing his cock against her belly. "I definitely noticed. I love seeing you in sexy lingerie."

He pressed his lips against her, forcing them open. With a soft groan, he pressed his advantage, sliding his tongue against hers and taking her mouth with a possessiveness that wiped away her resistance. Swallowing her moan, he reached a hand between them, breaking off his kiss only long enough to unclasp her bra and toss it aside. "I also love taking it off of you." Lifting her against him, he covered her mouth with his again.

The love and hunger Charity tasted in his kiss fueled her own need for him, a need that grew stronger as he deepened his kiss again. Pressing herself against him, Charity tried to wrap her legs around him, squealing when he broke off his kiss, and with dizzying speed, tossed her over his lap.

Holding her down with an arm over her back, he ran his hand over her ass, easily holding her in place, despite her wiggling. "And ripping it off of you. I want you naked."

With a jerk, he ripped the panties from her, the delicate lace no match for his strength. "Very nice."

Beau's primitive action and the sound of the material ripping as he bared her bottom threw Charity into a world of lust and sensation that had her writhing against him.

The hard slap to her ass cheek intensified the erotic mood, as did the firm hold that didn't allow her to escape. Both alarmed and excited by his arrogance and daring, Charity gripped his pant leg, using the leverage to turn her head toward him, grinning playfully.

"That hurt!"

The reverent look on Beau's face as he stared at her ass and the loving slide of his hand over the cheek he'd just slapped stopped her from saying anything more.

Turning his head to meet her gaze, he slid the hand at her back into her hair, pushing it back with a loving caress. "No, it didn't. It just warmed you up. By the time I finish with the spanking you so richly deserve, you'll be lifting this beautiful ass for more."

Bending close, he touched his lips to her upper back, smiling at her gasp when he slid the hand on her ass lower and plunged a finger into her pussy. "You're already wet, cher, and we've only just begun. You like being over my lap every bit as much as I like having you here."

Moving his finger inside her, he traced a finger down her spine, making her shiver. "I like having you however I can get you."

"Oh, Beau." Moaning in frustration when he withdrew his finger, Charity lifted into the hand he placed on her bottom again. "Sometimes, you just overwhelm me."

Beau chuckled and slapped her ass again, the arm at her back firming against her wiggling. "Tonight, be prepared to be completely overwhelmed."

Charity couldn't stop wiggling as Beau delivered several sharp slaps to her ass, warming every inch of it. After every two or three slaps, he massaged the heat in, spreading it, only to do it again.

Her pussy clenched with the need to be filled.

Her clit throbbed with the need for attention.

Her nipples ached with the need for his touch.

She ached everywhere with erotic hunger—a hunger only Beau could satisfy.

"Spread those pretty thighs, cher."

She did it without thinking, desperate for his touch. Expecting him to plunge a finger into her again, she jolted in shock when he spread the cheeks of her ass and delivered a series of light slaps to her bottom hole and slit.

"Beau! Oh, God." Stunned by the heat, Charity closed her legs again, groaning when her attempt to relieve the torment only served to hold the heat in. Wiggling, she felt Beau reach for something on the table above her head, and groaned again when she realized that she couldn't see what he reached for.

Knowing what they'd picked out in the store, and that he'd planned to add more, she stilled, tense with anticipation and trembling with excitement.

She'd wanted to play, but didn't know how much more of his erotic teasing she could endure.

Her stomach and pussy clenched, and another rush of moisture escaped to dampen her thighs even more. She opened her mouth to ask what he was doing, her words cut off by a gasp when he parted her bottom cheeks again and thrust a cold, lubed finger into her ass.

Gripping his leg, Charity cried out, her cry ending in a moan as the finger inside her began to move. "Oh, God. OhGodohGodohGod."

His touch, much firmer than before, and far more possessive threw her into a tailspin.

Reaching a hand under her, he cupped her breast, tugging at her nipple. "You've been wanting this for some time now, haven't you? Just didn't know how to ask for it."

Slipping his finger out of her ass with a speed that left her grasping at emptiness, Beau chuckled and reached toward the nightstand again. "You can be bad anytime you want. Just don't leave town again without telling me, or your spanking will be one you won't want to repeat anytime soon."

"Are you threatening me? Ahhh! Oh, my God. Beau!" Tightening her bottom on the finger he thrust inside her again, she found herself holding on to his leg for leverage and rocking her hips.

"Absolutely. I would be very disappointed if you left town again without telling me, and I wouldn't be shy about expressing that disappointment."

Charity stilled again when a sensation she'd never experienced before robbed her of reason.

Panting, she couldn't hold back a sound somewhere between a whimper and a cry, a sound she hardly recognized. "Beau? What—oh, God." Every nerve ending in her bottom came alive, the vibration against her anal walls so intimate and alarming that she couldn't even think. "Oh, hell! Oh, God! I thought it was your finger."

She couldn't believe the sensation, a sensation so overwhelming, she couldn't move.

She could hardly breathe.

His low chuckle sent ripples of pleasure racing through her. "I added a few things to the bag I brought home. Surprising how that feels, isn't it, cher?"

"Surprising?" Charity gulped. The vibrations in her ass had her juices dripping down her leg as mini orgasms raced through her. Cries and moans poured out of her as she struggled to adjust, but the hard rubber that filled her and vibrations against her inner walls overwhelmed her.

She cried out again and again when Beau began to fuck her with it. "I—oh!" Fisting her hands, she found herself kicking her feet against the feel of the vibrator sliding slowly out of her.

The inner walls of her bottom quivered, the nerve endings brought to life by Beau's play. Whimpering for relief, she lifted her ass up to him, unable to stop herself. "Beau, please!"

"Hmm. I'll take that as a yes. Very surprising for you, but I knew you'd react this way. You're too passionate not to." He ran a hand over her ass, sneaking a finger between her ass cheeks to press against her puckered opening. "I told you that the next time I had to spank this pretty little ass that I would use a butt plug."

The decadent awareness had her desperate to be filled. Bucking on his lap, Charity pushed against his finger, taking the tip inside her with a moan and spreading her legs wider. "Yes. Yes. Oh, hell. Oh, God." Her frantic movements took him deeper, but not deep enough to satisfy her. "Stop playing around with me, damn you!" She tried to get up, but the hard arm at her back didn't give at all.

Beau chuckled softly, a silky sound that sent a shiver through her. "I thought you wanted to play, cher. You've been trying to get me to play for weeks." He withdrew his finger, reaching above her to the table again.

"Yes, damn it. I want to play, but you're doing this just to torment me." Her clit felt so swollen and hot, she couldn't stay still. It throbbed, making her crazy, and rougher in her demands. She slapped at his leg, her frustration making her angry and more aggressive. "Why don't you just fuck me?"

Beau laughed softly and teased her opening, clearly enjoying himself. "Oh, no. That wouldn't be playing at all. You can't claim to want me to play, and then try to tell me how to do it. You've earned this spanking and you know it. You should be grateful. I'm being easy on you."

"Grateful? Oh, holy hell!" Charity stilled at the pressure against her bottom hole. "What are you—is that a butt plug? Oh, God. How big is it?" She tried to squeeze her bottom in an instinctive reaction to keep him out, but he'd created a need inside her that had her lifting into the pressure, moaning at the sting. Shocked that the burn of being stretched excited her even more, she pushed harder against the plug.

"Easy, cher." Beau slid the arm at her back lower, and used his strong fingers to pry her ass cheeks wide, exposing her bottom hole.

She could actually feel his gaze there.

Beau pressed the plug harder against her opening, stretching the tight ring of muscle, her position and strength of his fingers making it impossible for her to close against him. "It's big enough—bigger than my two fingers, but smaller than the rest."

"The rest?" Charity gulped, taking a shuddering breath and releasing it on a moan as he pushed the plug into her. "Oh, God. It's too big. Too full." Chills raced up and down her spine at the erotic feel of it, her entire slit burning for his touch.

"Too full?" Beau moved the plug in a circular motion as he pressed it even deeper. "You barely have it in you. Be still, and try to loosen those muscles. It's going to get wider as it goes into you, stretching this tight little hole."

"Oh, God. It's going to get bigger?" A shiver of anticipation raced through her. "I can't stretch anymore." Rocking against him, she cried out as the plug went deeper, hoarse cries and whimpers of both pleasure, and the overwhelming sense of vulnerability.

Even when he'd played with her in the past, he'd allowed her a small sense of control.

At least she'd thought so until now. Crying out at the slow, steady pressure, she lifted higher, her toes curled as the plug stretched her inner walls.

Beau had given her the illusion of being in control, but he had a wicked streak even wider than she'd suspected.

"Very good, cher. Only a little to go." He moved the plug from side to side as he pushed it deeper. "Seeing the way your ass is gripping this plug is making me crazy, cher."

His low, throaty tone seemed to rumble from deep inside him. "Just thinking about how it's going to grip my cock has my cock throbbing." He slid the plug the rest of the way inside her, releasing her ass cheeks to rub her back as he pushed against the base. "Easy. It's all the way in. Feel how it narrowed at the base. That'll keep it inside you and keep you from pushing it out until *I'm* ready to take it out."

Charity shuddered, finding it hard to focus on anything except the plug. "It feels huge. Oh, God, Beau. I don't know what to do. I need to come so bad. Please, do something." The brush of his fingers on her clit made her jolt, the sharp stab of pleasure driving her relentlessly toward the edge.

Shaking uncontrollably, Charity jolted when a hard hand landed on her ass again. Crying out as the slap seemed to reverberate through the plug and into her, she bucked against him, trying to fuck herself on the plug. Groaning in frustration when she couldn't do more than make the plug shift inside her, and struggling against the heat that consumed her entire slit, Charity tried to rub her thighs together to ease an ache so intense, it made her violent.

Using every bit of strength she could gather, she tried to get up again, cursing as she fought his hold. "Damn it, Beau. Let me up."

"There's my woman." Wrapping an arm around her, he held her firmly against him, a finger teasing her clit as a series of short slaps landed on her ass in rapid-fire succession, covering every inch of her bottom.

Through it, Beau moved his fingers over her slick clit, easily overcoming her struggle to escape. "You're going to come while your ass is full and I'm spanking you. Don't bother to fight it. I won't let you win."

Charity couldn't believe she could be so excited. She hadn't thought it possible to be this aroused. Shaking with it, she bucked on his lap, her mind fighting to get away while her body demanded more.

Her pussy clenched as the friction on her clit continued, the heat from her spanking spreading through her slit and making each sensation even more intense. She cried out in abandon, fisting her hands on the floor. Tears stung her eyes as the pleasure became so extreme, she wept with it.

Her clit burned under his relentless ministrations, the warmth spreading from the sharp slaps heating her buttocks.

The pressure inside her continued to build until she thought she would die of it.

She stilled, sucking in a breath as the wave hit her, crying out her pleasure as the tingling in her clit exploded in a shower of sparks.

Her body tightened, her abdomen clenching hard as the shimmering waves washed over her.

Beau stopped spanking her and released her clit just as she peaked, leaving her weak and still trembling over his lap. "That should end any claim that you don't like your spankings." Rubbing her hot ass, he reignited the heat while she still trembled. "Anytime you give me a hard time about something, I can put you over my knee. Very nice. You ready to play some more, cher?"

Charity was too weak to move, but the need in his voice had her struggling to turn to face him. "As long as you understand that I have every intention of tormenting you just as much in the very near future."

Beau chuckled and worked the plug out of her, easily overcoming her struggles and seeming to enjoy her cries as the sensations astonished her. With a groan, he gathered her against him, tossing the plug aside before lifting her to straddle him. Nuzzling her jaw and brushing his lips over hers, he cupped her breasts, rolling her nipples between his thumbs and forefingers. Sitting back, he smiled at her cries of pleasure, a smile filled with love, playfulness, and a need for her that stole her breath. "You already torment me, cher. Every cry from you is like a stroke to my cock. Every whimper excites me. Every moan only makes me want you more."

With clumsy hands, Charity worked to rid Beau of his shirt, and tossed it aside, her movements frantic. "I want you. I want you inside me."

Beau grinned and got to his feet, setting her on hers. "There's no place I like to be more." His body brushed against hers as he started to unfasten his pants, laughing softly as he slapped away her clumsy attempt to help. "I can do it faster. Get on the bed."

For the first time, Charity noticed that the wedge that they'd used in the back room of Beau's shop had been placed on the bed. Pausing, she looked back at Beau just in time to see him rolling on a condom.

Reaching out a hand, Charity rubbed his chest, thrilling at the feel of warm muscle. Wanting to touch him, she reached for his cock, frowning when he gripped her wrist.

His eyes softened, but his expression remained hard, the tension surrounding him even more intense. "No. Don't touch me. I'm already too close, and thinking about taking your ass has me even closer to the edge. Let me settle some, cher, while I pleasure you."

Cupping her jaw, he brushed his lips against hers. "Let me make this good for you, cher. Christ, I love you."

He nudged her, catching her when she fell, and lowering her to the bed. When she tried to lie on her belly the way he'd positioned her at the shop, he lifted her and flipped her over, once again surprising her with his strength. "No. On your back. I want to watch your face when I take your ass."

With the wedge under her, her ass was lifted even higher than before, the angle of it leaving her entire slit on display.

Spreading her legs, he made a place for himself between them and leaned over her forcing her thighs high and wide as he reached again for something on the nightstand. Braced on his elbows, he dangled the chain in front of her face, grinning. "Remember this?"

Charity smiled back, running her hands over his chest and her feet up and down his thighs. "You had a good time this afternoon, didn't you?"

Beau lowered his head, taking her mouth in a searing kiss that curled her toes. By the time he lifted his head again, she trembled with need and love for him. "I did, and more importantly, we had a good time *together*." Straightening, he ran the end of the chain over her breasts. "You excited the hell out of me this afternoon."

Slipping the loop at one of the chain to her nipple, he grinned. "Can I expect more of that in the future?"

Biting her lip at the gentle but unrelenting pressure, Charity whimpered and fisted her hands at her sides. "Absolutely. I loved it. I love playing with you. Oh, God, that feels incredible." Meeting his gaze, she moaned. "Damn, that feels good. I'm going to have to think up something else to keep you on your toes."

Beau fastened the other loop to her other nipple, tightening it securely before wrapping his hand around the chain and tugging, using his fingers to part her folds while keeping the chain pulled taut. "I'm very much looking forward to it."

Using his thumb to tease her clit, he pulled gently on the chain. "I love the thought of spending my life loving you. Playing with you. Think you can handle that?"

Watching him reach for the thin vibrator again, Charity sucked in a breath, her bottom clenching. "I'm a fast learner. Oh, God!" The feel of the slim rubber, well coated with lube, slipping into her bottom again had Charity struggling in alarm, but with the wedge under her hips, her legs kept falling back toward her chest.

Beau took advantage, thrusting his cock into her pussy and fucking her with slow, deliberate strokes. "Yeah? Let's see how fast." Still holding the chain, he caressed her clit with a slow, teasing thumb, and turned the vibrator on.

The slow tugs to her nipples drove her crazy, making the heat at her slit even hotter. The too-infrequent slide of his thumb over the sensitized bundle of nerves tormented her, her stomach muscles tightening as the pressure inside her became almost unbearable.

Her legs shook as the pleasure mounted.

Controlled her.

The vibrations in her ass and the firm thrust of his cock in her pussy drove her to incredible heights, the stretched, too-full feeling of having both her ass and pussy filled making the sensation even more intense.

Her cries of pleasure filled the room, cries that seemed to spur Beau on. Writhing beneath him, she called out his name over and over, shaking uncontrollably at the sensations bombarding her system.

"Beau, it's too much. God, I feel you everywhere!"

She clamped down on the cock and vibrator filling her, rocking her hips in time to Beau's thrusts, groaning in frustration when he released the chain and moved his hand away from her clit. "Beau, please!"

He slid a possessive hand up her body, holding her in place as he slid both his cock and the vibrator from her. "Easy, cher." His voice, hardly more than a growl, washed over her.

The awareness in her bottom threatened to drive her insane, and she couldn't stop wiggling against him, trying to get his cock back inside her. "Don't stop. More."

Opening her eyes, she stared into his, fascinated by the dark glitter in them. Struck by his tortured expression, Charity reached for him. "Beau?"

To her surprise, he shook his head and gripped her wrist before she could touch him. "No, cher. Christ, I want you so much, and the thought of taking your ass has me on edge. My cock's so hard it hurts. Just be still for a minute. I want to make this good for you but my control is being pushed to its limits." Gripping her ankles, he placed openmouthed kisses on each one before sliding his hands to the underside her of knees.

Warmed and humbled by his desire for her, Charity smiled and ran her feet up his side and to his shoulders, her pussy and ass clenching in anticipation. She couldn't stop moving, loving the slight tug on her nipples each time the chain shifted. "I love that you want me so much, but I don't think I can take much more."

Beau groaned. "You're going to get more—my cock filling your ass."

Her pulse leapt at the erotic intent in his eyes, a sharp look that made it difficult to breathe. Shivering with excitement when he pushed her knees back, almost to her chest, she gasped when the head of his cock pressed against her puckered opening.

Fisting his cock, he pressed harder, his other hand flattening on her abdomen. His eyes, nearly black, held hers, his face tight with sexual tension. Looping his finger around the chain, he tugged at her nipples while running his thumb lightly over her clit. "I want you more than I've ever wanted anything in my life."

The deep growl in his voice created an excitement and hunger inside her she'd never experienced before, as though her hunger and his combined, making each so much more. "And I'm going to have you—in every fucking way possible. Reach up and hang on to the headboard."

When she moved too slowly for him, Beau reached under her to slap her ass, and she would swear she could actually see his control slip. "Do it, cher. Now. I'm hanging by a fucking thread here."

Charity didn't hesitate, and raised her arms above her head, fisting her hands around the slats in the headboard. "Take me, damn you!"

Beau groaned and leaned forward, his features hard and his eyes narrowed to slits. "With pleasure."

Shocked at the feel of the head of his cock, so hot, so hard, so thick, forcing the tight ring of muscle to give way, Charity tried to push her legs against him, but Beau seemed ready for that and leaned more heavily against her.

Releasing her clit, he wrapped a hard arm around her thighs and held them firmly against his chest. "Be still. I don't want to hurt you, damn it!"

With a growl, he pushed deeper, sinking the head of his cock past the tight ring of muscle and into her. "So fucking tight." His expression looked tortured, his face hard and lined with tension, but his eyes never left hers. "Easy. Relax those muscles, cher. Easy. I've got you. I'll go slow, I promise. Just let me in, baby. Let me inside this tight ass."

Shivers raced up and down Charity's spine as Beau pushed deeper, his cock like hot steel as it forced her inner walls to stretch to accommodate him. She couldn't stop clamping down, her body fighting to get him deeper while at the same time trying to close against such a decadent invasion.

Her inner walls quivered all around him, but she couldn't stop. It was as if the cock stretching her ass controlled a part of her now, leaving her feeling even more vulnerable.

Shivers of delight raced through her, the need to come almost unbearable. "It burns! Oh, God, Beau. It's stretching me." Crying out as he pushed deeper, Charity tried to arch, but Beau held firm. "Let me move! It's so hot. Oh, God. I feel so full."

"Damned right, it's hot. Your ass is so fucking hot, it's burning me. So tight. Christ, Charity, you're killing me." Relentlessly pushing his hips forward, he continued to fill her. "Inch by fucking inch. I want it all. That's it, cher." Gripping her ankles, he spread her even wider. "Be still, damn it. You're not gonna be able to take it all and I don't want to hurt you."

She whimpered, writhing on the bed as Beau started to withdraw, crying out again when he thrust just a little deeper than before. She'd never felt so completely taken, the feel of his hard cock impaling her ass the most wicked and overwhelming thing she'd ever experienced.

"So full. Oh, God, Beau." Every shallow thrust took him a little deeper. The raw sexuality of the act and burning sensation of being stretched created a riot of sizzling heat inside her. The heat rippled through her, touching her everywhere.

She sucked in a sharp breath when Beau flattened his hand on her abdomen again, manipulating her clit and tugging at the chain attached to her nipples at the same time he worked his cock deeper. Dazed at the sharp pleasure that hit her from everywhere all at once, Charity didn't even try to hold back her cries at the alarming pleasure.

Her body felt as if it shimmered, every nerve ending tingling with the rush of warm delight as she came harder than she'd ever come before. Her shuddering cry went on and on as she rode the swell of pleasure. Tightening on Beau's cock, she reached for his hand, needing his strength to anchor her.

Beau groaned, gripping her hand in his as he sank deeper, his cock pulsing against her inner walls. "Oh, cher." Releasing her clit and the chain, he slumped over her, murmuring softly to her when she whimpered. "I've got you."

Trembling with aftershocks, Charity wrapped her arms and legs around him, needing the steadiness of his heat and strength to help her settle.

Lifting her against him with a groan, he pushed the wedge off the bed and gathered her close, kneeling on the bed and holding her on his lap, groaning again as his cock shifted inside her. "You okay?"

Smiling at the rumble in his voice and fascinated that the muscles of his shoulders quivered under her palms, Charity lifted her head. Wrapping her arms around his neck and leaning back to look at him, she sucked in a breath as his cock went deeper. "I'm fantastic. I can't believe we did that. Oh, God, Beau. We're going to kill each other."

Beau's chuckle ended on another groan, his breathing ragged. "Yeah, but I don't care."

Still trembling with the remnants of her orgasm, Charity cuddled closer, her bottom clenching when he moved her and his cock slid free. "You're a very naughty man."

Lifting his head, he pushed her damp hair back from her forehead. "You knew that before you agreed to marry me."

"I did." Charity giggled. "I just didn't realize how naughty you are." Pressing herself against him, she threaded her fingers through his hair and pulled his head down, to nuzzle his lips. "I just didn't realize that loving and play could go together this way. I was so scared, Beau. I was so scared that you couldn't possibly love me the way I love you. I was so scared of being hurt and making a fool of myself over you."

The arms at her back tightened, pulling her closer. "And that's why you didn't want anyone to know about us?"

"Yes. I was so stupid. I just never realized it could be this way. I love you so much." Her heart swelled with it until sometimes, she thought it might burst. "Promise me it'll always be this way between us."

Holding her against his chest, he rose from the bed. "No."

Striding to the bathroom, he met her startled look with a smile, his eyes filled with satisfaction and love. "I promise you, it'll be even better. Now, let's get cleaned up so we can go have some wine, and I can take you again in front of the fire."

"But, Beau. What about the things you left on my nipples?"

Beau grinned, his eyes flashing. "They'll look perfect with the one I bought for your clit. I want to see you wearing the whole set."

"You're kidding, right?" Her clit tingled with anticipation.

Beau set her on her feet in the shower, and went to rid himself of the condom. "You'll see."

* * * *

Almost two hours later, Charity struggled to get enough air in her lungs as she snuggled against Beau's chest. With the fire at one side, and him at the other, she found herself surrounded by heat. "You weren't kidding."

Beau reached behind him, retrieving a glass of wine. "I play. I don't kid."

Pillowing her head on his shoulder, he placed the glass of wine at her lips. "I always mean what I say, cher."

After sipping the wine, she nuzzled his neck while he finished the glass. "I can always depend on you, can't I?"

Reaching back, he set the glass on the table, closing his fingers over her nipples, still sensitized from the clips. "Of course."

She ran a hand over his chest. "You're very sexy, you know?"

Beau leaned back, to look at her, his eyes narrowed. "What are you up to?"

Charity smiled and leaned closer to nibble at his lips. "This time, I'm going to seduce you. Don't worry. I'll be easy on you. You just stay right here while I go get the paints. I want to make sure they taste the way they're supposed to."

"What?"

Laughing in delight at the look of shock on his face, Charity jumped up and raced to the bedroom.

"Charity!"

Gathering the paints and brushes, Charity ran back to the living room to find Beau reclining against the sofa and refilling their glasses.

Eyeing the paints, Beau groaned. "Charity, why don't you just lie beside me and we can cuddle?"

Charity hid a smile when she saw that his cock had hardened while she'd been gone. "You just lie back and relax. Just pretend I'm not here. I just want to paint your cock. When I'm done, I'll lick every bit of it off so you won't even have to clean it up."

"Holy hell, I've created a monster."

Minutes later, Charity couldn't stop grinning, her own body tight with need as Beau clenched his hands into fists beside him, throwing his eyes back and squeezing his eyes closed.

"Jesus, cher, you're killing me!"

"Be patient. We haven't tried the other brushes yet." She reached for the softest one and dipped it into the red edible paint. "I'm going to paint the head of your cock with the cherry flavor. Just be still, darling. I may show some of your products at the club, and I'm going to have to be able to answer questions about them. Once I'm done painting, you're going to have to be still so I can lick the paint off."

Giggling at Beau's string of French, most of it in guttural tones, Charity dipped the brush into the paint and stared at him, not realizing how long she'd just sat there and looked at him until he lifted his head and opened his eyes.

"You okay, cher?"

Charity smiled. "I've never been better. I adore you. Thank you for teaching me how to play."

Beau grinned. "You're *very* welcome." His smile fell, a harsh groan escaping when she touched the brush to the head of his cock. "You're fucking killing me!"

"There, there, darling. Just hang in there. You don't want me to think you can dish it out and not take it, do you?"

"I swear, I'll get even for this."

Charity dipped the brush into the paint again, knowing how cold it would feel. "Looking forward to it, darlin'. Looking forward to it. You don't scare me anymore."

Chapter Twenty-Two

Charity sighed, staring down at her cell phone as she disconnected. "Something's wrong." Her hands shook so badly, she put the phone down, scared of dropping it.

Why didn't he answer?

She pushed her glass of iced tea aside and looked up at her sister, trying to push back the panic that had gotten progressively more intense over the last hour. "Beau's still not answering."

Hope shrugged. "Maybe he's busy."

Despite her sister's nonchalant tone, Hope looked increasingly concerned.

Shaking her head, Charity flattened a hand on her stomach. "No. Something's wrong. I can feel it. You know it, too. He was supposed to call me this morning when he got done at the warehouse. He wanted me to go with him, but I had to straighten out the mix-up with the flowers. We were supposed to have lunch together, and it's already one o'clock. No, something's wrong."

Getting to her feet, she rubbed her hand over her churning stomach and began to pace her sister's kitchen. "It's two days until the wedding. He wouldn't pull something like this on me. He knows I'm a nervous wreck. Hell, he's been calling me almost every hour during the day. He knows I'm a nervous wreck about the wedding arrangements, and he still won't tell me where we're going for our honeymoon."

Beau always seemed to know when she needed him, and he'd spent the last several days teasing her and trying to lighten the mood.

Getting to her feet, Hope gathered their glasses and put them in the sink. "Come on. Let's go."

Charity spun. "Where?"

Hope took her arm, led her to the living room, and opened the closet door. "You're not going to feel better until we find him." She tossed Charity's coat to her before shrugging into her own. "Let's go look for him."

Slipping into her coat, Charity caught her sister's arm, struck by the concern in Hope's eyes. "You're worried, too." Frowning, she finished zipping her coat. "Hope, I'm scared. Something's definitely wrong."

Hope rubbed her arm. "It might be nothing, but it's not like Beau to disappear, and it's not like him to ignore his cell phone." She waved toward Charity. "I'm going to call Ace. Go warm up the car."

Charity nodded, her stomach clenching. She didn't know what she'd do if anything happened to Beau. Now she knew how he would feel if he couldn't get in touch with her, and vowed to herself to never do this to him.

She got in the car and turned on the ignition, staring down at her phone again.

Where could he be?

Had he been in an accident?

The thought of Beau being somewhere hurt made her want to throw up. She loved him too damned much to ever lose him.

A minute later, Hope came out and opened Charity's door. "Move over. I'm driving. You're shaking."

A few minutes later, they pulled into Beau's driveway.

Charity reached for the door handle, her hands shaking so badly that she missed the first time. "His truck's not here, but I want to go look inside."

As soon as she stepped through the door, she knew he wasn't there. She always felt him.

She had to look, anyway.

She went from room to room, calling his name, but there was no answer. As she started back out again, she looked up to see Hope standing just inside the front door. "He's not here."

Surprised that her voice cracked, she said it again. "I looked in every room. Let's try the store." As she started past the small table near the entryway, she saw that the light on the answering machine blinked.

"I wonder if all these messages are from me."

Hope strode over and hit the play button. "There's only one way to find out."

The first message began to play. "Beau, I really need to see you."

Charity stiffened at the sound of Anna's pleading tone.

"I need to talk to you about the divorce. I found the wedding invitation. Jeffrey hid it from me. Please don't tell me you're really going to get married to *her*. We need to talk, Beau. Today."

Charity blinked at the anger in Anna's voice.

Hope snorted. "Damn. That woman just can't take *no* for an answer, can she? Bitch."

Charity listened to the rest of the messages, all from her, each sounding increasingly frantic. "He hasn't been back here since he left this morning. If he had, he would have listened to these."

Hope gripped her arm and tugged, pulling her back out the door. "We'll find him. Let's go check out the store."

Rubbing her arms as she made her way back out to the car, Charity choked back a sob. "I knew something was wrong. Damn it. Why didn't I start looking for him sooner?"

After talking with Beau's employee and learning that he'd been expecting Beau to call him back, too, Charity was scared out of her mind. "Tim said he's been calling Beau for over an hour. Beau was supposed to talk to him today about the schedule. We've got to find him, Hope. Head for the warehouse. We'll check on the way to see if there's any sign of an accident. If he's not there, Hope, I don't know what I'm going to do."

She couldn't stop shaking, her knees rubbery and her hands shaking as she pulled the car door closed.

Staring straight ahead, she braced a hand on the dashboard as her sister pulled out. "Beau wouldn't have disappeared like this." Charity chewed on her thumbnail, ruining the manicure Hope had insisted she absolutely had to have.

Turning to glance at her sister, she shifted restlessly in her seat. "I can't stop thinking about that message from Anna. I'd hoped she'd given up. I wish I knew where the hell she lives."

Hope reached for her hand and squeezed, the look of fear in her eyes scaring Charity even more. "Ace is on his way there now. I called him when you were in Beau's store. If that fucking bitch—"

Charity whipped her head around. "What? What do you know that I don't know?"

Shaking her head, Hope sped out of town. "Ace and I were talking about her the other night. Her obsession with Beau is a little extreme. According to Ace, it's been going on for some time, but when Ace tried to warn Beau about her, Beau got defensive. He always looked at her as some kind of damsel in distress, but after what happened and Beau found out the truth about her, Ace is a little worried."

Charity swallowed the lump in her throat, but it was quickly replaced by another. "She's desperate now. Beau doesn't know what kind of effect he has on people. She's in love with him."

Hope released her hand, gripping the steering wheel with both of them as they hit the outskirts of town. Speeding up, she sat forward. "She doesn't know what love is. She's possessive. She's selfish. She wants what she wants and she doesn't give a damn about anyone else."

Every minute of the drive seemed to take forever, and with every mile, Charity became tenser, her imagination running wild. "What if she hurt him? He wouldn't be expecting that. He wouldn't feel threatened by her."

Hope spared her a glance. "Maybe he's just talking to her somewhere. Hell, maybe he has a flat tire and his cell phone's dead."

Charity nodded, clinging to any scenario in which Beau was safe. "Yes. He's usually good at charging his phone, though." Tapping her hands on her thighs, she turned her head from side to side, not wanting to miss anything. "He might have gotten tied up somewhere. He still would have called. Yeah. He would have called. It's not like Beau to stand me up. He'd answer his phone if he could. That means for some reason, he can't."

Sucking in a breath at the mental image of Beau lying dead at the side of the road, Charity whipped around to her sister. "What if he was robbed? What if someone knew he owned the warehouse and decided to rob him?"

Hope frowned. "Don't they just deal with credit cards?"

"What if the person robbing him doesn't know that? Shit, Hope. He just fired someone. What if the guy got mad and came back to get even with him?"

"Stop it!" Hope grabbed her arm. "We don't know until we know."

Charity knew Hope wanted to calm her, but the closer they got to Beau's warehouse, the more scared she became. "Right up here. It's on the right. There it is." Her heart hammered in her chest. "Look! His truck's there."

As soon as Hope stopped the car, Charity scrambled to get out.

"Charity! Wait!"

Ignoring her sister, Charity ran through the front doors, her heart stopping at the sound of Anna's voice. "No, Beau. You don't want her. You want me!"

The large aisles of the huge warehouse made it possible for Charity to remain hidden, and gave her room to move. Rushing to the first aisle, she ducked behind it, waiting for Hope to appear.

She listened to Anna and Beau talk, trying to judge their location.

It sounded as if they were in the next aisle.

As soon as her sister walked through, Charity put a finger to her lips and motioned for her to duck and hurry over, relieved to see that Hope carried a baseball bat.

Keeping her voice low, she leaned close to Hope. "I forgot you carried that. I want to get closer and see what's going on. Give it to me and you go call for help." She reached for the bat and tried to pull it from her sister's grasp, but Hope tightened her hold on it.

"No." Hope shook her head, keeping her voice at a low whisper that Charity had to strain to hear. "Stay put a minute and I'll text Ace. I'm not leaving you in here alone."

"Put the gun down, Anna, and we can talk."

Charity stilled, a cold chill going down her spine at Beau's soft command. Turning her head, she met her sister's gaze, a lifetime of experience enabling them to communicate without speaking.

I'm going.

Shit.

Hope started texting, handing over the baseball bat with a look.

Be careful.

Charity blinked back tears, fear for Beau threatening to choke her. She knew she had to get herself under control or she wouldn't be able to give him the help he needed.

She could do this. She had to do this.

He'd been there for her when she'd needed him and she couldn't do any less.

She did her best to push the mental image of Beau being shot to the side, knowing that she wouldn't be of any use to him if she fell apart.

Staying low, she focused on Anna's voice as the other woman pled with Beau to listen to her, and Beau's insistence that she put the gun down first. As Charity edged her way around the corner, she poked her head out, her breath coming out in a rush when she found the aisle empty.

She couldn't tell if they were in the next aisle or not, but she knew she had to be getting close.

She barely heard her sister's footsteps on the concrete floor, and didn't take the time to look back, just shaking her head to let know Hope they weren't in that aisle as Charity worked her way to the end of the next one.

Knowing that Hope had called for help, Charity thought about nothing except getting close enough to help Beau if he needed it, and possibly get a chance to let him know that help was on the way.

Her fear grew when she realized that Anna sounded more unstable and desperate by the minute.

Anna's voice also became stronger, her anger coming through and making her more uncontrolled.

"No, Beau." The cold edge in Anna's voice sent another surge of fear through Charity. "I can't let you make a mistake like that. I can't let you marry her. If I can't have you, nobody can. I worked too hard to get you."

"You never had me, Anna."

Charity sucked in a breath, spinning to look at Hope.

What the hell did he think he was doing?

"That's enough, Anna. Jeffrey loves you. He *needs* you." Beau's voice carried an anger and a hint of panic that hadn't been there before.

Peering around the display on the endcap, Charity sucked in a breath and held it, her heart jumping to her throat when she saw Anna, about eight feet away, holding a gun pointed at Beau.

Beau faced Charity's direction, but Charity didn't know if he saw her.

Ducking back, she gripped the bat tighter, closing her eyes and pressing her forehead against the smooth wood as she struggled to calm her breathing.

Anna stood only about eight feet away, facing Beau, who stood on the other side.

Hope peered around her, ducked back and tugged her sleeve, getting Charity's attention before motioning that she would go to the other end of the aisle.

Charity shook her head and tried to grab her sister to stop her, but Hope was already gone.

Inwardly cursing, she slowly straightened, pausing to wipe her damp palms on her pant legs before gripping the bat with both hands.

"I love you, Beau. You were supposed to marry *me*! I can't let you marry her, Beau. Don't you understand?"

"Anna, I love Charity."

Charity took a deep breath and let it out slowly, doing her best to ignore Anna's words and listen for whatever Hope planned to do. Easing her head around the corner just enough to watch Anna, Charity tightened her grip on the bat.

Suddenly, the display at the opposite end of the aisle came crashing down.

Anna cried out and whirled toward it just as Charity stepped out and raised the bat, hitting Anna's arm and sending the gun flying a split second before Beau could grab it.

Anna fell to the floor, screaming in pain as Beau smiled at Charity. "You broke my arm."

Charity nodded, never taking her eyes from Beau. "You stood me up." Out of the corner of her eye, she saw Hope racing toward her, and saw her sister pick up the gun from halfway down the aisle.

Beau's eyes seemed lit from within as he reached for her, his hands closing around her upper arms and pulling her against him. "Are you okay? You're shaking, cher. Come on. Let's sit you down."

Locking her knees, Charity buried her face against his chest. "I'm okay. Are you hurt anywhere?"

Running his hands up and down her back, Beau had to raise his voice to be heard over Anna's screams. "I think I aged ten years when you walked through the front door, but other than that, I'm fine. You scared the hell out of me. Why didn't you just call for help?"

Hope touched his arm as if assuring herself that he was unharmed. "We did. I did, at least." She winced at the sound of Ace's deep growl coming from the end of the aisle.

Ace strode straight for Hope, another policeman rushing along side of him. Snagging an arm around Hope from behind, Ace took the gun from her hand, handed it to the other policeman, and crushed his wife to his chest in one smooth move. "I told you to wait for help!"

Charity clung to Beau, watching the other policeman help Anna to her feet. "We couldn't wait. Anna was getting bolder by the minute and was going to shoot Beau. She said that if she couldn't have him, no one else could, either."

Beau's eyes were filled with pity as the policeman took Anna away. "She needs help. I feel sorry for her, and for Jeffrey."

Weak with relief, Charity poked him in the stomach. "You scared me, damn it."

Beau ran a hand over her hair, his eyes narrowed. "Not half as scared as I was when I saw the two of you come in."

Hope turned slightly, still held in Ace's embrace. "How did you see us?"

Beau gestured toward the mirrors in the corners. "I had to get Anna turned around so she wouldn't spot you."

Charity lifted her head, leaning back to look up at Beau. "Where are all your employees?"

Beau shrugged. "When I saw the gun, I sent them all home. Told them to get out and that I was closing for the day. None of them got a chance to see the gun."

With a sigh, Beau pulled out his phone. "I'd better call Jeffrey."

* * * *

Sitting on the hood of her car, Charity leaned back against Beau, watching as Hope finished giving the policeman her statement with

Ace hovering protectively at her side. "Thank God, you weren't hurt. Ace looks pretty grim, huh?"

"Men tend to look that way when their women are in danger. You and Hope scared the hell out of me, cher."

Hugging his arm, Charity shuddered, unable to get the image of Anna holding a gun on Beau out of her head. "You scared me. I thought for sure you were in an accident or something. I heard the message Anna left at your house. She really sounded desperate."

"She was. Something snapped inside her, Charity. I want to make sure she gets the help she needs. If Jeffrey can't afford it, I'm going to help him."

Charity blinked at the challenge in his tone. Turning to look up at him over her shoulder, she frowned up at him. "Why did you say it like that? Did you think I would object?"

Beau relaxed behind her. "I don't know. She's caused a lot of trouble, but I just can't let Jeffrey try to handle this on his own."

Charity nodded, enjoying the feel of him, warm, solid and safe. Leaning back against him again, she smiled. "You know, you really do have a thing for damsels in distress. It seems strange that you'd want to marry a woman who's perfectly capable of taking care of herself." She fought to hide her unease, wondering how a man who takes care of everyone around him would handle a wife who could take care of herself.

Beau tightened his arms around her and pulled her close, his warm, silky tone filled with love. "Afraid I'll get bored if I can't rescue you? I hope I never have to rescue you again, cher, and I know you're perfectly capable of rescuing me. I love you, cher. I'm not marrying you because you need me. I'm marrying you because I need *you*."

Epilogue

Smiling up at her husband, Charity ran her hand over his tuxedo as he turned her on the dance floor. "You throw a hell of a party, Mr. Parrish. I should have known you'd be good at this, too."

Beau grinned. "I know it was driving you crazy to turn the reception over to me, Mrs. Parrish. You're not used to giving up control. It was fun to watch."

Narrowing her eyes, she poked him in the chest. "You enjoyed tormenting me, didn't you?"

Faking a wince, he smiled and lifted her hand to his lips. "I plan to torment you in other ways, cher." Straightening, he ran a hand down her back. "This is the last song, cher. The party's over. Are you ready for our honeymoon?"

Grinning, Charity allowed him to lead her from the dance floor as the music faded away. "Absolutely." Her heart raced with anticipation. "I've never made love with a married man before."

Beau threw back his head and laughed. "And now, that's all you get." Bending, he put a shoulder to her stomach and lifted her over it.

Charity gasped, laughing so hard she could barely speak. "What the hell are you doing?"

Amidst applause from the other, Beau raised his voice to be heard. "Thank you all so much for making this day wonderful. Now, if you'll excuse us, I'm kidnapping my bride."

Charity stilled, lifting up to see her mother, fathers, and sister all watching with big smiles on their faces.

Hope applauded, she and their mother wiping away tears. "Yeah!"

Giggling, Charity, hung on to Beau's jacket and blew kisses to everyone as Beau strode through the ballroom and out the door. Once outside, she kicked her feet. "Okay, you can put me down now."

"You didn't hear me, cher. I said I was kidnapping you. You have just enough time to get home and change your dress before we have to go catch our flight."

Setting her on her feet, he helped her into his SUV, smiling when she waved at the crowd who'd spilled from the ballroom to wave them off. "I did promise to kidnap you, remember?" Lifting her chin, he held her gaze. "I'll always keep my promises to you."

Struck by his solemn expression, Charity nodded, blinking back tears. "I know that. Oh, Beau. I love you so much."

"And I love you." Grinning, he gestured toward the passenger seat. "And now, my darling wife, your kidnapping begins."

* * * *

Charity gaped, in awe of the size and beauty of the hotel in front of her. Lights shone from every window, and the large, circular driveway only added to the charm of the historical building. "This is beautiful. I can't wait to see it in the daytime. I'm so glad you brought me to New Orleans. I'd love to see where you grew up."

Beau smiled, his eyes filled with love and memories as he opened the door of the rental car and helped her out. "I wanted you to see where I come from. I want you to understand me, and see just how much I love you."

Gasping in surprise when he swung her up in his arms, she slapped at his shoulder, her face burning. "Beau! Put me down. What are they going to think when we walk into the lobby?"

Wrapping her arms around his shoulders, she pulled his head down for a kiss. "You know what? I'm so happy, I don't care."

Held securely in her husband's arms, and warmed by the love shining in his eyes, she couldn't imagine being any happier than she was at that moment. "I love you, and if people stare, I don't give a damn."

Beau grinned. "There's my girl." Lifting her high against his chest, he nuzzled her neck. "By the way, cher, this isn't a hotel. This is the home my grandfather left to me."

Charity stilled. "What?"

She whipped her head around as the front door opened, stiffening. "Um, Beau? Is that a maid?"

Beau chuckled. "Calm down. There's a staff to take care of things while we're here. You didn't really expect me to kidnap you and bring you here to watch you clean, did you? I have better ways for you to spend your time."

"Beau, I can't believe this." Fidgeting in his arms, she craned her neck, eager to see everything.

He carried her through the front door, and into a large living room before setting her on her feet, tightening the arm he kept around her when she started toward the massive fireplace, effectively keeping her at his side. "You'll have plenty of time to explore. We're spending a month here."

"A month!" The thought of having her husband to herself for an entire month proved an irresistible lure, but she couldn't imagine dumping the responsibilities of the club on her sister. "Oh, Beau. There's nothing I'd like more, but Hope…"

"I've already talked to Hope and she's hiring someone else to help out. She said that—and I quote—'Since we both have demanding husbands now, hiring someone just makes sense.' There. No excuses. I plan to come back here with you as often as we can get away."

Struck by the hint of uncertainty in his eyes, the first she'd ever seen, Charity blinked back tears. "I'd love that."

The tension eased from his big frame. "I'm glad. I want you and our children to know this place—love this place—as much as I do."

"It's a friggin' mansion." Charity looked around at all the beautiful furniture, the high ceilings and ornate woodwork making her feel out of place.

Cupping her face, he lifted it for his kiss. "It's a home, Charity. A home. There's always been a lot of love here, and I want to share it with you."

Blinking back tears, Charity sniffed. "Who would have guessed you could be so romantic?"

"You haven't seen anything yet, cher." He lifted her in his arms again. "Things are different here. *I'm* the master of Belle Fleur."

"Belle Fleur? Doesn't that mean beautiful flower?" She whipped her head from side to side, astounded at the beautiful, wide staircase.

Beau didn't even seem out of breath as he carried her up the long staircase. "Yes. My grandfather always called my grandmother his beautiful flower." At the top of the stairs, he turned to the left. "As I was saying, I'm the master here, and I've kidnapped you. None of the servants will help you escape."

Happiness bubbled inside her. "Wow, that sounds pretty sexy. I've always fantasized about getting kidnapped by a handsome rogue."

"Did you?" Beau's lips twitched. "And in this fantasy, what did your captor do to you?"

Sliding a hand over his chest, Charity looked up at him through her lashes, trying desperately to hide a smile. "He had his way with me. Over and over again."

"What a coincidence. That's what I plan to do to you." He continued down the hall and through a set of double doors.

Cuddling against him, she kissed his jaw. "I promise to be appropriately frightened."

Charity gasped at the opulence of the large bedroom, squinting her eyes to see in the shadows. The only lights came from the lamps on the nightstand on either side of the bed, old-fashioned lamps that made her feel as if she'd stepped back in time a hundred years. "Beau, that bed! It's so high. Oh, my God, this is incredible."

Beau chuckled and tossed her onto it. "That's so you can't escape me." He ran a hand down her thigh before going back to close and lock the set of doors before turning back to her, his eyes filled with desire as he slid the key into his pocket. "Now, you're all mine." His graceful strides carried him back to her, his eyes hooded as he removed her shoes and tossed them aside. "There's no escape for you." His dark eyes held hers as he unbuttoned his shirt and tossed it aside.

Need made her restless. Getting to her knees, she reached out to lay a hand on his chest, running it over the sleek muscle there. "So, I'm your prisoner?"

Beau gathered the hem of her sweater and began to lift it, inch by inch. "You are." Lifting the sweater completely over her head, he tossed it aside and with a twist of his fingers, unhooked her bra. "There's no escape for you."

Sucking in a breath at the feel of his hands moving over her breasts, Charity leaned closer. "I don't want to escape."

Touching her lips to his chest, Charity smiled at his own sharp intake of breath. "You're stuck with me." Heat shot from her nipples to her slit, her pussy clenching in demand. "I want you so much."

"Not half as much as I want you." Beau's fingers made quick work of the fastening of her jeans. "And I'm going to have you. Over and over."

"Promise? Oh!" Gripping his shoulders, she rocked her hips against the hand he'd slid inside, spreading her thighs as far as she could as his fingers parted her folds. "Beau!" With shaky hands, she undid his slacks and reached inside, closing her hand around his cock. "You're already hard."

Beau growled and jerked her jeans and panties down to her knees. "I'm always hard for you. And now, my sweet prisoner, I want you on the bed with those pretty thighs spread wide."

Squeezing his cock, Charity grinned when it grew in her hand. "Of course. I don't have any choice, do I?"

Shaking his head, Beau pulled her hand from his cock and urged her back, his movements hurried and impatient as he rid her of her jeans, panties, and socks. "None at all."

Watching him throw off the rest of his clothing, Charity leaned forward, running her tongue over the head of his cock. "Then I guess I'd better please you." Smiling when his cock jumped and he hissed, Charity licked him again. "So what's the ransom?"

With a groan, Beau threaded his fingers into her hair. "There's not enough money in the world to make me give you up. It looks like you're mine forever."

"And you're mine." Charity gasped when his fingers delved between her folds again. "Oh, God. Beau?"

"Yes, cher?"

"Promise to kidnap me again?"

Beau smiled and thrust a finger into her, tightening his hand on her hair and pressing his cock against her lips. "That's a promise. Prepare to be kidnapped and ravaged often."

Spreading her thighs wide, Charity lifted into his touch, clamping down on the finger he thrust inside her. Opening her mouth, she took his cock inside, crying out around it when he slid a thumb over her clit. Trembling with need, Charity fisted her hands on his hips and took his cock deeper, shocked at the warning tingles that already rippled through her.

To her surprise and delight, he bent and replaced his thumb with his mouth, his breath warm on her clit. "You're about to be ravaged, cher."

Crying out around his cock, Charity gripped him tighter as she came, her entire body trembling with pleasure, crying out again when he repositioned her and thrust into her moments later.

It was a long time later before she could even think again. Charity smoothed a hand over her sleeping husband's chest, staring at the ring he'd placed on her finger the day before. Sated and held firmly against the master of Belle Fleur's side, she lifted her head to stare down at his features, barely visible in the predawn light, and smiled.

She'd been well and truly ravaged, and couldn't wait to be ravaged again.

Her playful lover had returned.

THE END

WWW.LEAHBROOKE.NET

ABOUT THE AUTHOR

When Leah Brooke's not writing, she's spending time with family and friends, and spoiling her furry babies.

For all titles by Leah Brooke, please visit
www.bookstrand.com/leah-brooke

For titles by Leah Brooke writing as
Lana Dare, please visit
www.bookstrand.com/lana-dare

Siren Publishing, Inc.
www.SirenPublishing.com

CPSIA information can be obtained at www.ICGtesting.com
Printed in the USA
BVOW04s1006190514

353940BV00021B/1062/P